"Cecil Gomez has created a picture perfect story of his family's migration to America. The hope gestated in his grandfather's heart and soul was kept alive and culminated by his father's bold move to fulfill the family's dream. He gives the readers, through personal experiences, an enlightened insight in the hardships and trials of living in Mexico during those infamous years of the 1900's. Not only does his story "A Mexican Twilight" enlighten us about Mexican history during that period, it also provides us with a clear overview of the hardships immigrants faced and endured when they fled their country into Texas and Oklahoma.

"The history of West Tulsa, Oklahoma depicted in "A Mexican Twilight" is also worthy of note, as the author tells of his life in the "Y", as an example of a first generation Mexican in the U.S. At the insistence and sacrifices of his mother, he and his eleven siblings received a complete education and achieved success in the professional life and became models for others to come.

"The author tells the story vividly and holds the reader's attention through-out an exciting journey to America and to success."

—Ivo Greenwell
Author of "The Lucketts," "The Ancestor,"
and "Tsen Su and the 490th."
iUniverse Publishers

"A well written 'look back' at a desperate time in Mexican history for those poor people south of the Rio Grande. For those who chose to abandon their country, their decision to 'leave it all behind' took an incredible amount of courage—yet though it all, they maintained optimism and their gentle spirit. The story—a good read—reminds us 'gringos' to take a hard look at our prejudices."

—Shearl Barton
Local Business Man—Choteau, Ok.

I would like to congratulate you, Mr. Gomez, on your book "A Mexican Twilight." Your story has the potential to add a much-needed page to the history of Tulsa regarding the Mexican immigrant, not only in Tulsa, but elsewhere. The impact of Mexican immigrants has been overlooked for too long. It is important for us to remember that Tulsa has always been a vibrant town of many immigrants from many countries.

The story you tell so compellingly, relates the immigrant experience shared by so many, but always unique for each family. I welcome the addition of "A Mexican Twilight:" to the body of work about Tulsa. Although a work of fiction with non-fiction, the experiences and feelings your book conveys, resonates with all who empathize with the human condition and the high cost of the American dream. It is a wonderful success story, but it is no way, a simple road to that success.

—Sara Martinez—Coordinator
Hispanic Resource Center
Tulsa, Oklahoma

"A Mexican Twilight" is absolutely stupendous. Not only is it a beautiful story of a close-knit family becoming established within the U.S.A., but also worthy of a movie. The parents, although illiterate, had a deep-rooted faith in God that allowed them to overcome challenging obstacles and gave their offspring the education they needed to achieve the American dream. I enjoyed the story immensely and am looking forward to reading it again."

—Father James Greenwell
3rd Order Reg. Saint Francis of Assisi
(Priesthood & Missionary in Mexico 1955-1959)

A Mexican Twilight

A MEXICAN TWILIGHT

Cecil Gomez

Barbara & Vern

The pleasure is all mine. I hope you enjoy my book.

Cecil Gomez

7/13/07

iUniverse, Inc.
New York Lincoln Shanghai

A Mexican Twilight

Copyright © 2005 by Cecil Gomez

iUniverse books may be ordered through booksellers or by contacting:

iUniverse
2021 Pine Lake Road, Suite 100
Lincoln, NE 68512
www.iuniverse.com
1-800-Authors (1-800-288-4677)

ISBN-13: 978-0-595-38017-6 (pbk)
ISBN-13: 978-0-595-82388-8 (ebk)
ISBN-10: 0-595-38017-4 (pbk)
ISBN-10: 0-595-82388-2 (ebk)

Printed in the United States of America

ACKNOWLEDGEMENTS

Thanks to Universal Book & Bible House in Philadelphia, Pa., for their book, "History of World War II" Armed Service Memorial addition by Francis Trevelyan Miller, Litt. D., LLD, for providing a fantastic detailed history of the war.

Thanks to the Tulsa City-County Central Libraries in Tulsa, Oklahoma for their superb assistance in researching West Tulsa and the Depression Years with such books as:

"When Oklahoma took to the Trolley" by Allison Chandler and Stephen D. Maquire.

"Steam Locomotives of the Frisco Line" by Lloyd E. Stagner.

And many others, such as:

"The Fall of Japan" by Keith Wheeler

"The lawless Decade" by Paul Sann for their great rendition of the great depression.

"A Life of Their Own" by: Aylette Jenness and Lisa W. Kroeber describing the life style in Mexico during the 1930's.

"The Mexican in Oklahoma" by Michael M. Smith, a great depiction of the early Mexicans migrating into the State of Oklahoma.

"Mexico A History" by Robert Ryal Miller, a rendition of the history of Mexico.

"Independence—Revolution in Mexico" 1810 through 1940 by Rebecca Stefoff.

Thanks to Yale University's book authored by Benjamin Heber Johnson, "Revolution in Texas" a great rendition on how a forgotten rebellion and its bloody suppression turned Mexicans into Americans.

Thanks to Lupe Rodriguez, 95, for graciously sharing her memories of the Tulsa Race Riot of 1921 and her recollections of hard times during the great depression of the 30's.

Thanks to my dear old classmate of St. Catherine's Catholic School, James Alfred Mills, for his help and support in reviving old memories of West Tulsa, Oklahoma.

A very special thanks to—Roy Heim, Ivo Greenwell, Father James Greenwell, and Shearl Barton—for their kind words and gracious evaluation of "A Mexican Twilight." Each is a pillar of our community, and because they are all outstanding individuals in their own right, I greatly value and appreciate their unbiased opinions regarding my story about the hardships of Mexican immigrants.

A special thanks to my good friend Kent A. Schell, Planning Administrator for Urban Development Department of Tulsa, for his all-inspiring assistance and motivation in the creation of my historical novel and the telling of my parent's journey to America.

Thanks to my wonderful wife, Josephine, for her virtuous patience and endurance throughout the long, lonely hours while waiting up for me every night, but particularly, for her assistance in critiquing my story.

Also, thanks to my youngest son, Joseph Gomez—actor/playwright—for his ingenious ability to edit my story and his keen savvy of computers when I needed him.

Also, thanks to my little brother, Tommy Gomez, for his fantastic computer knowledge and technical assistance, and how he was never too busy to help.

Last, but not least, I must also express my appreciation to my young granddaughter, Sarah Gomez, for coming to my rescue each time I flubbed up on my computer.

DEDICATION

In memory of Juan and Edelia Gomez & Others

This book is proudly dedicated in memory of my incredible mother who nurtured and inspired me all the days of my life with her undying love and understanding, for her many sacrifices, and for the many times she did with less in order that I might have more. Her warm and gentle spirit was my pillar of strength and hope and it was through her wisdom and prayers that she passed along to me a legacy of righteousness.

And to my humble father, who labored and struggled unceasingly that his family might never go hungry or without clothing and shelter during an era of difficult times. And for his stringent rules of discipline, that I might learn the virtue of obedience and respect—the basic ingredients for sound moralistic values and guiding principles that will identify me wherever I go.

Last but not least, I want to dedicate this book to the many Mexican men and women who courageously cut a trail of woes and hardships when they left their beloved homeland in search of peace, freedom, and a better life. Because, without a single earthly possession and unable to speak a word of English, it was they who dared to cross over to a new frontier and challenge the uncertainty of life in a foreign country. Without them, many of us would have never experienced the American Dream. So, in their memory, I proudly salute them and those whom I knew personally, like; the Almendares, Casas, Casillas, Cervantes, Chavez, Fernandez, Garcia, Gonzales, Hernandez, Ledesma, Leija, Mendoza, Moreno, Morales, Murillo, Perez, Rodrigues, Salazar, Sanchez, and the Zunigas.

ABOUT THE STORY

A **Mexican Twilight** is the true-life story of Juan and Edelia Gomez that vividly encompasses three generations of a typical Mexican family who survived turbulent revolutionary times in Mexico in the early 1900's. Initially, the story tells of the disturbing unrest in Mexico when practically the entire country was being inundated by corrupt politics and a staggering economy that eventually resulted in an uprising of the people. Men like Pancho Villa and Emiliano Zapata emerged, coming to the rescue of the common man, and soon became leaders of a rebellious insurgency against a failing government.

With reference to the 'turbulent revolutionary times' mentioned above, it is only fitting that I briefly explain why the revolution played such a traumatic turning point in the lives of many Mexican citizens.

Those early years in Mexico when the land was ripe for growth and prosperity, by all means, should have been a time for establishing its own identity in the world. But that was not the case. Instead, it was a period of economic chaos and desperation. During those revolutionary times which spanned over six decades beginning in the mid-1800's, the country was struggling with the leadership of unpopular dictators, presidents, governors, and revolting insurgents. Among these were: Presidents Benito Juarez, Porfirio Diaz, Francisco Madero, and Victoriano Huerta—all of whom played a significant role—in their time—in a constant struggle for power that created an unsettling pattern of political maneuvering. It was during Diaz's administration that not only accelerated the pace of rebellion, but also caused many other factions to form—factions, who also wanted a piece of Mexico, but succeeded only to further destabilize the country. Throughout decades of political conflicts, it often appeared that Mexico had simultaneous rulers, each with conflicting ideas of governing and often at war with each other. Diaz resigned his presidency in 1911. Francisco Madero became president that same year, marking another phase of continuing unrest.

Causes of the revolution were numerous; corruption in government from the highest level on down, presidential atheism, nepotism appointments to high offices, loss of liberty, working conditions in shambles, and illegal expropriation of land by the government for gain. All of which, like a sweeping brush fire, created an uprising among the people desperately in need of social reform. Slow to ignite, revolts began to erupt in scattered parts of the country from Baja California to Morelos, and eventually to Mexico City and other States to the south.

When the masses of people felt they could no longer exist under tyrannical suppression, insurgents comprised of peons, teachers, students, factory workers, criminals, bandits, and deserters from the Federal Army, collectively joined two daring and courageous opposition leaders who later became the Robin Hoods of Mexico—as it were—destined to become instrumental in changing the course of Mexican history.

Francisco (Pancho) Villa and Emiliano Zapata led the fight against the rulers of Mexico whose corrupt and ineffective rule trampled the peasant masses. Their primary goal from the beginning was to recapture previously confiscated land and return it to the peasants, often making night raids on railroads and strikes against government and military installations. Using primitive methods of justice, Villa and Zapata often set up peoples courts denouncing cruelties and injustices against the people and dealt with opposition forces on the spot. In no time, they became idols for their courageous stance against the government—being loved by millions, but also, hated by thousands. Of all the many battles fought throughout Mexico, perhaps the bloodiest of all, took place in the town of Celaya, northwest of Mexico City in 1915, between President Huerta's forces led by Venustiano Caranza, against Villa and Zapata. In that battle, several thousand were left dead on the battlefield and thousands more were wounded or taken prisoners. Villa and Zapata were defeated but escaped.

As in earlier decades, most of the people of Mexico lived the country life as farmers and ranchers, away from the city life. Those of whom I speak, basically, had no allusions of grandeur, ambitions of fame or fortune, or even aspirations of greatness. Their simple goals from day to day were always the same; to be left alone to live in peace and contentment on their own land, to produce their own food, raise their own livestock, their horses, and to provide for their families. Ultimately, however, when the rulers took away their most prized possessions—the land, or control thereof—it severely decimated the very fabric of their existence and the basic identity of 'who and what' they were. Consequently, the infliction imposed by the rulers, in and of itself, created a simmering unrest and mistrust among the populace of Mexico, until a feeling of complete futility became prevalent nearly nationwide.

The period that followed, between 1910 and 1918, saw the broken spirit of many farmers and the common people, and for many, the choice was clear— move away or succumb to corruption and instability. Many chose to break away from the cruel, fruitless stagnation and hostilities that surrounded them, even if it meant abandoning their native land and facing total uncertainty ahead. Gradually, an exodus migration began. First, from the deserts of northern and central Mexico to the southern United States—principally, Texas—then, to New Mexico and California. It wasn't only to flee the wave of terror, but equally, to escape the chaotic aftermath that left so many families homeless, landless, and destitute in their own country.

Notwithstanding the Mexican revolution, the story also takes us through a concurrent uprising in the southern tip of Texas—namely, Brownsville/Matamoros. For the thousands of emigrants who deserted Mexico during the same time frame via the borders of Laredo and Brownsville, they found themselves entangled in another people's uprising—revolting Mexican-Texans (Tejanos) allied with Mexican Nationals from south of the border against Anglo American settlers. In dispute, was the southern boundary of the United States, namely: the Rio Grande River. This unrest caused many Texas-Mexicans and Mexican Nationals to disperse beyond the borders of Texas. The Texas rebellion, as it were, was a direct result of a spillover of ruthless, unsavory tactics of wealthy Anglo landowners seeking to uproot many of the original Mexican Tejanos from their land. In essence, the Mexicans in south Texas—mainly, the ranchers and farmers—were being squeezed out of their land, some, by economic pressures, title fraud, and others by outright forced evictions. Though the two revolutions were different, the causes were practically the same; greed of the powerful, over the weak and the powerless.

Caught up in the ongoing strife in Mexico and its economic stagnation, was **Juan and Edelia—my parents.** Their painful decision to abandon their beloved country would never have been their choice had things been different, but if ever there was to be a better life for them—at the time—it would not be in Mexico.

The story not only re-visits the painful exodus of Mexicans in the midst of great turmoil and unrest, but it also reminds us that an exodus of a different kind still continues today. The reasons and causes for millions who left Mexico in the teens, was, of course, the revolution and its consequences. But today, though the reasons are much different, the search for 'a better life' is still prevalent in many who aspire to make America their home—legal or otherwise.

The story will take us on a pleasant walk through two of Mexico's 'all but forgotten' villages, the lifestyle of its poor inhabitants, a day of celebration, tragedy, and a revolutionary encounter.

Basically, my story, which I consider a historical novel, is also a success story written in *plain and simple, easy to read* language, sprinkled with a variety of Mexican clichés and expressions. *'Historical'* in the sense that in the telling of Juan and Edelia's migration to America, their travels take us on a frightening, but true, step-by-step encounter with the infamous Race Riot of 1921 in Tulsa, Oklahoma, including a revisit of the desperate aftermath of the stock market 'crash of 29' that led to the great depression. Also included is a reminiscent historical flashback of the good ol' days of **West Tulsa, Oklahoma** during the 1930's. The story brings back a nostalgic remembrance of the simple, peaceful days of a unique little American town, and accurately describes the quaint down-to-earth community as though it was a famous city worthy of being on a United States map. It takes us back to the days of trolley cars, passenger trains, vaudeville shows, five cent movies, a seven cent loaf of bread, fifteen cent gas, when yes sir and no sir was still in everyone's vocabulary, back when an hourly rate of pay was only 35 cents, and when merchants could give change for a penny using mils— one tenth of a cent. Moreover, long before stop lights, four lane expressways, a congested metropolis, bikinis and mini skirts, atomic energy and bombs, and certainly before cell phones and John Wayne. Also, historically, is included is a detailed adventure that walks us through the troubling days of World War II and its victorious celebration over the defeat of Germany and Japan.

But the story is also a *'novel'*, in that it philosophically dramatizes the migration and journey of Juan and Edelia to the United States from deep in the heart of Mexico despite daunting challenges of language, illiteracy and tragedy. It includes a variety of unexpected dramatic conflicts, such as the fateful childhood days of Edelia whose life was like a rolling stone, having spent time in an orphanage and later falling into the hands of an abusive stepfather, and still later, her unintentional abandonment by her mother. Additionally, we'll see a beautiful, but explosive 'love story' between a very young girl and a much older man.

An essential part of the story, no less its theme, is the constant struggle with poverty and the unrelenting determination to find peace and happiness—and of course, the American dream. Having raised 12 children in the midst of it all, together, Juan and Edelia followed a 'beacon of hope' that constantly yearned for success and a better life. They never stopped believing that the dark cloud that constantly hovered over their allusive dreams would someday render its sweet reward. Thus, the title, **A Mexican Twilight.**

Down through the years, I never stopped wondering about my parent's past, their history, including the history of Papa's little village of 'Villa de Reyes'. Particularly, when he talked about his father, Cenobio, and his native land, and how it was always with the utmost anxiety and fervor as though each time, he was reliving that exact moment—and how the unmistakable sentiment on his face always revealed a pining to be back home in the old country. Somehow, I was never quite satisfied merely to embrace a photo of my parents, or a document they, too, had once held in their hands, or to stand on the same piece of ground that they, too, had stood on, or perhaps reading a yellowing, dusty letter from generations long past. Although all these things are priceless and will never lose their sentimental value, much of their fascinating past remained lodged in memories like an incomplete rhyme, or a book with missing chapters. That is, until I was finally able to draw a line between the dots that connect the unknown with the known, that ultimately led to the telling of their fantastic, unpretentious journey to the United States.

Undoubtedly, the stories of Mexican immigrants of the early teens have been told time and time again, and in many variations. And though their stories may not have been widely publicized or dramatized, I would venture to say that essentially, they all would convey the same sentimental tale of woes and desperation. Delving into the minds and concerns of those who wrestled with the decision to leave their beloved homeland, no doubt, many fears and worries surfaced at the very thought of; *where do I go after crossing the border, which way do I turn, can I find a job, will I be able to provide for my family, and how will I deal with the language.* But casting aside their concerns and ignoring the danger signs ahead, they came anyway. In this regard, the tale of my parent's grueling journey, almost in its entirety, can be viewed as an exact adventurous replay of the journey of thousands upon thousands who crossed the Rio Grande River between 1910 and 1918.

Was it easy? Did they do the right thing? The dynamic answers to these and many other perplexing questions are dramatically brought to light in my rendition of A Mexican Twilight. The story, to be sure, is by no means the only one of its kind. Heaven only knows how many families migrated to America from all over the world during the early 1900's, each sharing a commonality of hardships, hunger, and suffering.

Was the Gomez family any different? Well.....in many ways, they were the same, but in other respects, circumstances were much different, because when

Juan and Edelia came to America, they arrived broke, and not knowing one word of English—not to mention encounters with discrimination.

So…..from the quaint villages of Villa de Reyes, San Luís Potosí and Colotlan, Jalisco in Mexico, we'll follow Juan and Edelia's timeless journey to America, and through it all, we'll see that all is not necessarily gloom and doom, not when faith, hope, and love is alive and well. We'll see the fruits of their labor and perseverance despite disappointments and sufferings that stemmed from 'the hard life'. And in this regard, we'll also see a delightful presentation of how, in humble serenity, the hard life was taken in patient stride until conquered, one day at a time. From the beginning and to the very end, all Juan and Edelia ever really wanted was an uncloudy day, and that uncloudy day was in the offing when they finally settled in the little town of West Tulsa, Oklahoma. After years of living in a topsy-turvy world of ups and downs, success did come to Juan and Edelia and their children. From the day they first conceived the call for a better life—all the way from their sleepy little villages in Mexico, to the glorious day when the sun finally showered them with happiness and peace—*all that transpired in between, is what their beautiful story is about.*

The story of Juan Edelia Gomez is truly a delightful heart-warming success story rooted in true facts via fictionalized truth and presented in pristine settings that portray the realities of their past.

My attempt to preserve the memory of my parent's humble background is not only for my sake and satisfaction, but also for the benefit of my children and grandchildren that they might better understand the roots of their lineal heritage. Nor am I forgetting that these same migratory revelations, may also in some way, spark a fond reminder in the hearts and minds of thousands of other immigrants, and/or their descendents, who fled Mexico during those revolutionary times.

ABOUT THE AUTHOR

I, Cecil Gomez, am a native son of Oklahoma, born in the little town of Sapulpa, five miles south of Tulsa, Oklahoma. I am the 2nd offspring of Juan and Edelia Gomez's twelve children—eight boys and four girls. Namely; Juan, Jr., Cecilio, Cenobio, Manuela, Juanito, Virginia, Alberto, Miguel, Guadalupe, Felipa, Tomas, and Alejandro. I am a graduate of Oklahoma School of Accountancy having graduated with a Bachelor of Commercial Science Degree (BCS). I served three years in the United States Navy in the Aleutian Islands during World War II. I am married to my wonderful wife, Josephine, and have four beautiful children, eight grandchildren, and two great grandchildren.

I *self published my first book*—an autobiography—which was basically a documentary of the Gomez family and the little suburban town of West Tulsa. The book—exclusively a true story—was entitled, "Mama & Papa's Twelve Children and the Y", and published only for family enjoyment. Only one hundred ten copies were printed and all disappeared almost over night. And because of the historical significance that my book contained about West Tulsa back in the 30's and 40's, it received an overwhelming acceptance by the Southwest Tulsa Historical Society, which honored me by placing my book in each of the five West Tulsa Public School libraries.

It was the fantastic response from numerous readers, friends, and critiques that inspired the rewriting of the first edition into this expanded sequel. Because, as I delve deeper into Juan and Edelia's forlorn past, I find that a very important part of their story has yet to be told. I'm speaking now of how, when, and why, they left Mexico. Both migrated to the United States during the early 1900's. When they crossed the Rio Grande River into America, neither could speak one word of English. It was their harrowing experiences, before and after coming to America, that gave rise to my reasons for writing their complete story.

Vivid recollections of their ramshackle shack after settling in West Tulsa, still linger, because as though it was yesterday, I can still see Papa and Mama sitting in front of our wood-burning potbelly stove talking calmly about the days of the revolution, in and around their little hometowns, and how most the villagers lived in fear—fear of more fighting and killing. In this homely, picturesque setting, they talk about the harsh times left behind, but now they feel safe and out of harm's way. They consider themselves the lucky ones—luckier than the ones still in Mexico. Still....they can't completely forget. Mama continues knitting the holes in Papa's wool socks, and Papa is layering more wool patches on the earflaps of his winter working cap, as he prepares to face another frigid day at the Frisco Roundhouse. In conversation, without much emphasis on the staggering times, all of us, including the children, are talking quite casually in Spanish without concern that we now live in seclusion away from white people in town, or that we're poor and barely getting by. The evening is gleefully whiled away, as Papa's humorous wit is trying to trump Mama's jokes and laughter. We pretend to be happy with the way things are. Of course we want nice things too, just like everybody else—but we don't talk about it.

But the profound truth, however, goes unspoken. Each day, day after day, and year after year, things remain the same. Hard times still hover all around. But the wonder of it all, is that despite their disdainful circumstances, there are no broken fragments of hope for a better tomorrow in my parent's eyes. They wholeheartedly feel blessed for Papa's employment, the children, good health, and food on the table.

Me.....well.....I'm just like them. Just a happy go-lucky kid unable to do anything about our impoverished circumstances until.....until I returned from the war when I finally realized that no measurable progress in my parent's lives had been made. Their once beautiful dream of a better life in America had almost become a delusion. *It was then, that I took hold of their dream and made it mine,* breathing new life into their reasons for having left Mexico, long, long ago. I'm alluding to the fact that their dream, as we will see, did come true.

To tell their complete story, I had to find a way to weave myself into the interplaying of their early lives, way back then, and connect with the realities of their times. After wracking my brain to unlock the secrets of their beautiful past, I realized that I must first unlock my powers of concentration and tap into the magical works of an aspiring imagination. To do this, I had to keep reminding myself of the goal at hand, which was to convert their past into my present. Like: *Que pasó, Que pása, Que pasará.*

Cecil Gomez

Now that I have honed a keen mentality that will guide the story of the factual lives of Juan and Edelia and set their awesome journey into forward motion, I'll just blink my eyes a few times, and when my eyes stop blinking, all their past will be right there in front of me, pleading for a new awakening…blink…blink…blink…My eyes have finally stopped blinking and I see that I'm there with Mama and Papa—in the wings, of course.

But no kidding. In my mind and in my heart and soul, I think I've always been there. Now, in my writer's world, for the purpose of the fictional part of their story—I can permit all their different whims and secrets that cross my memory path to come alive once again. On any given day, my mind will be able to transform their intriguing past into my yearning present. Absolutely. When I choose to do so, I'll just close my eyes to remove the veil of obscurity and instantly, I'll be there participating in any special occasion involving Mama and Papa. That includes their exciting adolescent years, their friends, their loved ones, their hopes and dreams, happy times, disappointments and yes…even suffering. Even when circumstances around them involve tragedy, I want to be there. When they feel forgotten, or face failure, I'll be there.

I keep saying that I was there with Mama and Papa when they were growing up. But wait a minute. How could I have been there? I wasn't born 'til 1923, and papa was born 33 years before me. Surely I wasn't there when he was born. And yet, the many stories they passed on to me about their lives from the day they entered this world, I feel as though I was really there. So….I'll just close my eyes once again and let my imagination scan their beautiful past as though I was an artificial being invisibly snooping around like a sparrow from my lofty perch looking down onto their by-gone years.

So.....from the hard knocks of their poverty laden lives, to a new world of success and dignity, I'll be in the scene too, absorbing the whole truth of their past, subconsciously recording each precious moment. But even if I wasn't there, I must pretend I was, lest the fleeting memories dissipate and give way to the winds of the past. Because all the gold in the world cannot reproduce one glorious minute of their past—particularly when the past for Juan and Edelia was so unkind and yet so sweet.

Was I really there? If you'll give me just a second, I'll awaken my waiting imagination and see if I can see me there. Lets see now.....Ah! Yes! It's coming into focus, and.....there it is.....there's the answer. Yes! Absolutely! I was there.

And since I was there, I'll let you come along and you, too, can be an invisible observer as I redevelop this aging photo of the past.

Cecil Gomez

AUTHOR'S NOTES

Parts One and Two are Fiction
Parts Two and Three are non-fiction

It should be remembered that throughout the story, most of the characters are natives of Mexico, and with very little exception, none could speak English. In this regard, readers are reminded to read the story with the perception that the characters, when speaking, are speaking in Spanish.

Fictitious characters in the story have been given typical Spanish names and presented in bold print merely to emphasize the pride of their ancestral lineage that lends a spirit of Mexican heritage to the background in which the story takes place. Other bold impressions are intended to alert the reader of a certain significance to the story.

Throughout the story, some Spanish dialogue is used intermittently solely for the purpose of allowing the Spanish-speaking readers to identify more closely with the familiar characterization of back-home expressions. In every such case, these Spanish phrases are immediately translated into English so as not to interrupt the reader's trend of thought or flow of the story.

The word Don will be seen quite frequently. It does not mean Don, short for Donald. It means 'Mr'. The same goes for the word Doña which stands for 'Mrs'.

Finally—I dare say—my story has purposely been written in plain and simple, easy to read language. Readers won't find any words that are complicated, hard to read, or hard to understand. A dictionary on hand should not be necessary.

Juan and Edelia Gomez

Are you of Mexican decent or know someone who is?

Is it wrong to want a better life?

"from the rutted paths of Villa de Reyes, Mexico and the life-giving cornfields where Juan worked cheerfully beside his father...and from the night Domitila wandered aimlessly on the dark streets of sleepy Colotlan, Mexico waiting to give birth to Edelia...to the memorable little town of West Tulsa, Oklahoma—together, they obediently followed the call of their waiting destiny."

Through my mystical powers of concentration, I'll just swing open the dusty veil of transparency, click on the slumbering past, wait for Chapter One to come in to focus, and instantly, the forgotten past will begin to transform itself into a dynamic present with all the real-life splendor and sprawling backdrop of a memorable yester-year. The year is 1906, late summer, and it's hotter'n Hades. Cenobio has just returned from a week-long trip to the farmers market in San Luis, Potosi, Mexico.

PART I

▼

ORIGIN OF JUAN GOMEZ

CHAPTER 1

▼

REVOLUTIONARY TIMES— 1906

The dilapidated little sign on the edge of the dirt road read, **"Villa de Reyes,"** Village of Kings. The sign's letters—barely readable—were scrawled on a piece of eroding 2x4 protruding above the thorny thicket of weeds. Village of Kings? Nothing could be further from the truth—there were no kings living in this *pueblito*. In fact, the whole town's population was surely under 3,000, and covered an area less than two square miles. Of course, that's not counting acres and acres of harvested cornfields nor certain smaller parcels of rich produce land. As a matter of fact, the entire town was so small it could hardly be called a township. Although a suburb of the big city of **San Luis, Potosi,** it would never be paved over or modernized to double-decker buildings, nor would it ever be marked for national commerce. But even so, the townspeople were happy with their little town, just the way it was.

La Marqueta produce market was the most patronized. Another was the General Store, a small grocery store that included *botica y medicinas*, a barbershop, a blacksmith shop, a candy store, two *cantinas*, and a variety of other small time retailers. Of course, there were the usual stables and barns for the *caballero's* rodeo horses. But perhaps the most important, was the *Virgen de Guadalupe*

Catholic Church that provided daily *misas y confesiones* for the citizens of Villa de Reyes.

Cenobio stopped for just a minute to wipe away the salty sweat from his dark brown face after hiking over nearly fifteen miles of rutted earth on a sweltering hot August afternoon. And he thought to himself, *ay que bueno,* just a quarter mile to go.

Summer was extremely hot and unforgiving in Villa de Reyes country that day. The surrounding terrain was not mountainous country, not desert land, nor lush green pastures from here to San Luis, Potosi. It was just miles of scrub brush and *caca-brown dirt,* barren plains sprinkled with tuna bearing *nopales,* and *mesquite* that seemed to adorn the sleepy waves of the *cerro* countryside as it lay dormant against the broad skyline view. The profusion of millions and millions of smooth assorted rocks that lay on the stubborn soil, was not to be unutilized. Because thanks to the local hard-working residents, a large portion of the rocks were re-designed into long beautiful networks of bordering fences, walkways and stone walls—the likes of which were particularly pleasing to the eye in this nearly treeless part of the country. Essential to every family in town, was a burro or donkey if they could afford one. Shabby homes and huts made of adobe, lay in close proximity to the empty *milpas,* cornfields that lay in wait for next year's crops. Small statuettes of favorite saints and simple homemade crosses spotted along the way, bore witness to the sites of buried loved ones.

Cenobio Gomez, who had just turned 43, was by no means a large man. He was only 5'6" tall, weighing slightly over 160 pounds, but his broad shoulders that narrowed sharply at the hips, complimented his strong muscular build. A very handsome man with black wavy hair who wouldn't be himself without a perfectly trimmed thin-line black mustache, that when he smiled, his polite manners and friendly personality came shining through. His middle name could also have been 'toil', because to labor in the fields was the only thing he'd ever known, and—sad but true—this would be the only legacy he could ever bestow upon his family.

Cenobio had made many previous trips to San Luis' open market to sell his produce, since this was the largest and the nearest city established well enough to meet the demands of the area's food supply. Here, farmers and vendors of all kinds, from miles around, assembled daily and on weekends to sell their crops, their wares, and homemade crafts. This, too, was how Cenobio made his living. Every summer, he could hardly wait for his corn crops to ripen so he could take them to market, because this year—like most others—by mid summer, most of the family's savings would have been depleted. Primarily, it was the corn crops that provided his best opportunity to earn sufficient income to see his family through the non-productive winter months.

Cenobio, for a moment, turned and looked to the west as he shaded his eyes from the hot blaring sun. And as he did, many thoughts were rambling around in his head. Thoughts of the present, thoughts of the past, and particularly, one disturbing thought about the future—his future and the future of his family. *And how about the future of Mexico? Could it be that his entire adult life as a farmer had been no more than a mere exercise in futility? Suddenly, he recalled the political rally—a call to arms.*

On this trip to market, Cenobio had an abrupt awakening. It wasn't the fact that sales had not been good, after all, he did have 225 pesos in his pocket. And it wasn't the trek to market over miles of desolate country, by burros, pulling a two-wheel trundle loaded with corn and tomatoes. *No, it was something else. Something much worse,* he thought. In his pocket, he had tucked away a leaflet that had been distributed at the market almost in secrecy, asking for volunteers—young and old—to join in a political protest against Mexico's **President Porfirio Diaz.** Rumors had begun to circulate about two emerging young revolutionaries who were organizing and leading a rebellion against an unfair government, namely; **Pancho Villa,** 27, and **Emiliano Zapata,** 25. This in itself, however, was not Cenobio's big worry at the moment. Instead, it was an on-going revolution that seemed to be picking up steam and *could eventually spread to include his young son.* Already, there seemed to be an alluring fascination for daring young men seeking excitement and adventure, and this was Cenobio's big worry. There was no denying that previous revolts by the people during the last two decades were proof enough that many young men had fought and died for a cause that remained suppressed and unresolved.

Flashback...........

As Cenobio and his son **Juanito** continued on foot ever closer to home, he recalled how on the first night after arriving at the San Luis vending plaza, he had been approached by a group of local citizens strongly urging him to attend an important political rally being held at the convention hall. They said it was urgent and had something to do with the crumbling future of Mexico's people—meaning the 90% poor. Not only was Cenobio invited, but also many other young and middle-aged men were entreated to attend.

Cenobio, at the time, wasn't exactly surprised by the air of urgency. After all, *what else is new,* he thought to himself. But the over riding suspense of the matter prompted him to reconsider his personal views of a reckless government and attend the political rally.

That same evening, after having made the decision to attend the rally, he called out to his son, *"Juanito, ven aquí."* "Come here, son."

"¿Que quiere Papa?" "What is it, Papa?" answered Juanito.

"Hijo, Son, I have to go to a very important meeting and I want you to look after everything while I'm gone. I'll be back as soon as I can." *"¿No tienes miedo quedarte solo?"*

"No Papa. I'm not afraid."

So together they spread an old canvas cover over their corn and produce and closed their vendor corner for the evening, while Cenobio went looking for the convention hall.

Juanito, now in complete charge, unfolded his bedroll at the foot of the wooden produce stand and stood guard over their produce. With his shirt half-way unbuttoned and his wavy black hair waving gently in the breeze, he sat down beside their produce table and began tapping his foot, as he listened to the soft Mariachi music coming from the far end of the plaza.

The convention hall was not hard to find. Cenobio just followed the noise on the street and the steady stream of disgruntled residents, anxious to air out their frustrations with the government. On approaching the convention center, he immediately noticed a large gathering of *caballeros* on horseback, and a variety of horse-drawn carriages parked along the building. Men of all ages were huddled in small groups, talking loudly and unrestrained, as though arguing. Right away, he began to get nervous and could feel goose bumps on concluding that something serious was in the wind.

"Bueno, Compa, ¿De que se trata esta junta? Se parese muy urgente." "Hi, friend," he asked in a curious voice as he approached a passerby. "Do you know what this meeting is all about? Sounds urgent."

Showing Cenobio the flyer that he, too, had received, the stranger replied, *"Yo tampoco no se y por eso vine."* "I don't know either and that's why I came. I believe it has something to do with the revolution."

"Bueno, vamos a ver que dicen." "Lets go inside and find out"

On entering the building, Cenobio was amazed at the multitude of people who had come to hear the latest news on the status of a failing government. The smoke-filled hall was overwhelming, and the loud chatter of everyone talking at the same time vibrated the narrow hall, while tequila flowed freely. All the wooden benches and chairs were already occupied, leaving nothing but standing room in the rear. As darkness outdoors was about to set in, the announcement came that the meeting was about to commence. Immediately, everyone outside began to make their way inside and continued to pack the rear of the hall.

At the podium, stood a tall, burly, well-rounded man with a cigar in his mouth, stroking a graying mustache. He was wearing an oversize white shirt with pearl buttons, a black string tie, and badly in need of a hair cut. He was probably the town mayor, but at the time he introduced himself, his name—which sounded like **Enrique Salvador**—was not audible for the pounding of talk and clamor. Standing beside him, were four other local reps, whose names, too, escaped remembering.

The gavel banged heavily on the podium, time and time again, before silence could bring order to the meeting. Immediately, Don Enrique jumped right in on the crux of the meeting by announcing that on that very same night, similar meetings were being held in various other key cities like, *Morelia, Guanajuato, Irapuato, Guadalajara, Durango, Aguascalientes, and Chihuahua* to protest against the President's tyrannical government.

As the meeting was heating up, Don Enrique continued with a litany of allegations that he brought to the floor against a government 'not for the people', and right away, one could feel the fervor and anticipation building up in those present. Clearing his throat once again, pulling no punches, he began laying it on the line. Loud and forcefully, he declared that President Diaz had created a nationwide band of political bosses—'*jefes politicos*'—and was using them to force compliance with his demands, his false promises, and bullying. He also accused him of instigating a terrorist campaign of intimidation greedily designed to achieve only one goal—power at all cost. Don Enrique profanely criticized Diaz' unfair laws and land seizures that denied land rights to the peasant multitudes. He reiterated how land reform by Diaz had been set back years and years because under his rule, no peasant or farmer could lay claim to any land, unless he could produce legal title, even if it had been in the same family for generations. He sharply criticized land confiscations that were leaving many farmers without land and home, gobbling up millions of acres of prime land, then turning right around and selling it back to favored rich *hacendados.*

Continuing his contemptuous attack on Diaz, Don Enrique quite nastily harped on the way the President engaged in nepotism, an issue of common knowledge and a sore issue among the people. Particularly, when it was obvious that relatives and in-laws were being promoted to high-level positions, and that favorite friends in high places were being awarded huge rail and transportation concessions. Lastly, Don Enrique blasted the diminishing people's rights and freedom of the press, citing that editors who openly criticized the government, could possibly be arrested.

Wiping away beads of perspiration from his forehead, Don Enrique barked out in a hoarse voice, "Friends, tonight you're going to hear proof that I've told you the truth. Please! *No se vayan todavia!* Don't anyone leave yet. *No se rajen amigos. Aquí les presento Don Carlos Muñoz."* "Let me present to you my good friend, Carlos Muñoz."

After a roaring applause of unity, Carlos Muñoz took center stage.

Carlos Muñoz, a well dressed lawyer in his 60's, wearing a black suit, white shirt and black tie, and dark-rimmed eyeglasses, jumped up on the podium and waited for the applause to stop.

"Buenas tardes" he commenced, waving both hands at the crowd.

"Esta noche me presento aquí con ustedes con corazon muy pesado." "Tonight I come here with a heavy heart. Many of you already know me. But in case you don't, I am the owner and publisher of our local newspaper, *Prenza Democratica."* Trying to keep his temper contained, he began his argument with the government, saying, "Since the days of our former president, Benito Juarez, I've covered political news events from every corner of our great country; elections, political campaigns, and local matters. I have always tried to represent the voice of our people, and most recently, the tactics of our country's *jefes politicos."*

"Prenza Democratica has always taken great pride in reporting the news in a well-informed professional manner. It is your right to know what our government stands for, what it does, including what it fails to do. And that's why I'm here tonight—same as you. Our president has failed us. Today, we not only find ourselves in a political and economic crisis, but also, free enterprise is becoming a thing of the past. Everything you've heard here tonight is true. Also tonight, I have one more piece of evidence to confirm Don Enrique's summation of the hostilities going on around us."

After stopping for a moment to catch his breath Don Muñoz suddenly cried out, "Censorship!" "Yes, censorship!"

Unable to refrain from using profanity, he blurted out, "Now those dirty bastards have shut down my newspaper. Diaz's front men have padlocked my office for two weeks"

As he continued to condemn the government for interfering with freedom of the press, in his hand, he was holding a copy of a recent editorial he had just published.

"Here!" "Let me read this article to you," he barked out, shuffling through some newspaper clippings in his hand. "Here's what my article said."

What's happening to our country?

Time was, when there was peace in all our valleys and contentment on the faces of our people. But that's all changing. Time was, when we were all brothers in Christ without interference in our religion. But today, some of our priests are in jail for preaching against the wrong they see. Time was, when trust was a thing of honor and dignity, but now, we're becoming divided. Many of our people live in fear because our leaders rule by intimidation. Time was, when we could speak our minds freely, but today, we're forced to guard what we say or do, for fear of reprisal or retaliation. Time was, when we could walk our roads and our streets in peace, and work our fields with pride and dignity, but today, our land—the land of our forefathers—is in jeopardy. Even our horses and our cattle may be confiscated. Today, many of our young men have been either killed or imprisoned for refusing to bow down to dictatorial tactics. Our rich leaders have become richer at the expense of the poor. Our government rules with an iron fist and punishes those who disagree. Years ago, we were promised a constitution—a constitution that would protect and defend the rights of the people. But today, we're still waiting. And while we wait, the peace in our valleys and the contentment on the faces of our people, is disappearing. I repeat. What's happening to our country?

On concluding the recital of his newspaper article, Carlos Muñoz furiously raised it high above his head, shouting, "This is why they have closed my doors." "Friends!" he declared. "Can you see what's happening? Today, things are bad, but tomorrow they'll be worse if we pretend not to care."

He was still angry and trembly as he stepped down from the speakers platform amid thunderous shouts of cursing and feet stomping.

Cenobio was almost spellbound. Even though he too was applauding vigorously, what he'd just heard, was very troubling.

Suddenly, as the applause and uproar was still in a shouting match, to everyone's surprise, a man from the crowd stood up shouting obscenities about President Diaz.

"*Que vaya Diaz al infierno.*" "To hell with Diaz."

Jumping up onto the stage, hollering loud enough to be heard above the clamoring audience, "Wait!" he shouted. "*Esperense!*" "I'd like to say something too."

He was noticeably mad as hell at the establishment, and he, too, had an ax to grind. As soon as the clamor of the disgruntled audience softened, waving a piece of paper in his hand, he immediately began to lodge a serious accusation against the government.

"Yo me llamo, my name is **Jesus Timoteo."**

Don Jesus was a well-built *vaquerro,* casually dressed in a cowboy outfit and boots. *"Escuchen me."* he yelled. "Listen to me."

Then he began his protest.

"Look" he shouted, holding up a letter. "This is a letter I just received from my uncle in Aguascalientes. It contains very bad news. My uncle's eighty-acre farm has just been confiscated by a band of Federal troops because he couldn't prove legal ownership. They moved him out of his house, then, the *malditos soldados,* damned soldiers moved in. The bastards then offered him employment on his own farm." "Can you beat that!" he exclaimed. "He'll be arriving at my house soon, because he and his family have no where else to go. And listen to this," he shouted, "my uncle's neighbor, whose adjoining farm of thirty-two acres was also confiscated for the same reason. But he wasn't so lucky. He refused to surrender his farm peacefully, so they shot him."

Concluding his angry protest, he yelled, "Someday, someone is going to pay for this injustice." Still fuming, he went back to his seat on the front row, as the raging crowd cheered in agreement.

While the restless crowd was still shouting angry slogans, Don Enrique approached the pulpit once again and began pounding the gavel repeatedly, trying to silence the crowd. As soon as order was restored, he began his closing remarks.

"Amigos, tonight you have seen and heard the full truth, *la mera verdad,* about the state of our country. Instead of going forward, we're going backward, and if we don't take action soon, we may lose everything we've ever worked for—including our homes and our land. Time to act is now. All of you, particularly those of you without family, if you're not afraid to fight for your rights, leave your name with the *oficinista,* clerk, and he'll give you full details. And when the hour arrives, you will be contacted."

"Buenas noches amigos. Vayan con Dios." "Goodnight friends. Go with God."

Once again, profound bursts of thunderous applause from all directions began to vibrate the thin walls of the convention hall, as the meeting adjourned. Many of the men were still angry, shaking their fists and cursing the government with unrestrained profanity, while others demanded immediate retaliatory action. Truly the fighting spirit of the local residents had been awakened.

As the protesters' angry voices and scathing obscenities blended into a roaring shouting match, Cenobio quietly departed out the back door—more confused than ever. Even though he had begun to feel fear over the hostile action being contemplated, he also felt a sense of anger and betrayal by the government. And if it wasn't for his family—especially Juanito—he could easily have been motivated in joining the crusade.

As the sins of the government had been layed out one by one, Cenobio had listened intently, wanting to disbelieve all that he had just heard. There was no question that what he'd just heard was true, *but would a serious uprising of the people ever happen,* he wondered? *And even if it did, could the poor common man win against such power and influence as that of President Dias and his goons who were already bought and paid for?*

On leaving the all-fired-up rally, Cenobio tried to stop worrying. Of course, he already knew about scandalous corruption in government and their gangster type tactics, as well as plenty of other reasons that would justify a rebellion. But for the moment, he was satisfied that Don Enrique's remarks about '*wanting young fighting*' men wouldn't include him or his son, Juanito.

On his way back to the market, he stopped for a second under a dim gaslight to check the time on his pocket watch. "*Ay caramba,*" he whispered to himself. "*Ya son las nueve.*" "Oh my gosh, it's already nine o'clock."

When Cenobio finally arrived back at the market plaza, there was much idle meandering going on, certainly not much buying or selling. Live music continued to resonate throughout the square as people were still partying, instead of calling it a night. But Cenobio was tired and mentally exhausted after a night of troubling anti-government speeches and demonstrations. He worked his way through the noisy crowd, anxious to see if Juanito was alright.

As he reached his vending corner, he wasn't prepared for one more disturbing surprise. He found Juanito standing in the midst of three young soldiers in militia uniforms completely outfitted with boots, leggings, ammunition belts and rifles. The boys were talking to Juanito, showing off their military gear and filling his head with ideas of fun and excitement. They said they'd just joined the Army, and were waiting to be furnished with horses, and soon, they'd be going up north for training. They'd been told of certain bandits and outlaws that they would soon be engaging. To Juanito, these boys—not much older than he—represented a glorified life of adventure, without a single inkling as to the dangers that lay ahead.

"Juanito!" yelled Cenobio. "*¿Que estas haciendo?*" "What are you doing!"

"*Nada, Papa,*" "I'm just talking to these soldiers."

In an angry voice and waving his hand at the young recruits, Cenobio hollered, "*Vayanse!*" "*Vayanse de aquí!*" "Go! Get out of here!" By the tone of his voice, they knew he meant business, so off they went.

For the rest of the evening, neither spoke about the incident. Cenobio didn't scold Juanito, after all, he hadn't done anything wrong. But inside, he was mad. Not at anyone in particular, just upset with things in general. The rally at the convention hall had already planted the worry in his mind over imminent rebel mustering. And now, the thought of his young immature son seemingly being lured into a dangerous career, was just too much.

He couldn't sleep all night.

CHAPTER 2

▼

VILLA DE REYES

As Cenobio and Juanito were making their way home leading their two bur-ros—***Sonso and Flojo*** (Dummy and Lazy)—confusion was still unresolved in his mind. *Where is all this going?* he wondered. *Can we the people really make a differ-ence? Where do I fit in, in this complex equation? And how many men must die before responsibility in government is achieved?* In his mind, there was no quick answer—just confusion. But inasmuch as young restless teen-age boys were eagerly volun-teering to hook up with the adventurous rebels, the worrisome thought contin-ued to prey on his mind.

Cenobio was particularly worried for his son Juanito, who was growing by leaps and bounds, and in a few short years could also be drawn into the country's conflict. He would soon turn sixteen. Already his lanky frame had all the ambi-tious characteristics of a young adult, and in another year, Juanito would be taller than he. His features strongly resembled Cenobio's, and already, he was begin-ning to sport a little peach fuzz under his nose. He could hardly wait to grow a mustache to begin strutting around the village like other young men. And like any other teenager, his eagerness to grow up fast, was as obvious as a newborn colt. Early on, Cenobio had begun placing many responsibilities on young Jua-nito, whom he loved dearly. It seemed that with each passing day, he observed unto himself, the gradual changes in his son's budding personality. His obedience and keen sense of responsibility was showing great promise. But what really made Cenobio proud, was the fact that Juanito almost never left his side.

On this trip to market, Cenobio was greatly pleased with his little helper. Little Juanito had been very energetic and ambitious. He didn't have to be told to unload the wagon, or to take and tie it to the pole behind the leather store. He knew from previous trips, just exactly how to openly display the corn and how to arrange the baskets of fresh tomatoes. He loved showing off his artistic talents when posting sales prices on little pieces of cardboard found behind the local stores. Not only was he becoming a *take-charge little man*, but even unbeknown to himself, Juanito was becoming quite an effective salesman. As customers strolled by looking for bargains, he politely got their attention, persuading them to stop and examine the produce. Of course the usual price haggling always took place—but he expected that.

It was the common thread of love between father and son that had caused these worrisome thoughts about the on-going political troubles to stir in Cenobio's mind. He felt that the appeal for recruitment of young men was beginning to hit closer to home. He tried to cast aside these crazy thoughts, trying to convince himself that the dreadful scenario fabricated in his mind, was way overblown. After all, when he himself was younger, anti-government demonstrations and skirmishes had taken place, and to date, he had not taken part in any revolutionary movement.

So—*what's the big deal*, he thought to himself, trying to brush aside his worries. It's neither here nor there, at least not yet. And besides, *lo que sera, sera*— what will be, will be. And with this refreshing frame of mind, he found renewed comfort in just being home again after eight full days in San Luis.

It wasn't always easy for Cenobio to find a comfortable balance in his life, especially when problems never seemed to leave the horizon. And speaking of the horizon, as he squinted his eyes westward against the sun, it was difficult to smile and pretend to be happy. Because as he looked around, all he could see was the dismal effects of what the summer's unpredictable climate had produced. All bad. When he departed for San Luis a week ago, the cornfields were parched for lack of rain. But while he was away, torrential rains had practically inundated his little village. The creeks and gullies had swelled and running free. Some, tearing away at the cornfield borders and washing down whole acres of unharvested produce. A few local farmers saw their barns and sheds topple unto themselves, while other debris floated away. Even some pigs and sheep had drowned in the muddy water.

On seeing the rubble and debris scattered all around, Cenobio knew, all too well, that the storm had surely robbed many of the villagers—possibly himself also.

"Ahi te espero en la casa!" "I'll wait for you at the house," Juanito shouted, running on ahead.

"Tell your mother I'll be there shortly."

"Muy bien. Yo le digo."

Juanito was so glad to be home, he couldn't wait to see his mother. He had missed her terribly and could hardly wait to put his arms around her. He wanted to tell her everything about his weeklong trip—right down to the last detail. Including the twenty pesos he'd earned, and he couldn't stop thinking about how he would spend it.

Exhausted, Cenobio walked across the slippery dirt path, tied Sonso and Flojo to a nearby tree stump, and slowly inched himself down to rest in the stingy shade of a corner fence post of the corral belonging to his *padrino*, Panfilo Hernandez. Removing his dingy white *sombrero*, dripping wet from perspiration around the headband, he began to fan himself lazily, back and forth. At that moment of sheer hallucination, nothing could have hit the spot any better than *un vaso de agua fresca*, a cool glass of water, or better yet, *una cerbezita*, a beer.

After a few minutes of much needed rest in the shade, Cenobio slowly stood up, stretching his arms and shoulders from side to side to limber up his tired aching muscles. He unbuttoned the upper buttons of his long sleeve, cotton shirt and raised his collar all the way up to shield his neck from the hot sun. Slapping his sweaty hat against the side of his leg a few times, he walked over, untied the burros and headed for his house.

The last quarter mile would be the easiest of all, as he began walking lively, sidestepping the ruts in the murky wagon trail. After that 'five minute rest', he felt very much refreshed and could hardly wait to see his wife, Felipa. He loved her very much, and as usual, worried about her when he was away. As before, whenever possible he brought her and the children a little inexpensive gift; sometimes just a small trinket. But even that would be enough to bring joy and excitement to their faces, which was so important for him to see. Now he was thinking of the surprise for Felipa that he had traded for at the market; a beautiful *rebozo*, shawl. Knowing how badly she wanted one, he could hardly wait to present it to her.

No sooner had he started walking home, dodging the muddy crevices in the road, when he heard music to his ears. Yes, it was **Hilario** and his eight-year old daughter, **Gregoria,** running to meet him.

"Papa! Papa!" shouted Hilario, as he came running up the road leaving his sister behind.

With outstretched arms, Hilario sprang into his father's arms with much excitement.

"Papa, papa," he kept repeating. "You're back! You're back!"

Kissing and embracing his son only reminded him how much he'd missed them both.

"¿Hijo mio, ay mi'jo, como has estado?" "Son, my son, how've you been?"

Beaming with excitement and practically out of breath, Hilario said, "Papa, we sure missed you, and Papa, we had a real bad storm day before yesterday. We were scared. And Papa you know what, the storm caused a bad leak in our roof. Wait 'til you see it." "Papa what did you bring us from San Luis?"

As Hilario clutched his father's hand, Gregoria, running as fast as she could, finally caught up. Almost out of breath, she, too, was shouting,

"Papa! Papa!"

She jumped in her Papa's waiting arms, kissing him over and over and squeezing his neck. All the while, she was screaming at Hilario for running ahead of her. She wanted to be the first to greet her Papa.

"Dulce corazon, ay hija mia, que bonita te ves." "Oh, sweetheart, you look so pretty," Cenobio said, kissing her over and over with a tight squeeze.

"Te amo, chiquita."

"I love you too, Papa," said Gregoria, not wanting to let go. Jealous of Hilario and wanting all her Papa's attention, she pleaded, "Carry me, Papa."

Obligingly, he picked up his precious little angel and carried her a little way before putting her inside the empty wagon, saying, "Here, you can ride the rest of the way home."

"I wanna ride too Papa," said Hilario, as he quickly jumped in the moving cart.

"What's in this box?" he asked, noticing a drabby little cardboard box neatly tied with manila *cordon*. Cenobio had stashed it in the far corner of the cart bed hoping to keep it a surprise, at least until he got home..

"Don't touch it" he said. *"Esperate que llegemos ha la casa,"* "It's a surprise! Wait 'til we get home." Yanking at the burro's rein, he yelled, *"ahora Sonso, vamonos."*

The rest of the way home, Gregoria and Hilario continued teasing each other—in a playful way, of course—they were just glad that Papa was finally back home

It was nearing five o'clock on this late Friday afternoon as Cenobio steered Sonso and Flojo toward home. Soon, he would be passing in front of his godfather's ranch.

Panfilo Hernandez, Cenobio's Padrino and a prominent figure in the community, was nearing age 60, a little on the paunchy side with snow-white hair and a full mustache that still exposed a few strands of black—an absolutely friendly and amusing person, who had done quite well for himself. When talking to him, there could be no doubt about the air of sophistication he portrayed, nor the fact that he was also a man of high moral character. Besides being an influential leader in the village, he maintained strong political views. He was probably the best-dressed man in Villa de Reyes, and the only one who could afford tailor-made suits—traditional Spaniard styles, no less. Most of the time, he wore *tight-fitting* Charro suits that flared at the legs, and his silk *camisas,* shirts were of a variety of colors with ruffled cuffs. But for every day ranching, he could be seen in black square-toed boots, wearing a black leather *chaleco,* a vest that enhanced his image as a well-to-do rancher.

Don Panfilo happened to be outside, as Cenobio and the kids came by, still riding inside the empty cart. Hilario and Gregoria were still poking fun at each other when they spotted Don Panfilo behind the corral fence, walking one of his thoroughbred horses. "Hey Don Panfilo! Papa's back!" yelled, Hilario.

"Ay que bueno," he yelled back. *"Se los dije que volvia."* Kidding with them he said, "I told you he'd be back."

"Buenos dias Padrino, como le va?" I see you've been riding again," said Cenobio, greeting his padrino.

Don Panfilo walked closer to the front gate leading his favorite mare to chat with Cenobio, saying, "How did it go at the market this time, *ahijado*? (god-son) Was business good?"

"Si Padrino, it was alright. It took longer to sell my corn and tomatoes than I'd hoped. Too many people and too much competition."

"I know what you mean, *ahijado*, but that's the way it goes sometimes. I guess you noticed the rains finally came while you were gone. We had one hell'uva storm."

"I see that," said Cenobio, as he looked down at the muddy mess. "I can hardly walk around these puddles, and I'll bet it's worse down at my house."

"It probably is," Panfilo said, as he tried to settle down his restless mare. "But let's look at the bright side—we needed the rain."

"I know." Cenobio said. "I'm not complaining. See you later, Padrino. I'm really tired, and besides, I'm anxious to see Felipa. You know how she worries."

"Anda vete ahijado, te esta esperando." Panfilo agreed and urged Cenobio to go ahead. Felipa would be waiting for him.

"Ahi nos vemos, Padrino. Hasta luego." "See you later, Padrino." Then he gave a sharp whistle at Sonso and Flojo, and with a yank on the reins, he was on his way home again.

Panfilo Hernandez was a very prominent man in his own right and had become quite an influential staple of the town. He owned countless acres of tillable land on which he permitted sharecropping by many of the farmers who had little, or no land of their own. But even with all his success and wealth, he still enjoyed being a kind benefactor of the town. Living in a town where many of its people were illiterate, he served on the town council, organizing and coordinating fiestas, and sponsoring summertime rodeos. Panfilo was also a very religious man, having become godfather to a dozen or more children at their respective Baptisms, First Holy Communions and Confirmations. No doubt, he was the most respected man in all of Villa de Reyes—a true pillar of the community.

Don Panfilo lived on the outskirts of town, where he owned a Spanish-style adobe hacienda, by far, the most stylish in the entire village—artistically crafted with protruding round posts along the roofline, including arched corridors that guided the entryway to the front door. Black wrought-iron gates made of tall ornamental spears, signified the Panfilo horse ranch where the vastness of his estate proudly displayed an array of storage barns, sheds, stables and ranching equipment—including a bronco-busting arena. He had a passion for horses. Besides a herd of fine breeding horses, he also owned several well-trained thoroughbred trotters of pure Spanish stock. Sometimes he purchased wild horses and brought them to the ranch for taming by the *vaqueros*.

Closer to town, with the kids still in the cart, and the burros still pulling at the dilapidated, empty two-wheeled wagon, Cenobio's face began to beam with relief as he was nearing home. Now he could feel at ease amid familiar surroundings, and no longer would he have to put up with the hustle and bustle of the big city where dealing with strangers made him very uncomfortable.

To his left, he saw **Andres Luz** standing in front of his office talking to some friends. The sun had already begun descending in the west, and the men were taking advantage of the shady side of the building. One of the men was **Alfonzo**

Chavez, and another was **Jose Lopez.** Cenobio didn't recognize the third man, because he was facing the opposite direction. Alfonzo, 45, was the only barber in Villa de Reyes, who most people called *'peluco'*. He only worked part-time, usually in the mornings. The rest of the time, he worked on Panfilo's ranch as a horse trainer. Jose, 20, who had just gotten his hair cut, was a local vaquero and farm worker. Many considered him a big-mouth braggart with a know-it-all personality, and that's why he had been labeled *'el bocón'*.

Don Andres immediately recognized Cenobio and yelled out, *"Saludes Nóvo! Como te fue?"* "Hi Cenobio. How did it go?" he asked. At the same time, Alfonso and Jose also waved quite friendly with a *"buenos dias Cenobio."*

"It went good," he yelled back, without breaking stride toward home. "It could have been better though. I wasn't too happy with the prices, but it turned out alright. I'm just glad to be back" *";De donde viene tanta calor?"* "Where did this hot weather come from?" he asked.

"Mucha calor, verdad?" "Really hot, isnt' it?" Don Andres responded.

"Hay nos vemos" Cenobio yelled back, waving good-bye from a distance, "I'll see you later"

Quite often, merchants gathered in groups around closing time just to chat and pass the time of day; tell stories and joke with one another. Don Andres was the one who gave Cenobio the nickname of **Nóvo.** And he didn't mind it at all; in fact, he liked it and had become quite used to it.

Andres Luz, a very patriotic single man, had just turned 55. For a man his age, he was physically well preserved, not too tall, and his hair was starting to turn silver. He was lighter complexioned than most other residents; a self-educated man, a good horseman, part politician, and very friendly. He played a vital role in town, handling all civic affairs, tax records, property records, legal files, and he also resolved legal matters when necessary. His City Clerk's office was just a *one-man business office* that adjoined the fading white-framed courthouse. Of course, there were no paved sidewalks on the store fronts, just selected patches of gray flagstones articulately designed on the ground..

Looking ahead, still some distance away from his house, Cenobio was getting more and more anxious by the minute. He wished he could cut a path behind all the stores, so as to bypass the people milling around. But it wouldn't be that easy. Already he had spotted **Bentura y Josefa Cruz,** owners of the village grocery store: *Cruz Tienda de Comestibles.* Their storefront was trimmed in royal blue and displayed a mural depicting a lone peasant dressed in white, wearing the traditional Mexican sombrero, and pulling a weary donkey along a cactus lined trail. As Cenobio passed by, the Cruzes were busy gathering foodstuffs from their outdoor display, bringing them indoors at the end of the day. They hadn't seen Cenobio, so he didn't have to stop to visit.

At the *Tienda General*, he caught a glimpse of **Elena Gutierrez**, as she was walking away from the store. She, too, had probably just closed for the day

A little farther down the muddy road, Cenobio wanted to find a detour. He knew that if he stopped to talk to very many of his friends, he would be forever getting home. Exhausted and hungry, he was in no mood to kill anymore time.

But just as he turned into the narrow alley-way alongside **Concho Casemiro's Cantina**—out of the door came **Flaco (slim) Campos,** so named because of his long lanky frame which barely made a good shadow. The minute he stepped outside, he appeared to stagger slightly. It could have been the blinding sunlight that suddenly flashed in his face, or, it could have been that extra shot of *tequila*—the one for the road that he should have done without. Flaco was a slouchy dresser and didn't care who knew it. He was a good worker, however, and helped many farmers harvest their crops at various times. On seeing Flaco, Cenobio sped onward and pretended not to see him.

At last, Cenobio's familiar little house was in sight. His heart raced with excitement and his face brightened completely with smiles from ear to ear. His was not exactly a king's palace, but to him, *it was his palace—and his home. And even a king couldn't be happier at a moment like this.* Both of the kids, on seeing their house just a few yards away, jumped out of the wagon and ran on ahead as fast as they could, screaming and shouting,

"Mama! Mama!" "Papa's home!" "Papa's home!"

CHAPTER 3

▼

FAMILY

Felipa was standing behind the rustic screen door with her apron in her hand, as usual, exposing a faint silhouette of her petite body. Juanito had already broken the news to his mother that Papa was back. She was as nervous as a leaf in the wind, but excited nonetheless. She continued to peer out of the door, waiting to get a glimpse of her *viejo.* (ole' man) Brushing her hair away from her face repeatedly, she couldn't stop fidgeting with her hands. Just like the children, she could hardly wait. To her, it seemed Cenobio had been gone a month. She was afraid of being alone at night, but having him at home, by his mere presence, always reduced all her worries to pure triviality.

Felipa was a very pretty young woman and genuinely friendly. But for the most part, had lived somewhat of a closeted life. Despite being a reserved person, however, on occasion, she was capable of surprising people by coming out of her shell with streams of laughter. At 39, and only five feet tall, her face was still smooth as silk, complimented by her long shiny black hair that hung loosely on her shoulders after she unpinned it at night. During the day, she wore it in a *chongo,* a round bun behind her head with a pretty elastic silver band trimmed in red and gold. Cenobio had given it to her some time ago, and even though she had other hair novelties, this one was special. She rarely took it off.

The same was true of her apron. She wouldn't be Felipa without her apron securely wrapped around her waist. It was just a simple tie-behind apron with a thin, braided neck strap, but it too, was practically a permanent part of her every-day dress. On it, was embroidered a beautiful red rose trimmed in white and green with a monogrammed endearment which read, "*Felipa mia.*" To her, it was just one more treasured gift from her *viejo.*

Like most other women in Villa de Reyes, Felipa was an excellent cook. Especially when preparing her favorite specialties, like; chicken with mole, hot tamales, tacos, and enchiladas. She could easily whip up a fantastic meal from simple leftovers, and even when the family wondered *what's for supper* knowing the cupboard was nearly bare, she could come up with a tasty surprise. Daily, without fail, she could be found in her tiny kitchen making a stack of delicious corn tortillas to go with their meals.

Felipa—a very frugal person—had no formal education. She couldn't read or write and didn't really care to learn. However, she did learn how to count money and applied it very carefully when necessary. On the times when she went to the market to buy fresh vegetables, no one could cheat her. When making a purchase, she'd very meticulously, *untie the knot in her white silk handkerchief where she kept her money,* then start counting it out—right down to the last *centavo.*

As Cenobio stepped inside the door—his face reddened from being sun drenched—immediately his eyes were fixed on Felipa, his wife of 17 years. She, too, her eyes glistening, revealed her lonesomeness for her *Viejo.* Reaching out to her, he said, "*Ay querida, ven aquí.*" "Come here my love." Embracing her tightly and swaying her excitedly from side to side, he continued to kiss her over and over, repeating, "*Ay querida, como te quero.*" "I love you, I love you."

"*Tambien te quiero mucho,*" "Oh, I love you too," she said, as Cenobio gently put her down.

"Why were you gone so long? I thought you would be home two days ago."

"I know *querida,* but remember, this year's corn was not the best. I didn't think I'd ever sell it all" he said, taking off his sweaty hat and hanging it on a nail.

"Oh, yes. I remember now. Anyway, you're home now and I'm glad. How much money did we make this trip," she asked.

"225 pesos," he replied, handing her a soft, leather *portamoneda,* money pouch. "Not near as much as the last trip, but it's that much more to add to our savings. We should have nearly 650 pesos by now. Right?" he asked, taking off his sweaty shirt.

"That's pretty close," she answered, as Cenobio sat down at the kitchen table enjoying the cool breeze coming in through the open shutter.

"But we'll need some of it right away. Come over here and see what the storm did."

Still holding his hand, she led him into the bedroom where the damage had occurred.

The first thing he noticed, were two blue porcelain pans and a water bucket on the floor placed directly under the spot where the leaks had sprung. As he looked upward at the ceiling, bright rays of sunlight blinded his face. The wooden floor was rain soaked. Everything that previously belonged in the kid's cubicle had been moved to another room. Including the two *petates* that they slept on.

"*Caramba!*" "*Ay que maldita suerte,*" he blasphemed "What damned bad luck. That's why we never get ahead! It's always something!" Continuing his infuriated rage over one more problem to contend with, shaking his head in disgust, he said, "I should be mad at God for never letting up on us."

Scolding him humorously for swearing, Felipa quickly put her hand over his mouth, saying, "Shuush" "*No hables hacina, viejo, porque Dios te puede castigar.*" "Don't talk that way, viejo, God might punish you, and besides, it wasn't His fault."

After a few minutes, Cenobio retracted his anger and began to feel repentant. He didn't need to be reminded that it was, after all, God's generous bounty that gave him good health and food for their table—not to mention the roof over their heads and the 225 pesos he'd just given Felipa to put away.

"*Perdoname, Senor.*" "Forgive me Lord," he said, looking skyward; crossing himself with the Sign of the Cross.

Cenobio had always been a thankful person, never forgetting where his blessings came from. But this time, it caught him off guard, and momentarily, he felt abandoned by the Almighty. And, understandably so, because three years ago he lost his mother who died of cancer, he still owed his padrino for a previous loan which still hadn't been repaid, and for the last two years, crops had failed to produce adequately. Moreover, much needed repairs to the house still could not be attended to for lack of money. So, with all these worries hanging over his head, at any unguarded moment, he could easily feel burdened with one more costly situation. But being a righteous man, he promised never to show contempt for his God again.

"This is the worse yet, isn't it, 'Lipa?" he said, still halfway peeved, staring at the hole in the ceiling.

Felipa put her arm on his shoulder saying, "*No te apures viejo. Dios nos salvó,*" telling him not to worry, and to look at the bright side because, afterall, God did spare their lives.

"Go out on the patio where it's cooler, honey. You can rest out there while I fix supper. I'm glad you're finally home." Kissing him lightly on the cheek, one more time, she walked back to the kitchen.

"Me too," he said. "I'm so glad this trip is over. The heat was almost too much."

He kicked off the muddy boots from his tired aching feet; sat down in his favorite arm chair, and was just about to lay his head back to get comfortable, when Gregoria came running in all excited, interrupting his rest. She was carrying the little cardboard box that Cenobio had tried to keep secret. But in his fatigue and eagerness to be back home, he completely forgot all about bringing it inside.

"Papa, what's in the box? Is it for me?" she asked. "Can I open it?"

"It's a surprise *chiquita,*" he said. "No. You can't open it. Take it in the kitchen and we'll open it right after we eat."

Thoroughly exhausted, he leaned back in his waiting arm chair and within minutes, he was fast asleep. Gregoria took the box back in the kitchen like she was told, but sat down beside it, wondering what could it be.

Juanito went outside to talk to some friends and couldn't wait to describe his trip to San Luis with much enthusiasm—including showing off his new white hat. He had already curled up the sides on it, and shaped the tip to look exactly like his Papa's. Excitedly, he recounted the chat he'd had with the three young soldiers who had just joined the Army, and how one of them even let him hold his rifle. His little friends listened intently, as Juanito described his alluring fascination with the big city; with all its many stores, buildings, the streets, and, Oooh, so many people. Even he, was getting excited all over again reliving his market experience.

Hilario—Cenobio's 2nd born—was a good little boy—most of the time, that is. He was taller than his mother, but not yet as tall as Juanito. He was on the chubby side; didn't have wavy hair like Juanito, and didn't like wearing a hat. He could be feisty and temperamental at times and not always an obedient child. He tried to be obedient, but distractions by his friends sometimes got him in trouble. That was because his attention span was almost nil. His sporadic behavior at times required more discipline than the other two children, meaning more *azotes* with a leather belt.

Gregoria, on the other hand, was different still. True, she was the youngest, but absolutely the sweetest. She had a child-like innocence and such a sweet personality that one couldn't help but love her to pieces. Her Papa called her *mi morenita*; an endearing name for his cute, little, dark-brown angel. Much like her mother, Gregoria was petite, and her brunette hair was soft as silk and naturally wavy. Recently, she started school, attending only two days per week and already learning to read and write.

Cenobio had been fast asleep for about 45 minutes, when he felt a sharp tap on his left shoulder. Dead to the world in slumber, he jerked around clumsily, only to see Gregoria standing beside him, giggling at the way she'd startled him.

Still grinning, she said, *"Ya esta la cena, Papa."* "Supper is ready Papa."

"Ay Morenita you scared me," he said, shaking his head from side to side trying to regain consciousness. "Alright, I'm coming—let me wash up first. Tell mama I'll be right there."

He stood up slowly and began to twist his upper body slowly from side to side and stretched his arms back and forth trying to restart the circulation. Walking through the dirt-floored kitchen toward the back door, he couldn't help getting a whiff of that wonderful familiar aroma of supper waiting on the table—the same wonderful aroma he'd smelled a million times before; fried beans, chicken with *mole*, hot chili salsa, and hot corn tortillas.

"Ay Lipa, la cena huele muy deliciosa. Ya mero me muero de hambre." "Mmmm, Mmmm," he said. "Lipa, supper sure smells delicious, and I'm about to starve. Be right back," he said. "I'm going outside to wash up."

Just outside the kitchen door sat a white porcelain *lava manos* on a dried up tree stump. To the right of the stump, stood a 60-gallon wooden cypress barrel full of rainwater. Cenobio utilized rainwater for bathing, hair washing, and dish washing, but primarily, to preserve their precious drinking water He, like other residents, had built a rain gutter of sorts and installed it all around the house along the roof's eaves. It was a simple makeshift gutter, constructed of scrap metal and corrugated tin to catch the water run off and direct its flow to the waiting containers. All of Cenobio's three wooden water barrels and three metal drums had been spotted at key locations around the house and were full to the brim with rainwater from the recent storm. Now, if they used it sparingly, it should last a good long time.

Reaching for the water dipper, Cenobio scooped up several dippers of God-sent water out of the rain barrel and poured it into the wash pan and proceeded to splash water all over his head and face.

At the supper table, everyone was seated at their respective places, hungry as could be, and ready to dive in. Each one religiously made the Sign of the Cross, which was their custom before each meal, and as usual, Cenobio was first to pass the dishes around. For Felipa, having her *viejo* back home from the market, it was almost a reason to celebrate and a feeling of gladness had prompted her to use her new white tablecloth. Cenobio, now partially rested and wide awake after that cool dowsing, rubbed his hands together comically and with a cheerful grin, gave the order.

"Lets eat."

"Mama, these *frijoles* are really delicious. Are they different?" asked Juanito, as he tore off small pieces of his tortilla to use as bite-size scoops. *Of course, everyone else was using the same scooping method, since they didn't use forks.*

"*No, mi hijito.*" "The beans are the same. I just cooked them in some pork lard that I'd been saving."

"Mmmm!" Mmmm!" "This chicken in mole is really delicious" remarked Cenobio. "Why are we having chicken today?" he asked. "*Hoy no es Domingo,*" "This is not Sunday," referring to their Sunday dinners when chicken was considered a special family treat. Because, except for special occasions, they raised chickens primarily for selling.

"Today's just special," she replied. "I'm just glad you're home."

"Me too," chimed in Gregoria.

"*Yo tambien,*" agreed Hilario.

Juanito was the first to open the conversation at the supper table, saying, "Mama, I hope someday you can go to San Luis, it's a terrific city. You'd love their super *marqueta*. It's one hundred times bigger than ours, and I believe there are a lot of rich people in San Luis."

"*Hijo,* I have no desire to go to San Luis," she replied. "It takes a lot of money to shop in the big city, and you know we don't have any money. And besides, how would I get there." "*¿Trepado en el carreton como tú?*" "Ride in the wagon like you?"

"I know Mama," he continued, "I know it wouldn't be easy, but it sure would be nice if you could see how other people live. Everybody there seems to have more than we do, and I was just thinking how nice it would be for you to see the big city, especially the pretty dresses the women wear."

"*Pero quien quite un dia, si Dios nos da lisencia.*" "Maybe someday son. God willing."

"I hope so, Mama."

Cenobio could see that little Juanito was still overwhelmed about the trip to San Luis. Even though he'd been there several times before, this time, something must have made a lasting impression. In the back of his mind, he knew that his son had finally noticed all the difference in the world between the Big City and his little hometown of Villa de Reyes. And in his affectionate little heart, was merely wishing that his mother could also see the exciting City of San Luis. He was beginning to grow up and discern for himself that just perhaps—somewhere besides Villa de Reyes—there could be a more exciting life. Naively, he had interpreted the highly energized hustle and bustle of the market in San Luis as a place where money flowed freely, and where most people there were much better off. He didn't realize that the people that had impressed him so much, were just ordinary people like themselves, and all they were doing was simply selling their wares and produce in order to buy the necessities for tomorrow and the tomorrows to come—just as they were doing. In his heart, Cenobio could see the attraction for the big city building up in his young son and would never disillusion him. Instead, he just beamed with admiration for little Juanito's thoughtfulness and considerate nature.

Supper was great. And what made it so delicious was the chicken with mole that was added as a special feast for Cenobio's return from the market. But often times, meals were not usually that special, because every day, seven days a week, year-round, their humble meals seldom consisted of more than fried and re-fried beans and corn tortillas. At other times, however, if the family ever splurged on other dishes, it was at the fiestas. And of course, at the fiestas, they would all take full advantage of every single dish they could afford.

"*Ahora si, Papa?*" "Now?" asked Gregoria.

"Now what?" replied Cenobio, winking at Felipa.

"You know! My present in the box"

"Oh that!" "Alright sweetheart, bring it here," he said with a sly grin.

Impatiently, Gregoria quickly retrieved the mystery box from the kitchen and handed it to her papa.

"*Ahora es tiempo.*" "Now then, lets see what we have here."

Untying the box and dropping the loose string to the floor, Cenobio slowly opened the box and began pulling out each gift, one by one.

"Hilario, this is for you," he said, handing him a noisy little cloth sack.

"What's in it, papa?" he asked, as he kept shaking it.

"Oh boy!" he exclaimed. "*Canicas! Gracias Papa*" "You knew I wanted some marbles, didn't you?"

Reaching in the box again, Cenobio pulled out the *rebozo* and handed it to Felipa, "*Para ti, mi amor.*" "For you my love. I hope you like it."

On seeing the beautiful shawl, she was completely taken by surprise and overwhelmed by her *viejo's* thoughtfulness. Misty-eyed and joyfully laughing, she held it up for everyone to see.

"Ay viejo, te acordates." "Oh honey, you remembered," she said, reaching over to kiss him.

"Papa, what about me?" asked Gregoria.

"What about you, honey?" he asked kiddingly, again slyly winking at Felipa.

"Didn't you bring me a present?"

"Bueno, dúlce corazon," "Alright sweetheart" he said, pretending to search the bottom of the box "Let's see if there's something else in here."

"Ah, here it is," he said, handing her a small gift box containing a little hand-made bracelet decorated with tiny, green, jaded stones.

"Oh Papa!" "Oh, it's beautiful!" "I love you papa."

Juanito looked on, as he watched the gift presentation. But his present was the white straw hat that lay beside him on the floor, and until its newness wears off, it'll always be close at hand.

On seeing the happy smiles on the faces of his family, Cenobio—a proud Papa—gently eased back in his chair. Proud because if only for a brief moment he had removed the cloak of the poor life, *la pobre vida*, from his family.

Completely exhausted, he went to bed immediately after supper, wishing he could sleep the entire weekend.

CHAPTER 4

▼

REVOLUTIONARIES STRIKE

When Cenobio went to bed last night, he was so exhausted that he had every intention of sleeping at least until noon. But it was only wishful thinking, because as always by five O'clock in the morning, he was wide awake and ready for another day's work. For him—a workaholic—there was never a lack for work to be done, whether it was the cornfields, produce gardens, planting, harvesting, market vending, or needed repairs to his shabby *jacal,* little shack. Aside from the hot afternoon siestas, he found very little time for personal pleasure or relaxation.

Usually for Cenobio, after having labored in the fields all day, he could find peaceful relaxation playing his *mandolína.* Many evenings after supper, he could be found sitting in the privacy of his small court yard with his mandolin, playing soft romantic tunes, mixed with story-telling ballads, like *quatro milpas,* 'the four cornfields' and beautiful Spanish waltzes such as *sobre las olas,* 'over the waves'. For him, there was something naturally soothing about beautiful soft music, and the way it greatly relieved the weighty stress on his mind. Particularly, in the cool of the evenings when under a starlit sky, his music could drive away the troubling cares of the day.

Felipa was already stirring about in the kitchen, and the roosters were repeatedly crowing from the chicken pen announcing the start of a new day. The children were all asleep, as was Felipa's sister **Petra**, her husband **Pablo Manriquez**, and their two children **Roberto y Trena**. **Señora Victoria**—Felipa & Petra's mother—who also lived in the household, was also still in bed. As always, Felipa was first to rise and had made her usual morning trip to the chicken coop to gather eggs and had already dampened the dirt floor in the kitchen, which was just another early morning *quehacer,* chore that she could have easily performed half asleep. Next on her list of sleepy-eyed chores, was to stir the ashes in the earthen oven from the previous evening meal to boil water for Cenobio's coffee. This was her routine every morning, as automatic as *persinandose,* making the sign of the cross after praying *El Padre Nuestro* and *Santa Maria.*

Felipa's kitchen was nothing to brag about, but she kept it very cozy and inviting. It was furnished adequately, but only with the simplest of necessities. Her old upright cupboard with glass doors, nicely exposed her finest flower-designed dishes that she used only on special occasions, as well as the plain every-day dishes with cracked and chipped edges. Here too, she kept all her clay pots for cooking; her *vasos, copas, platos y ollas,* and *casuelas.* Her *horno,* oven where she cooked her meals was recessed into the wall nearly knee-high.

A crudely designed worktable sat in the middle of the kitchen floor and used primarily for meal preparation and for making tortillas and hot tamales. On one corner of the table, a *molino* had been mounted for use in grinding corn into meal. Underneath the work table, she stored her *molcajete* and *tejolote,* which was a simple mixing bowl made of black mortar rock, including a pestle, used for mashing chili peppers, cumin, and garlic.

Other necessary items included woven baskets, which *hung from the ceiling* containing certain foodstuffs such as chili, beans, eggs, half-dried beef and tortillas. She kept them covered at all times for protection from gathering flies and sometimes *cucarachas y ratas.* In the corner were buckets for carrying water from the communal well. In another corner of the room, lay a large metal basket-like cradle used for storing wood or coal, including a black stoking rod and a mini-shovel layered with coal dust.

The east exterior wall had no windows. Instead, it had adjustable wooden shutters, openable and closeable to let in the daylight or keep out the darkness of night—including the rain. Over Felipa's dinner table, hung a simple lantern made from a recycled tin can with cleverly designed holes punched all around for candle lighting after dark. She also had several of these hanging in other rooms.

An early morning breeze was gently finding its way past the open shutters and the sunrise was beginning to expose its beautiful rays of daylight, as Cenobio sat at the kitchen table, breaking fast with a small bowl of *avena*, oatmeal, and drinking his black coffee. On his mind, was repairing the roof. Slowly, he raised up out of his squeaky chair holding on to his half-full coffee cup, and began surveying the damage to the roof. Again, the very sight of the storm damage and the thought of the money needed for repairing it, caused him to shake his head in dismay. After staring at the gaping hole in the decking and rain-soaked floor for a few minutes, he quickly formed a mental list of the materials required: floor and ceiling planks, roll roofing paper and tar.

Sipping at his coffee once more, he inspected the rest of the house for damage. Besides a few broken slats on the window shutters, some uprooted outdoor plants, and a short section of the back yard fence blown down, he concluded that—yes, the windstorm could have been much worse after all.

On occasion, Cenobio had measured his impoverished existence, his humble dwelling, his age-old household belongings, and the two acres of land left him by his father, wondering if any gains in life had ever been made. But each time he did so, apart from his beautiful wife and three wonderful children, he saw none. But if there ever was any consolation to this pale fact of life, it would be that all other residents of Villa de Reyes were just as poor. In reality, their modest way of life, living in a town where riches are merely dreams, all the tomorrows are the same. That's why periodic assessments of his earthly possessions are not necessary, since he has no choice but to live out his life in a plain and simple state of coexistence with the other villagers. As a matter of fact, all of Cenobio's worldly goods, too, were just that—plain and simple. Even though no significant strides had ever been made, in one way, however, he was better off than many others, because his house, unlike many others, was a separate stand-alone residence.

Cenobio's home, by no means elegant, faced a narrow dirt road that not too many years prior was only a wide path and an oxen trail. Now the street was busy enough to bear the name **Saltillo Road,** which led to a much better road called **Camino Real.** This one led directly into town. Cenobio became better off than a lot of other villagers when his father purchased two acres of rich tillable soil directly behind his house and willed it to him on his death. This not only made him a legal landowner, but it provided much space and privacy, not too common in the village. His house, which was colorfully painted and better maintained, clearly identified it from the rest. The white front gate made of dry oak and hinged on a piece of steel pipe, noisily opened onto a narrow cobblestone pathway to the front door. His house was bordered on both sides with beautiful white stone, whereas, the rear yard's fence, while also serving as a boundary, was a crude display of a variety of wooden posts, an assortment of slats, and some corrugated tin. Off to one side of his piece-meal fence, was another wooden gate leading to two small sheds, roofed with fifty-year old corrugated, rusty sheet iron used for storing feed and farming tools. A small pigpen had been thrown together with random tree logs for keeping *el cochino* penned up Cenobio had also built a chicken coop for the family's three dozen chickens and another small barn for *Sonso and Flojo*. From a distance, it had the appearance of a small age-old *ranchito*.

Cenobio's modest little home—without electricity or utilities—was just barely large enough to accommodate a family of nine that consisted of 6 small rooms—two of which had never seen a wooden floor. Two of the bedrooms were comfortably furnished, while the others were still using bunks and petates for sleeping on the floor, all of which were used to sit on during the day. *La Sala* is where the family usually congregated after meals and before retiring to bed. No matter how humble the house or furnishings, Felipa kept it clean and beautifully decorated with potted plants and flowers. Most importantly, in the corner, Cenobio had built a *small prayer alter* which she had enshrined with saintly statues, pretty vases, fresh flowers, a bible, rosaries, an incense burner, crucifixes, and candles. It also included pictures of the family's patron saints—*La Virgen de Guadalupe* and *La Santa Familia, Jesus Maria y Jose.* Here, quite often Cenobio and Felipa knelt on a padded bench to pray—not to the statues nor the pictures on the wall, but to their heavenly Father.

The simple patio out back was also a beautiful picturesque setting, protected on both sides by 6' high adobe walls. Within the patio, Felipa had planted many pretty flowers and a variety of live cactus plants, which she kept in colorfully painted pots and old wash tubs. The sweet fragrance from her plants and flowers purposely intercepted the foul odor coming from the chicken pen and the burro's corral. An outdoor, cooking hearth, which was no more than a flat clay griddle supported by four earthen rocks, was used quite often. Particularly, during the summer months when they frequently roasted ears of fresh corn direct from the field. In the middle of the yard, stood a beautiful magnolia tree surrounded by an array of creeping phlox.

Other villagers, not quite as fortunate, lived in rows of connected units with absolutely no land of their own. Their frontage was no more than a narrow dirt road resembling an alleyway, dividing the tenants into opposite sides. That narrow road, however, was quite a valued piece of real estate owned by the town, but thoroughly enjoyed and maintained by its inhabitants. Early every morning found the women folk sprinkling water on their respective frontage, followed by sweeping it clean and sometimes relocating the surface dirt for the daily morning gathering of neighbors who liked to visit. During the day, the men folk used the road to get to their work place, hauling feed, tools and equipment, pulling or pushing wagons; some of which were horse drawn. And then again at day's end, the visitation started all over again, as neighbors carried wooden chairs and benches outside to the *calle* just to chat and enjoy the cool of the evening.

Farther out of town lived a cluster of indigents who made up the lower class district of Villa de Reyes. And for these poor souls, life, and their way of life, was a completely different story. Compared to the ordinary poor Mexican families in the village, these all-but-forgotten folks were literally the 'have-nots' living on hillside slums whose daily lives were deeply anchored in poverty. Theirs were not exactly houses—they were mere make-shift huts thrown together with a mixture of random materials in all shapes and sizes; some were square, some round, while others were long and narrow cubicles that accommodated their large families, and, of course, many with earthen floors. Sleeping mats made of thick fleshy maguey leaves were also used for thatching roofs for protection from the hot sun, with limited protection from the rains. Outdoor sheds, chicken pens and small barns still used a sod covering on their roofs.

Dressed in black pants and a long sleeve white shirt, Cenobio reached for his straw hat and yelled back at Felipa, *"Ya me voy!, Lipa. Voy a la maderería y la ferretería."* "I'm leaving now, honey. I won't be gone very long." A lumberyard and hardware store is where he'd find the needed materials to fix the roof. Already, the early morning sun was beginning to climb, as he was walking to the tool shed to pick up his two-wheel wagon. Not totally awake, he made his way to the front gate and onto Saltillo road.

At this early hour, not many people were yet milling around, except for those responding to the timely chimes of the church bells announcing start of the seven O-clock Mass. The fresh breeze that was coming out of the southwast still retained the fragrance of the dampened earth caused by the recent rains. In the low lying areas, fluffy clouds gathered as they floated across the sky. There were the usual number of early risers briskly scurrying in various directions; some carrying boxes, some carrying tools, and others walking lively to the church.. A few children were outside playing and some of the neighbors, too, were already outside on their front porches fanning themselves from on-coming heat of another hot day. Also, stray chickens roamed freely on some of the gritty yards, scratching around for strewn corn scraps and the like. Likewise, barking dogs were in their respective yards, guarding and protecting their masters. And because ordinances in town were loose and unenforced, all domestic animals, like; a few cows, horses, donkeys, goats and pigs were *commonplace* in most adjoining yards. All one had to do, was to stroll around the neighborhood to smell the presence of hay, barnyard *caca* and chicken *caca.* This type of country environment, however, was totally acceptable and commonplace for the people of the village. No one ever complained. .

At the other end of Saltillo road, near Camino Real, Cenobio could see several *vaqueros* at the *Sanchez ranch,* exercising their ponies in preparation for the Sunday's afternoon rodeo. Alfonzo Chavez was already putting 'chacho', his Palomino gelding, through his paces.

As the sun continued to rise, the morning's cool breeze had stopped, and from the looks of the clear blue sky, it promised to be another scorcher. This year, the entire month of August had been brutal in every way—for the crops, the stock, and the people.

As Cenobio made his way ever closer to town, he couldn't help but notice a peculiar cloud of dark smoke coming out of the eastward sky—perhaps from the direction of the nearby village of **Maria Del Rio**. Something like this was unusual, of course, but too far away to be concerned with. But as he walked along pushing the empty cart, occasionally, he stopped to shade his eyes from the rising sun and gaze at the distant black smoke. It puzzled him.

As he continued to look toward the direction of the smoke, he shuttered as a sense of fear came over him. It was as though he was seeing a familiar ghost. *Could this be a bad omen?* he thought to himself, increasingly wondering about the far away smoke. Something of this magnitude seldom happened around here.

The fear Cenobio was feeling, was brought on by recalling a tragic fire that destroyed **Soilo Manriquez's** house—Senora Victoria's husband—and how he fought the blazing inferno trying to rescue him. That fatal fire of three years ago left a *deep indelible* scar on his mind—the memory of which was now being relived on seeing the distant *billowing black* smoke. It just so happened that Soilo not only had a compulsive drinking habit, but also, a very bad temper. And on the night of the fire, a heated argument led to a drunken brawl with another town drunkard, turning over a lighted coal oil lamp. In a flash, the house was engulfed in flames, trapping Soilo inside. Being in no condition to escape, he perished that same night in that awful fire. Cenobio quickly shook these horrible thoughts out of his head and quit staring at the distant smoke.

Now Cenobio's little town of Villa de Reyes was a very old village. Ask anyone on the street how old their town was, and they'd probably respond with a *yo no se,*

I don't know. He had lived here all his life, as did his parents, and their parent's parents. The land itself was not exactly flat country, yet in some ways, it was like a hidden valley, surrounded by waves of slopes and hollows. In the center of town, as like other small towns, was a wide open space spared of private and business development for use as a public square. Of course, within very close walking distance of the square, was the Catholic Church—*La Virgen de Guadalupe*—which in essence, was the dominant driving force behind all things among the faithful. The **Santa María River** that once flowed rapidly along the edge of town and used to provide abundant irrigation for the crops, no longer swelled or sped to its destination as in years past.

As Cenobio turned north on Camino Real, which was the most widely used artery in town, he saw wives and daughters already gathering at the *pila*—a communal water well—with their buckets and basins for drawing their daily supply of fresh water; a self delegated responsibility of the women.

Closer to town, on the corner of *'Nieto Road'* stood what used to be the old one-room school house that until two years ago, held daily classes for those who could afford schooling. When the number of students dropped off dramatically, *Señorita* **Manuela Puentes**, moved away to San Luis to teach full time. After that, teachers were few and far between in Villa de Reyes.

As Cenobio passed by the schoolhouse, he waved a *buenos dias* to the children in response to those who recognized him. Smiling and waving with such a friendly greeting, they shouted, *"buenos dias, Don Cenobio."* Again, fond memories of the old school house—and **Doña María,** his old teacher—reminded him of the days when he attended school. He remembered how they used a miniature chalkboard when learning simple arithmetic, and how they dipped their pens in shallow inkwells when practicing penmanship, and how everyone washed their hands out of the same pan of water before lunch. And he remembered too, how silly he thought it was back then to always be sure to say *Sí Señor, No Señor, Sí Señora, and No Señora.* But the most enduring lesson of all was the consequences for misbehavior—*Azotes with a belt.* He never had an ounce of regret for attending school. His only regret was that he didn't complete his education.

Continuing north on Camino Real, passed **Vivora Road, Camaron Road, Ebodio Road, La Plaza de Armas, La Plaza de Gallos,** cock fighting arena, he finally reached **San Juan Road.** Now, **Reyes' Madereria,** lumber store was in plain sight, as was **Roberto's Ferreteria,** hardward store, so he decided to stop and rest for a minute in the shade of **Rico's Panaderia,** bakery. As he rested, he kept repeating to himself the materials he would purchase.

When he approached the entrance to the lumber store, he noticed some men standing in front, pointing to the north and talking excitedly. Cenobio turned and saw immediately what the men were concerned about. It was the same dark smoke in the distance that he had noticed earlier, and in the same direction of the village of **María Del Rio**. Obviously concerned, as he had been, they were making remarks like, *"¿Que sera esa lumbre?" "¿De donde vendra tanto humo?" "Yo creo que viene del pueblito de María del Rio"*

"I wonder what that fire is?" "I wonder where all that smoke is coming from?" and another would say, "I think it's coming from the little town of Maria del Rio." As the other bystanders began to gather around, they continued speculating, "Maybe we should go check it out" "Surely someone died in that fire". Then another bystander said, "Aw, it'll be all right. Someone over there is probably just burning a wood pile from clearing some land." After a few minutes of exchanging comments with the men, Cenobio proceeded to make his intended purchases, loaded them in the cart, and headed for home.

Already, the sun was beginning to get serious with its promise of another hot day. Cenobio yanked on the little silver chain attached to the fob at the upper front pocket of his trousers and looked at his watch. *"Ay caramba, ya son las ocho."* "Oh my, it's already eight O'clock." Sure enough, Mass had just ended and people were starting to appear everywhere. Hurriedly, he stepped up his pace, because he still needed to go by Don Andres Luz's office to take care of some business regarding two adjoining shanties on Camaron Road that he wanted to purchase. He had already made a down payment of fifty pesos and was anxious to see how *las escrituras,* the abstract was coming along. He'd always had high hopes of becoming a property owner someday, but, heretofore, it was never possible. This time, however, he made the supreme sacrifice by stepping out. Fifty pesos was a lot of money, but he badly wanted the property for Juanito's future, and prayed someday, it would prove to be a good investment.

Cenobio knocked on the front door of Don Luz's City Clerk's office and was surprised to find the door locked. He wondered, *how can this be? This is Saturday. He's always open on Saturdays.* No one answered the door, so he knocked again, this time, louder and longer. Again, he waited and waited. He was just about to give up and walk away, when the door cracked opened. It was Don Luz's brother, **Ramon Luz.**

"A, eres tú Cenobio, esperame un momento," Oh, it's you, Cenobio. Wait just a minute," Then Ramon closed the door behind him. *How strange,* Cenobio

thought, not expecting Ramon at the door. *He seldom comes around his brother's office.*

After a minute or two, Ramon opened the door again.

"Pasate" he said, in a mysterious whisper, as he peeked up and down the road through the half-opened door. *"Pronto!"*

Immediately Cenobio sensed something was wrong. On entering the poorly furnished office, he was not impressed. The only resemblance to a municipal office was one office desk, an antique typewriter, a hand-crank adding machine and one wooden file cabinet, besides the usual charts and maps, and stacks of legal files and documents. As he looked around, he wondered to himself, *why were the curtains closed,* and *why was the office closed for business?* Now, he was really beginning to worry.

"Ven con migo," "Come with me." said Ramon, leading Cenobio down the dark hallway and into a back room, *"Pero no vayas a decir nada,"* "But don't say a word about this to anyone."

When Ramon opened the door of the back room for Cenobio to enter, he got the shock of his life. His Padrino Panfilo, with blood on his hands and all over his shirt, quickly whisked him inside by the arm. Now his suspicions were really beginning to multiply. Especially when Panfilo reached over and softly whispered something in Ramon's ear, and how Ramon departed immediately out the back door.

"Pronto," Panfilo whispered, in a cloud of mystery *"Pasa para dentro."* "Quick, come inside."

"Padrino!" cried Cenobio, almost at a yell, as he suddenly tensed up with fear and felt his heart racing. *"¿Que pasó?"* he asked. "What's going on here? Are you in some kind of trouble?"

"Shush" he said, placing his forefinger over his lips as a sign to be quiet.

"No hables muy fuerte." "Don't talk too loud."

Looking around the dimly lit room, his eyes flashing from one side to the other, it was a scene of pure chaos. Cenobio saw spatters of blood everywhere. In the corner on the floor, he saw pistols, rifles and shoulder gun belts. On seeing boxes of ammunition and small arms strewn all over the floor, his heart almost stopped, especially when he saw several wounded men near death.

"Ay Dios mio" *"Padrino!"* he called out, as he made the Sign of the Cross. Then he noticed that Don Andres was one of the wounded men.

First off, he saw Doctor **Francisco (Pancho) Julano** bent over Don Andres tending to a gun shot wound in the shoulder, groaning in pain on a wooden cot.

Again, Cenobio pleaded with Don Panfilo, this time more forcefully, *"Padrino. Por favor,* tell me what happened! Who shot these men?"

"I can explain everything," Panfilo exclaimed. "But not now. Right now, I need your help. Please do what Doctor Francisco tells you."

'Quitate la camisa y ayudame." ordered Doctor **Francisco**, asking Cenobio to take off his shirt so he could help with the surgery.

Dazed, his hand shaking nervously, he held the lamp closer to Don Andres' open wound. It looked as if the flesh had been ripped open. Without any anesthetic, Doctor Francisco poured raw whiskey on the bleeding wound for sterilization, and instantly, Don Andres screamed and tensed in agony. All during the suturing, he lay grimacing in enormous pain and white as a sheet.

Cenobio looked down at two more bloody bodies on the floor. One man, whom he'd never met, but remembered seeing at Panfilo's ranch, was obviously dead, because his head had already been covered with a red-checkered bandana. A third man lay on the bare floor with only someone's coat to support his head. This man Cenobio did recognize. He was **Eduardo**, Panfilo's ranch foreman. He too had been critically wounded with a gunshot wound to the stomach. Still conscious and sweating profusely, he kept begging for the doctor, while lying in a pool of blood.

"Andale Don Francisco," he begged. "I can't stand it much longer. Is there some whiskey in the house?" *"Creo que me voy ha morir"* "I think I'm going to die." After a brief pause, gasping he asked Don Panfilo, "How did we do last night, *mi jefe?"*

He continued to gasp for breath and coughed continuously, as though his lungs were on the verge of collapsing. Don Panfilo knelt beside him all the while, wiping the perspiration from his face, trying to comfort him and keep him quiet. He was almost certain that his foreman would never make it, but kept saying repeatedly, "Hang on Eduardo. Hang on. The doctor's coming."

By now, Cenobio's mind was in a whirlwind trying to decipher what the heck was going on. All he could think of was, *who did this? Where did all this happen, and when?* And *why all the secrecy?*

"Padrino," he insisted, "won't you please tell me what happened?"

The only answer he could get was, "I'll explain later. Stay with Doctor Francisco and lets keep as quiet as we can. No one knows we're in here."

Another 15 or 20 minutes went by as Doctor Francisco continued closing the wound on Don Andres, who was now unconscious. It seemed like an eternity for Cenobio, as he held the lamp, listening to the doctor carry on about the art of suturing, watching each meticulous stitch as if it were in slow motion.

As Eduardo lay restless on the floor, still breathing heavily and in excruciating pain, it was obvious that Panfilo had begun to despair. He softly began praying the Our Father. Finally, after watching his young foreman fight to hold on, he noticed that Eduardo's blood soaked body was becoming relaxed. Then, with a final heavy exhale, his body became limp. He was gone. He died just minutes before Doctor Francisco had a chance to attend him. With his eyes misty, Panfilo bowed his head and crossed himself, as did Cenobio.

The whole unbelievable fiasco came upon Cenobio like a bolt of lightning right out of sky—stunning and sudden. It was like a scene from the devil's own fiery chamber of hell, or like a horrible nightmare where only in morbid dreams could he ever experience such a bloody scene with such sense of urgency. And in the aftermath of it all, he'd witnessed the whole bloody scene; three men shot, two of which had died in an apparent gun battle. And as fast as he had stumbled on to this bizarre stage of violence, so did it end—unbelievable and unexplained. After this horrifying event had subsided, the chilling silence lingered in the room resembling a wake for the dead.

The next 30 minutes were spent in haste. Don Andres had recovered consciousness and was attempting to stand. The two dead vaqueros were moved onto some white sheets and covered completely. The guns and ammunition were quickly thrown into a box and stashed under the wooden cot. When the cleanup was complete and all evidence of violence and death removed, Cenobio's entire body was numb. He wondered *how did I ever get mixed up in this anyway?*

Once again, he attempted to ask the question, *"¿Padrino, por favor?"*…but before he could get the words out, Panfilo stopped him. *"Esperate!"* "Wait!"

Momentarily, Cenobio had forgotten Panfilo's loss—the two vaqueros who had been so loyal to him. Now—they were gone. At that precise moment, he needed to be alone, a time to grieve. He found it extremely painful to deal with the death of his two ranch hands that lay dead on the floor. But after a few minutes, wiping away the tears from his eyes, and a couple of vibrant blows of his nose, he began to regain composure.

Putting his hand on Cenobio's shoulder in appreciation for all his voluntary support, and apologizing for such an abrupt calamitous episode, he said, *"Ahijado,* you have a right to know everything that happened and why, but its a long story. Tell you what, right after tomorrow's Mass, I'll send someone to pick you and Filipa up, and bring you to the ranch. I want to show you something that will explain everything. But first, I need one more favor." *"Por favor,* bring your wagon to the back door and leave it with me. I'll see that you get it back, and don't say a word of this to anyone yet." He knew immediately why he wanted the cart and nodded his head affirmatively. Then the two men embraced.

"*Anda vete.*" "Go" said Panfilo, patting him on the shoulder.

And with that, Cenobio retreated toward his house

As he walked hurriedly toward home, Cenobio was still trying to decipher the gruesome mystery, as all sorts of crazy thoughts flashed rapidly in and out of his mind. Suddenly he stopped and looked back. Something snapped. Out of the clear blue, a light came on in his head. The pieces of the puzzle were trying to come together...*the black smoke coming over the hill?...the people's rally in San Luis last week?...and how about the flyer in his pocket encouraging young recruits to join the revolution? And now, two men dead and Don Andres severely wounded?*

"No," he said out loud, "this can't be true—can it?" "*Ay Dios mio—Santa Maria.*"

"Has the revolution hit Villa de Reyes?"

Don Panfilo always kept his word. Sure enough, the next day—Sunday afternoon—around two O'clock, one of his ranch hands was at Cenobio's house with a horse-drawn two-seated coach for the ride back to the ranch. He hadn't yet said anything to Felipa about the previous day's bloody affair, but she was suspicious.

As they both hopped into the wagon, Juanito came running outside. "Wait for me, Papa. I wanna go too." But Cenobio ruled against it, thinking his son was far too young to discover the dangers possibly hidden at Don Panfilo's ranch.

"*Otra vez, hijo.*" "Not this time son."

After a delicious dinner and a casual hour of friendly visitation at the ranch, Panfilo invited Cenobio outside. He said he wanted to smoke a cigarette, but in fact, he was ready to keep his promise. Side by side, they stepped out to the back yard, through the black wrought iron gate and toward the main barn. In the stillness of this beautiful Sunday afternoon, Cenobio couldn't help but envy, the vastness of Panfilo's estate; the sturdy white barns, the livery stable, the grazing Appaloosa ponies, and the bronc riding arena nearby. As he looked around, noticing that no other employees were working, his mind was whirling was with anticipation to learn his Padrino's secret.

Once inside the barn, Panfilo walked straight to a sealed compartment within the building and unlocked the door. Stepping inside the dark room feeling his way so as not to stumble, he cocked his right leg and struck a match on his hip and proceeded to light two candles. As the room slowly brightened up, he said, "*pasate para dentro.*" "Enter." After a brief pause, he asked, "What do you see?"

Cenobio's mouth fell open.

"Padrino!" he gasped. *"Ay padrino, no lo creo"* "I don't believe this."

On entering, staring him squarely in the face was an arsenal of weapons, rifles, pistols, gun holsters, shoulder gun belts, daggers and enough ammunition to supply a small army. It was here, around a long wooden table surrounded with a dozen chairs and wooden benches that the seeds of revolt were sewn. On the wall were large maps and drawings of strategic locations marking specific targets in bold black circles. Picture posters of Zapata and Pancho Villa—small and large— dangled loosely on the wall, and others strewn all over the floor. On the table were decks of cards, broken pencils, half empty glasses, beer mugs, burnt candles and tiny red clay ash trays overflowing with stinky cigarette butts. The whole room smelled putrid and rotten to the core from the odor of stale cigars, whiskey, and gun powder.

"Padrino, I still can't believe all this. Is this for real?" he asked.

"It's for real alright, son. Come over here and sit down."

And with that, Panfilo began a full explanation and confession. From beginning to end, with a loud and angry tone in his voice, he profoundly reiterated the status of Mexico's greedy government and its deception at every turn. As Cenobio listened, he realized that he was hearing practically the identical warnings he'd heard at the protest rally in San Luis.

As Panfilo continued his rebuke, he told how the spark of the revolution had been ignited several years ago, north of the State of Chihuahua, and now, was beginning to spread south of Mexico City. Pointing to the pictures on the floor, he told about the two insurgent leaders of the protest movement, Zapata, and Pancho Villa, and their courageous quest for presidential reform. He said many young men; cowboys and roustabouts, had been recruited—mainly to attack certain Federales forces, cut key railroad connections, and burn government warehouses.

"Andres Luz and myself" he continued, "are some of the protesters. From here we organize in secrecy to get their attention. What happened last night was a raid on a warehouse near María del Rio. We learned they had been transporting guns and ammunition to the capitol. Our group rendezvoused at midnight near their warehouse, but someone must have tipped them off, because they were expecting us." "After a hell'uva gunfight, we got out of there fast, but not before setting the building on fire. Most of our men escaped, but as you saw, two of my men didn't make it. We rode like hell trying to get back here before sunrise. We thought we were being followed, so we didn't dare go back to my ranch—instead, we went to

Andres' office. We got there just shortly before you knocked on the door—that's when I sent Ramon to the edge of town to watch for Federales in case we were being followed."

"Ahijado" he continued, "war is hell, no matter how you look at it. For years the vast majority of our people have been forgotten, and until someone stands up to the President and his bunch, it'll always be that way. That's why I've chosen to fight. I'm not asking you to join—that's your business. But I am asking you to keep this under your hat, at least for now." "Promise?"

All the time he was talking, his anger remained aroused and his voice at a forceful pitch. He was dead serious in what he said. Cenobio was seeing a side of his Padrino that he'd never known before or even suspected.

After a long pause, with his head almost between his legs, Cenobio broke his silence.

"Padrino…you're a good man."

After another pause, and a deep breath, Panfilo asked, "Novo—how old is Juanito?"

"Fifteen" he answered.

"Go home," said Panfilo. "Go home and be with your family, and don't worry about me. I'll be all right." *"Vete a tu casa."*

Still confused over an awesome revelation, Cenobio gulped down the thickness in his throat and turned to leave,

"Adios, Padrino. Ay nos vemos."

All the way home, unable to shake the vision of Eduardo's lifeless body lying on the floor and Don Luz's open chest wound, he kept thinking of Juanito.

For the next entire week, it was pure mind-boggling hell for Cenobio. There was no denying that the revolutionaries really meant business. Rumors were no longer hearsay. He had now witnessed a real moment of truth and all the allegations he'd heard at the convention rally, were beginning to connect.

CHAPTER 5

▼

FIESTA—16 DE SEPTIEMBRE

Since that gruesome encounter, four weeks ago, things around the Gomez place had become rather stymied. Even Cenobio's appetite has been affected. Never in a hundred years, would he ever dream that such an act of revolutionary violence could occur in Villa de Reyes, at least, not before his very eyes.

Felipa knew. She didn't know the exact details of course, but from the very beginning—that Sunday at Panfilo's ranch—she sensed that something serious had happened, at least serious enough to have affected her husband's usually pleasant behavior. But she didn't push. She knew he'd come around when he was ready. Gradually, however, things were returning to normal, as Cenobio was becoming his jovial self again.

The beckoning bells chimed once again this Sunday morning. It was the first of three chimes signaling the nine A.M. Mass that was about to begin. When the first chime was heard, people started appearing from everywhere throughout the village, as though they'd been in hiding. **Juanito** had already gone ahead to the church. He promised Father Hidalgo that he'd serve Mass this Sunday, so he had to be there earlier than the congregation.

"Ya suena la campana de la iglesia," Cenobio said loudly so everyone could hear. He was reminding them about the church bell chimes. He didn't want anyone to be late.

"I heard them," replied Felipa. "We're almost ready. I'm making you some hot tea with honey for your cough," she continued.

This Sunday Felipa would be going to Mass without Cenobio, because lately he'd developed a nagging cough and a slight fever leaving him weak and in no mood to leave the house. Ever since his return from San Luis, coughing spells intermittently ripped at his throat.

The church was packed as usual. Don Panfilo and his wife, Doña Delfina, were there with their two children, **Chico** and **Estela.** Andres Luz was also at Mass with his arm still in a sling.

Father Hidalgo, 58, pastor of the beautiful Catholic Church, was a sweet little priest and totally committed to his mission in life as an ordained priest. The size of his small frame would never be interpreted by anyone as merely a man of the cloth, because after listening to his superb delivery of scriptural teachings, and how the teachings were intertwined with God's people, one always came away thoroughly convinced that this little priest was as tall as they come. He carried the full measure of religious authority when giving his homily, and invariably, hitting his mark when targeting the sins of the world. Masterfully, he could capture such total attention that even a church mouse might stop and listen. When he finished preaching his sermon, there could be no doubt about the difference between right and wrong. His concluding message was always tender and forgiving and sealed with a solemn blessing, saying, *"Vayan con Dios"* "Go with God." Acknowledging receipt of Father Hidalgo's blessing in the form of a bold Sign of the Cross, everyone in the congregation humbly crossed themselves twice, and concluded by kissing their hand. Short, and yet so tall, was Father Hidalgo, Villa de Reyes' 'most reverend' priest who had captured the hearts of all it's people.

Exiting the church on conclusion of the Mass, many stopped to greet their *'Padresito"* and to kiss his hand. When Juanito exited the church, he walked straight to Father Hidalgo, he wanted to visit for a second. After exchanging a few comments, he asked, "Father, I didn't see Eduardo in church this morning. Have you seen him?"

"No I haven't," he replied. "Come to think of it, he hasn't been here for several weeks"

Just then, Juanito caught a glimpse of Don Panfilo as he was climbing into his carriage and quickly bid farewell to Father Hidalgo. Hurriedly, he trotted over to

Panfilo's carriage, saying, "*Buenos dias, Don Panfilo, buenos dias, Doña Delfina,*" as he shook Panfilo's hand. "How are you?"

"*Muy bien,*" they replied.

"Don Panfilo," asked Juanito anxiously, "has Eduardo come back to work yet?"

"Not yet, son," he replied. "*Todavia no.*"

Leaving it at that, Panfilo continued, "Juanito, I hear your Papa is sick."

"Yes he is. He hasn't been feeling well at all."

"That's too bad, son. I'm real sorry to hear that. Oh, by the way, we have to start preparing for the fiesta soon."

He was referring to the annual celebration of the 16th of September at the central plaza, and all the preparations that needed to be made in such a short time.

"Since your Papa can't help me this year, do you think you can take his place?"

"Sure I can, In fact, I'd like to very much."

"Tell you what. Come over to my place this afternoon and let's see what we have to do. Alright?"

"*Muy bien*" "I'll be there right after dinner."

Juanito turned away and headed for home.

Gathered around the dinner table after Mass, Juanito was still troubled over the disappearance of Eduardo. "Papa" he asked, "Do you know where Eduardo went to? A few weeks ago, he promised to teach me horse roping, but he hasn't come back to work at Don Panfilo's ranch. I've been out there twice, but he's not there, and Don Panfilo doesn't know why he hasn't come back."

"*Pasame las tortillas.*" "Pass me the tortillas," said Cenobio, followed by a short pause. He wasn't quite sure how to respond. *Should I tell him now, or wait,* he thought to himself. Cenobio knew that secrecy was imperative to protect Don Panfilo and his vigilante riders. Finally, he said, "*Yo tampoco no se, hijo.*" "I don't know either son. But don't worry, he disappears like this once in a while, but always returns."

It wouldn't be that easy for Juanito to stop worrying because he knew Eduardo well enough to know he wouldn't just walk out on a promise. After explaining to his Papa about assisting Don Panfilo this year on the upcoming fiesta, Juanito left the table and headed toward the Panfilo ranch.

At the ranch, Don Panfilo, Don Andres and Juanito worked all afternoon, organizing and coordinating all events for the upcoming fiesta, like, assignments of exact locations and space for all the many food vendors, keeping them clear of the parade path, and other key areas of entertainment. They allotted exact time slots for all the performers and musicians for the entire two-day fiesta, after which, all participants had to be notified beforehand to avoid mix-ups. When all schedules had been made, it was Juanito's job to hand deliver written notices to all the participants desiring to take part in the fiesta.

"Juanito, you've been a tremendous help today, and I sure appreciate it," said Panfilo, expressing his pleasure for Juanito's eagerness to help. He had a lot of admiration for his young assistant and could easily see the exact reflection of his *ahijado*, Cenobio.

Was it really an independence day celebration? Independence from the conquering Spaniards way back when? Or was it just another reason to declare a fiesta? For the plain folks of Villa de Reyes, it didn't matter. One reason was as good as another. After all, when the vast majority of the people labor daily from daylight 'til dark, they feel like they've earned a day of fun and enjoyment. And who would deny them that right anyway?—a right that was also being celebrated in every city, every town, and every village in Mexico.

Saturday morning was a beautiful, bright sunny day, and the anticipation of a jubilant weekend was running high in the hearts and minds of everyone. The summer's heat and exhausting corn harvest had completely drained the community's energy, making this long-over-due fiesta as welcome as the arrival of fall. Now, the day everyone's been waiting for has arrived, a day of bodily liberation where the entire village could come together for a festive weekend of celebration and re-union.

Since daybreak, the peons, the peasants, the farmers, the hatters, the carpenters, shopkeepers, palm weavers, business men and even politicians were coming from every corner of the village and beyond. Some by carriage, some by buckboard, the wealthy by coach, others by horseback, donkeys, and many on foot. They descended on the plaza in such large numbers that in no time, the joyous atmosphere had been transformed into an air of flair and grandeur. Everywhere, scenes of embracing and spirited hand shaking told of old friends and acquaintances coming together once again.

The town flag waved proudly next to the *Red, White and Green Mexican Flag* that displayed the mighty bald eagle, along with colorful banners and streamers of all shapes and sizes strategically placed on every available building, wall, post and even trees.

Food preparations by the women folk had gone well into the wee hours of the morning for participants looking forward to a profitable fiesta. And that included Felipa and Gregoria, because until three A.M., they slaved over a hot oven making hot tamales to sell at the fiesta. By daybreak, participants all across the courtyard were scurrying in every direction, assembling and decorating their assigned cubicals, setting up food and snack bars, vending booths, including beer and tequila nooks.

At last it was ten A.M., and the fiesta was about to begin. Elbow to elbow were the masses gathered at the plaza waiting for the *paranda*. The chimes from the church steeple finally sounded—ding, dong......ding, dong......ding, dong. Suddenly, the drums began pounding away on Camino Real. The grand parade was on its way proudly marching along the tree-lined *paseo*, bordered by beautiful hollyhocks, marigolds, red-eye-hibiscus, and the radiance of the flowering Zinnias.

As the band led the way, the musicians followed, sharply dressed in their black Mariachi suits, studded with gold and silver buttons, wearing black wide-brim sombreros. As the band passed by playing '*La Jesusita en Chihuahua*'—accompanied by harmonizing trumpets, accordions, and guitars—it naturally awakened the musical rhythm in every bystander.

Marching behind the musicians and drummers were the dancers. All wearing beautiful full-length Jalisco-style twirling skirts with every conceivable color in varying sewn-in designs, including red ribbons in their cold black hair, long dangling ear-rings, and Cinderella dancing shoes.

And what parade would be complete without horses. Villa de Reyes was well represented with thoroughbreds strutting beneath their masters, dressed in charros, wide-brim black sombreros trimmed in gold beading, and adorned with fuzzy hanging tassels. Many of the horses and riders were from Don Panfilo's ranch, as he himself officiated as the Town Marshall, riding in his spiffy Victorian-style horse-drawn carriage, wearing a white suit studded in pearl buttons and a white gold-trimmed sombrero. Seated beside him, was the Number Two man of Villa de Reyes—Don Andres Luz.

On entering the plaza, every band in the parade joined in to play the famous marching theme, *Zacatecas*—including Cenobio and Juanito who were also in the parade. When the final beat of the *Zacatecas March* was played, it signaled the fiesta's commencement, and with loud cheers and thunderous applause, the paraders disbanded, integrating with the crowd already in the plaza.

For the next two days—almost non-stop—the fiesta continued constantly from one special event to another, consuming food by the ton and beer by the barrel. The music almost never stopped. Even though there was a wide variety of arts and crafts, leather goods, and other novelties on the grounds, by far, the most popular and irresistible were the food stands. And why not. Some of the tastiest Mexican food in the whole wide world was being served right here in Villa de Reyes. Here's where every lady in town tried to out-do the other by preparing such spicy dishes as; *Fajitas, Cabrito, Chorizo, Chili con carne, Chili rellenos, Mole, Chicharones, Carnitas, Picadillo* stew, *Caldrillo* soup, Hot *Tamales, Chili con queso, Nopales, Tacos, Burritos, Pozole, Quesadillas, Flautas, Tostadas, Sopapillas,* Spanish rice, *Huevos rancheros,* and the main dish of all—*Frijoles*—fried or refried.

By mid-afternoon, with their bellies full, everyone was ready to slow down, find a shady spot, and simply listen to the beautiful music. And of course, there could be no other music in the world prettier than Mexican music when being sung in three-part harmony from deep within the heart and soul. Especially when being accompanied by trumpets, guitars and violins, singing ballads that convey sad lamentations reminiscent of poverty, suffering, and painful departures from home, including stories of death, tragedy and revolutionary battles. And of course the beautiful romantic ballads that touch the heart with encounters of love.

At dusk, lamplighters went from post to post and from pillar to pillar, lighting the coal oil lamps all around the plaza. But just because nightfall was approaching, however, didn't mean an end to the celebration. In fact, the best was yet to come. Namely; the beautiful dancers—twenty or more—in their bright colorful twirling skirts and white blouses with red, silk waist bands. Their partners too, in flashy *charro* suits, their white sombreros with chin straps, and their black high-heel shoes for tapping and stomping—all of whom would soon take the spotlight performing the famous 'hat dance' to the *Jarave Tapatillo.* This was the highlight of the fiesta.

After two gorgeous days of jubilation, and as darkness fell over the plaza, a spectacular hour-long display of fireworks lit up the night sky symbolizing the triumphant sign of victory over Spain, as the Independence Day celebration was drawing to a close. .

Finally, preparations got under way for the grand finale—the peoples dance. Nearing the climax of a jubilant celebration, from the band stand came the introduction of the next group of musicians: **Cenobio Gomez** and his tocallos, Cenobio on the mandolina, **Juan Quiroz** on violin and vocals, **Eugenio Ortiz** on bajo sesto, **Gusman Lopez** on back-up guitar with his young student musician, **Juanito Gomez**, also, **Luis Navarro** on the trumpet. For weeks, they'd been practicing for this special performance. The applause was loud and long, because the crowd already knew that indeed, these *musicos* were good. As the band kicked off the fast peppy tune *Atotonilco,* immediately the dance floor came alive and over-flowing with exuberant towns people—young and old. As if musical rhythm had been inbred, they loved to dance. Some however, like *El Payaso,* the clown, and *El Chango,* the monkey, are not only acting silly, but they are also entertaining. *La Gordita,* little fatty, is having a great time dancing with her *flaco,* skinny husband, while others, like *El Mocoso,* the snotty nose, and *El Zorillo,* the skunk, are acting crazy; laughing and shouting. *El Borachón,* the drunkard, who's already had too much to drink, is dancing with a beer bottle in his hand, trying to stay in step with the music. And then there are the lovers, the *enamorados,* holding their partners ever so close as they dance the night away.

For the swingers of Villa de Reyes, there is no such thing as a *quiet good time.* During fiesta time, partying naturally had to be exhilarating and vibrant. For the rest of the night, culminating on the dance floor at the wee hour of two A.M., Cenobio and his band played and sang many beautiful love songs, including unforgettable favorites; like, *Maria Elena, Morir por tu amor, La Golondrina, Las Gaviotas, La Paloma, Adelita, Paloma Errante, Es Impossible, Tampico Hermoso,* and *Pajarito Baranqueño.*

The next morning, deafening quietness at the plaza was like the calm after the storm. It resembled an abandoned ghost town—asleep at best—with only two people in sight, cleaning up the strewn trash that possibly measured an inch deep throughout the plaza.. One of the men was Juanito who had been engaged to help cleanup the mess. No matter the headaches, the hangovers, the tired aching feet, or even the loss of sleep—it was worth it. Once again, the fiesta had served its purpose as a well-earned break from their daily lives of labor, poverty, and monotony.

For the next several weeks following the grand fiesta, it was back to basics for Cenobio and Juanito. Each day from morning 'til night, they mended fences, put in new fence posts, enlarged the chicken pen, built an extension to Sonso and Flojo's shed, along with other waiting repairs to the house. All these things needed to be taken care of right away because soon, they'd be back in the fields turning over the soil for the next corn crop. Already the long summer days were becoming shorter, making it imperative to utilize each daylight hour to the fullest.

Juanito's life, almost by choice, had become a lot like his papa's, work, work, work. He never learned the truth about the disappearance of Eduardo, until much later.

CHAPTER 6

▼

DEATH OF CENOBIO—
1910

Four years following that fantastic Independence Day celebration, almost to the day, Cenobio finally realized how ill he really was. He probably had known the truth long before now, but just wouldn't talk about it. Felipa kept pushing it out of her mind, trying to convince herself that his illness was only temporary and that he'd recover completely in due time. But his cough persisted, becoming increasingly worse, sometimes leaving him gasping for breath. He began losing weight. Just a little at first, but not too alarming. Lately however, his weight loss had become steady, and now everyone knows it's serious. Especially Cenobio. He wanted to talk to Juanito.

Straining to speak, and speaking with a raspy voice, he delivered his last piece of fatherly advice to his oldest son. Maybe it was more a message than advice. Or perhaps he just wanted to reveal a dream of his own. At any rate, for him, it would be too late—and he knew it.

"Querido hijo," he said. *"Quero hablar con tigo, porque siento que los dias que me faltan ya son muy pocos."* "Son, I need to talk to you. I feel like the days I have left are few and there's something I'd like to say to you."

Jaunito kept interrupting, saying, "Papa, please don't talk like that. You'll be alright."

"Hijo, por favor, escuchame." "Please son, listen to me."

Obediently, Juanito leaned back in his chair next to his Papa's armchair and relaxed, as he tucked the warm blanket around his father's lap.

"Alright Papa. I'm listening."

Cenobio paused for a minute, not exactly sure where to start. Then hoarsely, he said,

"*Hijo,* I want you to go to America."

Juanito was shocked when he heard these words. He was almost speechless.

"What?" he asked.

Now Cenobio was ready to talk. The essence of his last serious conversation with his son was one Juanito would never forget. Staring at the wall straight ahead, avoiding eye contact with Juanito, this was his message:

"Querido hijo." *"Con mucha lastima en mi corazon, quero darte este ultimo consejo."* "Son, it is with much sadness in my heart, that I want to give you these last words of advise."

"Mexico is my beloved country. It has been my whole life. I know of no other country in the whole world where people are friendlier or happier. Just like you son, I was born and raised right here in Villa de Reyes. Ever since I was a little boy, I roamed every inch of our valleys and plains, our hills and mountains. My roots here are deep and wide. The dirt beneath my feet has become a part of me, and I, a part of it. When I wake up to a beautiful morning, it's Mexico that I see. As well as the sun, the stars at night, and even the rain—they all belong to Mexico, just like our Virgen de Guadalupe.

"All my years of laboring in the fields and all the sweat of my brow, only made me stronger, and strengthened my belief in God. It taught me to be a man. A good man, as I've tried to teach you.

"But the truth is not always pleasant. Sometimes we close our eyes to the truth, and we would be like the ostriches burying our heads in the sand, if we knew the truth, and ignored it.

"Mexico is a boiling pot. It has become a country of the poor against the rich, the farmer against the greedy, and the common man against the government. There's much fighting to the south and to the northwest. All appearances tell of nasty revolution ahead. Right now, people are dying for what they believe in. Eduardo was one of those, and he died defending his beliefs. Also, Panfilo and Andres belong to the revolution, and God forbid, they too, may be killed one day.

"Yes, I love my country too, but Mexico at the present is lost. There's no longer a future here. Time was, when I thought I was sitting on top of the world, and if I worked hard, I'd have it all. But the harder I worked, the harder it became to make a living. I was right in thinking the way I did, but Mexico has too many problems.

"Were it not for your mother, and your brother and sister who need you, I wouldn't care if you fought side by side with Panfilo and Andres. Right now our country needs people like them, but not you, son. Your place is here with your mother and Hilario and Gregoria. In a few months, I'll be gone and the responsibility for their support and welfare will be all yours."

"Papa, please. Don't talk like that." Juanito interrupted. "You'll be alright."

"Please son. Listen to me," he insisted. "I want you to promise me something. **Promise me you won't join the revolution.**"

"Yes, Papa. I promise."

"Go to America, son. Go while you're still young. I hear there are many good opportunities over there. And someday, God willing, you can send for your mother."

With his head bowed, Juanito fought to understand the full meaning of his father's last request.

All during his final words, he had been coughing and struggling for oxygen, and after many pauses, he finally concluded his request.

"*Toma,*" he said finally, handing Juanito a letter he'd been carrying in his pocket for months. It was a letter from *un primo,* a cousin—**Rafael Peña**—who had left Villa de Reyes some years back and was now working at a ranch in Seguin, Texas.

For Cenobio, it was a letter of hope, a sincere wish for a life free of fighting and revolt, and perhaps, a fresh new beginning in America.

Sad and with an aching heart, Juanito put the letter in his pocket. He would read its contents later. For him at the moment, America was not even thinkable.

All during his talk—a talk with every hint of finality—Cenobio kept struggling to get his words out, and Juanito could see that his father's health had deteriorated much more than he previously thought. From that day forward, Juanito prayed like he'd never prayed before. Time became eternally slow, waiting for his father's recovery. But the miracle never came

On this cold January morning, there's a small procession making its way up the rocky, path of the hillside of *loma del viento,* windy hill, to **Tierra Bendita,** holy land—Juanito, Felipa, Hilario, Gregoria, Don Andres, Don Panfilo, Petra and Pablo and a few close friends. Felipa is wearing a black veil over her face sobbing quietly, as four men carry the simple wooden box containing the body of her beloved husband, Cenobio.

But for Juanito, only the redness remains in his burning eyes. There are no more tears left for him to shed. The deeply traumatizing death of his father has left him numb and motionless, with pain and sorrow pulsating in every fiber of his body. For him, his world has just ended, thanks to a fatal case of pneumonia. Tomorrow will only be make-believe, and the future a lie.

For the next several days after the burial, and the weeks that followed, Juanito could hardly grasp the reality of his father's absence. Like a zombie, he stumbled through his chores, forcing himself to function. Bitterness, sorrow and repentance all wrapped up into one, hovered over him constantly with accusatory notions that he had been cheated out his father. He searched for an explanation from the Almighty, but found none. Now, all is changed. Time is standing still, refusing to move on, and alleviate the knots in the stomach.

After his father's death, Juanito sought solitude quite often, insisting on keeping his memory alive. He reflected a lot on times past. Like the many times they walked the countryside chopping stalks of dried mesquite for firewood, harvesting fresh cactus from the fields for meals, plowing endless furrows with his father, and the fun times they had together when learning to play the mandolin. Particularly, he missed him on Sunday mornings at the Holy Communion rail. Juanito found comfort in recalling those wonderful memories, and for the time being, needed them to sustain him, day after day.

Juanito could only hurt so much, and when the hurting subsided, he found himself in a position he'd never dreamed of before. Now, at age 20, this untimely pivotal juncture has placed him at the head of the house. His father was right; the responsibility of the family's livelihood and future now fully rested on his shoulders, a responsibility he felt unprepared for. Always before, Cenobio had made all the family decisions and put food on the table.

Having been suddenly thrown into his Papa's shoes, he began to put into practice the things he'd been taught, like raising and butchering pigs, rendering the lard, raising and selling chickens, maintaining feed and hay for all the animals, and basic maintenance of the sheds, barns, and the house. Which included raising vegetables on the two acres behind the house, namely, beans, okra, tomatoes, onions and squash. But most importantly, he knew he had to join the other sharecroppers and take the place of his father. And this of course, meant laboring in the fields alongside adults, which in a few months, many farmers would be preparing the fields for the summer's crops. At first, he worried that he didn't have the farming experience as the others, but certainly, he was no stranger to hard labor.

After his father's death, things were gradually beginning to normalize. Felipa marveled at the way her son rose to the challenge of taking over the family's obligations, and rested her total dependence on his shoulders. At first, she worried, wondering how they'd make it without him. Now, however, she realized, she needn't have worried afterall. *Cenobio had taught him well*, she thought. Gregoria had always looked up to Juanito, and fully accepted his father-like position. Hilario, on the other hand, balked. He knew that Juanito was now the main voice of authority, but found it difficult to accept. He had always been stubborn anyway, and somewhat rebellious. Now, without his father's discipline, he wanted to be on his own, which only led to arguments. All these things about Hilario's nonchalant attitude only made things more difficult. But Juanito persisted in exercising his authority until Hilario gradually became more cooperative.

Two years later, Juanito was still struggling with chronic poverty and revolutionary times. A period of unbridled violence still persisted, keeping the country in a mode of fear and suppression. Churches were being desecrated and priests and nuns were being assaulted. People everywhere were restless and worried, including Villa de Reyes where some of its residents had already moved away. Despite the bleak outlook, however, Juanito tried to remain steadfast. But the more he struggled to meet the demands of supporting his family, the more he recalled his father's final words, *go to America, son*. Over and over, a voice kept repeating; *"Go to America"*

Finally, as he reached in the age-old wicker basket where he had placed the letter from Rafael Peña, he was ready to consider his father's last request. Though the letter was post marked several years ago and contained simply a trivial conversation, it did, however, also contain a clear message—a request for Cenobio to come to Seguin, Texas. Juanito had read the letter several times before, but beyond that, had never given it much thought. Now, the idea of America was becoming fixed in his mind, and the more he thought about it, the more convinced he became that he must go. The idea sounded good, but how about his mother. *How could he go away without knowing if she'd be well taken care of? And could Hilario step in and take over take over the reins of responsibility and obligation?*

In the back of his mind, Juanito wanted to go to America. In fact, he had already concluded that there was really only one choice to consider. Finally, after much wrangling with the idea of leaving, he decided that, yes, he would go to America. That was his father's wish. Now, he knew what he had to do. And even if it was the wrong decision, it couldn't be any worse than staying in Villa de Reyes any longer. Now, he had to talk to his mother.

Every day, when the subject of America came up, the answer was no. No matter how he approached his mother with his idea, it was always no. Respectfully, Juanito always dropped the subject, but invariably, as time went by, both he and his mother continued to come face to face with one hardship after another, until one day, like it or not, the writing on the wall could no longer be ignored. Finally, Felipa became lukewarm to the idea of America, and at last, was willing to discuss the matter.

Soon thereafter, serious talks got underway. Juanito explained again to his mother that the whole idea for him going to America was to find employment and send money home. And if all went as planned, they'd all be better off financially, and certainly alleviate the harsh conditions at home. Furthermore, hopefully, one day they could all go to America. Expanding on the idea, Juanito promised that he would return home as often as funds permitted. It all sounded so good and so easy, and the more they talked about it, the more possible it sounded.

"Aren't you afraid son?" asked Felipa. "Aren't you afraid of traveling hundreds, and perhaps thousands of miles to another country. You've never been there. Can you find America?"

"Mama, please. Please don't worry. I'll find it," answered Juanito, seeing the fear and worry on his mother's face. "I know I've never been to America, but I know where it's at. I'll find it. As soon as I get a job, everything will be alright. You'll see. You'll be proud of me, and Papa would be too if he were here, because this is what he wanted."

With mixed emotions, Felipa smiled at Juanito in agreement—thus granting permission for him to go to America. But her smile was immediately retracted as tears began to form. Nervously, she began wringing her hands and clutching a tiny crucifix pinned to her blouse. At that very moment, she could already feel the emptiness of his absence. The same emptiness that had persisted after Cenobio passed away.

Tentatively, the plan was that Hilario would take over the obligation at home. Also, Juanito would not depart until after Easter Sunday, which by then, this year's preparation of the fields for planting would be completed. For the next six weeks, Juanito worked harder than ever, including Hilario who had just had his 20th birthday. Word that Juanito was going to America spread quickly all over town, and wherever he went, people congratulated him and wished him well.

By the time Easter Sunday rolled around, Juanito was bursting with anticipation, and yet sentimental. All during Easter Mass, he knew it would be his last for a long, long time and was already starting to get homesick. After the conclusion of the Mass, Juanito waited in the sacristy for Father Hidalgo to change his vestments. He wanted a final word of advice, as well as his blessing.

"*Bueno, Juanito.*" "This is your last day in Villa de Reyes. We're sure going to miss you. Are you scared?" he asked.

"No Father. I'm not scared. I'm just a little worried. Worried about Mama. I sure hope I can make a difference by going to America."

"Father," he asked, "Would you give me your.....

"Blessing?" he interrupted. "Of course I will."

"Juanito, my son" Father said, "just like your father, you've always been a good Christian and a true son of God. Go to America and don't forget to pray. Wherever you go, my prayers will always be with you." "*Vete con Dios.*" And with these beautiful words of encouragement, Father Hidalgo gave Juanito his blessing—in the Name of the Father, the Son, and the Holy Spirit—after which he pinned a tiny medal of St. Christopher on the lapel of jacket to take with him as his traveling companion. The words spoken by Father Hidalgo, which most definitely breathed a new life of confidence in his worried mind, were exactly what he needed to hear. Now his anxiety eased and his departure would be much easier.

Easter Sunday, April 1913, was a gorgeous day, and very special. And with today's entertainment at the plaza, it would be like an unspoken tribute and farewell in Juanito's honor. The cold days of *El invierno,* had finally given way to Spring, *la primavera,* and today, the day he'd been waiting for, only a slight cool breeze fanned the hair across his face as he exited the church. With the warm sunshine slowly sweeping over the village, this was a perfect day for *El dia de la coneja.* Even the birds seemed to sense nostalgia in the air, as they chirped in close harmony with each other. And Juanito for the first time, noticed the pretty flowers and the flowering peach trees around the church. Even the smell of the dampened dirt in the flowerbeds had a welcome fragrance. As he looked across the plaza where today's fiesta would be taking place, seeing his friends dressed in their Sunday best, greeting each other as they walked by with a hearty *buenos dias,* and the men tipping their hats to the ladies, only added to the magic in the air on this Holy feast day.

When **Doña Josefa** passed by, Juanito caught a sharp whiff of her perfume as she smiled so pleasantly. Holding on to her white-laced bonnet she said, *"Buenos Dias, Juanito. ¿Como te va?"*

At that particular moment, his mind was somewhere else, but he quickly managed to turn and smile, as he returned her gracious greeting, *"Muy bien, Doña Josefa. ¿Y usted?"*

As he continued walking, he saw Dōna Delfina and sensed that she was about to say something, inspired by a perfect spring day,

"¿Como esta tu Mama, Juanito?" "How's your mother," she asked, stepping aside to let another parishioner walk by.

"Mama esta buena, gracias," he replied. "She and Gregoria finally finished making tamales for today's fiesta."

"Ay que bueno," she said. "I'm looking forward to this afternoon. It'll be great fun."

"Yo tambien," "Me too. I'll be there with the musicians."

"Bueno, hasta luego," "That's great," she said, tapping him on the arm as she started toward her waiting family. "I'll see you later."

"Ahi nos vemos al rato, Doña Delfina," "I'll see you after a while." Juanito replied, as he hurriedly walked toward Hilario and Gregoria who had been talking with some friends.

Yes—there truly was magic in the air this beautiful morning, and Juanito was a happy man. He was seeing and storing precious memories to take with him to America. But what really made his day, was Father Hidalgo's unforgettable message of inspiration by the symbolic ritual of **'La luz del Cielo'** at today's Easter Mass. As the church was filled to capacity, Juanito remembered how the two deacons, **Seferino** and **Paulo** had given each parishioner a tiny unlit wax candle as they entered the church, and how each person proceeded to their pew in the dark, 'til soon, there was standing room only. At the foot of the altar, Father Hidalgo first lit the traditional Easter candle and then blessed it. He then turned to the nearest person in the congregation and lit her candle saying, *"La luz del cielo."* And as soon as her candle was lit, she immediately turned to the person next to her, repeating the same words, *"Light from heaven."* One by one, this process continued until all candles were lit. And with each new flicker of light, symbolically, the entire church was transformed with new hope and reassurance. Total darkness had been consumed by new light, just like Father said.

"Vente Juanito! Se nos hace tarde." "C'mon Juanito! Or we'll be late," yelled Gregoria. Her concern was that they still had to go home and pack the food they'd be selling at the square. And besides, Juanito still had to rehearse the mandolin numbers that they'd be playing this afternoon and change into his charro suit.

"Esperame! Ahi vengo." "Wait for me! I'm coming!" he hollered, trotting toward them.

At the conclusion of the Easter Festivities at the plaza, by the time Juanito got home, it was late. On entering the house, he found his mother kneeling at the prayer altar. She was reciting the rosary. She had already lit two small scented candles at the foot of the statue of the Blessed Virgin Mary. Quietly, he stepped over to the kneeling bench and knelt down beside her and put his arm around her. He could see that she had been crying. On feeling his strong arm around her shoulder, she broke down again, holding her face in her hands while clutching the rosary. She tried to hold back the tears, but couldn't. The very thought of having to sacrifice her beautiful son to another land for their sake, was breaking her heart. Her voice was raspy and cracking, as she finally forced out the words, *"Ay hijo. Hijo de mi vida. Ya te vas de aquí. Solo Dios sabe cuando volveras. Ya me muero de tanta pena. Te encargo que nunca te olvides de tu pobre madre."* "Oh, son, you're going away, and only God knows when you'll return. I'm dying inside. Son, I beg of you, don't ever forget your poor mother."

"Ya no llores, Mama." he told her. *"Ya no te apures."* "Don't cry, Mama and please don't worry. I'll be alright."

"Hijo, ten mucho cuidado de los revolucionarios. Andan matando gente por donde quera." Brushing away the tears, she said, "Son, watch out for the revolutionaries, they're killing people everywhere."

"I know, Mama. But I'll be careful."

"Escribe me cuando lleges a los Estados Unidos." "Be sure and write me as soon as you reach the United States."

"I will Mama."

Embracing his mother one more time, he kissed her on the check and went to his room to start packing.

Early the next morning, the whole family was up to say good-bye to Juanito. Felipa could hardly speak without a choking in her voice. She'd hardly slept a wink from the pain in her heart that begged Juanito not to go. Deep inside, her intuition kept telling her that it would be years before she'd ever see her precious son again. She had prayed every day for some miracle to happen that would prevent her son from leaving, but the time for departure had arrived and still no miracle. She tried to be brave and strong like him, but how could she—she was a mother.

She had packed a lunch for the trip, several shirts, two extra pair of pants, some underwear, a small bible, and a dainty little black-beaded rosary that Cenobio had given her years ago. For identification, she handed him his birth certificate and his baptismal certificate issued by Father Hidalgo. As she placed 25 pesos in his hand, she said, fighting back the tears, "Come with me, son," "*quero darte la bendicion.*" She wanted to give him her blessing. Stepping up to the prayer altar, Juanito proceeded to kneel down. Felipa had already lit a small candle. After a final prayer, the '*Padre Nuestro*', she stood before him, crossed him with the 'sign of the cross' and wept again, saying, "*Te amo hijo. Que Dios te bendiga y te guarde.*" "I love you, son. May God bless you, and protect you."

Gregoria was not all that sentimental over Juanito's leaving. Instead, she felt the excitement and a little envious. Now at age 19, she'd gladly welcome the opportunity to go to America.

Hilario, on the other hand, remained quite neutral. He wouldn't be as courageous, at least until Juanito had proven the journey possible. But he still loved his brother and wished him well. Since Juanito had taken firm command of the family after their father's death, Hilario eventually conformed to Juanito's inherent authority and had developed a genuine respect for his older brother.

One more hug, and one more kiss, and with a lump in his throat, Juanito walked out the door tugging at the cloth cap that once belonged to his father. Flinging the small leather bag containing the letter from Rafael Peña and his personal traveling essentials across his back, he was finally on his way.

"I'll walk with you a little way brother," said Hilario, as he opened the gate leading to Saltillo Road.

At the edge of town, Juanito and Hilario affectionately embraced once more. "*Adios Hermano.*" "Goodbye, brother."
"*Adios.*"

Now—finally, Hilario was getting sentimental. He felt like crying as he stood at the barren knoll on the outskirts of Villa de Reyes watching the faint silhouette of his brave brother disappear over the horizon.

CHAPTER 7

▼

JUAN VENTURES TO AMERICA—1913

The death of his father had forced **Juan** (Juanito) to grow up very fast. Much faster than he'd realized. Now at age 23, he found himself a full grown man, and certainly much wiser as to the trials and tribulations common in the little world of Villa de Reyes. He was full grown alright. Very handsome, 5'6" tall, 165 pounds and physically stout as a horse, *but was he ready for America?*

The dirt roads and narrow paths en route to San Luis, his first stop, were very familiar. He had made this trip several times before with his papa, and several more times since his death, but he knew that this time would be his last for a long time. He had nothing of value in his possession, except the 25 pesos given him on his departure. Deep inside, he carried mixed emotions—courageous on the outside, but frightened on the inside, mostly because at the moment, his future was as bleak and uncertain as his final destination.

As he walked briskly down the road to San Luís, he wrestled with the thought of leaving his mother practically in a state of destitution with only Hilario's youthful inexperience to rely on. When he left home, he didn't have the slightest idea how long it would take to get to America. Any distance at all beyond the borders of San Luis would be new territory. Other things, like the lack of education, were also causing concerns, thinking that in America—a rich country—

everyone could afford to go to school on a full time basis, a luxury he never had. Because as a young boy, the possibility of going to school on a regular basis was out of the question. The only education he ever had, was the few years he attended school, off and on, until he quit to help his papa work in the fields. Quite naturally, however, he did have a compelling desire to become literate and never stopped striving to advance his self-education. As often as he could, he borrowed elementary textbooks from Don Andres Luz to study at home.

By mid afternoon, Juan had reached the outskirts of San Luis and would soon be heading toward **Fortunata's** house on **Lucio** Street. Fortunata was Rafael Peña's sister. All through town, the pedestrian traffic was notoriously congested on that warm April afternoon, particularly, the main business district. One would think there was a booming economy, the way local merchants eagerly displayed their merchandise on every street, every corner, utilizing every inch of frontage space for public attraction. Display tables were loaded with stacks of new and used clothing, shoes, shawls, linens, trinkets, and a million other items. Many grocers displayed strips of beef and pork hanging from the ceiling or outdoor trellises for customer selection. Also, the tantalizing aroma of Mexican food coming from restaurants, cafes, and tortillerias, saturated the air waves at every turn. Juan made it a point to hurry all possible, when making his way through the bustling business district. It seemed like every store-keeper he passed, persisted on making a sale.

On leaving the downtown district and passing along the outskirts of the big city, the scenery began to change, as did the fast pace of doing business. Here, Juan felt a lot more at ease and less intimidated because this was the poorer district—a neighborhood he could identify with more closely. Women were visiting in their front yards and the men were working away at odd jobs. Almost in every direction, could be seen young children running about playing games like; soccer, catch ball, jump rope and marbles. Also, it must have been washday, because most clotheslines were loaded with clothes hanging out to dry.

As Juan was leaving the outskirts of town, he was suddenly startled by a band of speeding caballeros on horseback, all with rifles and pistols in their holsters. It all happened so fast, that he didn't have time to count them or look to see if they were rebels or a friendly posse. Quickly, he dodged into the backyard of a nearby residence, knowing that rebel outlaws didn't always care who you were, or what side of the revolution you were on, just so you were of fighting age. As they galloped away at full speed, leaving a trail of dust, Juan noticed that in the midst of the riders, were two soldiers in black uniforms with their hands tied behind their back. He concluded immediately that an assault by insurgents had taken place somewhere and wanted to get off the road as soon as possible. Walking faster, he hurried toward Fortunata's house. It had been a long time since he'd been there, but felt sure he could find it if he could get there before dark. Another thirty minutes, and he'd be there. Rounding the corner on Lucio Street, he was much relieved on seeing a row of little adobe houses—one of which was surely Fortunata's.

As he walked along the row of *jacalitos*, wending his way through small children playing in the dirt, he could smell the familiar aroma of supper cooking somewhere. House number 129 was the one he was looking for. Soon, there it was.

Knocking on the partly opened door, Juan called out, "Fortunata!"

He waited for a couple of seconds and soon she responded with cries of delight.

"Juanito! Ay Juanito! ¿Que haces aqui tan lejos?" "What are you doing here so far from home? My goodness, it's so good to see you!"

After an affectionate embrace at the door, Juan stepped inside.

"You're just in time," she said, "we were just getting ready to eat supper."

"Ay que bueno, I'm really hungry. Something sure smells good."

Glancing at Fortunata's daughters who had been huddled behind their mother, Juan couldn't resist making a compliment, *"Ay que bonitas muchachas."* "My, what pretty girls."

Bashfully, they smiled and giggled at his flattering.

Juan was still concerned about having seen the band of insurgents, saying, "Fortunata, I think there's going to be trouble in town. I just saw a bunch of wild revolutionaries riding off with two prisoners. I think they were soldiers."

"Ay, Dios mio," she said. *¿Devuelta?"* "Oh, my God! Not again!"

"What is it?" Juan asked.

"It's those men again. They've been hanging around here for several days. Yesterday there was a lot of shooting south of town between them and the soldiers. It scares me when I see'em. Last week, there were hundreds of soldiers in town—I thought they were all gone."

"They may be gone," Juan remarked, "but two of them didn't make it."

"No doubt, they'll be paraded through town, then taken out and shot," she answered, "I'm so sick and tired of all this fighting and killing. When will it end?"

"I know what you mean, Fortunata. I hate it myself. We seldom see any fighting back home, but we hear about it when it happens in other places. I'm like you, though. I wish it would hurry up and end. Decades of fighting should be enough, but I don't think it will ever stop until our 'good for nothing' government starts paying more attention to the welfare of our country. I made a promise to Papa before he died, that I wouldn't join the revolution, but I'll tell you this, if it weren't for our family, I'd be out there with them."

"Juanito, I know they're fighting for our rights, and I should be proud of them, but I don't like the way those ruffians help themselves to whatever they want—the stores I mean. And when one of their soldiers gets captured or killed, the whole city lives in fear of retaliation. *Ay Diosito,* I sure hate violence."

Changing the subject, she said, "Did you say you were hungry?"

"Yes I did."

"Come on in the kitchen."

At the supper table, enjoying a delicious meal of beans and tamales, chili salsa and hot tortillas, the whole family was in a talkative mood. Fortunata's girls, **Sofia, Marta, Luisa, Concha**—all teenagers—were gabby little gals, and very polite. They were anxious to hear all the latest news from Villa de Reyes.

"There's not much to tell," said Juan. "Nothing very exciting ever happens back there any more. Mostly, just working like crazy in the hot summers. And in the wintertime, we just sit around waiting for the next summer so we can start all over again."

"Just kidding," he said with chuckle.

"Seriously though, nothing around the house has been the same since Papa died three years ago. Mama took it pretty hard and she still worries a lot. But truthfully, it's been hard on all of us. By the way, I've gotten to be a pretty good mandolin player. We play for dances once in a while. It's a lot of fun, but we don't do the cantinas."

"How about Gregoria?" asked Sofia.

"Gregoria is 19 years old now and learning to dance, and I think she has a boy friend."

"Hilario….well, I don't know about him. He's starting to like beer and sometimes, I think he's running around with the wrong bunch of boys. He's already been in a few fights. But I don't worry about him. He can take care of himself. As for Mama…well, she's still the perfect mother and still in good health."

"You know Fortunata," Juan continued, "it's been a real struggle ever since Papa died, making ends meet, I mean. That's the reason I decided to go north to the United States. There's got to be something better over there."

"But Juanito," she said, "things are tough all over. You saw that coming through town, didn't you? Look at us!"

"I know" he responded. "You're right. But…well anyway, I want to see for myself. Before leaving home, I talked to Don Andres Luz about America, and he said it was a young country, and therefore, should be open to new opportunities—much more than here. He said that sometimes, he, too, wished he could have traveled to America."

"Juanito, I sure hope you're right. But I don't know if America is really the so-called 'land of milk and honey'. From the letters I get from my brother, Rafael, making it in America is extremely hard for anyone who doesn't speak English, and even harder for the poor souls who have no money. Not me though, I like it right here in San Luis just fine."

"Fortunata," Juan said enviously, "I sure like your attitude. I wish I could say the same."

"Juanito, in the last letter I received from Rafael, he said there was some fighting going on down by Matamoros—some lynchings. Have you heard anything like that?"

"No, I haven't. I've heard of lynchings in Aguascalientes, but not in Texas"

"Well," she continued, "that's what Rafael said. I hope it's nothing like what we've had here in Mexico. Anyway…you'll be crossing the border at Laredo, not Matamoros, so you probably won't run into any fighting.

Fortunata, a delightfully charming person in her late 40's, was already a widow. Her husband Antonio, who had joined the revolutionary movement, was killed in battle in the State of Chihuahua over a year ago. She and her four daughters operated a weaving business out of their back yard under a wind-tossed canopy. And from the looks of her humble shack, business couldn't have been too prosperous. She was a peach of a lady, however, and never met a stranger. Anyone would always be welcome in her quaint little *jacal.* She wasn't the type of person to let her mind get all stressed out with worries she couldn't do anything about. Instead, she simply took each day's problems in patient stride. It was obvious that she didn't have much in the way of fancy clothes or stylish furniture, or even money. But then, she didn't require much. She was content just the way things were.

"Juanito," she said, "why don't you stay here with us for a few days. We'd love to have you."

"No, I'd better not." he replied."

"Why not. We've got plenty of room."

"Are you sure it's no trouble?"

"Absolutely! No trouble at all."

"O.K, Fortunata. That's really kind of you. I think I'd like to"
Thanking her for her persuasive invitation, Juan agreed to stay for a few days.

Two days at Fortunata's house were restful and enjoyable. In conversation, she brought back many memories of the days when she and Rafael still lived in Villa de Reyes. Especially when she pulled out some family photos from an old moth-balled trunk. One picture in particular of her and **Dolores,** her mother, standing next to Felipa. In the picture, they were standing near a cactus bush, each with a bouquet of flowers in their hands and with deadpan expressions on their faces which made the reminiscing somewhat nostalgic and yet so hilarious.

Juan also got to see Fortunata's fantastic weaving operation first hand. He found it so intriguing, watching the girls select each spool of colorful yarn and how they prepared the loom for threading, so professionally. Threading the loom, and the weaving itself, was so fascinating to watch, especially seeing the fin-ished products, like serapes, throw rugs, mats, and tapestry—each one, with it's own unique design.

After the 2nd day with Fortunata, Juan decided it was time to press on. He'd had a good time at her place, and being with her was the next best thing to being at his own home. He said good-bye to the girls, as Fortunata walked him to the door. After expressing his gratitude for her gracious hospitality, they hugged each other amiably, and Juan was ready to hit the road once again.

"*Adios Juanito. Que te vaya bien. Ten much cuidado. Escribe me.*" "Good luck Juanito. Be real careful and have a good trip—and don't forget to write."

"Here," she continued, handing Juanito a small envelope containing some recent photos of herself and the girls, "give these to my brother—and be sure to give him a big hug for me"

"I will, Fortunata, *Gracias por todo.*"

After bidding farewell to Fortunata, Juan was once again on his way. It took two full hours of walking through the narrow dirt roads, before reaching the cac-tus-lined *carretera* on the outskirts of town. All day, he walked, and he walked. By nightfall, after having passed through the little *pueblito* of Soledad, he finally reached Villa de Hidalgo, another tiny town that resembled Villa de Reyes. After two whole days, he had only covered a distance of 25 miles. Now for the first time, he was getting a taste of what the balance of the trip would be like. Yes, reality was becoming very clear. Food. What to do about food was his main con-cern, complicated further by the dwindling pesos in his pocket. It was a scary thought.

Just before dark, along the dusty stagecoach trail, he spotted a small ranch house. Hungry and tired, he ventured over to seek something to eat and hopefully a place of shelter for the night. On nearing their yard, it was the usual scene; children playing in the yard, barking dogs, chickens, and that old familiar barn yard smell of burros and goats.

Juan had never begged for food before in his life, but he would soon learn what it was like to be completely at someone else's mercy when in need of food and shelter. Now, looking back, he constantly longed for the comfort of his own home. Certainly, there could be no substitute.

As Juan was approaching the house, he could see a woman's figure standing in front of the window.

"*Alguien viene,*" she said to her husband. "Someone's coming."

Immediately, her husband went to the door and stepped outside. "It's gotta be some stranger," he said. "Look at the pack he's carrying."

Stepping off the front porch to greet the stranger, he was right. It was a wayward traveler.

"*¿Que tal, amigo? ¿De donde vienes?*" "Hi, friend, where are you coming from?"

"*Buenos tardes, Señor.*" "I've been walking all day and I was just wondering if…

"*Pasate.*" the man interrupted. "Come in."

Carlos Espinoza, the ranch owner, was a kind and friendly man. He appeared to be in his 60's, heavy set, rather tall, and walked with a slight limp. His faded blue overalls were much too small for the size of his large frame. Almost everything he said was followed with a short chuckle. His wife never had much to say, she just stayed in the kitchen talking to the kids. After exchanging a few comments about Juan's family, the revolutionary movements, and his journey to the United States, Don Espinoza asked, "*¿Tienes hambre?*" "Are you hungry?"

"*Ay, como no.*" Juan replied. "*No he comido en todo el dia.*" "Absolutely. I haven't eaten all day."

After a delicious hot meal, the two men went out to sit on the front porch swing, enjoying a cool southerly breeze. Juan thoroughly enjoyed the company of Don Espinoza—especially his generous hospitality. As their conversation was closing, Don Espinoza pointed to a nearby barn, saying, "You can sleep in my barn tonight if you like. It looks like it's gonna rain, and if it does, at least it'll keep you dry."

"*Don Espinoza, se lo agradesco mucho.*" "You've no idea how much I appreciate it. Thank you so much."

"*De nada.*" replied Don Espinoza. "*Mi casa es su casa.*"

All night long, it rained, as Juan kept trying to get comfortable in Don Espinoza's barn. This was certainly a new experience, sleeping on hay mounds in the company of goats and the harsh brays of donkeys. But he felt grateful to have a roof over his head. All night, however, he worried that tomorrow the rain would hamper his travel. Fortunately, by morning the rain had stopped and the morning sun was shinning bright from the east, leaving behind a sweet fragrance in the morning dew and a few silky white clouds floating in the sky.

As Juan was closing the wooden gate to the barn preparing to depart, Don Espinoza was already up and about. On seeing Juan, he called out,

"Hey Juan, how about some breakfast before you go!" He knew it would be a long day for the young hiker.

"Oh, *Don Espinoza,* that would be great. Are you sure it's not too much trouble?"

"Not at all. Come on in. My wife is also going to pack you some lunch for the road.

"*¿Deveras?*" "Really? *"Que Dios se lo pague."*

At the breakfast table, as they were eating *huevos rancheros with tortillas de maiz,* Don Espinoza, apparently feeling sorry for his foot-traveling guest, offered Juan some tips, saying, *"No eres el primero estranjero que pasa por aquí."* "You're not the first stranger to pass this way. If you're going to America, here's what I'd do, if I were you. When you get to **Nuñez**, which is the next big city 55 miles to the north, there you'll find the nearest railroad junction for freight trains going to the Texas border. When you find the train yards leading north, go to the outskirts on the other side of town and wait 'til the trains are leaving, then hop on one. But be real careful, because the railroad watchmen are vicious. If you get caught, they'll beat you up, and you may even end up in jail."

It certainly was good advice. Anything would be better than walking. Of course it sounded risky, but as Juan saw it, he had no other choice.

"By the way, Juan….here, take this with you," Don Espinoza said. "It's a rough sketch of towns and highways you'll be passing through. It might come in handy." "And here, take this. It's a small snack for the road."

"Muchisimas Gracias, señor.

Pitching his travel pack over his shoulder once again, he gratefully reached out to shake Don Espinoza's hand

"Adios, señor Espinoza. Gracias por todo."

"Adios amigo. Que te vaya bien." "Good luck."

Once again, Juan was on his way north

The next 55 miles, walking was absolute torture. Not just the walking, but also the hunger and fatigue. It took Juan five days of walking through wide-open country to reach the fair size town of Nuñez. During the day, after his arrival, he fed off a nearby apple orchard, eating shriveled apples off the ground. And at night, rest for his tired, aching body was wherever he could find it, either in an alley, a park, or the central plaza. Nights were by far, the hardest to deal with. He couldn't dispel the thought that each additional mile northward, would only take him farther away from home.

Every day while in Nuñez, he scouted the entire area around the railway yards, keeping mental notes on train departure times and watching all the movements of the heavy rail traffic. The train yard was much busier than he expected, so he was careful to maintain a safe distance from the center of traffic so as not to be conspicuous. Once in a while, he saw several guards checking the freight cars, peeking in the open doorways of the boxcars in search of tramps. The scary part was noticing gun holsters strapped around their waist and the billy clubs they carried. He definitely didn't want any part of that.

The night before, Juan had plans to sleep under a train bridge near the edge of town where the first morning freight train would be on its way north. The one he'd be waiting for usually departed at 5:45 A.M. He'd already spotted a hiding place near the tracks behind a pile of discarded barrels at a junkyard. The bridge would be a perfect place to spend the night where he wouldn't be seen. From here, he could see the train when it departed and he sure didn't want to miss it. He'd never hopped a train before and was already getting nervous just thinking about it.

Shadows on the ground were getting longer by the minute, as he climbed up the embankment underneath the bridge's steel girders. He looked around for just the right spot to spread out his bedroll and still be in full view of the freight yard ahead. He no sooner got settled, when he noticed another man approaching. Immediately, they noticed each other, but just like strangers, neither made any attempt to speak. Of course, each one knew right off that the other was also waiting for a train. Reaching this conclusion, the stranger made the first move. He walked over to Juan and asked,

"Mind if I join you? I saw you sitting over here, and I figured you were waiting for a train too…. are you?"

"Yes I am. Sit down."

"Would you have a light on you?" he asked. "I've got cigarettes, but I don't have any matches."

"No" replied Juan. "I don't smoke."

"How come?"

"I don't know. Just never wanted to I guess. Where you from?"

Placing his packsack down next to Juan's, he sat down and said, "**Cerrito.** Ever hear of it?"

"No I haven't," replied Juan. "Never heard of it. Where about is it?"

"Oh, it's about 70 miles west of San Luis. It's a pretty good size town, but there's nothing there for me. Where you from?" he asked.

Juan kept staring at the stranger. He wasn't exactly sure if he should even talk to this guy, although he seemed alright.

"Villa de Reyes" Juan answered. "Mine's just a little town down aways from San Luis, maybe 15 miles."

"Ever been there?"

"No. Nunca."

As the stranger began taking off his shoes, he remarked, "My feet are killing me. I've been walking and hitch hiking for two days. Gosh that feels good," he said, massaging his feet.

Juan was still a little bit leery about the stranger and wouldn't take his eyes off him. "Where you headed?" he asked.

"Don't know exactly," replied the stranger, "Somewhere in *Norte America*. It doesn't really matter. I'm just ready to leave Mexico. There's nothing here for me."

Stretching his hand out to Juan, smiling, he said, "My name is Pedro. **Pedro Morales.**"

"What's yours?"

Hesitating for just an instant, Juan cautiously returned the handshake with a firm grip and forcing a friendly smile, saying, "Juan Gomez."

The friendly handshake put a smile on both faces and immediately softened the cloud of suspiscion between them. Now, they were at ease with each other.

"How old are you, Pedro?" asked Juan, thinking that he couldn't be very old, at least not as old as he.

"I'm 21."

"Boy, you sure don't look it." Juan said. Amusingly, he added, "I thought you were much younger."

"Aw c'mon now. I'm probably older'n you. How about you Juan—how old are you?"

"23," he replied. "I'll be 23 next month, but I feel like I'm 33," he said jokingly.

Confidence was growing between the two men as they spread their bedding on the bare concrete next to the huge steel I-beams. It was getting darker now, but they still wanted to chat.

"Gosh, I sure wish I had a match. Cigarettes, but no matches, don't that beat you?" "Juan you never did say where you were going. Are you going to the other side too?"

"Yes" he replied. "I'm going to America also, but for different reasons than you."

"How's that?" Pedro asked.

"Well Pedro," he began, "mine is a long story. I love Mexico, and it breaks my heart to leave it. But like you said, there's no longer anything here for me either—work I mean. I'm tired of being broke all the time. So, even if I don't want to leave, for the sake of my family, I feel I must. My Papa died three years ago, and ever since then, it's been hell to pay."

"I know what you mean, Juan. Sorry about your Papa. You're right though, things are really tough in Mexico for a lot of people, not just you. And besides, the skirmishes by the revolutionaries don't make it any easier. Perhaps I am a little better off—my folks are still living. We own a small cattle farm and were able to make a fair living. But that wasn't enough for me."

"Pedro," Juan interrupted, as he began spreading out his bedroll against the concrete pillar. "I'm getting pretty sleepy, think I'll call it a night. How about you?"

"Me too." was the reply. "See you in the morning."

"Juan," Pedro asked, "if it's OK with you—since we're both going the same way, mind if I tag along?"

"Absolutely not. In fact, I was thinking the same thing."

"Good night, Pedro."

"Good night, Juan."

Juan began to feel much better after having met Pedro. He seemed like a nice guy and easy to talk to, at least now, he'd found a traveling companion and he wouldn't be going it alone.

"Pedro!" "Pedro!" "Wake up!" "The train is getting ready to leave," hollered Juan. "Hurry!"

In total pre-dawn darkness, Juan grabbed his tote bag and scrambled down the embankment in a frenzy. Pedro too, still half asleep, stumbled down the steep layer of concrete right on Juan's tail.

"*Esperame Juan!*" "Wait for me!"

Both men, at a full trot, were desperately running for the train, which was at least two blocks away. In the dark, they ran like crazy, circling the junk yard and waking the watch dogs whose ferocious barking sounded like they were right on their heels. Rounding the corner of the junkyard, Juan was running the fastest, and when he looked back, he saw Pedro stumble and fall, twisting his ankle. "*Valgame Dios.*" "Oh, Jesus." *Of all times for an accident,* he thought to himself. But no matter what—they had to make it. Juan turned back to help his friend who was grimacing with pain. With his shoulder to lean on, they made a dash for the hiding spot behind the pile of barrels. While they were waiting for the train, Juan quickly took a dirty shirt from his bag and wrapped it several times around Pedro's ankle.

"You may have to go on without me." Pedro said. "I don't think I can run fast enough to hop that train. My ankle hurts like hell. I think I sprained it."

"Don't worry Pedro. I'm not leaving you. We'll make it."

Luckily for the two young hobos, when the long black engine came rolling by, blowing its shrieking whistle, it came by at a creep. The black smoke they'd seen was only the engine's warm-up. They remained ducked behind a nearby water tank until just the right moment. As soon as they spotted the first boxcar with an open door, they made a run for it. Pedro tried several times to jump aboard, hopping and stumbling on one leg, but couldn't quite make it. But Juan, who was running alongside him, lifted his friend into the moving boxcar then jumped in after him. At last, they were on their way.

Once inside, they laughed and laughed, rolling all over the floor in belly-busting amazement for having accomplished their first train hop. Out of breath, and holding on to their sides from laughing so hard, they realized that they were both amateurs in the art of train hopping.

"Pedro, take off your boot, and let me look at that foot," ordered Juan.

Obligingly, Pedro unlaced his boot. "Damn," he said. "It's starting to swell. Gosh, it hurts."

Juan liked his newfound friend, but wasn't sure why. Always before, he'd tried to be selective with whom he associated, but this guy was different. He was good-looking, slender, not too tall, and wasn't afraid to say what was on his mind, which usually made good sense. He was a likable extrovert who seemed to find excitement in just being a carefree rover. Juan thought he was a little immature for a 21-year old, but found a touch of excitement and motivation in his personality. And on his grueling journey, he needed someone like that.

On getting settled on the floor of the boxcar, the two men continued getting acquainted. Being concerned about the cities and towns ahead where they could possibly encounter railroad guards, Juan pulled out the sketch of the highways given him by Don Espinoza. It outlined the route to Nuevo Laredo and listed most of the railhead towns in between. According to his list, the next train stop was about 80 miles away and considered a major interchange for freight trains. On seeing this, Juan was very relieved. He felt safe from the guards—at least for the rest of the day.

It didn't take long for the two men to get used to the humping and jolting of the moving freight train, even though the noisy clickety tracks and the whistling wind never stopped. For them, it was an all-new experience, watching peons at work in the fields and grazing cattle along the way. As they sat in the boxcar, legs extended and crossed, Pedro said, "Juan, I don't know about you, but I'm almost broke. I've only got 28 pesos. How about you? How much do you have?"

"Twenty eight pesos?" Juan asked. "You've got more than me, I've only got 12 pesos, and God help me when that's gone."

"Caramba." "It looks like we're gonna have to find work somewhere—and I'm not too crazy about working." With a grin on his face, he continued, "me and work don't get along too good."

Juan was learning something new about his friend all the time. *Reckon he's lazy,* he wondered?

"Where did you learn to read and write, Juan?" asked Pedro.

Immediately, Juan wondered, *where's this guy been all his life?*

"Can't you read Pedro?"

"Well"....he responded, "I can read a little bit, but I can sign my name real good. I never did like school. I didn't like being around smart aleck kids. And besides, the teachers were too strict. Papa never forced me to go, so I quit going. And you?"

"Yeah. I went to school part time for the first three grades, but I liked school. And I liked my teacher. I wish I could have gone all the way, but for us at our house, things were too rough—money, I mean. I had to quit school and go to work with my Papa. But I didn't want to grow up being ignorant. A lot of the people I knew were smart, and I wanted to be smart like them. Especially this one old gentleman named Andres Luz. He was really, really smart. He was my mentor. He helped me with reading and writing after I quit school. He's the one who gave me this other map. Also, he was my sister's *Padrino* when she received her First Holy Communion."

"Sister? You've got a sister?" asked Pedro.

"I sure do." Juan replied. "And she's a dandy. Her name is Gregoria, age 19."

"I've got a brother too—Hilario. He's a little younger than you. They're both back in Villa de Reyes with Mama. One of these days, I've got to be sure and write to them."

With a sigh, Juan continued, "someday I'm coming back to Villa de Reyes, and I want to visit Papa's grave every day. To me, there's no other place like my home town."

"How about your folks, Pedro?"

"Well," he replied, "they're still living, if you can call it that. They don't get along too good. I think it's Papa's drinking. Mama says he's too stubborn and bull headed. I don't have any sisters. I've got an older brother, but I don't know where he's at—somewhere up around Aguascalientes, I think. He was one of those fanatic rebels who thought he could help solve the problems of the world. The last we heard, he had joined up with the outlaw Zapata and his bunch."

Juan remained silent on listening to his friend's unsympathetic reference to the revolution.

It was getting dusk when the freight train was nearing the city of **Entronque**, and the two men were preparing to jump off before reaching the train yards. They didn't want to take any chances with the train guards. They would have preferred to jump when the train slowed down, but they had to jump at nearly full speed. First Juan jumped from the car, yelling, "*Ahora, Pedro!*" "*Brinca!*" Then Pedro jumped right behind him, trying to spare the blunt trauma to his twisted ankle, but instead, as he hit the ground, he bruised it again, cursing, "*hijo de la chingada.*" "Son of a bitch." Juan in the meantime had already stopped rolling down the soft embankment and rushed back to check on his friend.

"Pedro!" he hollered. "Are you alright?"

"I don't know," came back the reply.

As the train sped onward, disappearing in the distance, Juan and Pedro pitched their bags over their shoulders and commenced walking. Walking along the railroad tracks at a snail's pace—Pedro, favoring his swollen ankle—they headed in the direction of town.

"I'm awfully hungry," said Pedro. "How about you, Juan?"

"Me too," was the answer. "But don't worry. I've got us a snack in my tote bag. Yesterday in the town of Nuñez back there, I washed dishes at a little Cafe and I told the cook all I wanted for my pay, was something to eat, and something for the road. *El cocinero* was an awfully nice fellow. He let me get my belly full, then, fixed me an extra snack. I was saving it for an emergency, and now that you bring it up, I think the emergency is here. As soon as we can find a nice shady spot, we'll see what's in the sack."

A mile or so down the tracks, they spotted the shade tree they'd been looking for. And lucky for them, it happened to be near a stream of clear fresh water. Hobbling and hanging onto Juan's shoulder, they slowly made their way through the heavy brush toward the stream. In the sack were four tamales neatly wrapped, along with some green chili peppers.

"That cook was really looking out after you, Juan," said Pedro. "He must have felt sorry for you."

After finishing their short meal, which only took a couple of minutes, they walked down to the stream, and with the palm of their hands, helped themselves to a cool drink of water. Wiping his face with the back of his hand, Juan said, "*Gracias a Dios.*"

But Pedro, still splashing water on his face, said, "Thanks for the tamales, Juan." Kidding with a grin, he continued, "they'd been better hot. What do we do now?"

"Well, we're gonna have to find some place to sleep tonight." Juan replied. "When we get into town, we'll see if we can find the plaza.

The city of Entronque was big; lots of businesses, lots of people, and lots of streets. And for the two men, it seemed they'd walked them all, as they searched for the central courtyard where, hopefully, they could find a comfortable bench to sleep on. As they walked through town, they noticed groups of soldiers loitering around. Nothing for them to be concerned about, but still, Juan kept second glancing. Pedro grumbled occasionally about the pain in his ankle, and sometimes griped about the inconveniences of a hobo's life. Juan could tell that he wasn't used to the hard life. But he, on the other hand, kept a cool head, always focusing on the destination ahead. As for the next hitch on the freight train, that would be somewhere on the other side of town.

Early the next morning, after having spent the night on hard wooden benches, both men were dreary and still very fatigued. Four hours later, after having completely encircled the city's outskirts, they were again walking the dusty roads and trails leading out of town, where they would wait for the next opportune freight train leaving town.

The train yard at Entronque was huge. Train traffic was everywhere. Including guards.

"My! My!" said Pedro. "Did you ever see so many railroad tracks? It won't be easy getting out of this town."

"You're right," agreed Juan. "If we're going to dodge those guards, I think we better lay low until dark. Either tonight or tomorrow night, we'll hop a train that won't be so closely guarded."

The second night, in pitch, black darkness, Juan and Pedro finally spotted the freight train they'd be hopping but found it heavily guarded. Hiding on the ground underneath the freight cars, crawling on their hands and knees between rails and huge tandem steel wheels, they waited for the train to start moving. Pretty soon, they could hear the humping and crashing of each car taking up slack, and they knew the train had started moving forward. Instantly, they scampered out from underneath the cars to avoid being crushed to death, and began running alongside looking for a boxcar with an open door.

Suddenly, they heard guards blowing their whistles. Sure enough, they had been spotted.

"*Correle, Pedro! Correle!*" "*Ay viene la chota!*" "Run Pedro, Run! Here come the guards!"

Running as fast as his sore ankle allowed, Pedro high-tailed it in a direction out of the train yard, with Juan right behind him. The guards were not firing any shots as they chased the two men, but they sure made a lot of noise blowing their whistles. One guard threw his club at Pedro but missed. Both men, jumping wildly over track after track, never ran so fast in their lives. Off to their right, they saw their way out. It was a six-foot fence at the far end of the yard.

"*Siguele, Pedro! Siguele!*" cried out Juan. "Keep going, Pedro. Keep going!"

With the guards closing in, they scrambled over the fence like scared rabbits and continued running until they had cleared the railroad yard, then threw themselves down behind a clump of bushes. Looking back, they could still see the guard's flashlight beams flashing all around. With their faces pale from fright, they remained hunkered down until the guards had retreated. After catching his breath, Juan turned to Pedro and said, kiddingly, "*¿Que dices ahora, Pedro? ¿Nos devolvemos?*" "What do you say now, Pedro? Want to turn back?"

Also panting and gasping for breath, laughingly he acknowledged, "*Quita te.*" "Aw, get out."

Behind those same bushes, they spent the night, giving up on any train hop out of Entronque. The next morning, Juan, looking at his map, determined that the next town ahead, was **La Paz**, approximately 20 miles. It being a small town as the map indicated, they'd have a much better chance of dodging the watchmen. But the unfortunate part of this sad state of affairs was that they'd have to walk. And, walk they did, resting every so often to relieve the pain in Pedro's ankle.

By the time they reached La Paz, both men were completely exhausted. After finding a bench in front of a small restaurant, **Cafe Lindo**, Pedro said to Juan, "*Amigo*, I don't believe I can go much farther. I've got to get off of this foot."

"*No te apures.*" "Don't worry." replied Juan, "we'll stay in this town until your ankle gets better. We've got all the time in the world anyway."

"Are you sorry I came with you now?" asked Pedro.

"Absolutely not!"

After resting a bit, they made their way inside the restaurant, starving and ready to eat. The aroma of pure Mexican food coming through the cafe's screen door was irresistible. After finding a comfortable chair next to a drafty window in the little crowded cafe, Juan ordered two enchiladas, a bowl of beans with two tortillas, while Pedro ordered three enchiladas with chili. Each bite was like a feast, savoring each mouth full, as though they'd never eat again.

Again, it occurred to Juan that just perhaps the owner of the cafe could use some extra help in the kitchen. But the owner, a short fat man, wearing a chili-stained apron, didn't appear to be very friendly, nor easy to approach. And when Juan inquired about a job, immediately, the owner said no, even though he could see from their heavy beards and dirty clothes, that they had skipped a few meals. However, as Juan continued to plead for a couple days work, the cafe owner changed his mind, saying, "*Bueno*. I can't pay you anything, but if you want to work, both of you can work in the kitchen and your pay will be all you can eat. I need a dishwasher anyway. I never did like washing dishes."

"*¿Como se les parese?*" "What do you say?"

Smiling at each other, surprised at the *cocinero's* change of heart, Juan quickly answered, "*Ay lo tiene.*" "You've got it." "*Muchisimas Gracias.*"

After three weeks, still at Cafe Lindo and now working for pay, Pedro's ankle had greatly improved and they were ready to continue their journey. La Paz had been good to them, allowing them to earn some extra money for meals down the road. All this time, while working side by side washing dirty dishes, Juan and Pedro had become great friends. Before leaving, Juan wrote a letter to his mother and enclosed a few extra pesos.

Hopping another freight train north of La Paz, just as Juan had predicted, was easy as apple pie. They had no trouble finding an open-door boxcar, but then, neither did those other two guys already inside. At first glance, it didn't really matter to Juan, he figured they were just travelers like him, en route to the next town up ahead. But on second glance, he wasn't so sure. They both looked like thugs, which made Juan very uneasy.

Juan's intuition was right. Because within an hour of departure from La Paz, one of the men walked over to Pedro, as he and Juan sat on the floor of the boxcar, and demanded to know, "What do you have in that sack, *hombre?*"

It took Pedro by surprise. He didn't know how to respond. But resenting a hateful intrusion from a total stranger, replied, "None of your damned business." . The man repeated in a gruff voice, "I said, what's in that sack!" kicking Pedro across the foot. *"Dinero. Ay tienes dinero?"* "Money. Do you have any money?"

Instantly, as Pedro was springing to his feet ready to fight, Juan jumped ahead of him and unflinchingly faced the robber, saying, *"Oiga, Señor sin verguenza."* "Listen, you dirty bastard, I have 25 pesos in my pocket. How would you like to take it away from me?"

In a split second, the robber swung at Juan, but missed. Juan responded with a mighty right fist to the jaw that sent the stranger reeling, as blood spurted out of his mouth. Like an angry lion, Juan leaped on top of the thief, throwing fierce punches right and left, repeatedly calling him *un bastardo mugroso.* Enraged, Juan kept shouting, *";Queres dinero!"* *"Toma!"* "You want money!" "Here!" "Take this," hitting him again and again. Within seconds, the stranger knew he was no match for Juan's ferocious whipping, and yelled, *"Ya!"* *"Ya!"* *"Ya no me peges!"* With blood all over his face and shirt, he continued to cry out, "Enough!" "Enough!" "Don't hit me anymore!"

Juan heard the robber's screams of surrender and released his chokehold. Instantly, the man sprang to his feet and made a flying leap out of the open doorway. The other would-be robber had already jumped from the car, when he saw Pedro lunge toward him with an open switchblade knife. Angry, and his blood boiling, Pedro stood in the open boxcar door waving the knife at the scampering thieves, *ladrones condenados.*

Juan's blood pressure was still racing, as he got up off the floor, his shirt was torn in several places from the brawl, but otherwise, unhurt. Reaching down to pick up his cap, still panting heavily, he began brushing himself off. For the next few seconds, still in awe from the sudden robbery attempt, the two men slowly began to relax.

"Whooee, Juan!" Pedro shouted out loud. "Man, where did you learn to fight like that? That poor guy never had a chance."

"Pedro" he replied, "I don't know. I'm really not a fighter. I hate fighting. But that man was getting ready to rob you. And it just made me mad, I guess."

"By the way, Pedro, where'd you get that knife anyway?"

"I don't remember, Juan" he replied, still pacing the floor. "I've had it a long time, but I never used it. I think it used to be Papa's. But today, I came mighty close to cutting that bastard's throat."

"Yeah. You sure did. But the thieves are gone now, so please put the knife away. I don't like knives, they make me nervous."

"Alright, I'll put it up." he said, obligingly putting the knife back in the scabbard attached to his boot.

"And how about you, Juan?" Pedro asked. "Where'd you get 25 pesos? I thought you were broke?"

"I am broke" he replied, "but those guys didn't know it."

"Ay caramba, Juan." "You're something else. Sure you don't want a cigarette?" asked Pedro. "Right now, I gotta have a smoke to settle my nerves."

"No thanks, Pedro. I still don't smoke"

As the freight train chugged onward blowing it's shrieking whistle, calm finally came over the two men. Now it was time to try to rest.

An hour or so later, Juan decided he better consult his map again. After several minutes of studying it, pointing to a specific spot, he told Pedro, "Lookie here. Here's **Bella Union** way up here, and I'll bet it's several hundred miles away. That's the city Mr. Espinoza warned me about. He said it was huge and complicated, and to be real careful because they have security guards everywhere. And look at all the little towns in between, **San Cayetano de las Vacas, San Roberto, Providencia** and no telling how many more."

"Ay carajo," said Pedro. "Are you sure? At the rate we're going, we'll be all summer getting to the border."

"Don't worry Pedro, we'll make it. Here's what we'll do. After we get passed all those little towns, including Providencia, before reaching Bella Union we'll get off and walk into town. That will reduce our chances of getting caught. Does that sound OK?"

"OK. You're the boss."

As the freight train sped northward past mile after mile of wind-blown open country, there was plenty of time to meditate. Being hundreds of miles from home, and perhaps a thousand miles yet to go, it was comforting for Juan to have someone to talk to.

"Juan" asked Pedro, "What do you think America is like? Do you think all white people are rich?"

"Pedro, I don't know. I've heard so many good things about America. I don't believe they're all rich, but from everything I hear, they're all a lot better off than we are. However, my Papa's cousin Fortunata in San Luis said she wouldn't have any part of the United States. But in my heart, I really believe there is opportunity over there for those who want it and are willing to work for it. My Papa believed this, and I believe it too."

"You're probably right Juan," agreed Pedro, "but I've heard people say that America didn't want Mexicans over there. Do you think that's true?"

"I don't know, Pedro. It may be true. I've heard the same thing, but even if it were true, they don't own the whole world. Anyway, I'll take my chances. Before leaving Villa de Reyes, my friend Don Andres Luz, did however, caution me about white racist mobs along the Texas border. He read someplace where many white politicians in Texas were afraid that Mexicans wanted to reclaim some of their land."

"That doesn't surprise me." Pedro said. "That feud's been going on as long as I can remember."

"It doesn't surprise me either, Pedro, but I can understand why the bitterness. After all, south Texas did, at one time, belong to Mexico. Come to think of it, Fortunata's fears about America might have been justified, because she heard about a recent assault on a Mexican ranch along the border, somewhere near Matamoros, including a lynching."

"A lynching? Are you sure?"

"No, I'm not sure, but it's probably true. If there was a lynching, it was probably the Texas Rangers that did it. My friend, Don Andres Luz said the Texas Rangers were ruthless and brutal against Tejanos and the Mexicans from our side of the border. Especially those who still held a grudge against the Anglos."

"Juan, tell me. How in the world does your friend know all this stuff about Texas, when your little town of Villa de Reyes is so remote from the outside world?"

"I wondered about that too, Pedro, until he showed me an article in the Spanish newspaper *Generación* from San Antonio. I don't know how he got hold of this article—it was already several weeks old when he showed it to me. He said this is not the first time that the newspaper *Generacion* has reported news about rebellious encounters taking place in Texas."

"That doesn't worry you?" Pedro asked.

"No, not really," Juan replied. "But it does bother me that justice in the world is so hard to come by. Our people in Mexico—the poor ones—have been fighting injustice since the day I was born, and still yet, the rich and the powerful make us squeeze every centavo for all it's worth."

"I can't argue that," said Pedro. "I wonder how serious this thing is in Matamoros?"

"I don't know. But I'm not going in that direction. Anyway, I'm a peaceable man and they don't have to worry about me. I'm not going over there to make trouble."

"What's your goal, Juan?" asked Pedro. "I mean, how will we know if we did the right thing in leaving our homes?"

"I don't know about you, Pedro, but for me…..well, I have this dream. Somewhere, someplace in America, there lies a piece of ground just for me. And on this piece of ground, I see peace and contentment. I see a pretty little white house, all mine, and all paid for. And I think I can even see a whole bunch of little kids running around, all calling me Papa. But most of all, I dream of a life free of worry, because in Villa de Reyes, we worried about everything—mostly putting food on the table and making ends meet." "Someday, when my dream comes true, I'll send for Mama, so she'll never have to worry again"

"Gosh, Juan, you don't want very much do you? All I want is lots and lots of money so I can spend it all on good times—and girls."

"How come you never did marry, Juan?" asked Pedro. "Don't you like girls?"

Grinning as he continued, "I guess you know you've got to get married first, before you can have all those little *chamacos* running around calling you Papa."

Acknowledging Pedro's kidding with a blushing grin, he replied,

"Pedro, I like girls alright, but I've never been a ladies man and somehow, it never really mattered."

"You mean to tell me that you've never had a girl friend?"

"Yeah! That's what I mean. Well," he said, "I'll take that back. I did have a girl friend once, but I never told her she was my girl. I thought she was the prettiest girl in Villa de Reyes. She had the prettiest *chiches* I ever saw, and every time I got close to her, it was all I could do to keep from touching one. Once, I almost did, but I knew I didn't dare."

Laughing hysterically, Pedro barked out, "Juan, you crazy nut. You probably would've gotten your face slapped if you had've. But for your information, girls don't bite." he said teasingly. "I was going to ask you if you'd ever had a girl—in bed, I mean. But I already know the answer. What are you saving yourself for anyway?" he asked, "You're not getting any younger, you know."

Grinning bashfully, he replied, "Maybe I am crazy. Mama used to say I was too bashful. But I can't help it if girls make me nervous."

"You're a good man, Juan." Pedro said. "Someday, a pretty young girl will come along and sweep you right off your feet."

"You think so?" asked Juan.

"How about you Pedro, you ever had a girl in bed? Never mind. I already know the answer," said Juan, with a musing chuckle.

Pausing for a few minutes, staring at Juan and shaking his head in amazement, Pedro said, "Juan, you know, I like you. You're OK. Seems like I've known you for a long time. This may sound silly, but I'd like to go where you go. You're like an older brother to me. Especially the way you came to my defense back there against those two thieves. In fact, sometimes you remind me of my Papa. Sounds corny doesn't it."

For a second, Juan was overwhelmed.

"Pedro, I'm flattered. Maybe a little corny." he agreed, jokingly with a broad smile, "but I'm flattered just the same. That was a great compliment. Of course you can come with me—in fact, I insist."

Tearing off a small corner of the map in his hand, he began scribbling something

. "Here," he said. "If we should ever get separated before we get to America, here's the address of my Papa's cousin in Texas. He'll always know where I'm at."

The note read: Rafael Peña, Rte 3, Box 320, Seguin, Texas.

"Lets shake on it, Juan"

"You bet"

"Lets."

And so, a sincere pact of friendship was made between the two young hobos.

Four weeks later on a dreary rainy day, as they were approaching the southern tip of Bella Union city, Juan and Pedro could hardly walk any farther. From the day they left La Paz, misfortune seemed to follow them, starting with that frightening encounter with the two thieves. The trust they'd always had for everyone back home, had now turned into mistrust for the new faces they came in contact with. Particularly, when riding in boxcars with weird unscrupulous tramps. Hopping trains and dodging security guards had become a nightmare. Nothing seemed easy anymore. Many of the train yards were heavily guarded, forcing them to walk or hitch hike much of the way. They now knew all about the pangs in the stomach from hunger and lack of drinking water, and they learned how to swallow their pride and invite humiliation when asking a complete stranger for food—and a peso here and there. They learned to hop speeding trains in the middle of the day or night, in rainstorms, and they got good at running like hell from guards. Since leaving La Paz, at each stop, they had to seek odd jobs just to survive. And today, on arriving in Bella Union, they were still broke and hungry.

Looking up ahead at the business district—the traffic of horses, carriages, soldiers, and the multitude of people—Pedro began pressing for a change.

"Juan," he said, "we've been on the road now for over a month. What do you say we take some time off and see what this town is like? It looks like a pretty nice little town."

"You're probably right, Pedro. I'm ready to check out this town too. By the way, the map shows we've already come over two hundred miles."

"Really?" asked Pedro.

Bella Union was a nice town. Not nearly as over-crowded as others they'd seen. On entering the downtown district, they kept looking for a cheap hotel. Juan had decided that they had to get a job, before they could go any farther. By now, both were badly in need of a shave, to say nothing of the worn and smelly clothes they were wearing. Closer into town, Juan and Pedro found a cheap hotel, **Siesta Serena.**

Hunting a job in this strange town was totally exhausting. Walking the streets unsuccessfully all day long, day after day, was even more tiring than walking endless miles of railroad tracks. Finally in their third week, Juan and Pedro found work in a canning factory. Not much pay, but it paid for their past-due hotel bill and some direly needed hot meals. They continued their employment at the cannery just long enough to save up a few extra pesos for their journey.

After three weeks, once again, it was train-hopping time, and again, security guards were their biggest concern. By this time, they'd learned a few tricks about hide and seek—so they thought. Catching a freight train out of Bella Union in the dark of night went well, in fact, too well. Juan and Pedro were elated at the absence of guards and the ease in which they caught the train. This time, however, instead of a boxcar, they had to settle for an empty open-top gondola coal car. As the locomotive chugged its way through open brush land, Juan and Pedro were preparing to spread out their bedroll, when suddenly, Juan happened to notice a sign along the way that read **Saltillo.** Right then, he jerked around to take another look, and immediately realized that they'd hopped the wrong train.

"Pedro!" he yelled. We got on the wrong darn train! This train is going west, not north!" "*Ay Caramba,* we're headed toward Saltillo. As soon as this thing slows down, we're jumping off."

Within minutes, they got their wish. The train mysteriously came to a screeching halt. Juan and Pedro immediately started to climb out of the gondola, but instantly jumped back in, stone faced.

"*Alma mia!*" cried out Juan in an unsettling jolt. "This train is being robbed!"

Peeking out again over the top of the gondola, he could see approximately fifteen bandits riding on restless horses, as they kept yelling out orders and instructions to each other. All the while, gunshots were being fired at the train from both sides. Wild shooting lit up the sky with fiery red sparks that filled the night air with smoke and the smell of gunpowder. Juan could tell that most of the commotion was being staged around the flatcar behind the locomotive, while sporadic shooting continued. Suddenly, a loud explosion rattled all the freight cars. It sounded like dynamite.

"Juan!" Pedro yelled. "What are we going to do?"

"*Esperate Pedro"* "Wait a minute. Let's see what they're after." Peeking over the top once again, Juan said, "Look Pedro. They've surrounded that flat car up ahead"

"Well, I'll be, Pedro." Juan exclaimed in astonishment, "I know what it is! Why of course! These renegades belong to the revolution, and they're after those guns and canons I saw earlier on that flatcar."

"We've got to get the hell out of here."

In the black of darkness, they both leaped from the gondola and made a run for it. Not knowing which way to run, they scampered toward the nearest clump of bushes as fast as they could, but in their fright, they ran in different directions. Juan hadn't noticed that Pedro had lagged behind. After what he thought was a safe distance, he threw himself down behind a tall tuna mesquite plant and waited for Pedro, but he was nowhere to be seen. After waiting for a few moments, his heart pounding and crawling on his hands and knees, he inched his way back a few yards. Carefully hiding behind thorny cactus bushes as he went, he called out in a whisper, "Pedro." "Pedro." He waited a few seconds and called out again, "Pedro. *Donde estas?"* "Where are you?" Another minute went by, and still Pedro didn't answer. So again, Juan crawled up a few feet closer, hunkered down close to the ground so as not to be seen. Suddenly, by the light of the moon, he saw the silhouette figures of a gang of bandits beating Pedro viciously as he was fighting and resisting fiercely. For a moment, Juan was petrified. With all his heart, he wanted to go to his friend's defense, but he knew he was no match for the overwhelming odds. As he saw Pedro being dragged away on the ground, limp as though unconscious, he became mortified,. At that moment, his heart was still pounding away, not knowing what to do or which way to run. But after a few minutes of lying flat on the ground on his belly, the guns were silent and the riders were gone. As the train began emitting black smoke from its stack, it slowly disappeared into the night, until only the flashing red lantern from the caboose could be seen.

Juan remained in the same spot all night long, unable to sleep for keeping watch, should Pedro be released and return, but he never showed. Dazed and overcome with grief, his limp body felt unwilling to deal with the emptiness from the loss of his friend. And because their friendship had become so amicably intimate, a lump swelled in his throat from the very thought of his capture, and perhaps his death.

At dawn's first light, Juan searched the spot where Pedro had wrestled with the insurgents, thinking that perhaps, he would find some of his personal belongings. But the first thing he saw, were chunks of the canon's turret that lay strewn along the railroad tracks. Obviously, the insurgents' aim was to destroy the canon and other weapons belonging to the Federales. He was about to walk away, when he spotted a miniature gold watch in the exact spot where they had scuffled. It had the name 'Pedro Morales' inscribed on the back. Quickly, he picked it up and tucked it in his pocket. Someday, if they ever met again, he thought, he would return it to him. As he walked away from the scene of last night's awesome raid, still dazed, he kept looking over his shoulder hoping to see Pedro. But with no sign of his friend, he reversed his course and began walking back to Bella Union.

On arriving back in Bella Union once again, Juan returned to the canning factory and worked at his previous job, just in case Pedro should show up. But after two weeks of anxious waiting, he decided Pedro wasn't coming and decided to move on. After that frightening encounter with renegades, he decided to avoid hopping any more freight trains.

It was still some 200 miles to the Laredo border, and for many reasons, Juan dreaded the very thought of it with a passion—the eternally slow travel on foot. It meant more embarrassing pleas to strangers for handouts, plus lonely nights in god-forsaken places. He detested the humiliating instances he'd experienced all the way, instances like the time when he approached Don Carlos Espinoza's farm asking for a meal and a place to sleep. He hated the trudging appearance of a tramp. Now, it was like starting all over again—the hard way—because since leaving Bella Union, again, he began to experience the handicaps of his grueling journey through unfamiliar treeless prairies and sweltering plains, and sometimes, dangerous land. On occasion, he saw the remnants of what appeared to be a wealthy landowner's plantation reduced to rubble, presumably, by insurgents. Once in a while, he saw open-top motorized buses along the *carreteras* transporting paying passengers. Not only passengers, but also a variety of animals, such as goats, caged chickens and gamecocks, and the like. But very few times, could he afford their fares. Occasionally—on a lucky day—he got a lift from families also traveling north in a covered wagon being pulled by mules or horses. And though the jolting wagons trailed over well-used rutted roads, through choking dust, and sometimes, violent rainstorms, Juan felt every bump, rock, and pothole being crunched by the wooden spoke wheels. Despite the relentless drives, however, on a good day, he could cover a distance of fifteen miles. He always felt grateful to the wagon owners when given a lift, and often helped with miscellaneous repairs along the way, on occasion, hobbling the horses at night in open grassy fields so they wouldn't run away.

Three weeks later, after having left Bella Union and hitchhiking through the towns of **Lirios, Arteaga, and Ramos Arispe,** Juan finally made it to the big city of **Monterrey.** As he approached the city, off to the right near a blacksmith shop, he spotted dozens of horses and cavalrymen milling around the coral—some were in uniforms and others in casual wrangler clothes. In town, weary and broke, he began looking for work. He eventually found a job at a produce market, which didn't pay very much, but at least, it would pay for his food and lodging. Needing to save enough money for the remaining distance to Nuevo Laredo, he worked at the market for six weeks, until the day he'd been waiting for finally came.

When Juan finally reached the border at Nuevo, Laredo, he was exhausted. The dirt street in this dusty little border town was buzzing with excitement, as throngs of shoppers swarmed the merchants on the main thoroughfare in search of bargains. Music and jubilant laughter was abundantly loud coming from the cantinas. Juan's anxiety had finally pacified on his arrival at the Mexican border, and now for the first time, he felt greatly relieved at the very sight of the bridge that he would soon be crossing. In his relief for having made it to the border, the first thing he thought of was his mother—he wanted to write her a letter and share his incredible accomplishment. He knew how much she worried and prayed for his safe journey, and a letter from Laredo would make her very happy and relieved. But first, he had to find a church. He wanted to give thanks to God for his safe journey to the U.S., Mexican border.

The next morning after Mass at the little church of **Santa Maria,** Juan visited the parish priest. He informed Father Santiago about his plans of going to America and his gruesome experiences since leaving home, and in no time, they became good friends. Father understood very well the plight of this young traveler and immediately offered him lodging for a few nights of rest.

On the morning of his departure from Santa Maria Catholic Church, as he walked slowly toward the border crossing, he was somewhat bewildered and overcome with a strange sadness. It was as if he could hear distant voices coming from back home—perhaps the voice of his father, Cenobio. He sensed a peculiar omen—one voice saying 'you finally made it to America' and the other, saying 'you won't like it Juan'. As he walked aimlessly across the bridge, he stopped to take one last heart-wrenching look at Mexico—*la tierra de su Padre,* the land of his father—then proceeded to the other side.

CHAPTER 8

▼

UNREST IN SOUTH TEXAS

It was mid-August (1913) when Juan finally crossed the border onto **American Soil at Laredo, Texas**, and without question, a much wiser man. Naivety had given way to hard lessons learned, and to the longest day of his life, he'd never forget the bitter experiences encountered since leaving Villa de Reyes.

A passport was not necessary when he crossed the border, nor was a passport necessary for the other people walking northward, leaving a rebellious country all too familiar with the tragic remnants of a sporadic civil war. Juan's baptismal certificate was all the proof needed to declare himself a citizen of Mexico. Occasionally, however, when someone's identity was challenged and turned away, all they had to do was to go downstream of the shallow Rio Grande to a waiting ferryboat—or swim across the river.

Within blocks of the border crossing, Juan spotted a small cafe. Unsure of which direction to go, he entered the cafe and ordered a cup of black coffee and proceeded to make some inquiries. From the day he left Bella Union, and every town afterwards, he constantly looked back over his shoulder hoping to see his friend, Pedro. But nothing.

As Juan walked the cracked sidewalks of the streets of Laredo, he was greatly surprised to see the density of people in this bustling American border town which included the inescapable presence of numerous squads of boisterous soldiers gathered here and yon. If there was any consolation to be had on arriving on American soil, however, it was the familiarity of the Mexican faces that he saw. On seeing the faces of those of his raza—many sitting idle on the benches along the earthen roadway in shabby clothes and with their meager belongings at their feet—he wondered just how many of them were transients like himself, emigrating from south of the border. Because quite often, since leaving home, he had encountered a number of people traveling north; carrying satchels, suitcases and tote bags—some traveling alone, and on occasion, families with small children. While some were traveling on mules and horses, many were traveling on foot, and others who could afford horse-drawn wagons, carried as many personal belongings as possible, including pots and pans and odd pieces of furniture—some of which were strapped to their wagon. Every time he saw weary travelers going north, he wondered if they were leaving Mexico—and for the same reasons he was.

He should have been elated on having reached this distant land, and he should have been excited with feelings of rejoicing in the land that was to be his new home. But it wasn't that way at all. Because as he gawked up and down main street, the overwhelming number of Anglo Americans made him nervous and uneasy, particularly, the number of men carrying side arms and rifles. At different intervals, he noticed groups of armed white men appearing to be posses or law enforcers huddled together passing the time of day in haughty laughter. It was easy to distinguish the rich from the poor, because the poor seemed to be everywhere. The rich—all of whom looked like wealthy politicians or successful gamblers—were easy to spot. They were the ones wearing tailored black suits, white shirts, black string ties, and of course, smoking Havana cigars. Everywhere he looked; the street signs, storefront signs, window displays, and advertisements—all were in English. Unlike Nuevo Laredo, south of the border, where nearly one hundred percent of the people were pure Spanish speaking Mexicans, and where every business establishment had familiar luring commercials, all were in readable Spanish. Now, in Laredo, Texas, north of the border, it was completely the opposite—and scary, all because of Juan's inability to speak or read English. All of a sudden, a cold chill came over him and he felt more bewildered than ever. Now he recalled the words of Fortunata when she warned him that 'making it in America' would be extremely difficult if you didn't speak the language. *No truer words were ever spoken,* he thought, when seeing strange white people along the way unable to speak their language. Of course, he'd seen strangers before. In fact everywhere he'd been since leaving home, he saw nothing but strangers, but at least, he could speak their language. But now, he himself, felt like the only stranger in town. Without question, his confidence in pursuing his journey was deeply shaken.

On that very first day in Laredo, Texas, as he walked down main street—an overly busy road with cowboys, ranchers and farmers on horseback galloping the wide dirt road, horse-drawn carriages and wagons, dozens of horses tied to the side rails awaiting their masters, and a multitude of busy shoppers—he braced himself for the prejudiced environment he'd been warned about. He knew his appearance would raise questions to passersby, seeing his unshaven face, his shabby clothes and a wrinkled tote bag hanging across his shoulder. Walking along the wooden boardwalks of the shops and stores of this bustling Anglo town—trying to appear as though he wasn't lost amid the crowd of shoppers, the loud beat of Mexican music, and enthusiastic beer drinkers—he politely smiled at people when catching their eye, sometimes tipping his cap. Most of them returned his smile, and each time, a friendly smile from a white stranger worked wonders in restoring fresh confidence.

But that inspiring confidence changed abruptly when he stepped into a small shoe store seeking directions to Seguin, Texas. In a rocking chair, gripping an ivory smoking pipe between his teeth, sat the owner—a big fluffy white man who surely weighed 250 pounds, graying at the temples and balding on top. Making no attempt to get up, without hesitating, in a deep hoarse voice, said, "What do you want?"

Juan respectfully removed his cap and with a smile, handed him a piece of paper on which he'd written the name and address of Rafael Peña. Pointing to the note, he asked politely, "*dispenseme Señor, Mi primo.*" "*Busco dirección para Seguin, Texas.*" "Excuse me sir, but I'm looking for my cousin. Can you give me directions to Seguin, Texas?" Juan's presence had undoubtedly inconvenienced the owner, because as soon as he entered the door, the owner had apparently sized him up as being just another homeless drifter from across the river, and said gruffly, "Look buddy. You don't speak English and I don't speak Spanish. I sell shoes here, not information." With a deliberate shove on the shoulder and pointing to the door, he said, "Go somewhere else." Juan didn't need an interpreter to tell him that he wasn't welcome inside, so he meekly headed toward the door.

It so happened that at the same time Juan was asking for directions, a petite well-dressed Mexican lady had entered the store—presumably a customer. Overhearing the owner's rude treatment of the stranger, she was appalled and couldn't refrain from interfering. Turning to Juan, she said, "*Señor, vengase con migo.*" "Come with me."

Staring at the owner with a cold hard look on her face, she snapped, "Patron—wha su matta con ju. Ha cama ju talk to heem dot way?" Turning her nose up at him, she continued, "I go sum odder place too," and stormed out the door mumbling Spanish obscenities. Seeing that Juan was a stranger in town and no doubt from south of the border, she asked, *"De donde vienes, Señor?"* "Where are you from, mister?"

"Villa de Reyes." he replied. *"Cerca de San Luis, Potosi."* "Near San Luis, Potosi."

"Hombre, you sure are a long ways from home. You couldn't have picked a worse place to walk in to. That Gringo wouldn't give a Mexican the time of day. He thinks we're all stupid Mexicans and wouldn't lift a finger to help. Here, let me see the address of your cousin."

Handing her the slip of paper with Rafael Peña's address, Juan was smiling and much relieved. Immediately, he liked the woman. He marveled at the way she had confronted the store owner in his behalf. Obviously, she wasn't one to be pushed around. He admired this wiry 50-year old Mexican lady who could speak English, and though her English was badly broken, he knew she was a very capable person. At a glance, Juan couldn't help but notice how pretty she was, despite thin lines of aging around her green eyes, the way her pug nose turned upward when she talked, and the wavy strands of cold black hair blowing in the breeze from beneath a pink head scarf. Her perfume and the pretty full-length silken dress she was wearing, hinted of a woman of sophistication and perhaps a woman of means.

Visiting with her as they sat on a wooden crafted bench around the corner, they talked about their roots and their aspirations. Immediately, she was an inspiration to Juan, encouraging him to continue pursuing his dream—the same thing she was doing.

"Mire Señor," she said. *"Nunca sueltes tus sueños."* "Don't ever give up your dreams. America is a great country. You'll see. When me and my family left Durango, Mexico, 14 years ago, I encountered the same identical problems you're telling me about." *"Señor."* she continued, "please don't judge all the people in Laredo by that *pelado,* bald headed man in the shoe store. Most people here are friendly. They're all hard working people trying to make a living."

"Did you say your cousin lives in Seguin?"

"Yes."

"Caramba" "That's a long way from here. Do you have the money to get there with?" she asked.

"No señora. No tengo nada de dinero." "No ma'am. I don't have any money,"

"How are you gonna get to Seguin if you don't have money for the train?" she asked.

"I guess the same way I got this far—hopping trains."

"That's no good," she said. "Tell you what…by the way, my name is **Consuelo.**" "What's yours?"

"Juan," he answered, slightly tugging at the tip of his cap. "Juan Gomez"

"Juan" she said, "I know you're broke, and perhaps I can help you. I own the little cantina up the street—*El Rincón*—and in the evenings, I could use some help. Why don't you come work for me? You can work as long as you like—or at least, work long enough to buy some decent clothes and train fare."

"*Señora,*" he replied, "you don't know how much I appreciate that. I'm a complete stranger in this town, and still—you befriended me."

"Of course. I'll.come work for you. Absolutely!"

Juan was beginning to like Laredo, Texas. He met many nice Mexican people here, all of whom treated him fantastic, including a few white people who enjoyed trying to teach him to speak English. But were it not for his anxiousness to get to Rafael's place in Seguin, he would have liked to stay longer. After having worked at Consuelo's beer tavern for six weeks, the day finally came when he was ready to move on. He saved every penny he possibly could, and even bought some new clothes. On the trip to Seguin, instead of hopping trains, he would be a paying passenger. In his pocket, he had just enough money left over to buy train fare as far as San Antonio. From there to Seguin, he figured it was only about 40 miles and he'd worry about how to get there later.

Consuelo was a wonderful lady, truly, an angel in disguise. She came to Juan's defense when he was being mistreated, and also, to his rescue when he was broke and hungry. But most importantly, she made him feel welcome in America and put fresh new inspiration in his unfinished venture.

Consuelo accompanied Juan to the train station to make sure there were no mix-ups in communication. She knew how awkward he felt among white people, and not knowing the language, would make it even worse.

"*Bueno, Juan.*" Consuelo said, "*¿Como se te parese Norte America ahora?*" "Well, Juan, what do you think of America now?"

"*Me gusta mucho.*" "I like it very much. But I know I'll like it even more once I learn the language, and find my new home—wherever that is."

"Keep looking Juan. It's out there somewhere. You'll find it."

"Here," she continued, handing him a piece of paper, "give this note to the conductor on the train. It tells him where you're going. He'll tell you when it's time to get off."

The 'all aboard' sounded and it was time to say good-bye.

"Gracias Doña Consuelo. Que Dios se lo page por toda su ayuda." "Thanks for all your help, Consuelo. May God bless you."

"Dame un abraso, Juan. Te encargo que no se te olvides de mi. Y si algun dia pasas por aqui devuelta, quero ber te." "Give me a hug Juan, and please don't forget about me. If someday you should pass this way again, I want to see you."

With a tender embrace, Juan said good-bye.

"Adios, Consuelo. Muchisimas gracias."

"Adios, Juan. Que te vaya bien." "Good luck, Juan."

On the train bound for San Antonio, en route to Seguin, Texas, Juan felt very lonely. Not one day since leaving home had he forgotten his folks, especially his mother, and today, as he continued his journey farther north, he couldn't help but feel even more lonesome. Sometimes doubts entered his mind and he fought to reassure himself that he was doing the right thing. As for his friend Pedro, Juan still missed him immensely and wondered where he could be, occasionally stroking the small gold watch in his pocket as a reminder, and wondering if he was alright. Chances were, he'd never see him again.

From the first day he set foot on American soil, Juan observed many differences between the two countries, many of which he didn't like—particularly discrimination. In the first place, America was nothing like the people in Mexico thought it was—like, lots of money, and lots of jobs. It wasn't like that at all. And he soon learned that America was for white people who spoke English, not for brown people who spoke Spanish which always prompted him to seek people of his own skin color when asking for information. He learned, too, that it wasn't necessarily the snobbish white people that caused the dream of America to blur— it was simply a case of the 'haves' and the 'have nots'. Those with money had it made, and those without it, like him, were out in the cold. But the biggest hurdle for Juan, at the moment, was the English language, or the lack of it.

As the train was pulling into the station in San Antonio, Juan was beginning to get nervous all over again. He hadn't forgotten the 'stings' of discrimination in Laredo. Somehow, his naive notion that on approaching a stranger—whether white or brown would be the same as approaching a friend—was not necessarily true. He recalled the time when he was denied service at a restaurant and told to sit in a back room, and another time, when seeking directions to a certain highway, how he was shunned and told to *git*. Experiencing hateful discrimination was something new for him. It was like being told to his face that he was an inferior human being, intruding on someone else's property. On these occasions, the implied message *'you're not welcome here'* was always very clear and humiliating. And each time it happened, the feeling of being unwelcome, deeply wounded his pride. But he kept these ugly feelings of rejection to himself, and soon learned to expect it from time to time.

Stepping off the train in San Antonio, Juan still had 40 miles to go and once again, it was back to walking and hitch hiking. Three tiring days later, his long sought destination, all the way from Villa de Reyes had finally been reached. He now had both feet on the ground in Seguin, Texas.

In downtown Seguin, Juan approached several Mexican people showing them the return address on the letter from Rafael Peña, each time with no success. Until finally, an elderly catholic lady who knew of the Peña's as a member of her church parish, was able to give him directions to a cotton farm four miles east of town.

Walking anxiously down an old country road in the direction given him with cotton fields on each side, thirty minutes later from a distance he spotted the ranch. Immediately, he knew it was Rafael's place. Advancing his pace almost to a trot, he forgot all about the nagging weariness throughout his body. As he looked ahead, his heart was racing with relief knowing that, at last, he was walking that last, long, miserable, but beautiful mile. His answer to the challenge of coming to America was in sight, *Rafael Peña's ranch*. Excitedly within himself, he wished he could share this momentous arrival in Seguin with his folks back home. Especially Don Luz, who had given him the inspiration of America. He could hardly wait to write home.

Dusk was about to set in, when he saw a woman sweeping off her front porch, and a man sitting at a grinding wheel sharpening some tools. Approaching them both, Juan looked at the man and called out, *"Dispenseme por favor, pero usted es el senor Peña?"* "Excuse me Sir," he asked, "but are you Mr. Peña?"

"Juanito!" Cried out the man. *"Yo soy."* "Yes! That's me!"

"Rafael!" "Is it really you?"

Standing in the middle of the yard, Juan in his dirty clothes and scuffed shoes, and Rafael in his working *pecheras,* they both laughed aloud with a yell of excitement as they hugged each other vigorously, patting each other's shoulder.

"Juanito, porque te detenites?" "Juanito, what took you so long? We were expecting you a month ago" said Rafael, as they walked toward the front porch.

"Oh, Rafael, you'll never believe what I've been through." Smiling happily, he continued, "Would you believe I left home over four months ago? It was April, the day after Easter Sunday."

"Oh yes, I believe you." replied Rafael, also with a big happy smile. "I've been down that road myself. I know exactly what you're saying. Come on. Let's go inside. I want you to meet my family and I want to know everything about your Papa and Mama, and all about my old stomping grounds, Villa de Reyes."

"Here, I want you to meet my wife **Margarita**."

"Vieja, este es el hijo de mi primo Cenobio. Se llama Juan." "Honey, this is my cousin. Cenobio's son—Juan."

With a welcoming smile, she embraced Juan as though he was a long lost member of the family, saying, *"Gusto de conocerte, Juan."* "Juanito, I'm so pleased to meet you. We heard you were coming. Fortunata wrote us and said you were on your way. It's so good to meet someone from back home. My, you sure look like your Papa. Come on in and let's put some food in that stomach—you look pretty thin to me."

Margarita, a short but plump little woman, was the perfect housewife. She couldn't read or write, but it didn't matter. The only thing that mattered to her was her children and her *viejo*. And just like Juan's mother Felipa, she spent most of her time in the kitchen with her apron on.

"Muchachos—vengan aqui." Margarita called out, "Hey kids—come over here. I want you to meet our cousin." They had all been standing in an open doorway of the kitchen looking on, curiously. Smiling respectfully, they walked over to meet the stranger they had been expecting and shook hands.

"This is **Martin**, he's 21, the oldest. This is **Clara**, 18, and this one is **Maria**, she's 16."

"My, my," said Juan, still smiling proudly. *"Que familia tan bonita"* "What a pretty family."

With an affectionate embrace with the girls, and firm handshake with Martin, he said, "I'm Juan. It's all my pleasure. This is the day I've been waiting for."

Margarita excused herself and went into the kitchen.

"Sientate Juan. Sientate aqui junto de mi" "Sit down Juan," Rafael said, "sit here next to me. Tell me all about your trip. How's Cenobio?"

The children too sat down close to Juan, anxious to hear all about their new cousin whom they'd never met before.

"Rafael" said Juan, "I don't know if you knew that Papa died. He died three years ago of pneumonia."

"Ay Juan. No me digas." "Oh Juan, you don't say. I'm so sorry to hear that. You know," he continued, "in our letters, we talked about him coming to America someday, but he always said he couldn't afford it. I think he wanted to though. How about your mama, Felipa, how's she getting along."

"Mama is doing fine and is still in good health. Gregoria is grown up now and is a tremendous help to mama. Hilario is doing well too. He's looking after the place now, and just like the rest of us, farming is all he knows. I told him I'd write, once I arrived in America. By the way, it sure was nice seeing your sister Fortunata in San Luis. She's a great woman and very enterprising."

"Oh, and by the way, here's a package she wanted me to give. I think its some photos."

Reaching for the small package, Rafael asked, "Juan, tell me about Villa de Reyes, has it changed much? And how about Don Andres Luz? Is he still alive?"

"Andres Luz?" asked Juan, "Absolutely. He's very much alive, and he's still our City Clerk and looking after things at the courthouse. I have great respect and admiration for him."

Sipping on some hot coffee that Margarita just handed him, Juan said, "Rafael...Villa de Reyes hasn't changed a bit and I don't think it ever will. Lots of people have moved away. For us at home, things really got tough after Papa died. He always wanted the best for us, you know, but in Villa de Reyes, well...everyone there is so darn poor. I guess that's why I'm here in America—someplace, there's got to be something better. I'd like to make something of myself someday. At least, that's my hope."

"I hope so too" responded Rafael. "I really admire your courage. It reminds me of the same reasons why I left Villa de Reyes a long time ago, ten years ago in fact. But for me, besides not being able to make a living, it was the revolution, and how the country was so torn apart and everyone on pins and needles. I, too, was searching for a better life, and here on this ranch, I think I have found it."

Immediately, Juan was confused, because from what he could see of the old house and the farm, there seemed to be a lot more to be desired.

"Is this what you wanted, Rafael?" asked Juan. "This farm?"

"Yes," replied Rafael, "this farm. But let me explain why."

Leaning back in his easy chair, he began revealing words of wisdom that Juan would never forget.

"You see Juanito," he began, "this whole world is full of poor people, and no matter where you go, you'll always find poor people trying to make a living—and that includes Mexico."

"Look" he continued, "you've traveled more than *eight hundred kilometros* and tell me, how many rich people did you meet? No matter where you go, you won't see many, and even if you do, they're probably not happy because they all want more. More than they already have. Me? This is where I want to be. I'm happy here, and I've learned that no matter how rich we are, if we don't have happiness, then we might as well not have anything."

"Yes," he continued, "I'm happy here, and this is all I want." "*Gracias a Dios.*"

Juan was silent. He didn't know what to make of what he'd just heard. Then he said,

"That's great Rafael. I can see you're a happy man."

After that, Juan was speechless, trying to absorb Rafael's message. It sounded so satisfying and so blissful, as though he had already reached his dream goal in life. He was amazed at the truth and sincerity of Rafael's contentment. But for Juan—at least for the time being—his goal was still out there, somewhere else.

As Juan was seated at the dinner table eating his supper that Margarita had prepared, Clara and Maria sat close to him, asking questions about Villa de Reyes, what was it like there, and how about other young girls, did they go to dances, were they allowed to go out with boys. Also, they wanted to know all about hopping trains and his dangerous journey all the way from home. They were curious to know every little detail. Moreover, they were delighted to have a relative as their company. After a while, continuing to talk of old times, Juan and Rafael went back into the sala to relax. Martin had already gone to the barn to feed the horses.

Reaching for his pipe and smoking tobacco, Rafael said, "Juan, I want you to come work for me. I have a job waiting for you. As you saw on your way in, this is a cotton farm. This farm belongs to **Mr. Ralph Watkins**, but I own a small piece of it. We have 160 acres here, and we sharecrop a lot of it with other ranchers. Right now, I need you. If you want to work, I'll pay you the same as I do the other employees."

"Rafael" Replied Juan, grinning from ear to ear, "Of course I'll work for you. As you can see, I'm broke and I really need a job."

Rafael Peña was an older gentleman, in his mid-50s, well built, graying black hair along the temples, and super friendly. His face was slightly wrinkled, and obviously, the kick in his step was not that of a young man's anymore. But the smile on his face seemed to be the same smile of the people of Villa de Reyes. His house resembled many of the houses back home; small, cramped, and very old. They, too, had outside toilets, and no running water. They, too, collected rainwater from their roofs, same as in Villa de Reyes. The indoors was spotless and very comfortable. Pictures of relatives in Old Mexico hung on the wall and they proudly displayed a large statue of The Virgin Mary in the center of their prayer altar. Their small ranch also had the usual livestock, chickens, pens, sheds, barns, and several horses grazing in the pasture. For their transportation, Rafael had two open-top horse-drawn wagons that they used when going into town for provisions and to Mass on Sundays, and also, for transporting workers to and from the cotton fields. The setting was all too familiar to Juan, making him homesick for his own little 'ranhito' back home.

For the next several months, Juan felt very fortunate working for his Primo, Rafael. For the time being, things could not have worked out any better. He felt content living with his newfound relatives, and soon became a part of their every-day routine, as though he was another of Rafael's sons. Every day at sunrise, they boarded the horse-drawn wagons and went straight to the cotton fields. By noon, Margarita and the girls brought them lunch and a canteen of cool drinking water. After lunch and a short break, they continued working until dark. Another nice thing about living with the Peña's was that at last, Juan was able to attend Mass on a regular basis. Also, he became acquainted with some of Rafael's friends, occasionally making music with some of the local musicians. But most importantly, now with steady employment, Juan was in a position to send money home as promised.

One of Rafael's employees—**Jacob Santana**—was a Negro man. Juan had heard of Negros before, but had never met one. It was when he crossed the border at Laredo that he first began to notice one, here and there. Of course, Juan never expected to find a Negro working at Rafael's ranch, and even more surprised when he learned that a few other Negros were also employed at the ranch. Jacob, in his 40's, and a very friendly man, could speak both English and Spanish fluently. To Juan's amazement, Jacob's English and Spanish were almost flawless with absolutely no broken accent in either language. As Juan and Jacob became close friends, on inquiring about his origin, Jacob talked freely about his ancestors being from Africa, but never knew or remembered anything about his parents or relatives. He did know, however, that he was a descendant of Negro slaves brought to America from Spain during earlier generations of slavery.

For over a year, Juan and his new friend Jacob worked side by side, as Juan tried desperately to learn to speak English, or at least some English words. But as hard as he tried, the words he attempted just wouldn't come together. Of course by now, he had memorized a few words and broken phrases, but it was nearly a futile effort. He just couldn't quite pick up on the language. As a matter of fact, he had such a terrible accent, that every time he tried to speak English, he literally fractured the words. But the key word that was solidly planted in his limited English vocabulary was the word *work*. The way he pronounced it was 'weh-keh'—not even close to it's proper pronunciation.

Into his 2nd year at Rafael's ranch, Juan was eager to find a different kind of a job. To have left the fields of labor in Mexico, to have come to work in the fields of Texas, was not exactly what he had in mind when he left home. And so— armed with a few English words, and a few American dollars—he decided it was time to move on. The lure of money was not his reason for wanting to leave, however. God knows he never had any substantial amounts before, and even if he had a pocket full today, he would send it home to his family. No, it was something else he yearned for; roots of his own somewhere, a place of permanence. At any rate, he knew that Seguin was not it. So, at the next opportunity, he would notify Rafael of his decision to move on.

When that day finally came, it was a sad day. Juan and Rafael had become very close, many times reliving old memories of days gone by. It wouldn't be easy saying good-bye to this terrific man and his wonderful wife and family.

It was nearing the end of fall and cotton-picking season was over, when Juan decided the time had come to inform Rafael of his decision to leave the farm. The temperature outside had already begun to cool down, the last wagon load of cotton had be taken to the train yards for transporting to the cotton mills in San Antonio; hay had been stored in the barns for the winter, and the horses had been put out to pasture.

That November evening, Rafael and Juan, including Margarita, were relaxing in the sala, enjoying a dish of *Buñuelos*—a dessert. Juan was a bit nervous in breaking the news of his departure.

"Rafael" he said, finally, "I don't quite know how to say this, but I think it's time for me to be moving on."

"What?" asked Rafael, astonished, "you're leaving? I don't understand."

"Yes, Primo, (Cousin) I've been here two years now, and I think its time to move on to something else."

"Juanito," asked Rafael, "What exactly are you looking for? Aren't you happy here on the ranch?"

"Si, Primo. I like the ranch. I've been very happy here, but there's still something missing in my life, but I don't know what it is. I can't explain it right now, but I feel compelled to keep on searching."

"Where will you go, Juanito?"

"Probably San Antonio. I hear that in San Antonio the Mexican raza is growing everyday and perhaps there, I'll find the answer. If not, I'll keep on searching."

"I'll be leaving in the morning, if it's alright with you."

"*Bueno Juanito, Ay tu sabes.*" "That's fine," agreed Rafael, "Its kind of sudden, but you know best. I've loved having you here—you've practically become part of my family. I sure hate to see you go, but I think I understand."

After a brief pause, Rafael continued......

"By the way, Juan, yesterday when we were in town, did you notice that band of armed gunmen wearing a star patch on their shirt?"

"Yes, I did. Why do you ask?"

"Well—they were Texas Rangers. There's been an increased number of them around town, but more so, in south Texas near San Benito and Brownsville. Lately, according to the news, a lot more of them are gathering around Laredo."

"Why are you telling me this, Primo?"

"I'm telling you this, Juan, because there's something happening here in Texas. I don't know what it is exactly, but I think it could be serious."

"What do you mean?" Juan asked, with expressions of concern.

"South Texas. Looks like trouble over there."

The look on Rafael's somber face was beginning to worry Juan. The next few minutes, however, opened his eyes to a very serious matter—the growing unrest in Texas between Tejanos from both sides of the border, and the Anglos.

"Juan," he said, "I've lived here in Texas a long time. And even though things might look rosy and peaceable to you, it's not always so. Maybe that's another reason why I'm happy here on the ranch—away from the reality of harsh racial prejudices. Out here, I don't have to worry about animosity or the cultural difference between the Mexicans who were here before statehood, and the droves of Anglos who have converged on south Texas with all their wealth and power. Sometimes, it looks like they want to own every inch of Texas—as well as control of the Tejano. But here on the ranch, no one bothers me or bosses me around. Everybody treats me with dignity and respect.

"How about Mr. Watkins? He's white! Is he one of them?"

"Yes, he's white, alright, Juan, but thank goodness he has a good heart. I wish all whites were like him, then we wouldn't have so much friction in Texas."

"Primo," Juan said, "I think you're right. There does seem to exist an attitude of dominance in town, and for sure, it looks like the Americans pretty well control everything. Sometimes, a gringo gives me a dirty look as though I had the plague. But I've gotten used to that now."

"How serious is this problem, Primo?" Juan continued, becoming more concerned. "Is there going to be fighting?"

"Fighting! From the looks of things and what I read in the papers, it's already begun," he answered, shaking his head somewhat in dismay. He didn't want to be an alarmist or interfere with Juan's decision to leave, but at the moment, the road ahead seemed very unpredictable, and possibly dangerous.

"Juan," he commenced, "I think all hell is about to break loose down by Brownsville. I thought I'd better warn you before you head out. You know that new man I hired a few days ago? **Solomon Quiroz?**"

"Yes, I know him. He's a real nice man. Why?"

"Well…he saw first hand what's going on down there, and decided to get out while he could. But the important thing is, he pretty much confirmed what I've been reading in the newspaper—*La Cronica*—a Spanish newspaper out of San Antonio. I get a copy of their paper every two weeks. I've heard a lot about their publisher—Mr. Nicasio Idar. He seems to know what he's talking about."

"Juan," he continued, "trouble is brewing in Texas. It's all about territory. You may have read that Mexico has never accepted the Rio Grande River as the southern boundary of the United States. Mexico contends that the legal boundary is the Nueces River. The strip of land between the two rivers—referred to as the 'Nueces Strip'—is what all the unrest is about."

"Yes, I recall reading about it," Juan said, "but gosh, I thought that was settled a long time ago."

"It was." Rafael replied. "But ever since then, it's been like a festering open wound in the heart and soul of the Mexican. Not only those who were born here in Texas, but now, those same vengeances have crossed the border into Mexico.

"Primo," Juan asked, "What do you think about all this? Does it worry you?"

"No, Juan. It doesn't worry me. It does bother me though, when I see how indignant the Mexicans are treated over here. After all, they were here first."

"Did I make a mistake by coming to America?" Juan asked, as he was beginning to grasp a message of conflict between the two countries.

"Juan—I can't answer that. I don't know how things would have been if you'd stayed down there. Only time will tell. However, you may have left just in time.

Look what happened at Celaya.. Just when you think the revolution in Mexico is about over, Bam! Celaya! Several thousand men were killed in that horrible battle just this last summer. So, maybe it's gotten worse. And if that wasn't bad enough, it looks like the United States is forming a counterinsurgency to go after Pancho Villa. They're bound and determined to get him. In fact, they're already starting to mobilize pretty heavily around Laredo, and it wouldn't surprise me if they crossed the border into Mexico after him real soon.

"Yes, Primo. I heard about the battle at Celaya, and it makes me cringe. Sometimes, I think the revolution will never end. Do you think they'll catch Pancho Villa?"

"Yes, I do, I'm sorry to say—there's too many of them—they'll catch him, then hang him. Juan, I'm not trying to scare you, but before you leave the ranch, there's some other things you ought to know. You see…. there just might be trouble up ahead."

Pausing again for a second, he called out to Margarita, "honey would you bring us some more coffee, *por favor?*"

Then he continued…..

"Juan—it's like this. The stark truth is, that little by little over the past several decades, the stature of the Mexican—right here in Texas—is woefully waning. People around here don't like to talk about it, or admit it, but it's true. The pride and self-respect that they once had has been reduced to inferiority. More often than not, they're considered no better than the Indians or a slave like Jacob, and at times, they treat the Mexicans like racial degenerates. That's what all this is about, Juan. It wasn't like this before the Anglos began to settle here in droves and began crowding out the Tejanos. In some restaurants, train cars, or other public places, you still see signs that read 'Whites only', or, 'No Mexicans allowed'. Now tell me—how would that make you feel? Insulted! Right?" Can you imagine that? Just think—Texas has always been Mexican territory, now, with integration at the rate it's going, someday the Anglos will have it all for themselves. Think on this for a minute, Juan, they say that during the last ten years in the two counties near Brownsville alone—Cameron and Hidalgo counties—more that one hundred and fifty thousands acres were lost to the Anglos by way of economic pressures, title quarrels, and outright thuggary These are some of the fears the Mexicans are struggling with, Juan—segregation and outside dominance—and they don't like it……To quote an article in La Cronica, 'Mexicans view the attitude toward them by the Americans as an old race passing away and a new race on their departing footsteps'. And listen to what one of the Texas Rangers said, 'assert yourself at every opportunity to override the greasers'. So you see, Juan, all this is why the Mexicans feel like they're being pressed against the wall."

"Primo, you know…I've had suspicions of friction in America like this ever since I crossed the border. Discrimination, I mean. That first day I arrived in Laredo, I was given a good dose of it—one I'll never forget. What happens now, Rafael? Exactly how serious is all this?"

"Juanito, I wish I knew. But from everything I read and hear, it could be serious."

"Primo," Juan asked, "why can't countries get along? Does there always have to be fighting?"

"Juanito, that's a good question. Maybe the Mexicans are justified in wanting their land back, and maybe not. But me personally…..I don't disagree with either side."

"But you know, Juan, in my humble opinion, after all is said and done, the Euro Anglos—the ones we call 'gringos'—have done great things for Texas. They're a very ambitious bunch with great ideas for commercializing just about any product. Since they began settling in Texas—by the thousands—they've implemented many new ideas for farming and ranching, not to mention their aggressive push for expanding the railroads, bridges, the textile industry, and yes even cattle. Look how they ship mass herds of cattle to railheads for transporting to other states, like Kansas City, Colorado, and probably Oklahoma as well. It's too bad, however, that there are so many racist segregationists among them…..."

"Juan, you know," Rafael continued, "I personally don't have anything against white people. I used to, but not anymore. I just embrace the ones I like, and to heck, with the ones I don't like."

"Primo, that's the way I feel too. I think I could get along with anybody, given the chance. *I don't see why people can't live and let live.*"

"Me neither, Juan. But you know…the anglos are not exactly blameless in all this. In my opinion, the real kicker points to the things the Anglos have done, and the way they've done 'em, which is what the Mexicans don't like—especially, their blatant disregard for the Mexican as an equal human being. They pay very little attention to the rights of the Mexicans, as a whole. We're all supposed to be equal—and they say we are—but in the background and in the shadows—to some—we're like dirt under their feet. They take advantage of the poor Mexican at every opportunity by using their talents, their skills and all their energy for the betterment of themselves—and in lots of cases—the pay is an insult. When the chips are down for the Mexican farmers and ranchers, the Anglos are ready to gobble up their land with cheap prices then turn right around and hire them to work on the same land that once was theirs. And it's our fault, because we obligingly submit to them.

"A strong advocate of the deterioration of the Mexican image by the name of Aniceto Pizaña once said of the American rule that started some ten years ago, 'you are poor because a hand full of the rich have everything in their hands; they own the land, the mines, the ranches, the horses, the water, the railroads, and the machinery—and nearly all is in their power and possession. And if that weren't enough," Rafael continued, "as bad as I hate to say this, the same rule could be applied to our own country in Mexico

"Sad, but true, Juan. We let it happen simply because of the kind of people we are. Here in Texas, the Anglos want laborers—and that's what we are—laborers. And sometimes, the laborer works under brute force and harsh conditions pulverizing stone, digging water wells, building fences, branding cattle—and for what—for the simple pleasure and pride he gets out of showing off his ability, his talents and workmanship. They know the Mexican is a good worker, quiet, and asks nothing more than to be employed. Furthermore, he aims to please, because without satisfaction delivered, there's no satisfaction derived. They're probably not the fastest workers in the world, but they work continuously. On the whole, I think our people are kind and courteous, and in a slow, but steady way—industrious and reliable—and that's what they like. All this just makes the Mexicans more vulnerable. To put it bluntly, I believe that unintentionally, they become followers instead of leaders simply because of a natural inclination to blend with a luring society and readily attach themselves to anyone who may have befriended them. Ain't that pitiful? Yes—pitiful. But it's true......"

"Primo....will this fighting never stop! My God, the revolution in Mexico is still going strong, and now, it sounds like it's about to spill over into Texas."

"It already has," Rafael replied. "No one wants to call it a revolution, but it has all the earmarks of one. There's already a groundswell of fear spreading among many of the people in south Texas. Here's why I say this, Juan. Recently, La Cronica reported that Marauder bands of Mexican rebels were seen crossing from Mexico into Cameron County penetrating as far as 15 to 20 miles north of Rio Grande City.....in brazen raids, they've stolen horses and begun terrorizing citizens......many Anglo ranchers have moved into town for refuge.....gangs have forced open stores and robbed them of food, stole their weapons and ammunition. Armed rebel gangs on horseback—about fifty in each gang—are terrorizing farmers ten miles outside of Harlingen. Insurgents on the rampage have burned a railroad bridge, a railroad trestle, and cut telegraph lines outside of Harlingen. And listen to this," he continued, "the *sediciones*, the seditionists have killed dozens of Anglo farmers, and now, regiments of soldiers, including the Texas Rangers have been called in to do battle with the rebels."

"So you see, Juan," Rafael said somberly,"it may not be a revolution yet, but a dangerous hostile climate definitely exists in south Texas.. I wanted you to know about this before you left the ranch, because there's no telling where all this will spread to."

"Here's your coffee, *Viejo,* drink it while it's hot. You too, Juan."

"Gracias, Margarita."

"Viejo, how come you never told me any of these things before? You're frightening me."

"Oh, I don't know, honey—'til now, I've just considered it nasty politics, but not anymore. From what Solomon Quiros says, the insurgency by the rebels from across the border is for real."

"Primo," asked Juan. "Matamoros is several hundred miles away from Seguin. Do you think the fighting will spread this far?"

"Juan, I don't know. I hope not. I would like to think it's only a border dispute, but even if it turned out to be a widespread revolution, Mexico wouldn't have a chance against American supremacy."

As Rafael, Margarita and Juan sat in the living room, drinking coffee and pinching off bits of sweet Buñuelos, for a few moments, it was deathly quiet. The cold hard facts brought to light by Rafael regarding the revolting in south Texas, clearly took away any thoughts of going to bed early.

"Juan, I really do wish you'd stay longer—long enough to see how all this thing plays out. What do you say?"

"Primo, I probably should stay longer, but there's no telling where fighting will erupt next. I realize that the mass build-up of soldiers near Laredo could spell trouble, but while there's still peace and quiet in this part of Texas, I think I'd better move on. However, just to play it safe, instead of staying in San Antonio like I'd planned, I'll keep going farther north—perhaps to Oklahoma. What do you think?"

"Good idea, Juan. Oklahoma has no part in all this. I wish you well and much success, and please don't forget to write me. I want to know where you're at, at all times. If ever you need me, or if ever I can help you, I'll be right here. And don't forget, this is your home too, and you're welcome here, always."

"Thanks, Primo. That means a lot to me. I really have felt at home here."

After pausing for a minute, he continued, "Primo, I would like to ask a favor of you, if you don't mind."

"Of course I don't mind—just name it."

"You see, I gave a friend of mine your address."

After explaining in some detail the unfortunate capture of his friend Pedro by the insurgents in Bella Union, he concluded, "If he should write you looking for me, would you please give him my address. I'll write often to let you know what my address is."

"Not to worry, Juan," promised Rafael. "If he ever writes looking for you, I'll be sure to tell him."

Early the next morning, Juan was all set to continue his journey. This time, he was much better prepared. He had some extra traveling money in his pocket and a small suitcase given him by Margarita for his personal items. On departing, Juan hugged and kissed her on the cheek, and extended a warm embrace to Clara, Maria and Martin. Expressing his sincere gratitude for all their help, he could feel twinges of emotion starting to swell. After all, for two years, Rafael had completely taken him in. Margarita too, constantly looked after his laundry and personal needs, especially at the dinner table, always making sure he had plenty to eat.

"The horse is already hitched to the wagon," said Rafael. "I'm taking you to the train station."

"*Se lo agradesco mucho.*" "I certainly appreciate it," said Juan.

"Juan, do you have your birth certificate with you?"

"Yes, I do."

"Good. Keep it handy. You might need it."

One more embrace and a firm handshake, and Juan jumped aboard.

"*Adios, Primo!*" yelled back Juanito—"*Gracias por todo*"

"*Adios Juanito. Que te vaya bien. Ten much cuidado.*" "Good luck, and be real careful."

CHAPTER 9

▼

JUAN VENTURES INTO OKLAHOMA

As Juan boarded the train bound for San Antonio en route to Austin, Texas, he was surprised to see that both passenger cars were drastically over-loaded…mostly whites, but also, many Mexicans to be sure. Many passengers were standing, and a few were wearing gun belts and six-shooters. The mixture of passengers, which included the wild and the boisterous, was not discernable as to the farmer, the rancher, the rebel, or the bandit, and even less, the Texas Mexican from the Mexican from south of the border. The high-spirited voices of exuberance and arrogance, was far beyond normalcy, even though most of the passengers sat peaceably *platicando,* conversing with one another.

As the train departed from the station, Juan was deeply worried about some of the things Rafael had said about the strife between the Mexicans in south Texas and the white capitalists who seemed hell bent to downtrodden the Mexican by control and subjugation. The very thought of widespread racism throughout Texas, and now, the possibility of encountering fighting up ahead, tried to overshadow his intentions to continue northward. At the moment, however, aside from the loud, unruly behavior of some of the passengers, all was going well. When the train arrived at San Antonio, heeding his better judgment as to the unpredictable climate of hostility in south Texas, Juan remained on board throughout the two-hour layover. But his jittery concerns were soon justified, because shortly after the train pulled away from San Antonio and was nearing San Marcos, it came to an unexpected stop.. Within minutes, Texas Rangers who had jumped on board, were scrambling all over the train in search of two Mexican rebels—**Cisto Torres** and his brother **Giraldo**—who supposedly had lynched a Ranger the night before. With guns drawn, yelling, and forcibly barking orders for everyone to remain in their seats, they immediately seized all the guns from the gun-toting passengers and pitched them out of the windows. As soon as all the gun-toters had been ruthlessly relieved of their guns, the Rangers demanded everyone to produce identification at once. Some of the men who could not produce identification were ordered off the train into the waiting clutches of other Rangers. The two men they were looking for, supposedly had some connection to **Ricardo Simon**—a suspected instigator of the Texas uprising in Matamoros.

Juan had no trouble identifying himself. His birth certificate clearly stated the place of his birth in Villa de Reyes, Mexico—not Texas, and besides, he was not armed. By the time the train reached New Braunfels, his rattled nerves finally began to decompress, even though he wouldn't completely rest easy until he reached Austin, Texas—the last stop shown on his train ticket.

For the next two years after leaving Rafael's ranch, Juan again became a rambler looking for that all allusive niche in North America. In Austin, he had hoped to find employment of a different kind, but sparse field labor was the only kind he could find. After nine weeks, continuing his move northward through Waco and Fort Worth and working at odd jobs in the cotton fields, he eventually ventured into southern Oklahoma. It was here, that he finally found employment of a different kind—the railroad. Juan learned that the railroad industry was aggressively expanding northward using Mexican laborers, and since railroad labor was in such demand, he had no trouble finding work. However, after eight months of extra gang labor, unfortunately, all jobs were curtailed. But by this time though, he had reached Oklahoma City, where he again found employment of another kind—it was at a beef packing plant in an old section of town, called **'Packing-town'**.

Packingtown—probably better described as 'stockyards city'—was a well-trampled cattle distribution center and the final destination for an unending stream of cattle drives.

The tiny cattle town was constantly abuzz with cowboys and ranchers who brought herds of cattle from as far away as Central Texas. Throughout numerous cattle pens in the barren cattle yards, amid raunchy, stale stench, could be heard the constant drones of restless cattle, awaiting slaughter.

Packingtown's meat packing industry served cities as far away as New York, California, and Chicago. The packing plants were situated on approximately 120 acres parallel to the Canadian River that flowed directly through town and strategically located within the busy crossroads of the northbound Santa Fe and the St. Louis-San Francisco Railroad Companies that wended their way from south Texas. The plants employed a large number of Mexicans, mostly single men, besides other nationalities such as; Italians, Lithuanians, Poles, and French. Within a few blocks of Packingtown on Villa Street, Juan found an ideal location to lodge. It was in an all-Spanish neighborhood of Mexican immigrants where he felt comfortable, away from the dreaded awkwardness among English speaking people. Here, in Packingtown among his own people, it allowed him to socialize freely in an atmosphere much to the likes of his native customs back home; the music, the food, recreation, and particularly, the language.

Juan could have been happier at Packingtown, were it not for his iron-fisted bosses who seemed to have very little appreciation for their Mexican employees. It was hard, not to became disillusioned by their negative assessments, which claimed that Mexicans lacked ambition and were irregular in shop attendance, and also drank hard after paydays. This could have been true in some cases, but Juan resented this type of branding of the Mexican, but with tongue in cheek, he ignored their belittling opinions and set out to prove that most Mexicans—particularly the ones from Villa de Reyes—could surpass other nationalities in attendance and work performance. He made it a point never to be late for work, and quickly took hold of his assignments, assisting in the slaughter of cattle, and later advancing to the butchering process. The pay at the plant earning him $1.65 per day was far better than previous jobs. He soon began to grow in self-confidence and strived to satisfy his foreman, and after a few months, he succeeded. They loved his ambitious attitude and non-stop performance around other employees. His new job had served him well in many ways, because since crossing the border at Laredo, he was becoming more and more familiar with American customs, modern cities, including the value of the dollar, and most importantly, a sound government free of revolution. Furthermore, he was able to send money home more frequently.

After almost a year at the packing plant, Juan was beginning to feel as though Oklahoma City was his permanent home, until one day while eating his lunch in the men's locker room, the men began talking about a better opportunity in coal mining farther to the north in a town called Tulsa. At the time, it was believed that the coal industry was booming, and the towns of Tulsa, Anadarko, and McAlester were offering higher paying jobs for unskilled Mexican labor and sweetening the deal by providing free transportation for those who would sign up. At first, it was merely a rumor, which hinted of better pay, but considering the growing demand for laborers in the coal mines, the more Juan and the others debated the possibilities, the more enthusiastic they became. So they figured it was worth a try. Shortly thereafter, the attraction for better pay was irresistible, so Juan and two co-workers decided to make the move—to Tulsa.

Now in East Tulsa, in the vicinity of 15th & Yale Avenue, where numerous coal mines were operating, Juan and his two friends rented a small shack near the location of their new employer—the Adams Coal Mining Company—in a tiny all-Mexican community. Being among other Mexicans was just exactly what he needed, since he was again in a strange new town and still unable to speak English.

Juan's new job at the coalmines would take some getting used to. It was all together different than any work he'd ever done before. Primarily, because he wasn't used to working 100 feet underground under ever-present danger and in pitch-black darkness. Not to mention working in close, cramped quarters, unable to stand upright with only a tiny battery-operated headlight attached to his head-band. Nor was it easy breathing coal dust all day long throughout the tunnels where cracks in the low overhead timbers allowed water to seep through, creating a sea of ankle-deep tracks of squashy mud. The deafening hum of electric motors which constantly vibrated his eardrums was sometimes drowned out by the sounds of moving narrow gauge coal cars, air hammers and dynamite blasting. And he was so surprised to find mules working beneath the ground just like the men. But he soon learned that mules were an extremely essential tool for diminishing back-breaking labor He found it rather amusing sometimes, watching them trample mud underhoof as their floppy ears scraping against the low overhead shafts. He quickly learned how to handle the mules, training them to pull loaded cars repeatedly back and forth to the surface-bound shafts and elevators.

For a long time Juan didn't know what to make of these treacherous working conditions. At times, he regretted leaving the beef packing plant. And were it not for the much better pay, it certainly would call for reconsidering any kind of job above ground. But despite working in a dangerous environment, where quite frequently men were injured by gas explosions and sometimes killed, he eventually learned to cope with the hazards of coal mining. Also, since World War I had recently begun, this gave him all the more reason to remain employed where an essential commodity like coal, could guarantee steady work.

All during his employment as a coal miner—which had lasted almost four years—Juan became fairly content living among the Mexican raza. He made many new friends and soon became well known in the community. He loved dance nights, where nearly every Saturday night at someone's house, simple celebrations would be held. Spanish music could be heard throughout the neighborhood, as gala dances dominated the evenings. Often times, Don **Luis Eusebio,** the bandleader, asked Juan to join in with his mandolin. On evenings like this, however, much beer flowed throughout the houses, and sometimes created disturbances. All in all, however, the community was peaceful, and Juan found himself spending a lot of time with fantastic friends such as **the Casillas family, the Rodriguez family, David Lozano, the Mendozas and the Cervantes family.**

One day, in the **Spring of 1921,** a hundred feet below ground level, a gas explosion occurred in one of the tunnels. Instantly, a fire broke out causing a cave-in. Simultaneously, a layer of thick coal dust filled the mining tunnels and devastated the ventilators. It was as though all the lights had been turned off, except for one flickering ray of light coming from an undisturbed chute where Juan was working. Immediately, as the alarm began blaring away, pandemonium spread throughout the underground. Workers yelled out to one another in total blackness—coughing and choking as they fought for oxygen in a cave of thick dust. With only their remaining sense of sounds and direction, they scrambled in the opposite direction of the blast. Frantically, Juan began yelling out warnings to the men, trying desperately to help them to safety. He, too, was coughing and choking, as he helped them to the shaft elevators that had been activated for retrieving the trapped miners. He wasn't the first to go up, but after helping as many coworkers as he could, he too scrambled aboard a surface-bound elevator. Instinctively, as the shrieking whistles of alarm continued to sound all the way up to topside, like the others, survival was the only thing on his mind.

Had it not been for that earth-shattering cave-in at the mine, Juan might never have resigned. But after that dreadful, horrifying accident that took the lives of three men, he no longer felt safe. And because of the sweaty nightmares and the difficulty of shaking it from his mind, he took it as a warning—a warning that kept saying, *it could have been you, Juan.*

Since that awful day at the mine, Juan continued to languish at the loss of some of his friends and found it extremely hard to cope with the reality of such a fatal disaster. It wasn't as though accidents hadn't happened before, because they had. But Juan decided to put it all behind him and move on once again. He could no longer stand the thought of working in imminent dangerous conditions and possibly being buried alive. After gathering up his personal belongings, Juan would soon be on his way back to Oklahoma City, and hopefully return to his previous job in Packingtown. But first, he needed to say good-bye to a dear friend—**Demecio Almendares.**

CHAPTER 10

▼

RACE RIOT IN TULSA, OKLAHOMA—1921

Demecio, was another immigrant from Mexico, who, coincidentally, also came from a village not far from Juan's hometown of Villa de Reyes—a little town near San Luis, Potosi called Hermosillo Sonora. This coincidence naturally gave Juan and Demecio a pleasant kin-like commonality. Particularly, since they were both age 31, and familiar with revolutionary times. And since Demecio had fought in the Mexican revolution not too many years prior, there would never be a dull moment in conversation.

Demecio, much like Juan, who had also roamed all over Texas and Oklahoma seeking a better life, was now living on the north side of town and *operated a hot tamale wagon* at the corner of **Archer and Madison Street.** Since Juan had already learned his way around parts of Tulsa, the so-called **Magic Empire,** the five-mile walk would be a snap. The date was **May 31, 1921.**

From his little rented shack on East 15th street, Juan walked briskly to Peoria Avenue then turned north toward Independence Avenue, another two miles. He wasn't exactly in a hurry, since he wouldn't be catching the train until late in the evening. As he walked northward on Peoria, he noticed something that he'd missed on previous trips; Peoria seemed to be the dividing line between white people and colored people. He reached this conclusion from seeing poor, little colored kids dressed in raggedy clothes, playing in the dirt of their shabby yards on the west side, while at the same time, noticing that white families and kids on the east side lived in better surroundings. But Demecio, along with other Mexicans, like the Mendozas, the Garcia's, the Garnica's, the Carillo's, and the Lozano's, lived among the coloreds.

It was nearing sundown when Juan knocked on Demecio's front door. As he waited for a response, he was admiring a small vegetable garden that had been planted next to the front porch. After several more taps on the door, the door finally opened and there stood Demecio.

"Juan!" he cried out, with a friendly laugh. "Come in Juan. What brings you to the north side of town?" he asked. "*Pasate.*"

"*Buenas tardes, Demecio,*" replied Juan, as he opened the screen door and stepped inside. "*Que bonito dia, verdad?*" "Sure is a pretty day, isn't it?"

Respectfully shaking hands, Juan smiled and nodded at **Francesca,** Demecio's wife, who had also come to answer the knock on the door. Greeting her with a smile, he said, "*Buenas tardes, Francesca.*"

"*Sientate, Juan.*" "Sit down, Juan. How's everything at the mines? I heard about that terrible accident the other day. Several men got killed didn't they?"

"Three, was it?" he continued.

"Yes" replied Juan, "Three. That's why I'm here."

"What do you mean, Juan?"

"Well Demecio, I quit my job at the mines. I'm on my way back to Oklahoma City. Three and a half years of working those drafty back-breaking coal pits is enough—too many accidents. And after that cave-in the other day, they can have it." Kiddingly, he continued, "when it's my time to go, I don't want to go like that."

"I know what you mean, Juan," added Demecio laughingly. "I don't blame you one bit. You could never get me in one of those suicide pits."

"Have you had supper?"

"Oh yes. I grabbed a bowl of chili on the way out here. I just came to say good-bye."

With a surprised look on his face, Demecio asked, "Juan, are you sure you'd rather not stay in Tulsa? It's a great city you know. Surely, there are other jobs around."

"I know" replied Juan. "But I had a good job at the beef packing plant when I left, and maybe, with a little luck, they'll hire me back. Anyway, I'm going to try."

"Would you like some coffee Juan?"

"*Si, como no*" "Sure, why not. I've still got time. My train doesn't leave until ten O'clock tonight."

Pausing for a minute with a worried look on his face, Demecio warned, "Juan, if I were you, I wouldn't go into town tonight. There's some kind of trouble brewing downtown. A while ago, one of my hot tamale customers who'd just come from town said he saw a huge angry mob gathering at the courthouse, and he thought the Ku Klux Klan had something to do with it. It doesn't look too good Juan. As you may have heard, the last demonstration by the Klan ended up with houses being burned and a lynching"

"Why don't you stay here tonight Juan. I'd feel much better if you did. You know very well that those murdering Klansmen wouldn't give a damn for any Mexican."

"We've got room. Wait 'til tomorrow just to be safe. *¿Como te parese?*" "What do you say?"

Juan immediately reacted with concern as he tried to grasp the seriousness of possible violence in town.

"Thanks for telling me. I had no idea there was trouble in town. Perhaps you're right. It's probably best to stay clear of trouble, particularly the Ku Klux Klan. Are you sure it's alright if I stay here tonight Demecio?' asked Juan.

"Of course it's alright. In fact, I insist."

As the men enjoyed their coffee, cup after cup, they continuously reminisced about their old home place back home. And even though they never regretted leaving Mexico, that didn't mean fond memories were forgotten. As the evening hours swiftly passed, it became late and everyone, one by one, proceeded to their own sleeping quarters. Juan slept on a canvas cot in a screened-in back porch.

Early the next morning, as the sun was beginning to brighten up the sky from the east onto Domecio's little white house, *it marked the beginning of one infamous, horrendous siege on the City of Tulsa, as low flying airplanes awakened the entire north side of town with deafening roar of engines.* It had all the earmarks of a mysterious air attack on the city from an unknown source.

As Juan leaped out of bed, reaching for his britches, Demecio also came running in,

"Juan!" "Juan!" "Get up" "Something's happening!"

Immediately, they both ran outside to the front porch half dressed to check out the thunderous roar of airplanes and explosions, only to be confounded with the greatest shock of their lives. As they both looked at each other, startled and dazed, they could see that the hovering planes were dropping some kind of balls on just about every house in the colored community, which immediately exploded and caught fire. Before Juan and Demecio could sort out the frightful scene before their eyes, another house nearby exploded and immediately sent towering flames of black smoke skyward.

"Viejo!" "Viejo!" "¿Que Pasa?" cried out Francesca, still in her nightgown. *"Ave Maria Purisima,"* she prayed, as she too came running out to the porch trembling in fear.

"What's wrong Mama," cried out her little eleven-year old daughter, **Lupita,** who had also been awakened by her father's frantic yelling.

"Vayanse para dentro." "Pronto!" "Go back inside," ordered Demecio.

As he and Juan looked on in shock, scrambling back and forth to the middle of the street for a better assessment, all the neighbors had also rushed out to their front yards. And within a very few minutes, as Juan looked to the west beyond the Bethlehem Steel building to Greenwood Street, it seemed as though the entire fury of hell had been unleashed on the colored district, as houses and buildings were going up in flames.

As Demecio was trying to protect his family by ordering them inside the house, gunshots began going off in the same general area. It was at this point that Juan and Demecio fully realized that an assault against the colored people was taking place.

All up and down Independence Street, from Peoria to Madison, bewildered residents—mostly colored, some Mexican and a few whites—were in mass confusion and screaming hysterically in fear for their lives. Many had come out on the street with guns and rifles ready to protect themselves and their families.

Demecio also retrieved his shotgun from underneath his mattress and also handed Juan a 38 Smith & Wesson short nose revolver, just in case. Nervously, they continued their watch from the front porch, expecting the worst. But the worst was yet to come, as speeding buses and flatbed trucks packed like sardines with screaming colored folks in sheer panic, passed Demecio's house. And as the buses driven by colored drivers sped by, frightened colored people, including children, could be seen clinging to the outside, some on top of the buses, while others climbed aboard the hood. Bus after bus sped by with desperate coloreds, each bound for safer ground farther to the north of town.

As pandemonium continued to resonate throughout Demecio's neighborhood, creating further havoc by the scampering families, he, too, became deathly concerned for his family's safety.

"Quick!" he ordered, as he motioned to Francesca, "I'm taking you and the kids to Weaver's Dairy store. You'll be safe there because he's a white man." As frightening confusion continued to flash across his mind, he wondered if even a deserted shack next to the alley, might be safer.

On returning to his house from the Weavers', a band of white men carrying guns and rifles were coming up the street peeking through the windows of every house, banging on the doors, while others were ransacking the houses in search of colored people. As two of the white men approached Demecio and Juan, who were standing armed on the front porch, the men immediately saw that they were only dark-skinned Mexicans, so they weren't harmed, but not before barking out commanding orders using vulgar and profane language, demanding to know if they were harboring any colored...s...o...b's. When they were finally convinced that Demecio had not lied, they rushed to the next house.

The next house west of Demecio's belonged to Mr. Gibbs, and his house was the target of a thorough search all because one of the men knew that Mr. Gibbs—a white man—was married to a beautiful colored woman named Teresa. She was the one they were looking for. Earlier, Mr. Gibbs had seen that the mob was searching all the houses and quickly recruited the help of Don **Rodriguez** and Don **Carillo** to help carry their recently purchased furniture to the back yard. After piling it high, hastily they covered it with a tarpaulin in hopes the searchers wouldn't see it. Mr. Gibbs' was afraid that because of his colored wife, the gunmen would burn his house down, and if he couldn't save his house, at least he could save his furniture. Fortunately, because he had also taken his wife to the Weavers', his house was spared and the mob rushed to the next house.

By mid-afternoon, silence had almost been restored. Gunshots were only sporadic and the airplanes had disappeared. But only after dozens of colored people had been killed and hundreds of homes burned to the ground. *An awesome storm of violence had completely inundated the Greenwood business district, leaving behind only smoldering ashes of collapsed buildings that once identified the proud north side.* Only skeletal remains of what used to be multi-story buildings that housed theaters, barbershops, shoe shops and many other commercial establishments, lay burning. In the residential areas, only charred tops of smoldering refrigerators, wash machines, and hot water tanks, could be seen still standing in swirling smoke. The onslaught by angry, white mobsters had completely destroyed an entire colored town.

By late afternoon, hundreds of gawkers, absent of any coloreds, had gathered around the smoldering inferno, trampling through people's yards and getting in the way of fire trucks and city officials, as police and security officers tried desperately to bring order to a chaotic situation. Orders had been given to round up all *unharmed coloreds and take them to a place of safety* to prevent further bloodshed or retaliation. Many were afraid, hesitating to board the City vans for fear of being shot. Oddly enough, when the round up process reached Demecio's house, two white men who had mistakenly taken Juan for a colored man, grabbed him by the arm and tried to shove him onto a waiting truck. But Juan, who was afraid for his life, refused to go with the two men and immediately, a brawl ensued. Demecio, in broken English, kept hollering at the men, telling them that Juan was not colored and to release him. But when they wouldn't listen to his pleading shouts, he, too, joined the me-lee in Juan's defense. At once, a third man came to help force Juan into the truck, but on seeing him and Demecio, he knew instantly that they were not colored. *"Let'em go!"* he yelled.. *"These men are Mexicans. Can't you tell the difference?* Immediately, the two white men did as ordered, and released them. "Get off the street!" The man ordered. "Go back inside." Brushing themselves off, Juan and Demecio quickly went inside the house.

All day long, not a bite of food had been eaten. The day's dreadful violence had completely paralyzed all hunger pangs, as most people stayed indoors and out of sight, listening to the news on the radio—as did Demecio and Juan.

Late that night, as Juan and Demecio tried to sort out the day's frightening events, Demecio warned, "Juan, you'd better not go to the station tonight. It's still too dangerous, and besides, I'll bet every greyhound bus and every train in town will be loaded with coloreds trying to get out of town."

"I think so too," replied Juan. "From the looks of things around here, there's no safe place left to go to." adding that, "Mr. Gibbs said earlier that Teresa, his colored wife, has kinfolks in Muskogee, and he was going to try to sneak her out of town, but if I were him, I sure wouldn't try it."

"My God, this has been one hell of a day. As for me, I really don't know what to do."

"Demecio, is it alright if I stay here another night?"

"Absolutely! Stay as long as you like"

The next day after the riot, Juan and Demecio stayed close to the house, as did everyone else for fear of another violent eruption. Obviously, with shaky nerves still very much unsettled, Demecio didn't bother to peddle his hot tamales down at the street corner.

Finally, Juan was ready to attempt his return to Oklahoma City. He hadn't planned on such an awful parting, but with grief and destruction all around, it couldn't have been anything else but a worrisome good-bye.

As Juan stepped off the porch to leave, once again he and Demecio shook hands.

"Adios Demecio" he said courteously, "*Muchas gracias.*"

"*De Nada*" replied Demecio. "*Vete con Dios, y ten much cuidado.*" "You're welcome, Juan. Go with God, and be real careful. Write me when you get to Oklahoma City."

"Don't worry. I will."

Walking away toward town, he turned and waived one more time, "*Adios.*"

As Juan approached the Frisco train depot, he couldn't believe his eyes. Crowds of Coloreds packed the building trying to purchase one-way tickets to cities like Guthrie, Muskogee and McAlester. Unwilling to wait out his turn at the ticket office, he then walked to the Midland Valley Railway station, only to find all the platforms loaded with more Coloreds trying to purchase tickets out of town. As he approached the station, to his sorrowful disbelief, he witnessed a departing train packed beyond capacity, as some coloreds were hanging from the open windows. What he was seeing was no less than a mass exodus from Tulsa to God knows where. Not wanting to join the crowd of dispossessed Coloreds, he returned to Demecio's house, where he stayed three more days.

Finally in Oklahoma City, and still a nervous wreck from having experienced such a calamitous riot of killings and devastation, he set out to find a place to live. Fortunately, after staying in a cheap hotel for two days, he finally found his next home. It was an 8-room boarding house owned and operated by a Mexican couple by the name of **Manuel and Angelita Castro.** It was at this boarding house on **Villa Street** that he would meet a beautiful young girl by the name of **Edelia Almeida Flores.**

Soon after getting settled at the boarding house, Juan returned to the beef packing plant to inquire about reemployment, but unfortunately, it proved unsuccessful. For weeks, he was out of a job until finally, a job application with the **St. Louis-San Francisco Railway Company** was accepted. It was a job working on the railroad—again.

To be continued..........(in chapter twelve)

After eight years of following Juan on his timeless journey to America, I'll put him on 'hold' for little while,

Because........

A leap backward to 1906 is about to happen. There's something going on in Colotlan, Jalisco, Mexico, that we should know about.

Let's go check it out.

PART II

▼

ORIGIN OF EDELIA ALMEIDA FLORES

CHAPTER 11

▼

EDELIA ALMEIDA
FLORES—1906

Approximately 275 miles due west of Villa de Reyes in the wide-open spaces of western Mexico, an all-but-forgotten little town lies almost nonexistent in the eyes of the nation. A sleepy little town, '**Colotlan**', whose governmental jurisdiction falls under the State of Jalisco, is isolated almost completely from other cities in Mexico. At one time, the State's silver mines boasted abundant production that flowed lavishly among the mining tycoons. But when the mines quit producing—30 years ago—so did a roaring life style in Colotlan that had reciprocated from the wealth that trickled in from the booming silver mines. Now, this little town too, has nearly dried up. Many of its residents have moved away to the larger cities to find work, like; Guadalajara's textile industry, carriage manufacturing 130 miles to the south, and to the city of Puebla southeast of Mexico City, whose industry is glass, brick and soap. The remaining residents are the loyal ones who keep the town alive.

But on the bright side, even though Colotlan lies hidden somewhere in the open plains of Jalisco, the sloping ranges of colorful cactus and mesquite still reach across the beautiful sweeping mountains that eventually disappear into the Gulf of California. From here, every blessed evening can be seen the most magnificent spray of fiery-red sunrays as the sun sets beyond the sierras that keep the ocean waters to themselves. When evening shadows lengthen, the town is never forgotten by the cool evening breezes from the west. Dry, rainless climates, however, sometimes turn into sweltering summers that easily discourage enthusiasm, as well as the sweeping wind that doesn't mind chafing the faces of the poor Mexican *raza*, as it races across the town.

But for the remaining residents of Colotlan, they pay no attention to the elements; the occasional blown-in rains from the Gulf, nor the hot summer's relentless presence—each day is taken in patient stride by the happy people of this dusty little village—one day at a time. They work vigorously by day, just so they can play and celebrate at night. God meant for them to be a merry people; joyous and light-hearted.

But for one **15 year old**, dark-skinned little girl, barely 5' tall, on this cool November night, a good time was the farthest thing from her mind. The good times of her recent past had betrayed all notions that life was meant to be filled with fun and laughter among her teenage peers, especially among young sensuous and irresponsible boys. Her young foolhardy adventure of spring had taken away her innocence and forever changed a carefree life. Once, her slim and trim girlish figure could have easily been the envy of her friends, but no longer. Nine months ago, she made the mistake of her life, and the time for paying the fiddler his dues had arrived.

Domitila Almeida Flores was nine months pregnant and her hour of delivery was at hand. All alone, with a late night chill in the air, she walked the dark streets on the other side of town trying to avoid contact with anyone whom she might know. Her contractions were steadily increasing as she hurriedly searched for the address—**22 Calle Carbon.**

Domitila was a kind, easy-going young girl with a timeless attitude of innocence; free from worry and responsibility. Gifted with a delightful personality, she never lacked for affection from anyone, and though her personality was certainly not one of extroversion, her warm and friendly nature was ever present.

Her home was a mere two-room shack without utilities or running water, and not more than twenty feet from either house next door. The street on which she lived was only a narrow dirt road that closely divided a variety of little shabby two-room houses. In her young life, she had never taken poverty very seriously, and even though poverty was well rooted in her little town, she wouldn't miss any luxuries she never had, including an education in any shape or form—just a happy-go-lucky kid whose time for awakening was near.

On arriving at 22 Calle Carbon, she was extremely nervous and afraid, as she opened the squeaky wooden gate that led to a front porch. It was Rosa's house she'd been looking for—**Rosa Valencia.** She'd never met Rosa before, but learned of her previous practice as a mid-wife. And without a penny to her name, she prayed Rosa would have a big compassionate heart and come to her rescue at this eleventh hour.

Domitila knocked softly on the front door several times, hoping to awaken Rosa in the middle of the night. Finally the door opened—and there she stood— a big, chubby, 55-year old woman with long salt and pepper hair hanging way past her waist. She was wearing a pink flannel nightgown that hung loosely on her fat body and a pleated Navy blue seersucker robe. The after-supper aroma of corn tortillas and refried beans still lingered throughout the house.

"*¿Quien eres tú?*" "Who are you?" the woman wanted to know, as she peered out the slightly opened door.

"*Rosa?*" Asked Domitila.

"*Si…yo soy Rosa.*" "Yes, I'm Rosa."

"*Doña Rosa,*" continued Domitila, "*Dispenseme por favor.*" "Please excuse me, but I need your help, you see……"

Looking down at Domitila's unmistakable condition, Rosa knew instantly the purpose of this midnight visit, saying, "*Pasate creatura. ¿Como te llamas?*" "Come in child. What's your name?"

"*Gracias señora,*" she said, as she stepped inside. "*Me llamo Domitila Flores.*" "My name is Domitila Flores."

Looking around the dim-lighted room, she could tell that Rosa was not a meticulous housekeeper. At first glance, she could see shoes, stockings and a variety of magazines strewn all over the creaky wooden floor, a shaggy throw rug here and there, as well as a clutter of tiny statuettes and figurines on what-not shelves hanging on the walls. In the far corner of the room, however, was a beautiful prayer altar decorated with many religious articles, including a picture of Pope Pius X.

"*Sientate chamaca.*" "Have a seat," she said, as she tucked the collar of her robe closer around her neck to ward off the chill in the room. Then she walked over to the cast-iron stove and pitched in two pieces of *leña* to rekindle the dying embers. Waddling heavily from side to side toward the kitchen, with her *chanclas* dragging the floor with each step, she swung open a pair of white, dingy curtains made from bed sheets that hung across the doorway and proceeded to brew some coffee in a small saucepan.

"¿A quien le tirates flores?" "To whom did you throw flowers?" she called back from the kitchen, in a subtle expression for sexual submission.

Domitila didn't answer right away. She was still so embarrassed over her midnight intrusion on Rosa, and especially ashamed of her paunchy condition.

But after a brief pause, she said, *"Miguel—**Miguel Suarez del Real.** Pero ya se fue."* "He's no longer living in Colotlan. He's gone."

After another brief pause, she continued, *"No tengo dinero."* "I don't have any money."

"No te apures, Chamaca, Para esto naci." "Don't worry little girl," said Rosa, "this is what I was born for."

Rosa invited her scared little visitor into her tiny kitchen where they sat on some wooden stools. Domitila immediately saw that her kitchen was not very well kept either. Dirty dishes lay on the counter top from the previous meal and her well-worn linoleum floor needed mopping. Faded pink curtains dangled loosely across a small two by two windowpane.

"Didn't you know what you were doing the night of the dance?" asked Rosa, as she proceeded to pour out two cups of black coffee. "Or were you raped?"

"No." Replied Domitila. "I wasn't raped. I don't really know why I did such a thing. It all happened so fast. We just started kissing and it went from there. I guess I couldn't help myself. Miguel said he loved me and I thought he really meant it, but I was a fool to believe him. As soon as he found out I was pregnant, he turned cold and hateful and soon disappeared."

"How many times have I heard that story before," snickered Rosa.

As they sat in the kitchen sipping at their coffee, occasionally blowing at the swirling steam from their cups, Domitila was increasingly becoming more and more uncomfortable and waited nervously for her ordeal to happen. But Rosa kept saying, *"Todavia no es tiempo."* "It's not time yet. You'll know when it's time."

Domitila was gradually becoming at ease with Rosa. Her warm and friendly personality was ever so comforting, as was her patience and understanding. What had been a dreaded imposition on a total stranger had now become a feeling of confidence. She truly felt she'd come to the right place.

"Dime de tus padres, Domitila," asked Rosa. 'Tell me about your parents—are you living at home?"

"Yes I am."

"Entonces ellos saben que esperas cama, verdad?" "Then they know you're pregnant, right?"

"Yes, they know." replied Domitila, wishing they didn't. "But they don't know I'm here. I wanted to keep my pregnancy a secret, but there was no way. By the third month, I was beginning to show, so I had to tell them. First, I told Papa. Of course he was mad and scolded me for having made such a terrible mistake, but he knew there was no way to reverse my predicament and was willing to forgive me."

"Applauso para tu Papa." said Rosa. "I applaud your Papa."

"¿Y tu Mama, ella que dijo?" "And your mother, what did she say?"

"She was furious. Not only because I was pregnant with an illegitimate child, but I think it was mostly that she hated Miguel and detested him even more for having seduced me. She kept saying that he was already a grown man, while I was still a child."

"And what do you think, *chamaca*?" asked Rosa. "Are you just a child?"

"No, Doña Rosa," she replied. "I know I'm not a child, at least not anymore. But I think even a child would have known not to be swayed by a smooth talker like Miguel. I hate myself for what I have done. I'm so ashamed."

"No te des golpees, chamaca. Mañana veras que bonito es hacer una madre."

"Don't be so hard on yourself little girl, tomorrow you'll see how beautiful it is to be a mother."

Continuing with their coffee, Domitila and Rosa were getting to know each other a lot better, as they chatted freely about Domitila's domestic problems, until finally, the dreadful hour for her delivery arrived. Scared and trembling, Domitila began to perspire and pray, as Rosa led her into a back room just large enough for one small bunk against the wall.

"No tengas miedo, chiquita." "Don't be afraid little girl," said Rosa. *"¿Queres un niño, o una muchachita?"* "What do you want, a little boy, or a little girl?"

"I don't really care. But I hope it's a little girl."

After two full hours of labor and excruciating pain, Domitila's ordeal was over, as she finally gave birth to a seven-pound light-skinned baby girl. The blessed event came in the wee hours of the morning, but sadly, there was no one around to rejoice in the blessing. Not her mother, not Miguel, or even a close friend to applaud or offer congratulations for having brought such a beautiful child into the world. On seeing her beautiful baby girl, Domitila couldn't hold back the joyous tears that rolled down her cheeks. The pain was gone. It was over.

All went well for both mother and daughter at Rosa's house. Overnight, they had become great friends. For some reason, Rosa had taken a special liking to this sweet naive young girl.

"*Adios, Domitila,*" said Rosa, as she helped her bewildered young patient to the porch, carrying her newborn infant wrapped in a raggedy blanket.

"Come and see me when you can. And I want to know your baby's name. And by the way honey, if you ever want someone to talk to, you know where I live."

"*Adios, Señora Rosa. Dios se lo page.*" "Thank you, Senora Rosa. God bless you. No, I won't forget."

All the way home, Domitila was in a warm glow as she snuggled her infant daughter close to her bosom. She felt like a queen, and for a moment, all her previous cares were forgotten. She was still very weak and nimble, and her breasts were taut and sensitive to the touch, as she made her way home. Until now, she hadn't fully realized that suddenly over night, she had become a full-grown woman. Yes, a full-grown woman, with a newborn baby to care for, where before, she couldn't even care for herself.

On approaching her house, many concerns were crossing her mind; things about the future, about suddenly having become an adult, her little baby girl, and how would she provide for its needs. But mostly, it was the household that she was worried about, because frequently, her mother easily became irritable and frustrated over her illegitimate pregnancy. Moreover, it was a condition that her mother practically refused to accept, without constantly reminding her of her terrible mistake and making harsh remarks and accusations about the baby's father—Miguel.

Domitila's mother, **Maria Almeida de Flores,** a middle-aged woman, was not a happy person. She seemed to harbor an inferiority complex that always kept her on the defensive, creating unnecessary strife within the family. Ever since Domitila made that foolish mistake, Maria considered it a disgrace upon the family and found it extremely hard to cope with, and in so doing, created an uncomfortable atmosphere of discontent, instead of love and forgiveness.

Unlike her mother, **Cruz Flores,** Domitila's father, was a good-man, and certainly, very understanding. He was more on the positive side and could easily deal with most circumstances calmly. But over the years, unable to satisfy Maria's intemperate nature, he no longer insisted on control of the household, instead, he just stepped aside, solely to maintain peace and harmony. Ever since he was stricken with arthritis in his knees, he'd been unable to work, thus, unfortunately, putting all the household's financial obligations on Maria's shoulders.

Daylight was only minutes away when Domitila arrived back home. As she approached the house, she noticed a dim candle light in the window and instantly knew Maria would be waiting. On entering the house, scared and nervous, there she was, ready to pounce.

"Domitila!" shouted Maria, seeing a newborn infant in Domitila's arms. "I knew it! It was time for your baby to come and you didn't say a word! What's wrong with you child, I'm your mother! I told you I would deliver your baby!" Still fuming, she yelled, "Where did you go?"

Question after question blurted from Maria's mouth, but Domitila didn't hear a single word. The sleeping infant in her arms, at the moment, had brought such peace and serenity, that she didn't hear a single one of Maria's flurry of questions. Her only response was one sweet innocent smile. Removing the pink blanket away from the baby's face, she said, *"Mira, Mama, mira que chula salio mi muchachita."* "Look Mama. Look how pretty my little girl is."

Still mad and insisting on an answer, Maria once again blurted out, "Answer me! Who delivered this baby?"

"Mama, it was Doña Rosa Valencia. I know you've heard of her. She lives on Calle Carbon and she's a great lady. I like her a lot and she wants me to come see her again sometime."

"Yes, I've heard of her, and I'm happy to say, its all been good."

Finally softening her voice, she couldn't hold back the gleam in her face. *"Aber, dejame ver mi nieta."* "Here. Let me see my granddaugter."

"My, my. She's so beautiful." Immediately, Maria's anger turned into joy, as she cuddled the baby close to her face and rocked it gently from side to side. "Oh, she's so precious," she said. "And Oh, look! *"Se parese a una bolia."* She looks like a little white girl."

"Cruz! Cruz! Ven aqui." "Cruz! Wake up. Come see 'Tila's new little baby, it's a girl."

For the time being, all signs of Maria's previous discontent had disappeared. Domitila's precious little girl had completely wiped away nine months of scathing remarks that had built a wall of silence and uneasiness over an unwanted pregnancy. It had been a long time since Domitila saw her mother so happy.

"Have you picked out a name for the baby yet, *hija?*"

"No Mama, I haven't. But why don't you name her?"

"Me?" replied Maria. "You really want me to?"

"Yes Mama, I do. But make it a real pretty name—just like her."

"Alright. I will. I've always liked the name Edelia. Yes, Edelia."

"Mama, that's beautiful. I like it. Yes! That's what we'll name her—**Edelia.**"

The next two weeks around the house were simply fantastic. Maria was a completely changed person and all those months of griping and complaining were gone and forgotten. Immediately, Maria and Cruz made arrangements with the San Luis Catholic Church in Colotlan for the baptism of **Edelia Almeida Flores.** The date was **November 22, 1906.** Present at the baptismal ceremony were only the Godparents, **Rito Perez** and **Florencia de Avila.**

For the next several months, Domitila learned a great deal about caring for her child. At first, she knew absolutely nothing, but devoted all her time to the baby's needs. Breast-feeding came naturally. Diapering too came easy and she tried hard to keep her baby immaculately clean and pretty, responding quickly to all its cries, day and night. She was a proud little mother and simply adored her little girl, often singing to her when she cuddled her and rocked her to sleep.

One day in early Spring, Domitila remembered that she'd promised Señora Rosa a visit, and was anxious to show off Edelia—the little baby girl whom she delivered one dark night five months ago. With a slight chill in the air, she wrapped her baby snugly in a warm pink blanket and started walking to 22 Calle Carbon, two miles away. On arriving at Rosa's house, she was surprised when no one answered the door. Time and time again, she tried knocking, but no response. Pretty soon, she heard a faint voice which sounded like it was coming from far away, saying, *"P a s e n."*

"Doña Rosa!" called out Domitila. *"Soy Domitila! Se acuerda de me?"* "It's me!" "Domitila!" "Do you remember me?"

Again Rosa called out in a weak voice, *"Pasate Domitila. Pasa"*

When Domitila opened the door to let herself in, she immediately saw that Rosa was sick in bed.

"Valgame Dios, Doña Rosa. ¿Esta Mala?" she asked. "Oh my God, what's wrong? Are you sick?"

"Si, estoy mala," "Yes I'm sick," Rosa responded. *"Ay Domitila. ¿Como has estado?"* "What a nice surprise to see you again. Of course I remember you, and I've thought about you a lot. It's my back, honey," she replied. "I fell down a few days ago and hurt my back."

"Enseñame tu niña." "Show me your little girl. What did you name her?"

As Rosa slowly sat up in bed, Domitila placed little Edelia in her arms and immediately, the pain was forgotten, as Rosa smiled from ear to ear, cooing and kissing the baby.

"Edelia. I named her Edelia. That's the name Mama liked," said Domitila. "Do you like that name?"

"Oh honey, that's a beautiful name. Of course I like it."

"Who's taking care of you, Doña Rosa?" Domitila wanted to know. "Is there something I can do?"

"Domitila, you're the first person I've seen since I fell. No one has come around 'til now. Yes, I could use someone to help me. I can hardly walk."

"Bueno," said Domitila. "I'm going to take care of you. I can cook and do house work. You'll see. I want to help you, the same way you helped me the night I needed you."

"Child? Would you do that for me? Take care of me, I mean?"

"Absolutely," replied Domitila.

"Honey, you don't know how grateful I am. In fact, why don't you move in with me and be my housekeeper? I'll pay you."

Domitila didn't have to consider the offer very long. Shortly thereafter, she and her baby moved in with Rosa with every intention of repaying a tremendous favor the night of her delivery. Having moved in with Rosa allowed Domitila much more freedom from her parents and saw it as an opportunity to become self-sustaining. Since her mother Maria often grumbled about working conditions and low wages at the tortilla factory, now perhaps, becoming employed would relieve some of the burden at home. And besides, she wouldn't have to put up with her mother on the days of her cranky flare-ups. Domitila loved taking care of Rosa—the little fat lady—and all the time she was there, she never had to worry about money.

A year later, Domitila was still housekeeping for Rosa. At Rosa's she was happy, and it allowed her to be herself and independent of Maria's control. But like any other young girl, she still longed for fun and excitement, and the company of her friends. That's when she started seeing a 22-year old man named **Tacho Tibursio.** Their relationship grew quite rapidly, and on the surface, it appeared that she and Tacho might have been meant for each other. Genuine bonds of love, however, never developed, but neither one placed much importance on it at the time. He wasn't too crazy about Domitila's little daughter, but he proposed. At the time, Domitila was still searching for an independent life of her own, and when Tacho proposed, she really believed that together they could build a good marriage and eventually find love for each other. Wanting to build a meaningful life, which included a father for her *one-year old daughter,* she accepted his proposal.

Tacho was a handsome young man and well-known around town. Unfortunately though, his reputation was not for any outstanding quality, but instead, it was for his flamboyant attitude among his peers; impulsive, immature, and lazy.

For a while after their marriage, it appeared that they had both made the right decision, but difficulty in trying to make a living, complicated matters in many ways. As should have been expected, there were no jobs in Colotlan. So, after constant financial struggles, Tacho finally had enough of the same daily drag and wanted to move away from Colotlan. To him, it didn't matter where. So he came up with the idea of moving to the United States, where he supposedly had some wealthy friends in San Antonio, Texas who could set him up in some kind of small business. After having made the hasty decision to journey to America, and without giving any serious consideration to the hardships and hazards involved in getting there, they left their little rented shack in Colotlan. It was in **early fall of 1908.**

Tacho was not prepared for the eternal problems encountered on their journey. Had he known, he never would have left Colotlan. Furthermore, he was not a man who could easily deal with hardships. It was bad enough that he was immature, but to be lazy, also, only caused problem after problem on their journey. Right away, Domitila learned many unpleasant characteristics about the man she married. From the outset, he griped and complained at every inordinate situation, no matter how big or small. Primarily, to her dismay and disappointment, she learned that he wasn't capable of taking on the obligations and responsibilities of a husband. He often hinted of missing the freedom of the single life and the good times he used to have before he got married.

Tacho's first mistake, was having depended on a friend, **Alfredo,** for transportation to the big city of Zacatecas via one horse-drawn covered wagon. At first, it appeared that the wagon was capable of making the one hundred twelve mile trip, but from the beginning, they had to deal with one breakdown after another, which made the frustrating trip even more miserable, particularly, with a small child along. First, it was the gearbox in the wooden spoke-wheel that cracked and wouldn't hold grease very long, nor let the threaded axle nut to stay in place. But the worst, was when the hitch bars kept slipping off the swingletree, disabling the horse's ability to pull the wagon. At each breakdown, stopping for repairs or walking long distances for parts, much precious time was lost, often stranding the family in desolate prairie land. After six days and five nights of bumpy wagon trails and camping alongside the road in wide-open country, they finally reached the little town of **Huejúcar**, a distance of only forty-two miles. Here, the faulty wheel had to be rebuilt—a terrific expense not anticipated. Nor was it ever anticipated that their trip would also be delayed for two weeks. From Huejúcar to **Tepetongo** to **Zacatecas**, it was the same story—wagon problems and a three-week grueling grind.

After having reached Zacatecas, his friend, Alfredo, changed his mind about continuing the trip and refused to provide transportation any farther, leaving Tacho and Domitila in a terrible predicament. They remained in Zacatecas for almost six weeks before Tacho finally found another traveler going north with his wife and two children—also in a covered wagon. From this day forward, all the way from Zacatecas through ferocious wind-swept desolate country to Monterrey, many times hitching rides for only short distances, it was pure hell for Tacho who felt burdened with a wife and her kid. He regretted his decision to go to North America, and often considered returning to Colotlan. Being a fair-weather person, he couldn't cope with the burdening stress of daily problems, particularly, when at each stop, he was forced to look for work before heading out again. This, of course, was his biggest problem—work. He could never find a job to his liking; the ones he found were either too hard or didn't pay enough. And, due to his lack of ambition or motivation, the family was often forced to remain in small towns for extended periods of time, often indicating an end of the line. On several occasions, he imposed on complete strangers along the way for accommodations, supposedly, for only a few nights, and sometimes longer. But even worse, was the time he over stayed his welcome with the **Ramirez Family** and was politely told to find some place else to live.

After more than two miserable years of grim harshness en route to America, via any number of wagons, coaches, and perhaps hundreds of roads and highways; with a young *pregnant wife and a four-year old step-daughter,* Tacho and Domitila finally made it to San Antonio, Texas.

On arriving in San Antonio, they moved into another two-room shack, much like all the others they'd stayed in. But Tacho soon discovered that San Antonio was not what he'd expected. The friends that he supposedly had were nowhere to be found. Thereafter, when seeking employment, the jobs he found were none to his liking. Little by little, he began to despair and started drinking heavily, until he became totally indifferent about providing for his family. It seemed as though he could care less if the family survived or not, thus, turning over the responsibility of earning a living to Domitila. He liked the idea of being idle and able to loiter at will, at home, or wherever he chose, usually at the Cantinas with his friends.

Domitila's marriage to Tacho was gradually falling apart. During the four years of marriage, thus far, she had tried to be a good wife, making allowances for all his shortcomings, and never complained about their impoverished conditions. And now, she had given birth to two more children—two boys, **Faustín** and **José,** the youngest. As a husband, a father, and a provider, Tacho turned out to be totally worthless. Skepticism about the good life in America nurtured his refusal to work, or even look for work. He became obnoxious and tyrannical, practically making slaves of Domitila and his now *seven-year old* step-daughter, Edelia. He made them do all the dirty work, like haul and cut firewood, while he loafed and drank beer. Often times, he made them walk for miles for provisions, or in search of food. When he felt mean spirited, he'd make Domitila or little Edelia wash his dirty feet as though he was their lord and master. He had no conscience when it came to exercising dominance over them. Moreover, he became very abusive, often beating Domitila, and extending his abusiveness to young Edelia.

It was easy for Domitila to concede that her marriage to Tacho was a failure. But despite her marriage going awry, she felt she had no choice but to live with his physical abuses and his unscrupulous code of morals, and fully accepted her marriage as simply a bad marriage. But the one thing that she would never accept or condone, or even forgive, was Tacho's molestation of young Edelia. Though not yet serious, she knew she must do something about it, before it became worse.

After much worrying over just what to do, she decided to pay a visit to the priest at St. Joseph's Catholic Church where she had been attending Mass on Sundays. Perhaps he could help.

Father Browning was a sweet bilingual priest—in his 50's. He even looked rather handsome in his black vestment with red beaded stripes on his button-down cassock, with his white priestly collar and a small stainless steel crucifix pinned to the upper left side.

"*Sientate Señorita.*" he said. "Have a seat. I've seen you in church before, haven't I?" "*¿Como te llamas?*" "What is your name?"

"*Domitila*" she replied. "*Domitila Flores.*"

"Ah, *Domitila.* That's a nice name. You don't hear that name very often. "*Dime. En que te puedo ayudar.*" "Tell me, Domitila, how can I help you?"

Pausing for a second, unsure of how to begin, she said, "*Padresito*, it's my husband. I don't know what to do about him. He's become very mean and impossible to get along with. He drinks constantly and when he gets drunk, he beats me and my little daughter.

Pausing for a deep breath, she continued, "I wouldn't have come to you if that's all there was, but Father, he's beginning to molest my little girl, Edelia, and that's why I'm here. I've got to do something about his molesting her, but I don't know what to do. She's told me how, when I'm not home, he touches her inappropriately and makes her cry. When I confront him about it, he denies it, saying she's just making it up. But Father, my little girl wouldn't lie about something like this."

All during her visit with Father Browning, she was nervous and stuttery, occasionally clearing her throat and brushing away the tears from her misty eyes. It wasn't easy talking to Father about Tacho's abusiveness, especially the embarrassing details about his repulsive touching and fondling of little Edelia, his stepdaughter.

"How old is Edelia?" Father asked.

"She's almost nine years old."

"How long have you two been married?"

"Almost eight years, Father."

"Is your husband Catholic?"

"Yes Father, but he never goes to church."

"Has he always been like this—abusive, I mean?"

"Yes Father. And it gets worse every year."

"Father, what am I going to do? I'm deathly afraid of my husband, and so is my little girl."

For a few moments, Father silently pondered Domitila's dire circumstances, as he sat in his leather armchair, puffing occasionally on his pipe, sending little white clouds of smoke across the room, filling it with a delightful aroma of Prince Albert tobacco. From the tears in her eyes and the squeak in her voice, he could see that she was desperate.

"Domitila," Father said, after breaking his silence, "It looks like you have a serious problem. Marriage should be sacred and not made a mockery. But I agree no one should have to live under those conditions. You know the Church doesn't permit divorce, but I believe even the Church would understand if you didn't live together. Have you considered leaving him?" he asked.

"Yes, Father," she replied. "Many times, but I'm afraid to. And besides, I don't have any money or any place else to go."

Again, there was nothing but silence in the room as Father continued to mull Domitila's troubling situation. Suddenly, he began to scribble something on a note pad.

"Domitila," he said, finally, "I can't help you in your marriage. I know you have a problem with your husband, but you'll have to work that out yourself. And I know you will. But as for your little girl, I can help you there."

Father slowly rose up from his chair and walked over to a brewing teapot. From an antique china cabinet, he took out two flowery demitasse cups and proceeded to fill them with *Canela tea*, handing one of them to Domitila. Father began to chat casually with his young visitor, reassuring her that everything was going to be alright. As he handed her the cup of tea, immediately, her composure was returning the blush on her face. Father had understood perfectly, because Domitila was merely repeating a similar story he'd heard several times before.

When she saw Father walking toward her with that comforting smile, it was like a ray of sunshine. She could sense that he was going to help. Reaching for her hand, he handed her the note that he'd been scribbling on, and said, "No child should be abused by their parents. Bring your little girl here where she'll be safe. *Toma* Domitila. Take this to Sister Beatrice. You'll find her at the orphanage across the street, and try not to worry. Things have a way of working themselves out. You'll see. And don't forget to pray."

With laughter and tears in her eyes, Domitila raised up and respectfully kissed Father's hand, thanking him over and over again.

"Gracias, Padrecito. Gracias."

Walking her to the door, Father said, *"Adios, Domitila. Nos vemos en la misa el Domingo."* "I'll see you at Mass next Sunday."

Tacho was furious when he found out about the arrangements Domitila had made with Father Browning. Immediately he knew why she wanted Edelia out of the house. He threw a fit, calling her every *mal-dicion* in the book. He started pushing her around, slapping her in the face, and pulling her hair. Defenseless in every way, she cried and screamed, trying to fend off his blows as the boys looked on. They too, were screaming. After the fighting stopped, Tacho threw a chair across the room and rushed out, cursing and calling her names as he slammed the door on the way out. On the floor, Domitila sobbed bitterly holding her face in her trembling hands.

St. Joseph's Orphanage had been founded by the Order of Discalced Carmelites in the prior year for the under-fed, the under-privileged, and for many others in the same situation as Domitila. The note in her hand was Sister Beatrice's instructions to accept one more child at the orphanage. The note authorized a free stay of 6 months.

The next morning as Domitila approached the front gate of the orphanage holding little Edelia's hand, the playground was absolutely alive with young children laughing, screaming, and playing games. The clothes Edelia was wearing, though not new, were clean and neatly pressed. She was wearing knee-high stockings, with black patent-leather shoes—the ones reserved for Sundays only.

Sister Beatrice was a sweet compassionate nun, very congenial and understanding. Father had already explained Domitila's troubling circumstances at home, so she was expecting a new little resident. When Sister reached for little Edelia's hand, she started crying and jerked away, tugging at her mother's dress. She had never been away from her mother before, but she knew she was being put in a special home for children and feared her mother would never be back. When Domitila reached to embrace her little girl and to kiss her goodbye, little Edelia began crying and screaming violently, resisting Sister's hold on her arm and fighting to break away. At that precise moment of fear and desperation, both their hearts were breaking, as Domitila turned and walked away with tears in her eyes.

All the time little Edelia was at the orphanage, she was scared and very lonely, often, seeking a secluded corner of the playground where she cried. She missed her mother tremendously, including her two little brothers with whom she'd become so attached. As the days came and went, however, both would adjust. Domitila made it a point never to be late on Saturday mornings—visiting days— to spend two whole hours with her little girl—two hours of hugs and kisses and making plans for the future, reassuring each other that the day would soon come when they would be together again.

The next few weeks were absolutely horrific for Domitila, living in the same house with a man obsessed with anger and dominance. For the first time, she was thoroughly convinced that sooner or later, she would have to break away. All she needed was the means to survive and the courage to make it happen. Until then, however, all she could do was to pray and wait. She never forgot Father Browning's words: *Have you ever thought of leaving him?*

Diligently, every morning she went looking for work; most of the time…. nothing. Sometimes a few hours work at a local cafe, either cooking or waiting on tables. When these played out, she'd roam her neighborhood looking for customers who needed maid service, or washing and ironing, never forgetting her goal to become self-sustaining and take her little girl out of the orphanage.

Perseverance finally paid off. One day as she roamed the business streets of San Antonio, she found a job **at a local boarding house**, operated by a couple named **Manuel and Angelita Castro.** She hired in as a waitress, a maid and a cook, including dish washing. Her job with Angelita, (hereafter called Angela) came after four months of placing Edelia in St. Joseph's Orphanage. At last, she was filled with new hope.

Manuel was a good and righteous man, very friendly and compassionate. He was tall, heavy-set, and with a light complexion. He had a great sense of humor, a contagious laugh, and when he talked, it was always with warmth and respect

Angela on the other hand, was a rigid commanding woman. When she barked orders around—people moved quickly. Everyone knew that Manual was hen-pecked, but despite their outward appearance of incompatibility, the two did seem to have a mutual love and respect for each other.

Soon after Domitila's employment with the Castro's began, **in the Spring of 1916**, Angela became dissatisfied with her business in San Antonio. She wanted to move north to a better location, which would be no problem for them, because she and Manuel had money. Maybe not a lot, but at least they never wanted for anything. Angela liked Domitila's dependability and her ability to cook and keep house, and especially, the pleasing *cariño* she showered on her boarders.

After breakfast one morning, as they all gathered in the sala, Angela broke the news about her intentions to move farther north.

"Domitila," she asked, "*¿Como te gusta trabajando aquí con migo?*" "How do you like working for me?"

"*Ay Angelita, me gusta mucho.*" "Oh, Angela, I like it a lot," she replied without hesitation. "I don't know what I'd do, if it weren't for you and Manuel."

"*¿Porque me pregunta?*" "Why do you ask?" Domitila wanted to know.

"*Bueno Tila,*" she said, "I don't want to do business in San Antonio any longer. I want to move to a better location."

"*¿Porque?*" Domitila asked, "Why?"

"The people here are too poor," she answered, "and can't afford to pay me. I need to go somewhere up north where there's lots of money to be made."

"*La semana que entra, nos vamos ir mas al norte.*" She continued to explain her plans to move farther north the following week where business, supposedly, was much better—preferably Waco, Texas.

"Domitila, I want you to come with me. You're a very good cook and you're good for my customers. Would you like to come?"

Without hesitation, Domitila replied affirmatively, "Of course, I'll come. I like working for you, and right now, I need a job more than ever."

"Don't be too hasty," Angela said, "That's not all. I want you to come and I would like for you to bring your little girl with you, but not the boys. I can't afford the whole family. Anyway, I think you need to get away from that 'good-for-nothing' husband of yours. He's nothing but a leech. He'll let you support him for the rest of his life, as long as he has you. He needs to be taught a lesson. As for the boys—Faustín and José—they can stay with their father. And later on, he and the boys can come to Waco."

The excitement immediately disappeared from Domitila's face, only to be replaced with regret. She needed a job, but how could she go away and leave her two little boys behind, who were just **4 and 6 years old**. Her mind was running rampant, trying to decide whether to go or stay? Deep down, she really wanted to go, because how else could she manage, Tacho was no help. But needless to consider the matter any further, she quickly responded, "Angela, I would dearly love to go with you, but...*Angelita, no puedo dejar mis hijos.*" "I just can't leave my boys behind."

"Of course you can," Angela persisted. "The boys will be alright with their father, you'll see. And I promise you, if he doesn't take care of them, we'll come after them."

Reassured by Angela's promise, after two whole days of a mind-wrenching quandary, and considering the constant friction at home, she finally decided that, yes, she would go with Angela to Waco, taking Edelia with her, but leave the boys with their father. Very possibly, this could be the break she'd been waiting for. Her decision had become easier with Angela's promise, which sounded like a guarantee that she wouldn't be without her boys very long. The big question now, was, *how was she going to tell Tacho* without another violent reaction. She tried time after time to get the courage to face up to him, but each time, fear got in the way.

Early one morning, however, as she was getting ready for work, without thinking, she said quite casually, "Tacho, Angela is moving away. She's shutting down her business and moving to Waco."

"What did you say? Moving away?" he asked, turning around and nearly spilling his coffee.

"I don't believe it!" he roared back.

"It's true. She told me a few days ago, but not only that, she wants me and Edelia to go with her."

"What?" he shouted, jumping to his feet, "just you and Edelia? She must be crazy."

"Well...how about me and the boys? What are we supposed to do?"

Scared and trembling, she mumbled barely above a whisper, "She doesn't want the boys to come," then waited for violence to erupt.

"Well I'll be damned! That old freckled-face bitch!"

Waving both arms wildly, he grabbed her by the shoulder, swung her around and got right in her face.

"Well?......what did you tell her? Did you say you'd go?"

Again, taking a deep breath and turning her head the other way, she replied, "Yes. I told her I'd go." then waited for verbal lashing.

His face reddened with rage as he began pacing the kitchen floor back and forth like a caged lion, fuming and cursing out loud. Domitila knew that just any minute, he would explode.

"That old bitch!" he yelled repeatedly at the top of his lungs. "That fat bitch."

"To hell with her and to hell with you too. Go!" he shouted. "Go! And don't come back." With a fever pitch in his voice, he continued to roar.

"Me and the boys don't need you anyway. Go with that damned old woman. I never did like that stingy old bat. Sure, she wants you to go—all she knows how to do, is sit back and order people around."

Short of a physical confrontation, he stopped dead in his tracks and stared sharp daggers at Domitila, as the veins of anger pulsated in his neck. Suddenly, he stormed out of the house in a verbal rampage, cursing God and everyone else as he went. She knew he would come home later, drunk, and fully expected another fight. But this time, he stayed out all night.

At work the next day, she told Angela how furious Tacho became when she broke the news about leaving. Now she was more scared than ever before and having second thoughts about the whole matter.

"Don't worry about that big mouth, 'Tila," Angela said, in a voice of assurance. "He's just crazy in the head and can't be taken seriously about anything. Just remember, he needs you more than you need him."

Angela might have been right about Tacho, Domitila thought, because the next evening when he finally came home, he was drunk alright, but strangely enough, he was not in a fighting mood. On the surface, it appeared as if he'd reconsidered his hateful remarks and was willing to step aside. All day, Domitila had been nervous and afraid, expecting a raging temper...but it didn't happen.

At first, Tacho was quiet. But pretty soon he turned around and looked Domitila straight in the eye, and said gruffly,

"Alright. Go on with Angela, and take Edelia with you. But don't expect me to follow you to Waco. If you ever want to see the boys again, you'll have to come back here. And if you wait too long, we may not be here when you get back." On concluding his threatening remarks, stammering, he walked into the kitchen and started banging the cabinet doors open and shut, searching for a bottle of whiskey that he had stashed away.

Domitila was dumbfounded at Tacho's angry, but yielding attitude toward her going away. *Could this be his idea of a separation?* she thought. *Could this be a threat? Was this really Tacho, no longer in a fighting mood?*

She tried to appear grateful in his change of heart, but her intuition didn't like the sound of it. Nevertheless, after seven years of marriage—threat or no threat, she knew him well enough to know he could never make it on his own, and that sooner or later, he would relinquish custody of the boys. And with that settling consolation, she tried to think positive and prepare for the move.

A few days later, on the date set for departure, Domitila had already picked up Edelia at the orphanage and packed her things, then waited for Angela and Manuel. She didn't have to wait very long until their horse-drawn buckboard pulled up in front of the house. The wagon was already loaded with all their suit-cases and ready to make the trip to Waco, Texas. As Manuel politely assisted with Domitila's suitcase, he looked around for Tacho expecting interference, but nothing happened. Tacho had refused to say good-bye and secluded himself in the kitchen.

Finally it was time to go and Domitila began hugging and kissing the boys.

"You boys be good, now, and do what your Papa tells you."

She had already explained that she was going to work in another town and she wouldn't be gone too long. Faustín seemed to be comfortable with her leaving, but not José.

"Mama, do you have to go?" he asked in a slight whimper.

"Yes, honey. I have to go. I won't be gone too long."

"Mama, please, can I come too?" he pleaded, as he began to cry and tug at his mother's arm.

"No, honey, you can't, now give me a kiss."

"I love you, Mama." He said, clinging to his mother's waist.

"Faustín, now you be sure and look after your little brother while I'm gone, Ok?"

"Yes, Mama. I will—Love you."
"Love you too, my little man."
"Bye, children."
Little Edelia too, anxious about the trip, squeezed the boys with a tight hug.
"Bye Faustín." "Bye José."

As the buckboard pulled away, Faustín finally broke down with tears in his eyes, and José was screaming for his mother, "Mama! Mama!"

Waco, Texas—at the time—was a booming cattle town. Angela knew that cattlemen didn't make good boarders, so she sought a location closer to town, preferably near some railroad yards. She knew that railroaders were frequently on the move, and therefore, would bring in more business. She finally got her wish. She found a satisfactory location at the edge of town near a busy train yard.

Six weeks had passed since Angela opened her new boarding house, and with each passing day, Domitila anxiously waited to hear from Tacho and her two boys. She frequently checked the General Delivery window at the post office, but never, was there a letter. The letters Angela had written were never answered. She tried telling herself that any day now, she'd receive a letter from Tacho, but it was only wishful thinking. Finally, she grew tired of waiting, and because the worrying was driving her crazy, she went to Angela for permission to return to San Antonio to pick up her boys. She remembered Angela's promise that she wouldn't lose Faustín and José.

Angela was very understanding. She knew exactly the torment that Domitila was going through and said, "Yes, 'Tila. We're both going. Don't worry any more, you won't lose your kids."

Together, they made the trip back to San Antonio. But on arriving at the house where they had been staying, they found it empty. Tacho and the boys were gone. And after five whole days of making house-to-house inquiries, no one in the neighborhood could offer any information as to their whereabouts. Domitila was devastated and nearly collapsed when all search attempts were exhausted.

The trip back to Waco without her two boys was agonizing beyond words. Domitila, sick and grief stricken, cried most of the way, and for days on end, wept silently, languishing at the very thought of never seeing her boys again.

After more than a year in Waco and another unsuccessful attempt to operate a profitable boarding house, Angela again became dissatisfied and wanted to move farther north. After firmly deciding to relocate one more time, she invited Domitila to come along to seek yet a better location. But this time, Domitila didn't want to go. Secretly in her heart, she still yearned for her boys and would never abandon the thought that someday they would find her. She wanted to be there when that day came.

Domitila had come to love Waco, with its robust Mexican flair and was profoundly happy with the numerous friends she'd met. She thought she'd finally found a place to plant roots. **Only at age 25,** and still a young woman, she wanted to find the right man—a decent man whom she could love and be happy with. Indeed, that was the case, because now, there was a man whom she'd been seeing a lot of.

Angela was surprised that Domitila would refuse her offer. She wasn't accustomed to being rejected. Trying to hide her displeasure, she exclaimed, "How will you manage all by yourself? And how about your little girl, have you thought about her?"

"Yes, Angela," she replied. "I've thought about it a lot, but I don't want to travel any more, going from one place to another. I want to plant roots somewhere. Ever since leaving Mexico, I've never had a place I could call home—until now. I love you Angela, and I appreciate all the years you've helped me, but really—I want to stay here in Waco, and besides, there's a man in my life now."

For the next few days, Angela remained upset and angrily stormed about the house unable to persuade Domitila to change her mind. In one sense, however, she really was concerned about their welfare and hated to leave them alone to fend for themselves. She remembered their destitute days of the past, and truly wanted to prevent the same thing from happening again. But Domitila's mind was made up. She did not want to move again. That's when Angela came up with a different request.

"*Bueno Tila,*" Angela said. "*Yo comprendo tu razon que te queres quedar aquí en Waco, pero por favor, dame permiso a llevar tu hijita Edelia con migo. Yo la quido muy bien hasta que tú vengas por ella. ¿Como te parese?*" "Tila, I fully understand your not wanting to leave Waco, but please, if you don't want to go, then let me take Edelia with me. I'll take good care of her until you can come for her. What do you say?"

Domitila balked instantly at the idea. In no way, would she ever be separated from her precious little girl again.

As time went by, Angela remained very persistent, hoping Domitila would change her mind, but her decision remained firm. The answer was always no. Still, Angela continued to press, and after frequent discussions and more promises, Domitila began to weaken in her decision. Finally she questioned,

"If I let her go with you, how will I know where you are?"

"I'll write you," she replied. "You'll always know where to reach me."

"Angela," continued Domitila, "I've already lost my two boys, and if I should ever lose Edelia, I'll never forgive myself."

"Domitila, please don't worry. You won't lose Edelia, I promise."

"Angela, I still don't like the idea of being without my little girl, but give me some time to think about it."

After several days of deep consideration, Domitila's nerves were becoming unraveled. But in the end, trying not to seem unappreciative for all of Angela's help in the past, she finally gave in.

"Alright, Angela. You can take her," she said, "but as soon as you get settled, be sure and let me know where you'll be."

When Domitila gave Angela permission to take her little girl, she sincerely thought that it would only be temporary. In the back of her mind, she felt confident that in a few months she would re-marry and would pick up Edelia—*wherever she might be.*

The day of parting was truly a heart breaker, especially for Edelia who was just a ten-year old child and still very much in need of her mother. Screaming and crying, she desperately clung to Domitila, refusing to let go.

"No Mama!" "No!" "Don't make me go. I don't want to go without you."

As the tears continued to stream down her trembling cheeks, she couldn't stop tearing at Domitila's dress, begging, "No Mama!" "No!" "*No quero ir*"

Embracing her little girl tightly to her bosom once more, Domitila tried to reassure little Edelia that everything would be alright and not to worry.

"Don't cry my little Angel," she kept saying. "You'll see. Everything will be alright. Now you go along with Angela and be a good girl. As soon as I can, I'll come for you. You'll see. It won't be very long."

"I love you sweetheart."

With her little heart breaking in two, she cried, "I love you too, Mama."

After one more embrace and a final kiss, with tears in their eyes, they said good-bye.

As Domitila slowly walked away and closed the door behind her, the excruciating sounds of her little girl's mournful screams came crashing through the walls, painfully piercing her heart to pieces. She felt guilty, as if she was deserting her little child. Inside, she felt like dying as she leaned against the house and wept. And, for good reason too, she never forgot those awful days of separation at the orphanage. Now, today, another agonizing good-bye that would break little Edelia's heart—one more painful pivotal juncture in both their lives.

And so it went. Domitila remained in Waco, permitting her little daughter to relocate with Angela, *even though Angela admittedly didn't know exactly where her next place of business would be.*

The next stop for Angela was Fort Worth, Texas. Little by little, Edelia was becoming accustomed to Angela and Manuel, but it wasn't easy. She missed her mother tremendously and wept frequently. As promised, after getting settled, Angela wrote Domitila informing her of their new address, hoping that she would reconsider and rejoin her at her new boarding house. But after two months, Angela had still not heard from Domitila. All the letters mailed to her last known address were never answered. Finally, at the insistence of little Edelia, who grieved unceasingly for her mother, Angela and Manuel began writing to previously known friends in Waco. But as time passed by without a word, Angela began to worry and decided to dispatch Manuel back to Waco in search of Domitila. But to his great surprise, on his arrival at her previous residence, she was no longer there. He made every inquiry possible within the neighborhood, going from house to house, seeking the slightest clue as to her whereabouts, but all attempts were to no avail. All traces of Domitila had vanished.

Angela loved Domitila and blamed herself harshly for having come between mother and daughter. Her intuition told her that this separation had every sign of being permanent. And now, looking back, she also blamed herself for having persuaded Domitila to leave her two little boys with Tacho in San Antonio, never to see them again either.

It would be a long time before little Edelia stopped grieving over the disappearance of her mother, but she never stopped praying. Every day, she waited silently for some word to come, but word never came.

In **Oklahoma City, five years later,** Angela had again relocated and opened up another boarding house located near a beef packing plant called 'Packingtown' near downtown, and also, near a small, but thriving, Mexican Community. **Edelia now at age 15,** tried hard to accept her new foster parents, but it wasn't easy. She loved Manuel. She thought he was a real gem and felt loved by him in return. He was always kind and understanding when she needed comforting. But with Angela, it was different—all because of her strict unyielding personality. Their new relationship never really blossomed into a genuine love as between mother and daughter. It was more like a respect for Angela's authority—mostly because she was such a commanding person and hard to please. There was no doubt that Angela loved Edelia, but it wasn't always apparent. She possessed not a single ounce of charm and her bossy ways always kept them at arm's length. But despite Angela and her rigid personality, she had provided a very comfortable family environment for little Edelia who had just about forgotten all the hardships of earlier years. Little by little, she began to accept Angela and Manuel as her parents—and the stark reality of her mother's disappearance.

Nowadays—living with her new parents—there seemed to be an upswing in Edelia's life. At last, it seemed as though a breath of new life was dissipating the lingering pain of her mother's disappearance. As a typical young teenager, she now yearned for fun and excitement, flaunting a wardrobe that she could never have known before. She was beginning to spread her wings and began feeling all the anxieties of a budding young girl. She sought thrills and excitement with other young girls in the neighborhood, going for short strolls after her days work at the boarding house, visiting and chatting about things like hair-dos, lipstick, pretty dresses—and boys. She always made it point to look nice when the railroad workers came in at suppertime

As for Angela—**childless all her life**—she had now taken complete control of her new foster daughter, and she was happy.

It was here at Angela's boarding house in Oklahoma City, that Edelia would become fascinated with one of Angela's boarders who worked for the St. Louis-San Francisco Railway. His name was **Juan Guerrero Gomez. The year was 1921.**

CHAPTER 12

▼

LOVE AND MARRIAGE—
1921

Angela's boarding house on **Villa Street,** on the edge of town in Oklahoma City was quite an impressive building—old perhaps, but still in excellent condition. It was a two-story white frame house completely surrounded by a white picket fence, complimented by a ranch-plank boardwalk on three sides and enclosed by a white picket railing. On the front porch hung a porch swing and several old rustic benches for evening relaxation. The upstairs consisted of four bedrooms—for men only. Neither Edelia, nor Angela's other two female employees were ever allowed upstairs during evening hours. **Linda Reales** was 24 years old, and **Rebecca Cortez** was 27.

Angela's boarders were all Mexican railroad workers ranging in age from 25 to 45, each with his own distinct personality. Some were quiet and well reserved to themselves, while others were enthusiastic and interesting talkers who liked to engage in conversations and debates dealing with politics, conditions in Mexico, and world affairs in general. On the evenings when some of the men indulged themselves in a few beers, they were always well behaved and certainly respectful of Angela and her rigid house rules.

Angela had eight boarders, all with the same commonality; they were all originally from south of the border. Most had transferred from other Railway Companies to work as 'extra-gangs' repairing broken down railroad foundations around the Oklahoma City area.

The boarders were: **Chon** 25, and **Rosendo** 28, who were the youngest. When they weren't sitting around playing cards, they'd go into town looking for a good time, or maybe, just to check out the cantinas. They could speak more English than the others. **Gordo** 33, the fat one, was the comedian of the bunch who always supplied the laughter that helped pass away the time more quickly. **Antonio,** 35, was usually pretty quiet. Often times after dinner, he would excuse himself to the quiet of the sala to write letters to his folks back home. **Angel,** 40, was short and stocky built, and never seen without a crucifix on a small silver chain hanging around his neck. It was he who detested foul language and kept conversations above board. **Chino** 42, the one with curly hair, was the flirty one. Even though he had a wife back home in the old country, he still liked the feeling of being foot-loose and fancy-free. **Jesus** 45, was the literate of the group. They called him '*el professor*'. He also liked to retire to a secluded spot after dinner just to read.

*And then there was **Juan**.....*

Juan was different from the others. He was the musician—the mandolin player who provided melodious memories of life back home with his music. He loved to sing. Often times after supper, he retreated to the front porch with his mandolin where he liked to hum and strum favorite *rancheritas*. He wasn't an extrovert by any means. In fact, he was quite the opposite. Even though occasionally he could be comical and amusing, most of the time he was just a quiet mild-mannered man who liked to be alone. Sometimes however, he readily chimed in on an interesting conversation, especially if it was about Mexico. And that was because of his one track mind which was always centered round his folks back home in Villa de Reyes. Juan was a bashful man. Being around the girls at the diner

Juan Gomez

always made him nervous, and he simply shied away when they got too close.

Ever since he left home, Juan had been steadily driven onward. *Keep going! Don't look back! Straight ahead lies the place you're looking for!* These were the voices that provided the motivation to reach his goal. His goal being......well......whatever. Surely he'd recognize it when he reached it. And when he found it, it might be riches, if not riches, then perhaps just a plain and simple little cottage somewhere in some peaceful valley like the ones in Villa de Reyes. Likewise for Edelia, who had onstantly been led in a direction of someone else's choosing—a long and bumpy road of sorrow and sadness. She too, yearned for a life with a meaningful purpose and fulfillment.

Now, at long last, Juan and Edelia's hidden desires would be sharply awakened. This spring would long be remembered as a victorious milestone in their long and trifling journey. Heretofore, they both had ventured almost in any given direction as aimlessly as the shifting winds in search of something, or perhaps someone. But neither would ever have guessed the prize that lay in store, nor would they recognize the magic hour or the thrill of the moment, if and when it finally arrived—until......

Until one day out of the clear blue—there it was—the missing link. A missing link that would suddenly re-ignite their lives into an all-new world of dreams they never knew existed. Just when they least expected it, as though an answer to a prayer, Juan and Edelia found a beautiful piece of their destiny waiting just for them.

It all started at the boarding house in the **Summer of 1921**. Juan was 31 years old, and Edelia was almost 15. The blossoming month of June had finally overtaken the cold of winter, bringing with it all its majestic beauty that anointed all the pretty flowers and countryside. Sure enough! Spring had sprung. It had made its magical debut, depositing jillions of tiny bubbles of inspiration and romance in Juan's and Edelia's unsuspecting hearts.

Angela's boarding house wasn't all that big of a deal for Juan. Not at first anyway. It was just another place to hang his hat with a fairly nice bed to sleep on. The added services of boarding, which provided his washing and ironing, were by far, the best convenience of all. So, in that regard, Angela's boarding house was the next best thing to having his own place. As time went on, however, it became a beautiful memory; a house of fanciful dreams, where he felt as though he was prince charming waiting for his princess to awaken, and if not a prince charming, then surely someone very special.

When Juan first checked in at Angela's, he immediately captured the attention of all the other boarders, including her two employees, Linda and Rebecca, but especially, her beautiful young daughter—**Edelia**—whom most everyone called 'Lela'.

Juan had already been engaged at the local dance hall—*Casa de Baile*— where on Saturday nights, he and a few other musicians played their hearts out for the local folks. Each dance night filled the dance floor with Mexican raza, young and old, who would never pass up a night of fun and dance. Angela and Manuel also liked to dance and permitted their young daughter to join in on the merry good times as well. Juan, too, liked to whirl the girls around occasionally, when he took breaks from the spotlight on the bandstand, especially when the musical tempo on the dance floor was loud and lively. After all, good old Maria-chi country music always did rejuvenate the Mexican spirit, including Juan's.

Edelia never had a dance partner. If she ever danced at all, it would be with either Angela or one of her girl friends. Most of the time, she just sat near the bandstand, tapping her feet, maybe clapping her hands, or swaying from side to side. She loved music and loved listening to the beautiful words of the love songs that Juan sang. One night in particular, on seeing Edelia, Juan remembered her as the waitress from back at the boarding house, but never thought too much about it at the time. He could see, however, that she enjoyed the music when in pantomime, she sang along with him from the sidelines.

Juan liked that little girl from the beginning, remembering her cute smile and how nice and polite she was. But never before, had he noticed anything beyond that, until that night at the dance hall, when he noticed that she hardly ever took her eyes off him. Seldom did anyone ever pay that much attention to him, but this young girl was different. Her gazing and her smiling seemed to say things to Juan that played tricks with his feelings, making him self-conscious. But despite the goose bumps and stirring emotions, it still gave him a warm glow. He enjoyed every minute of her attention and didn't hesitate to return her contagious smile. The night he asked her for a dance—the memorable dance that she accepted— was the night everything began to change. It was just a simple two-step to the pretty ballad '*Porfiria*' that awakened a dormant longing in both their hearts.

After that, something completely strange was happening to Juan. Or perhaps, I should say his mind. Strange feelings and impulses were coming over him like a sweet welcome scheme, causing weird anxieties and giddish moments. He was quite sure it was Edelia that was causing all those throbbing heart palpitations. But why— they'd never talked in private before, much less, had conversations of affection or intimate feelings toward each other. And why was it

DELIA
1930

Edelia Gomez

that her flirtatious kidding every evening at the supper table bothered him, making him nervous and bashful liken to that of a little boy. He kept thinking, *how absurd it would be for a man his age to even remotely entertain emotional feelings for such a young girl.* He continued to wonder why, and each time, he reached the same conclusion. Yes, it was that sweet, crazy kid, Edelia—the one he danced with the other night that was dominating every corner of his mind. And for good reason too. She was such a pretty girl, physically in full bloom, and matured far beyond her age. She could say things with such excitement and exuberance that always delighted everyone in the diner. It was certainly no wonder that all the boarders looked forward to her spontaneous remarks and silly wisecracks when they gathered around the dinner table.

Since the night they danced, Edelia's presence was more and more noticeable and becoming friendlier than ever. That's when Juan began to recall some of the things he hadn't noticed before. He was almost certain that since the night they danced, she had been giving him special attention. Like reserving him the special place at the head of the table, the one nearest her serving counter, and always serving him first with leading remarks such as; *you look nice tonight, Juan. Do you have a date?* She already knew he was bashful and surely didn't have a girl friend.

Kiddingly, sometimes she'd say such things as; *I wish I had a date. How come you never married Juan? You're very handsome, you know.* And when she joked, somehow that wink in her eye and that radiant innocent smile always found its resting place on him. Sometimes that touch—the touch across his shoulders when she'd pass by...and when supper was over, how she followed him outside to the front porch when Angela wasn't looking.

Yes! It was her fault. She was to blame for all those crazy sensations he was having. But despite those strange but wonderful feelings of excitement, each time, on remembering their age difference, he just knew that Edelia was way too young and bubbly to ever get romantically involved.

During the weeks that followed, Juan discovered the truth. Edelia really did have an attraction for him. He hadn't just been hallucinating. The gleam in her eyes for him was real. And all he could think of was *how sweet it is.* Soon, those wonderful feelings of anxiety began reciprocating back and forth through unmistakable gestures; flashing of the eyes, and yes—a touch here and there. As for Edelia, each day, she could hardly wait for the men to come home from work. She wanted to see Juan. Even a glimpse would do. Unconsciously, she pranced in front of the mirror every time she went by just to make sure she still looked pretty, and made it a point to wear her prettiest blouses and dresses. And her long flowing black hair—it too had to look just right. She never stopped to ask herself why she was doing these silly things, or even wonder what was causing giddy sensations. Nor did she ever realize that it was only natural for a pretty young girl, such as she, to become breathless and light-headed when enchanting voices of romance kept putting songs in her heart.

And it was the same way with Juan. Although he didn't realize what was really happening either, he gladly welcomed her warm and charming presence. He surely wouldn't stand in the way of the effect she was having on him—not for a single minute. Every day at work, while moving steel rails from one spot to another, setting railroad ties one after the other, and pounding hundreds of railroad spikes, he could think of nothing else but to be at the supper table, waiting and watching for sweet little Edelia to appear.

Angela Castro

As time went on, the evening meal became more and more the highlight of their day, as each one waited for supper time in child-like anticipation, merely to glance and smile at each other, and to pitch cupid's little darts and arrows of enticement back and forth. And even though their kidding around was frivolous and flighty, there could be no doubt about the romantic tendencies implied. They each knew that all those tingling skips of the heart were genuine.

But there was one big problem. Seemingly, a thorny blockade wall was standing in the way of happiness—standing in the way of an open door that led to freedom and an all-new encounter with a budding romance. That wall was Angela. Ever since the night Edelia and Juan first danced together, Angela became suspicious of her attraction for Juan and gave her strict orders not to get too chummy. She strongly disapproved of anything resembling romance. From that night on, Angela watched Edelia's every move, taking away a lot of her free time and deliberately loading her with as many chores as she could handle. When she went for walks or on errands, Angela made sure Edelia was accompanied by Linda or Rebecca.

Angela's supervision over the girls at the boarding house had always been strict. And being such a demanding woman and needing to be in control at all times, for Edelia, it meant 'you either obey, or else'. When she made an innocent mistake—something as trivial as spilling a glass of water, or breaking a dish—she scolded her harshly, and sometimes gave her a *cachetada,* a face slap. Most of the people at the boarding house knew that Angela was capable of being mean and hateful, especially when she got mad. They, too, had felt her sting at one time or another.

Angela knew that Edelia was very pretty, and catching the eyes of all the men at the boarding house, and all the more, watched her like a hawk. Many times when Edelia was punished for a simple mistake, it immediately reminded her of her malicious stepfather, 'Tacho'. On occasions like these, she would run to her room, crying her heart out, desperately longing for her natural mother, Domitila, and with rushing thoughts of running away. Angela probably meant well most of the time, but obviously, didn't possess the tolerance or understanding essential to raising children. Her stern punishments were never meant to be hateful, but she just didn't know any other way. Her business ambitions always came first.

All the years that Edelia lived with Angela, dating back to the time when she was taken out of the orphanage, she had tried hard to love Angela and please her in every way possible, but somehow, she was never able to penetrate her uncompromising personality. It was as though she didn't need affection from anyone. So...**after 6 years**, tiny scars had begun to form in Edelia's heart, and her love for Angela seemingly remained unanswered.

The end result of Angela's overly stern discipline only brought resentment and rebellion from Edelia. She knew she couldn't hold back those urges to be around Juan, because every time she saw him, she wanted to reach out to him. So…she would not deny herself the call of romance any longer. Instead, she would let her feelings go unbridled every time she got the urge. Thereafter, when Angela was away from the diner or away from home, Edelia felt liberated. Free from Angela's choking reins and free to express her self in whatever way she pleased.

It didn't take long for the boarders to take notice of what was going on between Juan and Edelia. After all, it was so obvious that all that kidding around was more than just fascination—they were actually romancing each other. Chon and Rosendo seemed to get much pleasure in poking fun at them, and sometimes, broke out in belly laughs. They thought the relationship looked so silly…like Edelia being just a child, and Juan being old enough to be her father. To Chon, it was childish and so ridiculous. He was the big teaser, sometimes saying, *I'm gonna tell Angela on you.* Or, *You're gonna be in big trouble.* At other times, he'd say something like; *will you marry me,* which only brought more laughter from the others. She couldn't stand his teasing and never thought it was funny. She resented it, sometimes throwing a wet dish-towel at him, or thumbing her nose at him. At times, even Chino couldn't resist chiming in with a teasing remark, like; *I'm better looking than Juan, don't you think?"*

Of course, all the fellas were just teasing in a friendly way. They all knew that neither had ever had a serious relationship with each other, beyond what went on in the presence of everyone at the diner. They had the deepest respect for Juan and knew all too well that any motives or intentions he might have would be sincere and honorable. And they loved Edelia too, knowing her predicament with Angela. Every day at dinnertime, they could see how pretty she was, and how she pranced around the table from chair to chair, unable to conceal a perfectly proportioned figure. So…perhaps the guys were a little envious and jealous of Juan for being the *chosen* one.

The magic moment for Juan and Edelia came one evening after supper in mid-July, when Angela had gone to visit some friends. Juan was feeling very romantic that day, as he trotted upstairs to fetch his mandolin. Humming a beautiful Spanish tune as he came skipping back down the stairs, he walked out on the front porch and sat comfortably on the porch step. Looking back, he could see that Edelia had followed him outside and motioned for her to sit next to him.

As Juan began to sing the beautiful love song—*Solemente una vez,* "You belong to my heart"—there could be no doubt that the words to the song were from the heart, and every word meant for his sweetheart. As for Edelia, she was basking in ecstasy, absorbing each and every word.

Solamente una vez, ame en la vida	You belong to my heart, now and forever
Solamente una vez, y nada mas	And our love had its start, not long ago
Solamente una vez en mi huerto brillo la esperanza	We were gathering stars, while a million guitars played our love song
La esperanza que alumbra el camino de mi soledad	When I said "I love you" every beat of my heart said it too.
Una vez, nada mas, se entrega el alma	T'was a moment like this, do you remember
Con el dulce y total renunciacion	
Y cuando ese milagro realiza el prodijio de amarse	And your eyes threw a kiss, when they met mine
Ay campanas de fiesta que cantan en el corazon	Now we own all the stars, and a million guitars are still playing
	Darling you are the song, and you'll always belong to my heart.

By the time Juan finished singing his love song, Edelia was in a trance, sighing deeply in a cloud of heavenly bliss. She was in love.

Putting his mandolin aside, he asked, "Lela, let's go for a little walk. You want to?"

"Yes! Let's do," she replied without hesitation

At last......the moment they'd both been waiting for. Finally, they could be alone and together without worrying about Angela. As dusk was approaching, side by side, they walked down Villa Street, the dirt road that led toward town, each with overflowing anticipation as though they might never get this chance again. As Edelia accelerated her pace to keep up with Juan, occasionally, she turned to look back over her shoulder to see if anyone had noticed, but she ignored the inner voices that warned of Angela's wrath. At that sweet moment, she was too excited about her indiscreet date with Juan to care. Juan, however, was a bit worried about being alone with Edelia, thinking that he might later be accused of luring her away from the house.

After walking a short distance from the house, Juan had to ask

"Lela, are you sure you don't mind going for a walk? You know Angela will have a fit, if she finds out."

"I don't care," she replied. "We're not doing anything wrong."

"But if she finds out, she's not going to like it," he warned.

"I don't care what she says. She hardly ever lets me out of the house, and besides, she's not home tonight. She won't find out."

Edelia waited until they were out of sight of the boarding house before reaching for Juan's hand. She couldn't resist any longer. As they walked arm in arm, they soon spotted a grassy spot near a huge pecan tree. Carefully, they ducked through the barbed wire strands of a nearby neighbor's fence, and upon finding a soft spot beneath the tree, Juan invited Edelia to sit down—he wanted to talk. He had some things he'd been wanting to say, because from the beginning, he felt guilty for his infatuations and perhaps improper advances. Despite the hunger in his heart and his desires to court beautiful young Edelia, he felt bad for allowing his emotions to get out of hand, thinking all along that a relationship with her could never be.

"Lela" he said, "forgive me, but there's something I've got to say."

But before he could get out the next word, she interrupted, saying, *"No digas nada, Juan."* "Don't say anything" Then she kissed him.

At first, it was only a slight affectionate kiss. But the second was filled with explosive passion. As he held Edelia close in his arms, he could feel the pounding in his chest. For him, it was a moment beyond belief, when deep in his heart he knew he couldn't deny the feeling. He knew right then, that someday she'd belong to him

And likewise for her, the kiss said it all. She also felt like she'd finally found a place in the sun, as all the yearning and longing, and the fondest dream of her life, had suddenly come alive.

The minutes that followed, found them cuddled cozily in each other's arms as Juan began telling his *dulce corazon* all about Villa de Reyes and his family in Mexico.

"Someday," he said, "I'd like to take you back to Mexico. I want you to meet my mother." Continuing, he said, "I have a dream too." *"Si Dios me da licencia,* God willing, I want to settle down somewhere in America…own my own little home, and start a new life…a life of peace and success, without having to worry every day about putting food on the table.

"Don't stop dreaming, Juan," she replied. "I like your dream and I know someday you'll make it come true. Yes, I'd love to meet your mother."

For the time being, they were totally relaxed and the fears of the world no longer weighed heavy on their minds. The enchantment of being in each other's arms had taken away every single nightmare of the past. In the quietness of the hour, as each one talked freely about their past and all the hardships they'd faced, they soon realized that they had many things in common, especially being lonely and their need for meaningful life where they could be truly happy.

But as they continued to savor the sweetness of each other's affection, all of sudden, Edelia was in a panic. She jerked away from Juan and sat straight up. She was frightened and shocked when she heard a familiar voice in the distance. On recognizing the voice, cold chills ran up and down her back, as fear filled her entire body. It was the same fear of Angela that she had felt many times before.

"Le......la"….. "Le…..la"….. "Lela…..where are you?" It was Rebecca. She was yelling for Edelia.

Scared and trembling, she instantly pulled away again, saying, *"Ay Juan, Angela is back."*

She didn't know whether to run or stay hidden behind the tree. She began crying, as though fearing for her life.

Still shaking, she said in a voice of urgency, "I've gotta go Juan. I'll see you tomorrow." *"Adios."*

"Le…..la"………"Le…la"…Rebecca was still calling for Edelia.

Edelia began running as fast as she could toward the house, scared to death. She knew she had disobeyed Angela and feared for the worst. She ran passed Rebecca without stopping.

As she ran by, Rebecca noticed Juan. He was still standing beside the tree.

The next day—back on the railroad—Juan was still floating on a cloud. There were no birds flying or playing around the railroad yard, but he could hear them singing anyway. The clouds were hanging low overhead, but he could swear the sun was shining. His heart was still asleep, resting from all the excitement of the day before. At last, he too had fallen head over heels in love.

The workers now knew about Juan's increasing fascination for Edelia, and how in recent weeks all that hanky-panky stuff was becoming more serious. What they saw in the beginning was merely her infatuation with Juan, but now, it appeared they were both getting into deep water. They often wanted to talk to him about it, but didn't want to meddle. Until today . ….After finding a shady spot to eat their lunch, not too far from their job site, Antonio brought up the subject of Juan's seemingly unwise fling with Edelia. He sensed serious implica-tions ahead and couldn't resist offering Juan a word of caution regarding his new love affair, saying, *"Juan, ten mucho cuidado. Esa niña es muy joven y todavia no sabe lo que es amar, menos los dolores de un corazon quebrado."* "Juan, you'd better be very careful. That little girl is too young to know about love, much less, the pain of a broken heart."

"I hear what you're saying, Antonio." replied Juan, "and I know you mean well. But I wouldn't do anything to hurt her. And I certainly wouldn't break her heart. I'm fully aware that she's very young, but she thinks she loves me, and I think I love her too. But for now, that's as far as it goes."

"Well, that may be true," said Antonio, "but don't you think Angela can see what's going on? She ain't blind you know. Aren't you afraid of getting her in trouble? There are lots of rumors going around about you two."

"Yes, I know," said Juan, "but if just being her friend is going to get her in trouble, then it's Angela that's in the wrong, not me. And besides, you've seen how Angela treats her. She keeps such a tight rein on her that if she even looks at a guy, she makes it look like she committed a mortal sin and punishes her for it."

"I know," said Antonio "I've seen how she mistreats Edelia, and I really feel sorry for that kid. But even if we don't like it, she's still her daughter, and how she raises her own daughter shouldn't be anybody else's business."

"Antonio," said Juan. "I don't know what to do. All I know is that Edelia is very unhappy with Angela and she badly needs more freedom. I don't know how all this got started or where it's going, but it really does my heart good to know she likes me the way she does. I know I'm a lot older, and I know our friendship doesn't look right, but neither of us can help how we feel about each other. It may be love, or it may not be love, but one thing is for sure, our feelings for each other are real. All I know right now is that Edelia is very unhappy with Angela, and someday, she's going to lose her anyway. But Antonio, I can promise you one thing, which ever way it goes, I'll always do the right thing by Edelia."

"I know you will Juan," said Antonio. "And in a way, I envy you. She's such a beautiful girl and mature way ahead of her time. I've seen the way she looks at you, and believe me, I'm convinced she really does love you. Too bad things have to be the way they are—she deserves better."

"You're absolutely right Antonio," replied Juan. "She deserves better, but she'll never have it as long as she's with Angela. If I had my way, I'd marry her tomorrow if it were possible. But I know it's impossible."

"I'm afraid you're right Juan."

It was 7:00 O'clock, and all the workers were gathering at the dinner table, as they did every evening after work, noisily chatting about the sweltering heat of the day, including the long hours of working on that stupid old railroad. Juan, as usual, was waiting to get a glimpse of Edelia, but only Linda and Rebecca were serving. After waiting patiently as long as he could, when Edelia never showed up, he began to worry and decided to ask Linda.

"Donde esta Lela?" "Where's Lela?"

She looked at Juan pretending not to hear him and continued setting up the table with the usual routine of dishes and silverware.

Juan asked again, "Linda, what's wrong." "Where's Edelia?"

Immediately, Linda turned to face Juan with a mysterious look on her face and pointed to the kitchen, saying, "In the kitchen, Juan, but don't go in there."

For a second, he was dumbfounded, but sensed immediately that her absence in the diner had been perpetrated by Angela to keep them apart. He turned toward the kitchen abruptly, intent on seeing Edelia, when Antonio took his arm.

"Sientate Juan!" *"Esperate!"* "Sit down, Juan," he said, speaking with strong voice of caution. "Wait. Don't be to hasty."

Juan's intuition was right. Angela was punishing Edelia for seeing him the night before. He was angry, and also worried. As he looked around the diner, all eyes were focused on him, as if to say, *Juan, you're in trouble,* immediately causing him to wonder; *what's wrong? Why is everybody acting so strange? Why is everybody looking at me like this?*

But he knew. In his heart he knew the real reason. It was he. It was his age. It was the appearance of an older man seducing a young innocent girl. Losing his appetite, he merely picked at his dinner, and after a few minutes, went upstairs to his room.

Juan couldn't sleep a wink all night. But because his conscience was clear, he was determined to talk to Angela and explain. He knew she was always in the kitchen by 5:00 O'clock every morning.

Early the next morning, as he walked through the swinging doors leading into the kitchen, Juan saw Angela putting some firewood in the cook stove and approached her very respectfully.

"Angela, can I talk to you for a minute?" he asked.

"No Juan!" she blurted out angrily. "I'm busy!"

"Angela, please," Juan insisted, "I just want to explain about yesterday. It's not what you think."

"Juan," she roared again, "I told you I'm busy. Now get out of my kitchen!"

"No, Angela!" Juan yelled back, becoming more persistent, "I'm not leaving until you hear what I have to say. It's about Edelia."

"Juan," she growled back, "I don't want to hear one word you've got to say. Now, for the last time, please leave!"

"Angela!" Juan snapped back, "Edelia is innocent and so am I. We've done nothing wrong. We just went for a little walk."

Angela bristled. She was still steaming from having found out about Juan and Edelia's romantic stroll. She looked at Juan straight in the eye, and said, "Juan!" "Now you listen to me!" "I've always respected you and I know you're a good man, but I forbid you to see Edelia again. She's only 15 and far too young to be seeing anyone, much less, someone your age. She's not to see you again, and I want this whole business between you stopped. If you continue leading her on, you'll have to go live somewhere else!"

"Leading her on!" exclaimed Juan. "Angela, you're badly mistaken. I did not lead her on, but even if I had, she's better off. For the first time since I've been here, she's now a happy girl. Can't you see that?"

"Juan, tú tienes toda la culpa que mi hija sea tan loca y toda volada!" Still hollering, she continued, "Juan it's all your fault that my daughter has become so flighty. Ever since you came here, she's been acting wild and crazy in the head. You've got her living in a fantasy world, and that's got to stop!"

"Where's Edelia?" Juan angrily insisted in a loud voice. "Where is she?"

Angela's temper had been rising steadily and was about to explode over Juan's refusal to leave, when she shouted out in anger at the top of her voice.

"Get out!" Pointing toward the door with a shaking fist, she shouted out again, "Get out!" "Now!"

At that moment, Edelia came walking through the door. She had heard Angela's shouting at Juan and almost retreated in fear.

On seeing Edelia, Juan quickly called out, "Lela. Don't leave!..... Why...you've been crying! What's wrong?"

"Nada" she replied, turning her head the other way.

"Como que nada. ¿Porque lloras?" "What do you mean nothing's wrong? Why are you crying?"

Angela became even more infuriated when she saw Edelia come through the door.

"Lela!" she shouted angrily, rushing toward her ready to pounce. "What are you doing here? I told you to stay in your room!"

Picking up a leather strap, she dashed toward Edelia, yelling, "I'll teach you to disobey me!"

As she was about to strike her, Juan jumped in between them to stave off her advance, saying defiantly, *"No Angela. No le pegues. Mire, Angelita. No es justo maltratar tu niña cuando no ha hecho nada mal."* "No Angela, don't whip her. It isn't right to punish your daughter when she hasn't done anything wrong.

Angela yelled out again at Edelia, *"Vete!"* *"Vete a tú cuarto!"* "Go to your room!" "Now!"

"No," she yelled back sharply, still crying, "I hate you! I'm not going and you can't make me! I want to talk to Juan."

Angela, fuming more than ever, was about to make one more attempt to strike Edelia with the belt, when Manuel stepped in. On hearing her angry shouting at Juan and Edelia, he instantly intervened.

"No, Angela. Ya no le pegues! Deja el cinto!" In a forceful commanding voice, he shouted, "No, Angela! You're not whipping her again! Now put down the strap!"

Mad as could be, and with the veins in her neck about to burst, she shouted angrily at Manuel, *"Salte de aquí, Manuel!"* *"Salte!"* "Get out of here Manuel Get out!'

Walking toward her, he warned her again.

"Angela, I told you to put down the belt. You whipped her last night, but you're not going to whip her again. Now give me the belt."

Suddenly, Angela was bursting with rage. Now, even Manuel had diminished her authority in front of Juan. Shouting obscenities at Juan and Manuel, she flung the strap across Manuel's chest and stormed out of the kitchen, pushing Juan to one side as she went out, saying, *"Que vayan todos al infierno"* "All of you go to hell"

When Manuel came to Edelia's defense with such striking authority, Juan was startled. Always before, he stayed out of Angela's way, but not this time. Obviously, at long last, even Manuel had taken objection to the harsh mistreatment of Edelia and overruled another whipping.

"Ven para aqua, Niña." "Come over here, little girl,"

"Lela," he said, "You're growing up very fast—almost too fast. I know you don't hate Angela, and I know how you feel. Anyway, this is your home and we are your parents, and as long as you live with us, you must do as you're told. As for your feelings for Juan…well…hold on to them. He's a good and decent man, but don't be too hasty. He isn't going anywhere."

Turning to face Juan, he continued.

"Juan, I hate to say this, but I think the best thing right now for all concerned is that you find some place else to live. For you to remain here only means more problems, not only with Angela, but also for Lela. As for you to continue seeing Edelia, well…we'll just have to wait and see."

Juan had much respect for Manuel, now, more than ever before. And much to his regret, he knew Manuel was right. He knew he would have to leave the boarding house.

On hearing Manuel's advise to Juan, Edelia ran to Manuel's side, pleading, "No Manuel!" "Please let him stay!" "Please!"

"Callate" "Hush," Manuel ordered.

Juan knew what he had to do. Turning to Manuel, he said, "Alright, I'll go." "You're right. I've already caused too much trouble."

As Juan walked out of the kitchen, he could hear Edelia pleading desperately with Manuel to let him stay. She was still crying and threatening to run away

An hour later, as it was getting dark outside, Juan walked away from the boarding house carrying his suitcase, still angry and hurting immensely. As he walked toward town, the ache in his heart repeatedly asked; *"is it over, will I ever see her again."* These were the anguishing thoughts going through his mind. Never before in his whole life had he ever been even remotely touched by the pure sweetness of a girl's affection, and now, he couldn't help but feel it was over. In town, he spotted a small hotel where he decided to check in. He rented a cheap dreary upstairs room.

For the next two weeks, it was pure hell for Juan, not being able to see Edelia every day as before. He missed her tremendously. The sweet memory of her young smiling face followed him wherever he went. The only consolation remaining was that his fellow workers kept him informed as to Edelia's miserable situation with Angela. The men felt sorry for Edelia because they knew she was being unduly punished. But they didn't exactly feel sorry for Juan. They couldn't feel his pain at all. In fact, at times they still teased him and poked fun over his romantic fling. Jokingly, someone would say something like; *Juan, you naughty cradle robber,* then laugh. Another time, on noticing Juan's self-detachment from the others, Antonio began to worry and asked, "Juan, are you alright?"

Antonio later became the 'go between' for Juan and Edelia, sending messages back and forth. Being their contact, he had already informed Edelia where Juan was staying. After several days of this type of indiscreet communication, one morning at the job site, Antonio surprised Juan with an important message.

"Juan," he said, "Lela wants to see you. She says it's very important. She said she was coming to see you tomorrow night. I don't think it's a good idea" he continued, "but what should I tell her?"

Juan replied, "I don't care what anybody thinks, Tony. I can hardly wait. Tell her I'll be waiting."

On seeing each other again, it was a rendezvous of desperation as they kissed and embraced unceasingly. The past two miserable weeks, filled with heartache and emptiness, had proven without a doubt, the depth of their feelings. At that moment, they each knew that there was no turning back.

"Juan," she said tearfully, "I hate Angela. She makes my life miserable. I don't want to live with her anymore. I'm going to run away."

"Run away?" Juan asked, "You can't run away! Where will you go?"

"I'll go with you," she said.

Shocked on hearing these beautiful words, Juan paused for a brief moment. Smiling finally, and gleaming as though his prayers had just been answered, he asked, "Lela, do you really, really want to leave Angela, your mother? Do you really want to run away with me?"

"Yes! Yes!" she answered pleadingly, as tears continued trickling from her cheeks

"Yes, I do! And besides, she's not my real mother."

Again, Juan paused for a minute, trying to sort out the extremely complicated situation they were in. Finally, he said, "Lela, I love you. And if that's what you want, then that's what I want."

With tears in her eyes and laughing with joy, she jumped in his arms, as if to dare anyone to ever separate them again.

"Yes," he repeated. "We'll get married. And Angela will never hurt you again. But listen, running away is not proper. That just makes matters worse, so let's do it right. We've got to at least try to get Angela's permission. She might say yes. After all, a lot of people back home *often get married real young*—younger than you sometimes. Her problem is, she just doesn't want to give you up."

"I love you Lela," Juan repeated, "and try not to worry. Everything is going to be alright. I want you to go back home and wait. And when the time is right, I'll come and talk to Angela. We've got to give her time to cool off. If we can convince her that we're both serious, and that this is not just some 'spur of the moment' illusion, she may say yes."

"If she says no, then that's her problem. We'll get married without her permission and she won't have anyone to blame but herself."

"Juan," she answered, still misty eyed, "I don't want to go back home. It's awful back there. I feel like I'm in a cage being watched every minute. And besides, I miss you so much. Each day seems like an eternity."

"Sweetheart," Juan said, "I miss you too, more than you know, but we've got to do it this way. So get back home right away before Angela misses you. I promise you, it won't be much longer. Please?"

Embracing each other tightly once more, Edelia, for a minute felt completely relaxed and comfortable in Juan's arms. She knew he was right and trusted him implicitly for his wise judgment. From here on, she thought, the waiting wouldn't be near as torturous.

"Alright Juan. I'll go," she said hesitantly. "I love you."

"Love you too, Lela," he responded, as he walked her to the door.

And so, the stage was set for a visit with Angela and possibly another confrontation. On his next day off, Juan would deliver his appeal in person.

A week later, Juan was ready to face Angela. It was 10 O'clock on a warm Sunday morning when he approached the boarding house. He was nervous, but mostly anxious to know what Angela's answer would be. After knocking on the front door, Juan waited for a minute and pretty soon, the door opened. It was Rebecca at the door.

"Hi Juan," she said with a surprised look on her face, *"¿Que Pasa?"* "What are you doing here?"

"Hi Rebecca. Is Angela in?"

"Yes she is, Juan. Do you want to see her?"

"Yes. I'd like to talk to her for a minute. Please tell her I'm here."

"Come in," Rebecca said.

Stepping inside, Juan began clearing his throat and looking around to see if Edelia was anywhere in sight. He'd hoped to talk to Angela in private.

Pretty soon, Angela came walking in the room. On seeing Juan, she came to a dead halt. Instantly, she stiffened up and her face became an icy glare. For a few seconds, the room was deathly quiet. Then suddenly, she snarled in a hateful voice, *"¿Que quieres?"* "What do you want?"

Seeing that Rebecca was still in the room doing her house cleaning, Juan asked, "Angela, can we talk in private?"

"No!" she growled back. "Not in private, not today, not tomorrow, not ever. Why did you come back here?" she yelled.

Instantly, Juan's frustration shone all over his face. On seeing that Angela was still mad as ever, he knew it was hopeless to continue, and barked right back.

"I don't know why I came back. I was going to ask your permission to marry Edelia, but I see you're still a stubborn old mule. Talking to you is a waste of time. I'm sorry I came!"

Immediately, Juan did an about face and angrily stormed out of the house as Angela began calling him names. He was thoroughly convinced that reasoning with her was impossible.

On his way out, stomping off the porch, he could see Rebecca standing at the front door. He knew she had seen and heard everything, so he yelled back,

"Rebecca. Will you please tell Edelia I was here? She'll be glad to know I tried."

"Wait, Juan." Rebecca called out, as she caught up to him and walked along side.

"What is it, Becky?"

"Well," she said, "Maybe I shouldn't be saying anything, but I heard that Angela is putting the boarding house up for sale."

"What?" he answered, "Why are you telling me this?"

"I don't know," she replied. "I just thought you'd like to know."

"Thanks, Rebecca."

On his way back to his hotel room, Juan was mad at himself for going to all the trouble of talking to Angela. Edelia was right, he thought. Angela was impossible. And now, there was only one thing left to do. If they were to get married, Edelia would have to elope. And if the rumor was true about Angela wanting to sell her boarding house, they had better hurry.

With Rebecca's help, the elopement became much easier. She had become very sympathetic toward Edelia and her unfair punishment, but especially, her sudden awakening to a beautiful romance and desperation to be with the man she loved. Edelia confided completely in Rebecca on revealing her plans to elope, and together they schemed a plan to make it happen. Since Edelia was so closely confined, Rebecca could leave the house freely, facilitating the runaway. Little by little, Rebecca began sneaking a few clothes out of the house—a dress or two, here and there—and taking them to Juan's hotel room, and waited for the precise opportunity.

One week later, in the dark of night, the daring escape happened. Late in the night, when Angela was asleep, Edelia sneaked out of the house and quietly walked away from the smothering restrictions of the boarding house—frightened, but nonetheless, excited.

As she hurried to Juan's hotel, Edelia couldn't help but feel sorry for Angela. Deep down, she loved her in spite of her rigid discipline. Deep down, she knew that Angela loved her too, and would like to forgive her for all the times she'd been harshly punished, and also for her hasty disapproval of her relationship with Juan. But now it was too late. Nothing could justify turning back now.

As Juan paced the floor back and forth, the minutes seemed like hours. She was late, he thought, and perhaps something went wrong. Nervously, as he watched from his window on the second floor, he prayed that all would go according to plan. Suddenly, out of the shadows, he saw a figure running toward the hotel. Yes! It was Edelia. She was carrying a small satchel. Stomping noisily all the way up the echoing wooden stairs, she saw Juan waiting at the open door to his room and leaped into his outstretched arms—scared, but excitedly happy.

"I did it!" "I did it!" she shrieked in a triumphant, jubilant voice. "I'm free."

Juan's heart also was racing with excitement as he embraced her tightly, swinging her round and round. Now he knew that she belonged to him.

"Ay dulce corazon, como te amo" "Oh, how I love you sweetheart."

The next day, **August 8, 1921, Juan and Edelia** were secretly married by a Justice of the Peace in a simple ceremony in Oklahoma City. Now, they were husband and wife. They never realized how blissful it would be to be crazy in love. Silly and giddishly, Edelia joked about being in 'love forever after', and dancing with Juan and swooning over his beautiful love songs. That memorable day marked a new beginning for them both, as a missing link in their lives had just been discovered. No! It wasn't riches or fame—for her, it was Juan, and for him, it was Edelia. And even though their journey of dreams had been suddenly interrupted, now they each had a new guiding light firmly secured by their love for each other.

Unfortunately for Angela, however, the only true happiness she might have known, had been centered around Edelia—and now she was gone. On Edelia's departure, Angela became extremely bitter. Her spiteful obsession became callous and vengeful as though daring anyone to ever challenge her authority again. She bottled up her anger inside, when in reality, she really did love her little girl. But unfortunately, she mishandled Edelia's love, causing her to run away. The newly-weds attempted several times to meet Angela half-way towards obtaining at least a lukewarm blessing on their marriage, but she refused forgiveness of any kind. Before the year ended, Angela and Manuel sold their boarding house and left Oklahoma City. Destination unknown. It was rumored that she moved north.

CHAPTER 13

▼

A RETURN VISIT TO MEXICO

After their marriage, the newly-weds remained in Oklahoma City, and time seemed to be passing by quite rapidly. Juan's employment with the Frisco was slowly solidifying into a permanent status. He felt fortunate having a full-time job, especially now that he had a wife to support. He loved being married, and his love for Edelia continued to grow and strengthen his ambitions. But new and unexpected events continued to develop. For one thing, the Frisco was making preparations to move its operations to a newly completed freight yard 100 miles to the north in a little town called **Sapulpa**, not far from Tulsa where the recent race riot had taken place. The Frisco had been growing by leaps and bounds and on the verge of becoming one of the largest railway companies in the Southwest. So when they completed their move to Sapulpa, Juan and Edelia had no choice but to do the same, if he was to keep his employment in tact.

By 1925, and still employed at the Frisco, many wonderful things were happening for Juan and Edelia. **Four years of marriage had blessed them with 3 beautiful young boys.** Beyond all the fears and struggles from Villa de Reyes to Sapulpa, the dream of success in America was still alive and well. Juan's seniority with the Frisco had finally earned him free traveling privileges, and since it had been many long years since Juan last saw his family, not wanting to wait any longer, he submitted an application for a travel pass to Mexico. Now, a married man with a beautiful wife and three wonderful children, bursting with pride, he could hardly wait to show them off to his mother, Felipa.

After a hectic four-day trip on the train and several train transfers en route, including the last desolate 15 miles by horse-drawn minibus from San Luis to Villa de Reyes—for Juan and Edelia—it was an indescribably joyful day. Especially for Juan, who was wildly elated to be home again in his own village—the one he left behind, **twelve years ago**. Saltillo Road in front of his old home place was truly a sight to behold. On opening the front gate to the house, he immediately spotted his mother. With out-stretched arms and tears in her eyes, Felipa came running to greet her long lost son, crying out at the top of her voice, *"Juanito! Ay Juanito, hijo mio!"*

Juan couldn't hold back tears either, nor the tremendous joy of his mother's tight embrace, saying, *"Mama mia! Ay Mama! Dejame verte!"* "Oh, Mama. Here, let me look at you." The sounds of her trembling voice told of the painful, empty years of the past. Both were practically speechless and disbelieving that Juan had finally made it back home to Villa de Reyes.

Once inside, with jubilant cries of delight, the jabbering was almost out of control, as everyone excitedly tried to speak at the same time. For the longest time, Gregoria, in her gibberish excitement and gladness to have him back home again, couldn't let go of Juan's arm. And Hilario, who had also married and now with three children of his own, was still living at home with Felipa. But despite all the excitement and jubilation, Juan's eyes were constantly fixed on his mother as they both tried to absorb the wonder of his return. Then in a soft tone in his voice, he asked, *"¿Mama, como has estado? No te imagjnas lo tanto que te he hecho menos."* "Mama, how've you been? I've missed you so much. You'll never know how much I've worried about you, wondering if you're alright."

"Ay, hijo," she replied, still forcing back tears of joy, *"¿Poque te fuites tan lejos?"* "Oh son, why did you have to go so far away?"

"Mama, please don't cry anymore. I'm home now, and you'll see, everything's going to be alright."

"Look, Mama," he continued. "Look at my beautiful wife. Isn't she pretty? Her name is Edelia."

Just then, Edelia reached out to Felipa, also gleaming from ear to ear to embrace her husband's dear mother.

"Saludes, Señora Felipa. Tengo mucho gusto de conocerla." "Greetings, Señora Felipa. I'm so pleased to meet you. Juan has told me so much about you, and I've

really been looking forward to this day." *"Me robé su hijo,"* she said, jokingly. "I stole your son."

"Sientate hija." "Please sit down," Felipa said in a happy voice. Welcome to our humble home. You're a very pretty young girl, and lucky besides." Laughingly, she said, "Juan never looked at girls before, so tell me, how did you catch him?"

"Well," she said, "one day I just winked my eye at him, and he came running. After that, he was all mine. I'm just joking." she added. "But Yes, I'm a lucky girl, and I love him very much. And to prove it, I want you to meet our three wonderful little *muchachitos"*

"Vengan aquí, hijos." "Come here, children."

"This one is Juanito. I named him after his Papa. He's four years old." *"Andale hijo, dale un beso ha tu abuelita."* "Give your grandmother a kiss, son." Bashfully, Juanito Jr. allowed his grand-mother to kiss him on the cheek then pulled away.

"And this one is Cecilio, he's two years old. We named him after Saint Cecilia because he was born on her birthday, November the 22nd." Felipa reached for her next grandson, and giving him a ten-der squeeze and a kiss on the cheek, she said, *"Ay que hijito tan precioso."*

Handing Felipa the baby, Edelia said, *"Tenga, Doña Felipa. Este bebe apenas tiene tres meses, y todavia lo tengo en la chiche Preguntele a Juan como lo llamamos"*

*Juanito, Jr., Cenobio and Cecil
Sapulpa, Ok.—1927*

"Here, Doña Felipa, This one is barely three months old and I'm still breast feeding him. Ask Juan what we named him."

Cuddling the baby most tenderly, pinching its little nose, and plucking at its puffy brown cheeks, Felipa was all aglow and couldn't help but marvel at such a wonderful surprise from her son and his new wife.

"Ay que bebe tan chulo," "My, what a pretty baby."

"Juan," Felipa asked "What's the baby's name? Edelia said for me to ask you"

Hesitantly, with a proud smile stretching across his face, Juan said, "Mama, I named this one for you. His name is **Cenobio**."

As soon as she heard the name—Cenobio—her face beamed with joy, but immediately began sobbing again. She hadn't expected such a sweet surprise. *"Ay Diosito de mi vida"* she uttered, pressing both her hands against her face.

"Mira, Mama, lo que te traje." "Look what I brought you, Mama" said Juan, reaching inside a little white paper sack and handing her a dainty ivory beaded rosary. *"Lo compre en los Estados Unidos."* "I bought it in the United States, and I've already had it blessed by *El Padresito* at Sacred Heart Catholic Church in Sapulpa. That's the little town where we live."

"¿Te gusta?" "Do you like it?" he asked.

"Ay hijo, como no. Este rosario lo voy a usar y guardar para siempre. Gracias hijo." "Yes. I'll use it and keep it always. Thank you son."

"Here Gregoria, this is for you," handing her a silk scarf with a bouquet of roses design. "I hope you like it."

"Oh Juan, I love it. Its beautiful."

"And Hilario, this is for you" Juan said, handing him a burgundy necktie with white silvery diagonal stripes. "And look what it says here on the back, 'Made in USA'."

"Ay caramba. ¿A mi tambien me toca?" Hilario asked. "I get something too?"

"Gracias hermano" "Thanks brother."

Lastly from the sack, Juan pulled out a hand full of black candy-flavored licorice sticks, saying, "These are for anyone who has a sweet tooth."

As the joyous celebration continued, Juan reached inside his coat pocket and took out an envelope containing some important papers. Looking at his mother, all smiles and about to pop the buttons off his vest, he said, "Look Mama. You'll never guess what this is."

"What is it son? She asked with much curiosity.

"Here…take a look."

"Son, you know I can't read. Please! Tell me what it is!"

Playfully dangling it in front of her face and grinning from ear to ear, he finally cleared up the suspense, saying, "Mama, it's my new identification card from America. It means that now, I'm a permanent resident of the United States. Look! See here! It's got my name on it—Juan Guerrero Gomez." Continuing to explain, he said, "This is my permanent residence card issued to me by the United States Department of Justice and the Immigration and Naturalization Service of America."

Awe-struck with immeasurable pride, Felipa let out a shriek of joy.

"*Hijo*! ¿*Deveras?*" Oh, son!" "Really?"

Her face beaming, she reached for the card, kissed it playfully, and reached for Juan. Laughing out loud, she said, "I knew it! I knew you could do it! Son, I'm so proud of you." Her eyes glistening, she passed the card around for everyone to see.

"Look, everybody!"

With both hands in his pocket and his chest expanded, Juan momentarily basked in a cloud of swelling pride.

Following the awesome return home and the gift presentation, happy smiles remained on every face in an air of sublimity. Glancing outside through the open kitchen shutters, Juan couldn't wait to see his old familiar yard. As he looked around, seeing the barn, the shed, the chicken house, and their rickety old fence, he was overcome with sad and sweet nostalgia, recalling his childhood days working side-by-side with his father, and remembering that his hand print and foot print was still on every inch of their humble *hacienda*. As he continued to look around, he saw that hardly anything had changed. Even the kitchen floor was still a dirt floor.

"Juan" said Hilario, "*el mismo dia que recibí tu carta diciendonos que ibas a venir, matamos el cochino.*" "The same day we received your letter saying you were coming, I butchered a pig. For the next few days, we're going to feast." With an affectionate pat on the shoulder, he continued, "It's so nice to have you back home again, brother. We've really missed you.

"By the way, Hilario" asked Juan, barely above a whisper. "Tell me the truth, how have things been going? Are things any better around here, or are we still just getting by?"

"*Hermano,*" he replied, "*casi que todo es lo mismo. y a veses es peor. Si no fuera por el dinero que nos mandas, no se que hicieramos. Las milpas ya no queren dar maiz. Esta pobresa no nos suelta.*" "Brother, everything is still the same, and sometimes worse. If it wasn't for the money you send us, I don't know what we'd do. The cornfields don't yield like they used to. Poverty just won't loosen its grip on us. But we manage" he continued. "It's not just us, the whole village is in poverty, the same as it was when you left."

"Hilario," Juan interrupted, "while I'm here, I want to see Don Luz. I want to transfer *las escrituras,* the title to those two little houses that I own. The ones Papa gave me. I'll put the deeds in your name and you can either sell them, or rent them—it's up to you. Hopefully, you'll have enough to put a wooden floor in Mama's kitchen."

"That's great," said Hilario. "Thanks. I certainly appreciate it. I'll see that it gets done.

Back home in Villa de Reyes, it was impossible not to relive some of his old memories as a young lad, as Juan strolled nostalgically across the cornfields that had once provided the life-blood of existence for his family, including a sentimental visit to Cenobio's grave site at Loma Bendita. And just like his father Cenobio, the small town of Villa de Reyes was deeply rooted in his veins also, and he could almost hear its greeting of welcome home.

Old friends were called to come and say hello to their long lost native son who had dared to cut a trail to the good land of America. Hilario and Gregoria began making the rounds, starting with Don Andres Luz. Others were Jose Lopez, Alfonzo Chaves and his wife, Bentura and Josefa Cruz, Elena Gutierres, Concho Casemiro, Flaco Campos and of course, Don Panfilo, and especially, Father Hidalgo All his old friends, just like himself, were a lot older now, but still, it was a great joy to be reunited again.

On seeing Juan again and his beautiful wife and three little boys, Don Panfilo was shocked, but also elated.

"Juanito," he said, "I'm so proud of you. You've done well, you remind me of your father Cenobio. Let's celebrate! If you'll let me do the honors, we'll have a fiesta at the ranch. I have lots of room out there and we'll need it, because I'm calling in the **Torres Mariachi Musicians** for a big dance. How about it? We can get started right away. What do you say?"

Looking at Edelia, with a proud and hearty smile, Panfilo continued, "*¿Como te parese, Lela, te gusta bailar?*" "And what do you think Lela? Do you like to dance?"

"*Como no, Don Panfilo. Ya estoy lista. Usted tiene la pimera polka.*" "Yes," Edelia answered kiddingly, "I'm ready now—and you can have the first polka."

"Padrino, you haven't changed one bit," said Juan. "Absolutely! Why not! Let's have a fiesta."

Word had already gotten out that Juan was in town, so when the invitations were announced, many of his old friends were only too eager to come shake his hand. Panfilo immediately set the gala event in motion by instructing his chef **Ronaldo** to butcher a hog and prepare for an outdoor hog-roast at his pavilion adjacent to the corral. The chef had been busy all day long cooking pork fajitas, cabrito, carnitas, burritos and pozole for the special guests. For dessert, he prepared individual servings of delicious buñuelos. As other guests begin to arrive,

Juan was the center of attraction, answering question after question about America. They all wanted to know down to the last detail, his experience in getting there. As the socializing was abuzz throughout the pavilion, Panfilo went to the wine cellar and retrieved six bottles of his finest imported wine. Interrupting the musicians while they were tuning up, he stepped to the center of the floor for a special announcement.

"Amigos" he said, *"Amigos...por favor."* "I'd like to propose a toast. Everyone—please fill your glass, because this toast is for our dear old friend, Juanito. He's one of us—a son of Villa de Reyes. I want to congratulate him for his triumphant journey to America, and I wish him the best when he returns." *"Salud"* "Bottoms up." *"Para arriva."*

As a round of applause roared for a few seconds, Panfilo signaled for the waiters to begin serving dinner.

After a fantastic dinner and nearing dusk, the musicians kicked off the dance with the favorite *corrida, Atotonilco,* and immediately, the dance floor came alive with Juan's old friends in celebration of his return. Once again, it was like old times in Villa de Reyes.

For the remaining days of his vacation, Juan spent much time at his mother's side. At every opportunity they reminisced about Cenobio, old times, and the hardships of the past, as well as discussing plans for the future. He reassured her that the day would come when he would send for her. Felipa beamed constantly for having her son back home, and if only for a few more days, happiness filled every corner of their little house once again. She loved Edelia to no end, including her three little grandsons whom she continually smothered with hugs and kisses.

All along, however, she knew that the day was fast approaching when Juan would again say good-bye. And each time she thought of it, heart-wrenching emptiness gnawed in her stomach. When that dreadful day finally came, again for Felipa, it was a day of profound pain and sorrow—much worse than Juan's first departure. All she could think of was *how many more years would it be before she saw here son again.* In any event, it would seem like an eternity, despite Juan's assuring promise to return more frequently.

The following year after returning from Mexico, just as Juan and Edelia were making permanent plans to settle in Sapulpa, the Frisco was preparing to make, yet, another move. This time, to a little town to the north, called **West Tulsa**. It came as a big surprise that the Frisco would abandon their freight yard in

Sapulpa, but they did. Once again, however, Juan was one of the lucky ones. For him, there was no disruption in employment because he, too, made the move to West Tulsa. Edelia never complained. She was still very happy and in love with Juan, and of course, very much preoccupied with their four young children—three boys and a latest addition, a girl—Manuela. Their marriage had remained fantastic, and Edelia stayed pregnant most of the time. Child bearing was becoming her specialty. As a mother, she was fantastic, and as a wife, absolutely superb, completely contented in being a poor man's wife.

The year was 1927.

Thus far, at the blink of an eye or a flashing thought, by blending true facts with fiction, I created a true-to-life portrait of Juan and Edelia's early unsettled lives just to see for myself the troubled waters of their past.

But no more blending. Henceforth, their story will continue in non-fiction as I personally witnessed it growing up in a forlorn section of West Tulsa, Oklahoma. Throughout the end of the story, I, Cecil, will be one of the leading protagonists next to Juan and Edelia—my Papa and Mama. I realize it sounds strange for me to be a part of their awesome story, but as will be seen, it was undoubtedly destined that I play a vital role in their long and tiresome journey— a role dictated by demanding times and circumstances necessary to propel their lives to higher level.

But first…let's take a look at the simple life of my parents—and mine—as we casually make our way through fun times and difficult times in a place called the "Y".

PART III

▼

FAMILY STRUGGLES TO MAKE IT IN AMERICA

CHAPTER 14

▼

A SETTLEMENT CALLED
THE "Y"—1927

From the teens of the 1900's, through 1927, all the way from Mexico to Oklahoma, Juan and Edelia's world has rotated to a degree reaching far beyond anything they'd ever imagined. Marriage had never been anticipated, nor was a fast growing family. And there still remained a monumental problem—a problem far removed from their native land. It wasn't the fact that they were still living in a world of poverty, either, because for them, that was acceptable since that's all they'd ever known before. No, it wasn't that. *It was the language, further complicated by the lack of education,* a problem they knew that they would eventually have to overcome, if they were ever to make it in America.

The early years in America, roaming from one job to another, never taught Juan much English. Fortunately, he and Edelia had always been able to find a Mexican community along the way, not necessarily needing to know the language, because at every stop, there was always a leader among them to interpret or intercede. Even his job doesn't require much English communication with his supervisor, since all he wants, is for him to put in a good days work. To this day, Juan still struggles with English, and many times, were it not for clumsy hand gestures and body language he might never get his message across. Edelia likewise, had yet to learn the language.

It was with these handicaps that Juan again set out to find a place to live. After several days of walking and hitch hiking highway 66 back and forth from Sapulpa to the little community of West Tulsa, he finally found a vacant one-room shack located *smack dab in the middle of the Frisco train yards*—a place called the "Y".

The landscape of the "Y" was anything but flattering. First of all, for Juan and Edelia, the "Y", with its squalid-like surroundings, sharply resembled many of the places where they'd previously lived—either in Mexico or America. Secondly, the *"Y" was merely a small colony of Mexican migrant railroad workers all crammed together in a sunken hollow with restricted access to the town.*

The "Y" itself was just what the letter implies. That being a Y formation of railroad tracks located on the north side of the **1500 block of West 21st street**, not too far from the Arkansas river that flows easterly, dividing West Tulsa from East Tulsa. Descriptively, it was the train line coming in from the west that formed a Y effect—one leg of the Y going south to the Frisco's roundhouse, while the other leg of the Y went north to Tulsa. A bird's eye view would reveal a perfect Y formation of railroad tracks. Additionally, the "Y", as it were, was completely cut off on the east by Frisco's main arterial rail traffic, thus enclosing the "Y", and converting it into a triangle. *This triangle affect completely enclosed all residents within it by borders of railroad tracks dealing with heavy train traffic 24 hours a day.* Thus, Juan and Edelia's newfound colony—a mere five acres neatly isolated inside the borders of the triangle—virtually closed them off to any exit. During all hours of the day or night, the constant rumbling of switch engines, chugging, puffing, bumping and humping, including the lonesome freight train whistles that constantly warned of their presence, almost never stopped. Many times, pedestrians and automobile traffic would be completely blocked off for long periods of time, which only created a constant annoyance for those who had families on either side of the train crossing.

The railroad crossing at 21st street was so notoriously dangerous, that it became labeled by the Mexican community as **'Cruzero del Diablo'**—the Devil's crossing. Flagmen directed traffic of motorists and pedestrians around the clock, and many times, guards patrolled the crossing area to prevent violators from jumping on freight cars while still moving. But impatient violators couldn't always be stopped, because sometimes, it seemed that the freight trains kept the crossing blocked for hours.

Every mother in the "Y" lived in constant fear of 'Cruzero del Diablo,' particularly after one horrible night when a boxer who lived in the colored community just south of the "Y", lost his life in a most tragic way. Warning signs against jumping onto moving freight cars had always been conspicuously posted, but even that didn't stop impatient pedestrians who had no desire to wait out the timeless switching of freight cars. But on that dark and rainy night when there didn't seem to be any end in sight to the spotting of freight cars by the switch engines, it happened. Mr. Sampson, a colored man, daringly jumped onto one of the moving cars despite the warning whistles being blown by the crossing's flagman. Now this wasn't his first time to jump onto moving freight cars, but this time, as he defiantly tried to make his way between two freight cars to the opposite side of the tracks, he lost his footing on the rain-soaked wooden walking planks and fell to the ground between the two freight cars. In an instant, he was rolled over by the train and died a horrible death. Within minutes of this tragic accident, floodlights appeared almost from out of nowhere. Guardsmen's whistles were blowing and ambulances with their shrieking sirens were blaring away, scurrying frantically to the scene of that horrendous accident. For the next hectic hour, traffic remained at a standstill, as the lighted area where Mr. Sampson had been mangled, became a spot of intense shock and even tears. Flagmen, police, and railroad officials immediately rushed to the scene and cordoned it off to keep away shocked onlookers who had rushed in from every corner of the "Y" and from the colored community. Yes, it was an awful night, a cold and rainy night at *'el crusero del diablo' that lived up to its name.*

Juan and Edelia's newfound settlement was just a tiny little ghetto neatly hidden on the outskirts of West Tulsa where poverty continued to thrive. Their little colony was in a setting all its own and totally separated from the mainstream of other West Tulsa families. At least, the town of West Tulsa was up to par with other small American towns; it had paved streets, streets with names, stop signs, sidewalks and the like. The houses had numbers on them to direct the postman to the correct address, most of which had pretty yards and lawns and white picket fences that added a flavor of peaceful simplicity to their cozy little town.

But not the "Y". The "Y"—a mini-hamlet totaling at least 45 people living in eleven one and two-room ramshackle shacks all bunched up together—never enjoyed such special benefits of living in an upper class neighborhood. No doubt about it, Juan and Edelia, along with their neighbors, as the saying goes, *lived on the other side of the tracks.* By any stretch of the imagination, the "Y" at best, was no more than a slummy little barrio comprised of poor humble Mexican families.

There were no streets in the "Y", nor any sidewalks. None of the houses ever had an official address, they were simply numbered like, 1,2,3,4, etc., but only for the convenience of outsiders. *The postman never came to the "Y".*

There was only one way in or out of the "Y", and that was one little narrow rutted road descending into it liken to a pit. Much of the ground surface was loose dirt or sand, and when it rained, the terrain became treacherous. Rainwater always collected in the low spots, and many times, people with cars unfamiliar with the muddy road, got stuck axle deep and had to be pulled out by the local "Y" folks, sometimes with horses. The "Y" was never a place of beauty, at least not to outsiders. The only beauty around—*besides the hierba buena and the quelites,* (wild vegetables)—might have been the abundance of pretty yellow sunflowers growing wild along the banks of the railroad tracks. Weeds and thorny thickets of stickers and sand burrs grew uncontrollably. Never, ever, was there a single blade of Bermuda grass anywhere in the "Y", much less pretty green lawns.

The "Y" never had any such thing as environmental protection against the emission of soot being discharged from the coal burning switch engines. Nor were there any controls against the offensive odor of creosote coming from tarred railroad ties—new ones or old ones—sometimes strewn in all directions. Also, when the daily breezes were just right, the "Y" automatically absorbed the oil stench coming from the nearby Mid-Continent Refinery, as it burned off excessive basic sediment from their sludge oil ponds. When at its worst—which was most of the time—the stench smelled like rotten eggs. *And everyone knows what that smells like.*

Juan and Edelia's house was far too small for the size of their family. *It consisted of only one long 20' room, 12' wide, which was utilized as a living room, bedroom, or any other kind of room.* The red tar-papered roof over their little house had waves of unevenness as though it would cave in at any moment. And the same was true for the floor—it, too, was uneven and without a sub-floor. Doors had no knobs, just door latches. The exterior walls of the house had been thrown together with random oak studs and siding that never saw a coat of paint. Indoors, the walls were covered with thin, wavy wallboard, the color of powder blue.

Their little house never had an ounce of insulation for protection against the hot summers. Every day, all day long, the windows and doors had to be kept wide open to allow cool breezes—if any—to circulate through the house. This in turn, simply invited the flies and mosquitoes inside. Trying to keep cool in hot afternoons wasn't easy. Sweaty clothing clung to their bodies and the smothering heat at night sometimes forced them to sleep outdoors with the mosquitoes just to get relief.

The winters were worse than the summers. It was bad enough just trying to keep warm, much less, coping with other problems brought on by freezing tempera-tures. At night, the children sometimes slept on the floor next to the stove to keep warm. Often times, ice had to be chipped off lumps of coal or firewood before a fire could be started. During the night, Edelia, in her heavy flannel gown and heavy wool stockings, had to get up several times to put more wood or lumps of dirty, black coal in the stove. Cracks in the windows had to be stuffed with papers, and even that didn't keep the windows from crusting over with thick lay-ers of ice. Around the doors, Edelia tucked rags along the cracks to keep out the cold draft. Their pot-belly stove stood squarely in the middle of the floor, and on cold winter nights, when Juan crammed it full of wood, newspapers, and a dash of coal oil, red hot crackling heat roared through a black stove pipe and exited through the ceiling. But worst of all, was water freezing. Invariably, their drink-ing water froze and had to be thawed out over the cook stove.

Edelia's kitchen, which took up the far corner of the room, was comprised of one three-burner kerosene stove and a small kitchen table. *The house had no electricity; therefore, no radio, no music, and no bright lights.* All they had for night lighting was coal oil lamps that provided dim lighting at best, and when their kerosene supply ran low, candles were used.

Edelia

They had no running water, and of course, no plumbing. In the back yard stood a manually operated water pump whose oily tasting water was not fit to drink and had to be primed each time before using. Still yet, pump water was viewed as a blessing because it provided ample water for bathing and washdays. Standing beside the pump, was a black 20-gallon, cast-iron kettle, which on washdays gathered all the household laundry, including Juan's dirty *pecheras,* overalls. A rip-roaring fire under the kettle brought the water to a boil, to which Edelia added shaved slices of P & G soap. Clotheslines were stretched from tree to tree with supporting poles mid-way on the long stretches.

Fresh drinking water and water for cooking, had to be carried in from two blocks away in two and five gallon pails from the Mid-Continent Oil Refinery across the tracks, who provided us with free drinking water. Fresh drinking water in a two-gallon water pail always sat on the edge of the cabinet with a tin dipper in it, which everyone drank from—including friends and visitors. *Germs? No one could be that particular.*

Modern toilet? No. They didn't have one of those either. *All they had was a pathway in the back yard leading to an outdoor toilet supplied with old newspapers and magazines—a two-holer with two half moons—standing in an isolated cloud of rancid air of caca stench that hardly anyone ever paid any attention to.* A very popular place at times, not only for the family, but also for the wasp's who liked the indoor protection from the weather elements for building their bee hives. In the house at night, surely to come in handy, was a white porcelain *vacinilla—* porta-potty—complete with lid that always rested at the foot of the bed.

As the family grew, Juan and a neighbor added a 10' wide lean-to room to the south side of the house that included three 'push-out' windows and served exclusively as bed space for the kids. Eventually, the room occupied several beds pushed against each other. What a sight it was, when all the children jumped in bed on cold winter nights, after which Edelia tucked them in with blankets, quilts, including coats and jackets. What was so funny, was all those little brown faces sticking up out from underneath the covers. It wasn't easy going right off to sleep with kids laughing and giggling, and others fighting and kicking. In the far corner of their new bedroom is where Edelia bathed all the children behind a white bedsheet suspended from the low ceiling. Eventually, Juan added another small room to the rear of the house, which was to be the family's new kitchen. At first, it only had a dirt floor.

Even though their little house was no more than a shack, Edelia kept it remarkably tidy and cozy. Of course, there was no fancy furniture, just antique wooden chairs, none of which matched. The beds—made of metal head-rails, foot-rails and coiled bedsprings—also served as seating for company and guests. Odd sizes of linoleum were placed on the floor for added insulation, which Edelia constantly kept mopped with rags on one end of a mop stick. In her own unskilled fashion, she quilted pretty bedspreads and made lace-trimmed curtains for the windows which nearly always absorbed the smell of Vicks and kerosene. Her treadle type Singer Sewing Machine stored a variety of colors and size of buttons, spools of thread, scissors, needles, pincushions and crotchet needles, including colorful strings of embroidering thread. Among these, she kept scraps of remnant material for patching the children's clothes. Also, on the walls, she hung pictures of favorite saints, a picture of Pope Pius XI, a current Mexican calendar with a beautiful scenery of a *toro and matador*, a 1927 almanac, religious crosses made of palm branches, and a variety of other colorful knick-knacks. Juan's old cap from Mexico hung on a nail next to his Mandolin. **On another nail, hung a**

small gold watch and chain that once belonged to a dear friend of his, by the name of Pedro. At the foot of the bed sat an old graying trunk where Juan and Edelia kept their best clothes in moth balls and a variety of other family relics and mementoes of Old Mexico. Edelia's *chanclas*—the ones with the squashed heels—she kept tucked under the bed.

All together, besides Juan and Edelia's house, there were ten other shanties in the "Y". The general description of one quite accurately described them all. Most families were Mexicans who had also migrated from somewhere in Old Mexico.

Doroteo and Jesus Perez were close neighbors. He was a stocky built man with an over-grown mustache, very polite and friendly, and with a fantastic sense of humor. His wife Jesus, a very inhibited woman who most people called 'Chewy,' was short and on the chubby side, and always wore her hair in long braided pigtails that hung to her waist. She was seldom seen outdoors, but that didn't stop her from being nosy and gossipy.

Pablo and Salome Rico Flores had six children; Alberto, Julia, Rudolfo, Ramon, Lucio, and Socorro. All were fine people whose lives also had been scarred many times over. Dealing with severe poverty was their biggest battle. Pablo, a big paunchy fella, was very likable and amusing, but on the lazy side. His inability to hold a job very long only contributed to their impoverished circumstances. Mrs., Salome, on the other hand, who was so light complexioned that she could easily be mistaken for a white lady, was an extremely hard worker and a great mother.

The **Edisons** were white neighbors. Their children were: Sherman, Floyd, Ethyl, Jerry and Louise. They didn't visit very much with their Mexican neighbors, probably because of the language difference. But they bickered among themselves quite a lot, often loud enough to be heard throughout the "Y", especially their daughter Louise, whose profane, vulgar language seemed to be the norm around their house. Mr. Edison, a quiet, mild mannered man, was one of the train flagman at the 21st street railroad crossing.

Juan and Roberta Valencia, a middle-aged couple, had no children and neither could speak hardly a word of English. They were very devout Catholics and never wandered too far from the "Y". Their only pass-time seemed to be evening visitations with other Mexican neighbors in the "Y". Mr. Valencia was very dedicated to his job on the railroad.

Arcadio and Viola (Persky) **Gonzalez** were next-door neighbors. She was white. They had two sons; Raymond and Edward. Arcadio was a short heavy-set man, very dark complexioned, self-educated, and a part-time barber. He had a touch of sophistication, but often times, very stern and rude. He wasn't very popular among other Mexican families, probably because of his arrogant demeanor. He was, however, a very thrifty person, and like Juan, he always raised a beautiful vegetable garden.

Mrs. **Strickland**, a widow, was another white neighbor. Her children, who were all adults, were: Lawrence, Edith, and Ethyl. Lawrence was already working for the Frisco, making him the primary breadwinner in the family. Mrs. Strickland was a prejudiced, snooty old woman, very cranky, and never socialized with any of her Mexican neighbors. She didn't like Mexicans and made no bones about it. No children were ever allowed in her yard, and many times, if children played too close her kitchen window, she deliberately pitched dirty dishwater at them through the window screen. Sometimes hot water.

The **Harrises** were another white family, great, friendly Christian people. They had eight children: Bessie, Leona, Virgil, Luther, Veda, Derrel, Charlene and Ronnie. Mr. Harris was a Section Foreman for the Frisco, which allowed him to live in the biggest of two company-owned section houses in the "Y". Unlike Mrs. Strickland, the Harrises were very neighborly and hospitable, and graciously accepted all the Mexicans in the "Y" as brethren.

Antonio Chavez, a very dedicated Frisco employee, was a real nice man, dark complexioned, very short, stocky, comical, and a joke teller. His wife and family still lived in Mexico. His job with the Frisco was an Inspector, walking miles and miles of railroad track daily, searching for trouble spots in need of repair. Tony could play the guitar a little and liked to sing sad Mexican country songs, especially when he'd been drinking. He lived the life of a bachelor, of course, and also sent money home to his wife and family every payday.

Claudio Camberos was a bachelor and a rounder who thought he was a ladies man. He always wore neatly pressed shirts, splashed with cologne, and hardly ever seen without a flashy necktie. He didn't mingle too much with other Mexican families, but every Saturday night, he headed straight to the beer joints on 1st Street in downtown Tulsa where other Mexican males gathered on Saturday nights. Once in a while, he would be seen in the company of a white lady at his house.

Antonio and Maria Fernandez were fair neighbors. Tony was a nice man with a pleasing personality, and very handsome. But he liked his beer and his freedom, staying away from home for months at a time. Their children were Nicholas and Petra. Maria, who was not very neighborly, was an unhappy person, seemingly disgruntled over the lonely life that she lived. Much of the time, she appeared mad at the world for her destitute situation, and understandably so, because first off, she couldn't speak English, thereby making it impossible for her to seek employment, and secondly, Tony was seldom around to help raise the kids or put food on the table.

All of the above folks were hard working families living free of rent and property taxes on land belonging to the St. Louis-San Francisco Railway Company. As described, one can readily see that the dreadful living conditions in the "Y" were no paradise. But for the "Y" families, who at the time had no other choice, it sufficed. They never paid much attention to their humble lifestyle…they were content living among friends of their own *raza*. For entertainment, it was not uncommon for them to hold an evening dance party at someone's house just for fun, and they didn't need a special occasion to celebrate. Someone would simply suggest, "let's have a party," and so they did. Once, however, partying almost got out of hand.

It was one evening when Juan had invited some friends over for a music and dance party. The musicians were all in place, playing and singing beautiful Spanish *rancheritas,* and by all accounts, the party was well underway and everyone having a swell time…not too much dancing, just a lot of visiting and laughter. Juan wasn't one of the musicians on this occasion and stayed outside hanging out with some of the men. As the party continued, it got livelier and louder, and began to disturb Mrs. Strickland across the road. When the police arrived, Juan immediately concluded that this old biddy had reported their little shindig to the cops, probably as a drunken disturbance. This, of course, was not the case, because the party was well behaved and none of the men were intoxicated. Nevertheless, the police loaded up eight men in a paddy wagon, including Juan, and took them to jail. The others, were; Sylvestre Garcia, Juan Garcia, Antonio Chaves, Frank Moreno, Tony Fernandez, and a couple of others. Each of the men were fined $10, and released. Back at the house within the hour, the party continued 'til the wee hours of the morning, but this time, more contained.

In the beginning, when Juan and Edelia moved into their little house in the "Y", it had a very little yard. But as their family grew, obviously, Juan needed more yard. So, when his neighbor Don Garcia moved away, he immediately took possession of his little house and yard, and also took possession of Doña Salome's yard after her house burned down. But despite the increased size of his yard, it was never enough to satisfy his ambitions of raising pigs, chickens, goats, and a vegetable garden. Ultimately, the fence was quite different from other fences. Actually, it was just whatever

Edelia holding baby Juanito. Standing; Cecil 6, Manuela 2, Cenobio 4

material he could find that would establish the boundaries of his yard. It might consist of old railroad ties, rusty old bedsprings, old raw lumber, wooden slats, oak timbers, wire, etc. It wasn't a very pretty fence, but it served his purpose, which was to keep all his children in their own yard.

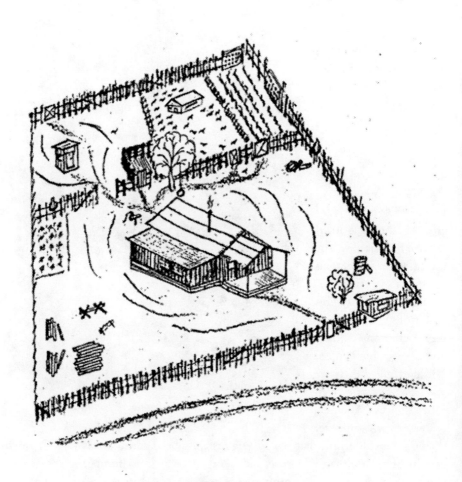

Gomez House in the 'Y'
1931

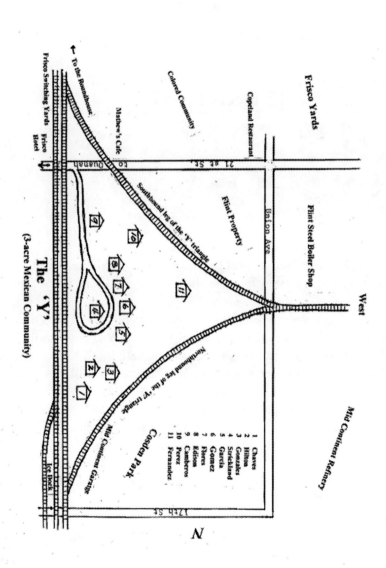

CHAPTER 15

▼

LIFE IN THE "Y"

Settling in the "Y" was easy for Juan and Edelia…all things considered. They were barely getting by, living from paycheck to paycheck, and living a quiet lifestyle nicely secluded from downtown. The easy part was being among other Spanish-speaking people. Every family needed each other, and somehow, found strength and confidence by the mere fact that they weren't alone in the strangeness of an all-white society that didn't always reach out to them. Just being around other Mexicans gave them the moral support so badly needed to cope with an outside world that they couldn't feel comfortable in. But in the "Y"…in their own little Mexican community…yes, it was easy—and they were contented.

Being contented in the "Y" was one thing, but being satisfied and fulfilled, was a whole different story. At times, Juan entertained thoughts of uncertainty about his future, like; *is it always going to be like this?* Ever since he returned from his visit to Mexico, the warm lingering memory of his family and Villa de Reyes just added confusion to the reasons why he left Mexico in the first place.

But be that as it may, he fought to shut out these nagging thoughts and tried not to worry about the 'right or wrong' of the matter. After all, he'd always been able to send money back home to his folks. Also, he now had a wonderful wife who loved him dearly, and thus far, had given him five beautiful children, the latest, another boy. And in the children, he found great pleasure in watching them grow. In their own sweet innocence, they were his pride and joy. And his pride swelled even more when they'd run to meet him everyday as he approached the yard coming home from work. Hastily, they'd look through his lunch pail to see if he brought them a treat, and seldom, did he disappoint them, even if the treat was no more than a cookie, or perhaps a lollipop. Often times, when surrounded by his children at his feet, he recalled his own childhood, and how he was always at his father's side. Nowadays, when he looks at Cecil, the eldest, he sees the image of himself as the identical little boy he once was, with his father Cenobio. Now, he was the father…and he felt proud.

By the way, where's Cecil?

Romping around in the "Y" with my little friends was something I always looked forward to during the summer. That's when I could get down to some serious fun, like going swimming, or going 'junkin'. I thought God must have surely created summers just for kids, because each morning, I'd wake up in a new world itching to find something to do or someplace to go, or maybe a project to get into. Restlessness was all over me. Surely Papa and Mama could see that summertime was for kids and not interfere with my busy childhood plans. On the days we didn't have chores to do, we could find lots of ways to have fun. Sometimes we—me, Noble and Nick—would talk Mama into letting us go swimming at a little swimming hole we called 'rocky dive' at the foot of Chandler Park. Sometimes we'd be joined by Burtis and Wayne Carpenter and Jack Walls. On the banks of this murky stream that emptied into the Arkansas River, there was a large tree with branches that extended over the water. From this tree, we'd tie a rope to an overhanging branch, swing out over the water, let go the rope, and 'splash', right in the middle of three feet of muddy water.

The other swimming pool we liked a lot, was a bit more risky. I'm speaking now of the swimming pool across the tracks from our house in the Cosden park. Now this swimming pool was strictly private and patrolled at night by security guards. It had always been off limits to families living outside the Mid-Continent residential compound—like us. And because of constant patrolling during the summertime, we wouldn't dare go swimming in their pool in the daytime, *but at night, after dark? Well…now that's a different story, because that's when we took our chances.* Let's see now, there was me, Noble, Nick, Ernie, Burtis, Wayne, Jack Vanhook, and Jack Walls. This was our courageous bunch who liked to live dangerously. On the nights that we'd risk being caught, we'd sneak over there very quietly after dark, and most of the time, if we didn't make too much noise, we'd get away with it. And believe me, there's nothing like a nice cool swim in the shadows of a moonlit night in someone else's pool, except when we had to swim with our heads under water every time we saw the flashing headlights of cars going by. But once in a while, one of the guys would forget to stay quiet and out of sight, and get carried away as though he owned the pool. Of course that was a 'no' 'no'. Invariably, this would attract the attention of the guards, and instantly, we'd make a run for it. A bunch of kids never scrammed the way we did, trying to get to our side of the railroad tracks. One night, the guards almost caught Jack Vanhook. They were chasing him across the park, and when he came to a four-foot chain link fence, he made a flying jump and cleared it completely without breaking stride. Scared? Absolutely! Those guards were right on our tails, which explains why Jack cleared the fence so picture perfect.

In the "Y", behind our backyard fence, tall weeds and sunflowers always grew very tall—in fact-taller than our heads. This particular summer, Nick and I decided to cut a tunnel through the tall weeds and sunflowers. It was a rather clever idea, I thought, so we cut out a path low to the ground by clearing out the short weeds, and leaving the tall ones for overhead cover. At the end of the tunnel was our make-believe den totally secluded in the wilderness of an imaginary forest. In our new den among the tall weeds, we'd hold important kid-talks and meetings, tell wild stories, and map out a strategy for our next day's venture—usually junkin'.

One day, out of one of these important kid's meetings, came a super kid's idea. Nick came up with an ingenious idea that would keep us from oversleeping, because whenever we went junkin', it was essential that we start out early so as to beat some of our competition. Since on these hot nights when we slept outdoors, Nick brainstormed an idea on how to set an alarm. A 'pulling alarm' might be a better word because his idea was, that before going to bed, we would tie a kite string to my toe that reached all the way to his toe, at his house…probably 60 feet away. That way, whoever awakened first, would pull on the string, thereby waking up the other. At first, I thought it was a great idea, but forget it. It was a crazy idea. It didn't work. Either too much slack in the line, or too many loose splices. *Or maybe it was the red ants, or the frogs, or maybe the lizards that gnawed our line in two.* But it was a good try.

Not too far from the front of our house, was a sandy spot in the road. Cars going through it usually had to 'gun it' to keep from getting stuck in the dry sand. This particular spot became a favorite of ours, and many evenings after the sun went down, kids from all over the "Y" would gather to play sand games. Burtis and Wayne, from the Frisco Hotel, would also come and join us. Wayne was the 'story teller'—a bookworm. *He liked to read books about African Safaris, jungle adventures, spooky ghost stories, Rin-Tin-Tin and the like.* And this, we thought, qualified him to play like he was our great orator for the evening. So with these qualifications, we wouldn't interfere in his story telling. He really was an interesting kid, combining all sorts of gestures and facial expressions as he brought his stories to life. Many were the times, when on starry, moonlit nights, Wayne entertained us with his non-stop stores of fantasy and adventure, despite the fact that I didn't always understand the big words that he used.

Also, I recall going barefooted in the "Y", as did most other kids. Each time Mama sent me to the grocery store or to the drug store, I'd go barefooted. I could care less that my feet would get dirty and black from tromping throughout the "Y" and on some of the blacktop streets of West Tulsa. But going barefooted also had its draw backs, because when running errands in the middle of a hot afternoon, nothing could burn my bare feet more than hot sand or hot concrete. This is why it paid to be a fast sprinter when dashing from one spot of shade to another. Even the shade of a skinny telephone pole could be a lifesaver.

As I was growing older, I began to put away some of the kid's stuff. It wasn't exactly my idea either, because, **work, work, work** is all I ever heard Papa say. He kept me so busy that there wasn't time to get into mischief. Until now, I only thought I had worked hard around the house, but now, it would even get harder. Come this next November, I'll be **11 years old,** and I'm beginning to notice my body stretching and developing both in size and in strength. Papa sees this too, and don't think for a minute that he didn't make full use of every muscle in my body. I knew all along that he himself was a work-a-holic, and now, I was beginning to believe that he was also a relentless slave driver. It seemed that all I ever heard him say was, chop wood, clean out the coal shed, fix the fence, weed the garden, feed the chickens, slop the pigs, go buy some kerosene, and on and on. He never let up. If there was anything he hated to see, was to see me idle. But there was good reason for all his commands. First of all, I was the oldest and I should have known without being told that these working chores at home would never get easier, much less go away. As a matter of fact, the urgency of our daily work routine had always been there, it's just that now, the family had not only grown in numbers, but also in size. And so—the workload too, had gotten heavier and harder.

Papa was not only a work-a-holic at home, but he must have been the same fireball at the Frisco. His job title at the 'round house' was *"Locomotive Engine*

*Wip*er." Quite simply, all it meant was that his job was to wash and scrub loco-motives after returning from out of town runs. Now this title doesn't sound like much, and of course, it didn't carry any important classification or special func-tion, but to Papa, it really was special. And despite the times when his foreman treated him harshly, sometimes jerking him around discriminately, he continued to carry out his duties very diligently. You'd think his was the most important job in the whole system. *Yes, that's the way Papa was; a hard worker from the word 'go'.*

In a way, I didn't exactly mind doing all those chores around the house. I should have suspected all along, however, that Papa was molding me into a work-a-holic like himself. One of the hardest chores of all was **hauling and chopping wood,** because for us in the "Y", firewood was such a precious com-modity, essential for heating and cooking. We knew that throughout the Frisco train yards, they never ceased repairing railroad tracks, discarding old ties and replacing them with new ones, and this meant that there would always be old weather-beaten ties for us to haul in for firewood. The trick was to get to them before someone else did. *All summer long, it seemed we were like squirrels gathering nuts for the oncoming winter.*

Now Papa had an eagle eye for spotting old, worn-out railroad ties, and when he did, he immediately swung into action. As soon as possible after work, he'd get out our old wooden flatbed cart, grease the axle's thin steel wheels, and off we'd go, to the location of the pile of discarded ties. Sometimes the ties were as far as two blocks away, but most of the time, a lot farther. Six to eight ties would be the most we could haul at one time, because pushing that two-wheel cart along the steep banks of the Frisco tracks was absolutely brutal. And it got worse as we approached the house making our way through the sand and rutty road. Once inside the gate, however, unloading the ties was easy. After a brief rest and a cool drink of water, we'd start out again, wringing wet from perspiration. *By the end of summer, we would have gathered several huge piles of railroad ties.*

Stock piling railroad ties was only the first step. The hard job hadn't even begun, because now, we had to start the sawing process. Papa had built a 5' saw-horse designed for this purpose. Brother Cenobio had not yet grown enough in size to be of significant help at the other end of a 6', push-pull, cross-cut saw, so this meant that Papa and I had to do all the sawing. As one can imagine, sawing hundreds of railroad ties into 16" blocks, was hard work. Even though Papa helped with the sawing, most of the chopping and splitting was left up to me. So, each day, I had no choice but to chop up the wood blocks into smaller pieces, and—as needed—carry them into the house.

I gradually became resigned to this chore of chopping wood. Sometimes grudgingly, but still, I knew it was my responsibility. And so—having chopped an awful lot of wood for our family—I learned to do it proficiently, and later, I would earn good money chopping wood for other "Y" families.

Right after breakfast every morning—usually a bowl of '*Avena*'—oatmeal, flavored with cocoa—it was my responsibility to **fetch fresh drinking water** from the Mid-Continent maintenance garage. How unfair, I thought, that other people in West Tulsa had running water at their fingertips, and yet, for us in the "Y", it was always out of reach. Mama and I were the ones stuck with this chore, and it seemed we never had enough fresh water. But to ease our burden of carrying heavy pails of water, Papa made us a 5' long, wooden 'shoulder bar' carved from an oak tree limb to carry across our shoulders. And on each end of the crossbar, with a light chain, we hung two 5-gallon water pails. Of course, it was just a simple primitive shoulder crossbar, but that ingenious tool worked like a charm and greatly eased our load. Hauling water in the summer time through blistering heat was bad enough, but even more dreadful during the howling winds and frigid temperatures of winter. Particularly, when deep snows blanketed our path, causing us to step into waist-high snowdrifts.

The order of each summer's day didn't always offer a change of pace to our usual routine. Every morning, Mama went straight to the kitchen to put on Papa's eye-opener—coffee. No breakfast, just black coffee. And, boy, did he like it hot! For Papa, on the mornings after the night before when he'd had just a little too much 'gusto', Mama knew immediately that he would be asking for some **Ponche.** Now, Ponche, the way Mama made it, must have had somewhat of a kick to it because it always seem to jolt Papa's head when he guzzled it down. Actually, it was no more than a 'hot toddy' or spiked black coffee. First, Mama would beat an egg to put in his coffee, add a little cinnamon, and then pour in a generous jigger of whiskey. When Papa gulped it down, 'great balls of fire', that would do it. The day could now begin.

"*Andale Juan, ahi viene ya* **La Marana,**" Mama would say to Papa every morning. "Hurry Juan, here comes the sow." La Marana was the name given to an all-blue steel freight train locomotive that headed West  every morning and passed within a hundred feet of our house at exactly 7:45, blowing that ear-bustin' train whistle. This was Mama's signal for getting Papa off to work. Some mornings, it was rather comical watching him get ready. He hated being late, but once in a while, he'd oversleep, and when he did, you'd better step aside. In a frenzy, he would put on his overalls and hi-top work shoes, quickly slurp down his coffee, slam the back door on his way out, and trot up the bank of the railroad tracks near Don Doroteo's house. From a distance, we could see him high-stepping it to work. All the while, La Marana would still be blasting its whistle. Now, 'La Marana' in Spanish means 'sow pig'. And because of its squealing pig-like whistle, is why Mama labeled it La Marana. Amazingly—rain or shine—that darn train was never late. Every morning promptly at 7:45, it kicked in our day.

Most every day during the summer, I had to **take Papa's lunch** to him at the Frisco round house, and I had to be there at 12:00 noon sharp. I wasn't too crazy about this chore, because no matter where I'd be playing, or what I'd be doing, I always had to be ready to drop everything. Papa was only allowed 30 minutes for lunch, so I didn't dare be late. The Mid-Continent Refinery always blew a siren-like whistle at exactly 12:00 O'clock noon, and if the whistle ever blew before I got to Papa's lunch spot, I was in trouble.

As with most of us, Papa never had a wide variety of dishes that he liked. His lunches were always the same. Even though we couldn't have afforded a greater variety in our meals, he wouldn't have had it any other way. Mama always fixed him a delicious lunch, consisting of two hot tortillas, a white porcelain cup full of hot juicy pinto beans, Spanish rice and hot chili. Sometimes she'd add green chili peppers fresh from the garden, and other times, green chili salsa. And of course, she never forgot a thermos bottle full of steaming black coffee. Papa always ate so hearty, and just to watch him eat, also stirred up my appetite. After each meal, he'd take out that little red flip-top can of Prince Albert smoking tobacco from the upper chest pocket of his blue *pecheras,* and roll up a cigarette. He wasn't a heavy smoker, by any means, but he certainly enjoyed his 'smoke' during the last five minutes of his lunch break.

Papa had several favorite spots where he liked to eat his lunch, and he always picked a secluded spot as if to be out of sight of other workers. Sometimes, he picked a spot outside the tools warehouse, and on rainy days, he ate inside. On cold winter days, he always chose the warm boiler room, where we'd both sit spraddle-legged on the floor in the midst of steam chutes and the roar of motors and compressors. But my favorite spot was in the engineer's seat inside one of those giant locomotives. I remember climbing up the smelly steel steps amid all that smell of coal, soot, and oil, and how I would climb up into the engineer's cab and pretend I was the engineer. I remember too, how the engine's front bulkhead was literally cluttered with the likes of throttles, gauges, valves, and piping. The intricate network of engineering controls, such as this, was awesome. To be an engineer, seemed like an exciting job and a young man's dream.

On the days when I could escape my chores, my friends and I, could hardly wait to go **Junkin'.** For us, this was a very important summertime kid's project. The whole purpose of going 'junkin' was to earn some spending money. We always liked to be able to rattle a little change in our pockets because summers could get awfully hot, and we needed to stay prepared to buy a popsicle or a cool Nehi soda pop at Fred Walkers Grocery store, or maybe some Cracker Jacks at Doc Reynold's Drug Store. Or perhaps a western movie on Saturday afternoon— we couldn't miss one of those either. So there were a lot of compelling reasons for us to go junkin'. Sometimes, even my parents benefited from my junkin' trips.

The objective in junkin' was to go through all the back alleys of the West Tulsa behind the stores looking for discarded goods. All of the stores periodically cleaned up their shelves during restocking and threw away damaged or obsolete items. Taking into account the wide variety of stores in West Tulsa, this could virtually consist of hundreds of items being thrown away. An example of items found, could be hats, shoes, pots, pans, clocks, coffee pots, dishes, faded clothing, and many other such goodies. Any of these—if I found any—I tossed in my junk wagon. Items useful in the house, I gave to Mama. Other items, depending on their kind, I threw in my own junk pile at home, which usually consisted of iron or steel, brass, copper, and brown beer bottles.

The West Tulsa Iron & Steel Company—a junkyard—would buy just about anything. They may not have known my name, but they sure recognized me when I'd be coming into their yard pulling my squeaky little wagon loaded down with rusty iron and stuff. Junkin' was a lot of fun and a profitable pastime. *I'll bet that on a good day, I could earn 15 cents.*

Papa was quite a scavenger in those early "Y" days, always on the alert for spotting salvaged items useful around the house. And if he ever spotted anything with any sign of remaining usefulness, whether it be steel or wood, he'd take it. And, as a matter of fact, many other families did the same thing. A good example of this is when Papa shingled our roof with metal **Wonder Bread Shingles.** I had been out junkin' one day, when I spotted two large stacks of discarded, razor-thin, 12" x 24" tin sheets. Each sheet had an advertisement embossed on the topside—in color—"wonder bread." When I told Papa what I'd seen, he immediately wanted to have a look. Sure enough, it was just what he needed to shingle our roof. The next evening, with our home-made 2-wheel push-cart, we loaded up both stacks of metal shingles and took them home. Soon afterwards, Papa hired a colored man to help shingle our roof using these tin sheets advertising wonder bread. At the time of 'the find', I thought it was a good idea for Papa to see them, but now, watching the shingles being installed, with Papa and I as helpers, I wasn't so sure. But there was one consolation, the colored man at least remembered to put the red, white, and blue, colored letters to the underside. It was humiliating enough when I got caught by my friends Burtis and Wayne cleaning cactus, now, all I needed, was for them to come by and see this ridiculous shingling job, and ask, "wha'cha doin', Cece?" But as I thought about it for a minute, I realized they would never have gotten past the front gate if Papa was around. He never hesitated for one second to holler at my friends, like "go home", when there was work to be done. When he'd holler at them, instantly they'd turn around and skedaddle.

There was another summertime chore that I hated with a passion. **Cleaning Cactus.** Besides it being ridiculous and stupid, so I thought, it was most embarrassing. Back in the ole' country, as Papa would put it, poor people in the hill country and in the arid regions of Mexico, resorted to eating cactus—a form of vegetable. Now who would have ever remembered that anything like prickly cactus with jillions of tiny stickers would not only be edible, but also delicious. Of course, it would be Papa. Papa loved to eat cactus and Mama did too for that matter. Sometimes jokingly, she reminded us of an old Mexican expression, *cuando uno tiene hambre, hasta las piedras son buenas*—"when one is starving, even the rocks might taste good."

I don't know where Papa got his information leading to possible cactus locations. He knew they were rare around Tulsa, and somehow, he managed to find them. Once, he found a cactus field in Sapulpa near the old elementary school house. Each time we went, we always ended up trespassing across a barbed wire fence into an open brush-field belonging to someone else. Papa didn't see any harm in it, so quite innocently, he ignored the 'no trespassing' signs. He just never thought of it as stealing, because why on earth would anyone care if we helped ourselves to a little cactus. We always went prepared. Leather gloves, pliers, and several buckets were the tools needed to harvest the thick fleshy cactus leaves. *Every time we discovered a field of cactus, for Papa, it was like a kid in a candy store…he just gleamed from ear to ear.* Hurriedly, we would trample through the knee-deep, brush and weeds, snipping fresh cactus leaves until all our buckets were over flowing, then we'd quickly scamper back through the barbed wire fence to avoid being caught. Papa would be beside himself for having found such a thriving field of delicacy.

Arriving back at the house, Papa put his cactus bonanza in pails of fresh water for soaking those tiny, fuzzy stickers. After a day or two of soaking, we would be ready to start the cleaning process—and this is what I hated the most. I just never did seem to get the hang of it, but that didn't disqualify me from that dreaded chore. Papa would usually start the cleaning process in the seclusion of our fenced-in back yard, each with our own individual bucket full of that awful cactus. Just looking at each blade of cactus, one would think it's no big deal…removing all those little stickers, but it's not necessarily so.

The way Papa did it, first he would put a leather glove on his left hand, and using a pair of pliers with the other, he would pluck a cactus leaf out of the water pail. Then he would lay it down on a flat rock, and with a razor-sharp knife, he'd start slicing away at each little patch of stickers until all were thoroughly removed, after which, he'd take every one of those slimy edibles and pitch them in a pan of clean water. When thoroughly clean, Mama would take over for cooking.

Mama's favorite method was to dice them into small quarter-inch cubes and put them in a frying pan, adding red chili powder and favorite spices like; garlic, cumin, oregano, cayenne pepper, diced onion, salt, and a little water. Another favorite way was to take pre-cooked cactus and add to scrambled eggs. *At this point, I should probably say, Mmmm good…but I won't.*

Every meal, with cactus as a side dish, was a speial treat for Papa and Mama. Mama often canned cactus during the summer, if we could find enough for canning. And for sure, she always shared our cactus with our Mexican neighbors who really appreciated this rare treat.

Did I mention earlier that this summertime chore of cleaning cactus was most embarrassing? Ok! Let me explain. You see, Papa never liked to see me idle while he was at work. He expected me to stay busy—like cleaning cactus for example. And that would be Ok, I guess......nicely secluded in our back yard where my little 'white' friends couldn't see me. Surely they'd never see me or 'catch me in the act', so to speak, because, if they ever did, how on earth could I ever explain to them that this was our food?

Invariably, though, it happened. Like the time Burtis and Wayne came over to see if we could go out and play. *Red handed, they caught me knee deep in cactus and stickers. Grinning from ear to ear, again, Burtis asked, "wha'cha doin', Cece?"* In utter humiliation, my face would turn from brown to red, because here I was, trying to learn the American way of life in an all-white society, and all the time, Papa is hung up in the old days on an ancient Mexican dish—cactus. Inside, I would be angry at Papa for allowing me to be exposed to such embarrassment. *Then Wayne chimed in to further mortify my sinking pride by asking, "You gonna eat those things, Cece?"* Now you know how small this made me feel. I could have sunk right into the ground with humiliation. I thought to myself, how could Papa let my shinning reputation sink so low among my little white friends? But for him, this was the norm. He couldn't feel a thing. Eventually, I'd live over it.

During these days in the "Y", when our family kept growing and growing, it occurred to Papa one day to build a **cradle for the baby.** What seemed at first like a silly idea, it really was handy and practical—and perhaps ingenious. He built it just large enough for a newborn, and just deep enough so the baby wouldn't fall out. Next—of all things—he hung it from the ceiling directly over their bed in the front room. This way, when the baby cried during the night, all they had to do, was to reach up and give the cradle a little swing 'til the baby went back to sleep. *Great idea, huh! But wait, there's more.* Now the kitchen was only about ten feet away from the cradle, and here's where Papa really got clever. He tied a heavy chord to the cradle and strung it across the ceiling through some metal eyelets all the way to the kitchen to Mama's fingertips. *You guessed it! Every time the baby cried, all Mama had to do, was to tug on the chord and the cradle would rock. Ingenious, huh!* Well—maybe not. But as funny as it was, it definitely was unique—and it worked.

Papa had to try it all, including **butchering pigs. Ah yes, pigs!** But it didn't take long for him to realize that raising pigs required too much time and attention, and constant feeding of slop. In the first place, our two male pigs were kept penned up in a very small pen behind the chicken house with a divider between them to keep them separated. Sometimes at night, however, they'd break down the divider and fight ferociously, and believe me, nothing can be more nerve racking than two pigs fighting in the middle of the night. And of course, each time it happened, here we'd go, Papa and me, to get them separated. When Papa finally realized that raising pigs was not meant for us, he decided to butcher the swines. Of course, he'd butchered pigs before in Villa de Reyes, so he knew it would require some additional help. That's when he recruited the help of one of his colored friends that lived behind Mr. Mathew's Café in colored town. His name was Dan. Their plans for butchering seemed simple enough...as soon as the pig was out of its misery, they'd slit his throat, dip him in a vat of boiling hot water to soften his bristly hide, then hang him from a tree for quartering. So they brought in a round steel vat, propped it up off the ground, filled it full of water from the hand pump, and then built a roaring fire under it. The next step was to fetch 'Porky'.

Now Papa didn't own a gun, and apparently, neither did Dan. So, to kill this poor animal quickly, it would take a flat-headed ax for knocking him unconscious by a blow to the head, plus one heck of a sharp knife. Up to this point, all the details seemed to have been taken care of, and theoretically, all should have gone smoothly as planned...now if only they could just get Porky to hold still. And this is where all hell broke loose, because Porky wasn't about to hold still. He must have known something harsh was about to happen, so he had different ideas, because for the next fifteen minutes, Porky squealed like a stuck pig, loud enough for all the "Y" to hear. He must have been scared, because the instant Papa opened the pigpen gate, Porky made a mad dash for freedom. He couldn't hold onto the 200-pound pig and neither could Dan. The way they grappled all over the ground with him, huffing and puffing, you'd think Porky had been greased with Pure lard, because neither Papa nor Dan could subdue this poor thing. Squealing and snorting, running crazily all over the back yard, Porky tore down part of the chicken yard fence, trampled Mama's flowerbed, and half of Papa's garden. By this time, he had a dazzled audience—us and the chickens. Mama, with Virginia at her side, stood on the back door steps with a broom in her hand ready to stave him off, should he come her way. Noble had a stick in his hand, and I had one too, while Nellie and Johnny were laughing and screaming.

It was like trying to corner a mad bull, almost impossible. Porky made a lunge at the fence near the outdoor toilet that divided the back yard from the front yard. Head on, he went clean through the fence and headed toward the front gate with the speed of a greyhound. Next, he decided to circle the house, and did just that—round and round—with Papa and Dan, Noble and I, right at his heels. This scene was so hilarious, like; Act 1, of "Chase the Pig." *If any of the neighbors had been watching this circus-like chase, it would almost be worth charging admission.* All of a sudden, Porky reversed his direction and headed straight toward Noble. Now Noble wasn't afraid because he still had the stick in his hand. Poor Noble! Desperately, Porky charged Noble right between the legs and up-ended him as though he was a chicken feather. It was like a perfect cartwheel, maybe two. Did we all laugh? You bet! I'm still laughing.

Moments later, Papa and Dan simultaneously made a lunge at Porky and hogtied him. Needless to say, that day was certainly a day of thrills and excitement, and one less pig to feed. The other pig, Papa gave to Dan for all his help. *In memory of Porky, however, all I can say is, "he sure was delicious."*

Ice in the Summertime. *One thing for sure, summers in the "Y" were hot—I mean really hot, especially, on the days of 100 degree heat waves when our little shack seemed to absorb the sweltering temperatures like a sponge.* It was next to impossible to find a cool spot anywhere, except, in the back yard in the shade of our sycamore tree. Ice water was never available at our house, and since we only kept a small chunk of ice in our tiny icebox, Mama wouldn't allow us to chip at it for ice water. The **Ice Truck** always came by our house at about 9:30 in the morning. The small wooden ice box that Papa had purchased from one of his colored friends for one dollar, only measured two feet square across the top and stood only four feet high. At most, a fifty pound piece of ice would be its capacity. But not to worry, we could never afford that much anyway. Under the icebox, Mama kept a porcelain pan directly under the drip tube to catch the water as the ice melted. And, of course, the pan had to be emptied at least daily. On our screen door, we placed our order for ice on a 12"x 12" orange card, indicating our desired order; 12-1/2 lbs., 25 lbs., 38 lbs., or 50 pounds. All we had to do was to spin the card so that the quantity desired would be at the top. This way, the iceman, in his old-timey yellow ice truck, could see at a glance our order for the day, if any. Most of the time, we only bought like 12-1/2 lbs. for 8 cents.

On certain hot days, however, it was just possible for us to strike it lucky. Because in the "Y", the Frisco operated its own **Ice Plant** that produced large commercial-size, 400-pound blocks of ice for packing refrigerated boxcars. About once a week, they brought in boxcars loaded with produce and other perishables to be packed in ice and placed them along side a 14' high ice-chipping platform. The ice dock, which was the same height as the boxcars, could accommodate eight or ten cars manned by six Frisco employees. On the days for packing the cars with ice, by conveyor, here come all those huge chunks of precious ice, slowly ascending from ground level to the top of the chipping platform. Once the ice reached the top, the workmen opened the rooftop doors at each end of the boxcars for packing the produce compartments. With narrow conveyor ramps, the men steered the 400 pound ice blocks into the open top doors, chipping at it simultaneously into small chunks, until each compartment was full.

Now most of the families in the "Y" instinctively learned to keep a watchful eye on the Frisco's ice-packing days. It was extremely important to get there as soon as possible when in operation, because the whole purpose was to be there just in case a piece of ice accidentally fell to the ground. Only poor people like us, living in over-heated shacks, could appreciate what a small chunk of ice could do. So...when Mama heard the ice conveyor motors start grinding away, immediately in a hasty voice, she'd yell at me, *"andale hijo, ya estan picando hielo."* "Hurry son, they're picking ice." At once, I knew to grab my tow sack and my ice tongs, and beat it to the ice dock, knowing that other people of the "Y" would be doing the same.

Now the Frisco didn't want anyone near those boxcars while they were chipping ice, particularly standing on the ground in between two cars while they were being packed. But out of desperation, we ignored their warnings and usually stood as close as we could. So, we'd stand there, looking straight up at the ice pickers while they worked, hoping that at least a small chunk of precious ice would miss its mark and fall to the ground. Sometimes we'd get lucky and sometimes we got nothing. But we never stopped trying. Once in a while, one of the more compassionate workmen on seeing how desperate we were for ice, would deliberately push off a big chunk to the ground below, then pretend it was an accident. And, of course, everyone below immediately scrambled for it. Like I said, sometimes I'd get lucky enough to retrieve several fair size chunks of ice. Arriving at home with my catch for the day, Mama would fill our little icebox to the top, and if we had any leftover, I'd take it to Doña Jesus, who would pay me quite generously for it. Needless to say, ice in the "Y" in the hot summer time, was almost as essential as water for relief from the heat. *Praying for a small chunk of ice to fall in my tow sack, was like a farmer praying for rain—sometimes it did, and sometimes it didn't.*

Whenever possible, Papa looked for ways to show us a good time. I remember one time when the circus was in town and Papa took us to see it. The circus grounds then, were located near Archer Street and Peoria Avenue. We had a super great time watching the clowns, the pony trick riders, and the man they shot out of a canon. Papa loved to watch the acrobats and trapeze artists, particularly, the high-wire acts. He used to tell us stories how as a young boy, he too, used to do tight-rope walking and other acrobatic tricks. Although I never saw him perform, I could tell by the way he told his stories so excitedly, that he surely must have been a good performer. He wasn't exactly the athletic type, but he did like swimming. I remember he had gotten acquainted with an auto mechanic, named Arthur, whom he referred to as *El Mecanico*. On occasion, Arthur and his wife came by to take us out for a drive. He knew of a secluded lake called Camp Partheñia, located East of Highway 66. At the lake, Papa would put me on his back and swim out into deep water, and gosh, how Mama would scream at him and order him to come back to shallow water. But he paid her no mind. She couldn't swim, of course, and was awfully afraid of the water.

Besides the good times, the hard times, and the fun times in the "Y", sometimes extremely bad luck would strike. I'm speaking now of a terrible tragedy that happened to our next-door neighbor, **Doña Salome.** One evening, in the early fall of the year, just before dark, we heard terrible screams coming from her house. Suddenly Doña Salome came running outside screaming frantically, jumping up and down and running in all directions yelling for help. When we heard the screams, we all came running outside and immediately saw clouds of smoke coming out of her front door. Within minutes, her small house was completely engulfed in flames. And without ample water supply, there seemed to be no way to contain the fire. The closest source of water was from manually operated hand pumps—hers and ours. Papa, and one of the neighbors, kept the pumps going, filling buckets as fast as they could, while others carried the water to the burning house and pitching it on the flames. In just a few minutes, other neighbors had come to help, and they too, started pitching water. But despite all efforts to save her little house, it was not to be. She cried so pitifully, watching her house burn to the ground, helpless to do anything about it.

All the while, pandemonium was also building up at our house, as we watched the swirling flames occasionally brush against our roof. Fearing that our house would be next, with lightening speed, all of us started carrying our belongings outside. Papa carried out mattresses and some of the heavier things, while I carried out anything I could lift. Mama single-handedly carried out her upright sewing machine.

But despite the chaotic intensity of Doña Salome's burning house, we were lucky that night—our house was spared. Scorched on one side, but otherwise in tact. This was a horrible experience for all of us, but most devastating for Doña Salome and her family. She was already in poor health, and now on losing her house, it would be a most grievous blow. And besides the fire tragedy that took her home, that loss would be even less hurtful compared to the events that followed.

The cards were certainly stacked against this fine lady. Because after the loss of her house—homeless and broke—her failing health would not allow her to rebound against chronic poverty. With nowhere else to turn, she decided to put her two small children—Lucio and Socorro—up for adoption. Accordingly, within the year after the fire, this was accomplished. Lucio, age seven, was adopted by a family in North Tulsa by Mr. and Mrs. Pedro Nieto, while Socorro, still a very young child under age four, was adopted by Mr. and Mrs. Doroteo Perez from the "Y". Soon after her two small children were established with their new adoptive parents, Doña Salome requested her oldest son Albert to take her back to Mexico. This is where she wanted to live out the rest of her life. Sometime later, we received word that she had passed away.

CHAPTER 16

▼

A YOUNG INTERPRETER

Those early years in the "Y" for Papa and Mama were coming and going very rapidly. Neither had yet learned to speak much English. Mama was gradually learning it, but Papa still couldn't get it together. He still found himself shying away from white merchants in West Tulsa in order to avoid embarrassment. He preferred seclusion most of the time, and if he couldn't be in the company of his Mexican friends, then, he'd rather be alone. Papa and Mama willingly accepted the ways of poor people to which they had become accustomed and never pondered too much on luxuries for themselves. In their humble way, they, and all the "Y" families became very close, often enjoying lively evenings together, sharing stories of the days back home in the 'old country'. For the time being, integrating with the white community of West Tulsa never entered their minds. But even if it had, there was no escaping the language barrier, which made it unthinkable. So, a switch over to a better life outside the "Y", for now, seemed out of the question.

But they continued to dream of someday advancing to something better than the "Y", and never stopped believing that someday it would happen. Occasionally, they retreated to the back yard after supper to discuss ways to get ahead…owning nice things and laying out their hopes and plans of someday owning a modern little house all their very own—at least, away from the "Y".

Despite their hindered dreams, however, they never gave up. Slowly, things began to improve. It was through me—**Cecil**—that the forward push for a better life remained in motion, even though none of us ever saw it happening. *As time went by, the barrier of language finally began to yield its hold on the Gomezes. At first, by way of education.*

From the day I began learning how to speak English, and from the day I started getting an **American Education**, my parents began depending on me in a variety of ways. and even more so, as I grew older, because almost overnight, this Mexican boy had become an American boy. And for Papa and Mama, who had previously lived in constant seclusion and inhibition, it couldn't have come too soon. Unlike them, I was free of confining inhibition and intimidation beyond our borders and easily integrated with people outside the "Y". Thus, I quickly became my parent's connection and easier access to broader reaches into an all-white society that previously had not been easy to penetrate. At long last, language and education in our home had finally begun delivering on its promise.

Until now, both my parents fully realized that they had floundered enough without any significant sign of progress. Especially Mama. She knew that sooner or later, they'd have to face an outside world before better times could ever be achieved. Her entire life had been completely void of any education, and needless to say, many times she experienced embarrassing moments, all because of her inability to read or write. This is why, now, she is bound and determined that all her children will have the opportunity that she never had, no matter what the cost and no matter how great the sacrifice

Until the age of 7, I was just like my parents. **I spoke Spanish only. No English.** I was just a happy-go-lucky kid with not even a thought, much less a desire, to learn to speak English. There was no need to at the time. After all, we were all Mexicans living in an all-Mexican community. But when I reached this age, that all started to change. Beginning with religion.

Mama had not forgotten to teach us to pray. Of course, all prayers were in Spanish, including recital of the rosary. In the corner of our front room, she had a tiny prayer altar that she kept beautifully adorned with a large crucifix; a picture of the Blessed Virgin Mary and other saints, candles, and a variety of religious articles that collectively complimented her prayer station. It was here that all of us learned about Jesus.

It was during those early childhood days that Holy Family Cathedral in East Tulsa, which was considered our 'mother church', began to address the needs of a growing number of Mexican families to have their own Spanish speaking priest, not only their own priest, but also, their own facilities. Eventually, this was accomplished. When they finally got their own church, they named it *Virgen de Guadalupe* ', after the patron saint of Mexico.

Our first 'all Mexican church' was just a small country church located away from the mainstream of downtown Tulsa on East 15th street, 1/2 mile East of Harvard Avenue, near the Tulsa Coal mines. This specific area was chosen because it had become a small, but thriving community of Mexican nationals who worked the coal mines. Of course, not many families had automobiles, and for them, they would have a long walk, since eastbound bus service didn't go beyond 11th street and Harvard.

Father Tapia was our new priest. He was a native of Mexico and therefore, all the Masses were said in Spanish. Serving under the authority of Holy Family, he immediately began to organize teams of volunteers to initiate and teach Catechism classes to as many young children as possible. A little old man by the name of *Jesusito Morales*, who was partially blind, became my Catechism teacher, and eventually became my *Padrino*. Every Sunday afternoon, he came to the "Y" where all the young children, ages five and up, gathered at our house for religion classes. In our back yard, we'd find a shady spot and seated on wooden benches, he conducted our Catechism classes—totally in Spanish

Later, when I reached school age and enrolled in **Celia Clinton Public School,** it was like stepping into an all-different world—a world full of English speaking white kids. Of course, I was scared, and to make matters worse, for the first time I came face to face with some prejudicial young kids. Now, I remembered what Papa had warned me of many times, when he himself faced harassment. Not necessarily because of the language, which was bad enough, but primarily, his nationality. I should have expected something like this, because I was with Papa one night when he tried to flag down a taxicab on his way to the hospital to see Mama. When the driver of the cab saw Papa was a dark-skin Mexican, he quickly swerved and sped away as though Papa had the plague. Now, it was my turn to deal with prejudice—and I didn't like it. I couldn't help it if I had trouble speaking English, nor the fact that I was a dark skinned Mexican boy, but it continued to bother me, especially when embarrassing, smirky giggles and sneers came from two little white brats. Being the only Mexican boy in the classroom seem to single me out for their wisecracks. Prior to starting school, I never gave it a second thought about racism or rejection. How naive I was to think that all kids—white, black, or brown—were all the same. To me…we were all just kids who liked to play…we all had mothers and fathers…we all wanted and needed the same things...we all lived in the same town. So I wondered, *why are things different? Why bigotry?* Fortunately, the painful jeers and insults were few and far between. Papa never held a grudge or animosity toward racist comments or incidents. Although he didn't like it either, he understood their feelings of superiority over Mexicans. Nevertheless, he instructed me not to be too critical of those who harassed me, reminding me that these young kids were merely a reflection of the attitude of biased parents, and that *someday, it'll all go away.* "Don't pay any attention to them" he said, "*just keep on being who you are. Be proud of your nationality.*"

That first day of school was a bad day. Especially when each kid had to stand up and recite his name. My name had always been Cecilio—'Chilo' for short. But when I finally got the courage to speak my name out loud in front of the whole class, it sounded pure Spanish in the way I pronounced it. Right then, my teacher Mrs. Wilbanks, changed my name from Cecilio, to the English translation of Cecil. She was very patient with me on that first day, and also, very understanding in my frightfulness.

On that first day of school, there was also a problem for Mama. The enrollment card called for our home street address, but of course, we didn't have one. The "Y" was just considered a part of the Frisco railroad yards, and how could you have a street address where there was no street? For the first few days of school, and perhaps weeks, Mama watched over me very closely, knowing how nervous and frightened I was of school—especially the language. Each day when school let out, she was always waiting for me at the railroad crossing, worrying about the constant traffic of freight trains.

For the remainder of the school year, I began to settle down. But most importantly, I was learning to speak English. At first, however, I was thoroughly confused. I remember many times hearing certain words that I had absolutely no idea what they meant. Being too timid to ask Mrs. Wilbanks, when I'd get home, I'd ask Mama. But of course, she wouldn't know either.

That first year was a struggle, but like any other young kid, I learned quickly. The second year, I was much better prepared and no longer frightened. By the time I reached the 3rd grade, I was becoming more and more at ease around white kids. I learned to stay away from bullies and trouble-makers, and made friends with the ones who liked me the way I was. My teacher, Mrs. Trolinger, was terrific and I liked her a lot. She liked my performance at the blackboard during math exercises, and because she completely accepted me and treated me equally to others, it gave me much self-esteem and confidence. No doubt, it was because of her that I began to shed the cloak of inferiority around other people.

And this is where it all began. At last, the English language was finally spreading throughout our shabby little house. First it was me, then it was Cenobio, then Manuela, and so on, until we would all tap into another nationality and unlock the secrets of their language. By the time my younger brothers and sisters started learning to talk, they were now hearing two separate languages...Papa and Mama speaking in Spanish, and the children responding in English—the English they'd learned from hearing me and other little white kids. Oddly enough, this method of communication in our house became quite permanent. What happened as a result of this type of two-way conversations, was that Papa and Mama greatly learned to understand English, even though they couldn't speak it, while the kids on the other hand, learned to understand Spanish, but never quite learned to speak it fluently. English would be their only language. But for me, however, it was different. Spanish was always my primary language and I never stopped speaking it, even after English came along.

When Mama vowed that all her children would receive a good education, no matter what the cost or sacrifice, no doubt she meant religion also, even though she never realized that both the costs and the sacrifices would invariably be beyond all expectations Particularly, when I reached the 4th grade and enrolled at **St. Catherine Catholic School.**.

When Father Landoll came to visit at our house, he wanted to know why the Gomez children were not attending a Catholic school. And understandably so, because it was his duty to see that all catholic children receive a Catholic education, besides just reading and writing. Mama had known all along that the day would come when she'd enroll us in a Catholic School, and now that Father was here asking about it, perhaps this would be the right time. So, it was settled. This fall we would enroll at St. Catherine—I in the 4th grade, Cenobio in the 3rd, and Manuela in the 1st.

Besides the one-mile walking distance, there would be other concerns. Tuition. Something my parents hadn't heard of before. Always before, books had been furnished free at Celia Clinton Public School, but now, Mama came face to face with that humiliating situation of making arrangements with Father Landoll to pay for our books and tuition. And this was always so embarrassing for Mama. She was a proud person and never liked the slightest resemblance of begging or asking for charity. But still, she swallowed her pride, requesting installment considerations. Fortunately, her pleadings were never denied, and through Father and the grace of God, she was always given full consideration. Often times, she bartered this obligation by doing Father's laundry and ironing.

That first day at St. Catherine, Mama packed us a lunch and put it all in a brown paper sack, which I was responsible for. On arriving at school, I didn't know what to do with it, so I put it under my seat on the floor. All morning, I felt awful. I was thoroughly confused and intimidated by the Sisters, especially, Sister Theopholus who wore a solid black habit from top to bottom, totally concealing all but her hands and face, and how her little watchful eyes peered from behind those thick rimmed glasses. And from a leather strap around her waist, hung a giant size rosary with beads as big as marbles—the likes of which I had never seen before

When the lunch bell rang, I picked up our lunch sack, took my little brother and sister by the hand and walked them across the street to an open grassy field where we ate our lunch in the shade of a huge oak tree, away from all those strange new faces. We never ate biscuits at our house before. In fact, I didn't know they existed, but I'm sure Mama did. Tortillas was always our bread, but this time for lunch, I found six biscuit sandwiches in our lunch sack…three with scrambled eggs, and three with jelly.

The next day, we didn't eat across the street as before. This time, Sister Theopholus led us into the dining hall to eat our lunch with the other kids. After that, we stopped bringing our lunch. Father had made arrangements for us to eat at the cafeteria. Everyday, it seemed we had soup or stew for lunch, and it only cost us three cents apiece. I don't believe it was their regular price, but it was the price Father said we could pay.

For the rest of the year, things were very different than what I'd known in public school. To begin with, we had to attend Mass every morning, which started sharply at 7:30. And it wasn't as though we had a choice either, because Father insisted that we go, as did our parents. The biggest difference was the discipline. There were so many rules of conduct laid down by the sisters, to say nothing of the strict compliance of homework assignments. Paddling was permissible, and if you had one coming—you got it—either from Father or the Sisters. The utterance of a bad word could get your mouth washed out with soap at the water fountain.

Mama was on cloud nine every time I served Mass as an altar boy. And she always made it a point to be there on the days when it was my turn to serve. I know she would have been extremely happy if I had received a 'calling' for the priesthood, but that was not to be. Every Friday morning, immediately after Mass, all the children who had previously made their First Holy Communion, had to go to confession. I don't remember confession being voluntary....we just knew we had to go, so we did. I don't think any of us ever had any serious sins to confess either, but when we examined our conscience thoroughly, we would know if we had sinned, like; telling a lie, spoken bad or dirty words, if we'd been disobedient to our parents or our teachers, or if we'd been mean, ugly, or disrespectful to others.

The season of Lent held a very special meaning for Mama. Each year, she participated in all the Lenten activities as much as she possibly could, including the fasting. She completely accepted her Catholic faith and believed every word of God. *How can this be?* I thought. *She never went to school, she never attended any catechism classes, nor could she read.* But despite all of this, by her deeds, by her prayers on bended knees, and by her devout participation at the Mass, she set a shining example for me and all my siblings. Sure, she didn't know how to read, but she had children who could, and frequently, she would ask me to read to her from my textbooks and my little bible. It was as though she had a yearning to learn the things we were learning, including the spiritual word of God.

By the time I'd reached age 11, something new and exciting was taking place for me regarding language. I was becoming a **Young Interpreter.** All this time in America, neither my parents nor the "Y" families, had learned to speak English beyond a smattering of comprehensibility, but not me, at least not any more, because now I'm speaking two languages. What with all my little white friends and colored friends, English had become easier by the day. And I never realized that I had become bi-lingual Unintentionally, I had acquired a new skill that later became very rewarding and beneficial to my parents and other Mexican families, in and out of the "Y". It all started by running errands for the Mexi-

Cecil—Young

can families, mostly the women in the "Y" who were too timid to risk embarrassment with the white merchants in town. Not me though, I was too eager and too bold to let it bother me. From the beginning, I gradually earned their trust and confidence, and later, their dependency on my bi-lingual skills. Like anyone else, they too, had important commitments and appointments away from home that needed to be taken care of. And even non-business, such as a visit to a friend's house in Sapulpa, Sand Springs, or Red Fork. On paydays, they'd come to our house and ask Mama if they could borrow me for the day. This was so they could go pay some bills, go see a doctor, sometimes to the hospital in East Tulsa to visit a sick friend or relative, or other times, just a leisurely day of shopping. Another big reason why they needed me was because they couldn't read the street signs or the destination signs of the buses and trolley cars. On many occasions, I'd get quite a workout from the doctors, nurses, or clerks, who would tease me, thinking it was cute to see such a young interpreter.

Electric Trolley Cars was our primary mode of transportation. The boarding station for my lady customers and I, was parallel to the railroad tracks on 21st street at the Frisco Hotel, a two-story hotel, which at the time, accommodated many transient railroad workers. After boarding the eastbound trolley, it slowly meandered **across the Arkansas River, squarely in the center of the 11th Street Bridge that divided the red brick, paved street into two lanes for two-way auto traffic.** I remember on the days when the ladies used me as an interpreter, it cost us a nickel to ride to our downtown destination. The price for small children was only 2-1/2 cents. Also, this being the era of the 'mil', which was worth only one-tenth of one cent, the Conductor could even give change for a penny using mils. Police, Firemen, and Postal carriers were admitted free, if in uniform. Conductors and motormen operating the trolleys earned only 22 cents per hour. The urban interchange for us when we went to Sand Springs was located at Archer and Boston Avenue. It was a transfer station, named "The Archer Alley Depot." After boarding the yellow trolley, we could settle down for a delightful swaying ride, as the trolley cut its way through the tall weeds and brush-land. The slatted wooden seats weren't exactly the last word in luxury, but enjoyable nonetheless. The back seat-rest of each seat was pivotable to allow passengers to see where they were going or where they'd been.

I'll always remember Doña **Porfiria Murrillo** who used my interpreting skills the most. Of course, she couldn't speak a word of English, but on the days when she came to get me, she liked to tease me, tickle me in the ribs, and play with my wavy hair. I liked all her endearing attention, but it always made me blush. One day as she was teasing me and making me blush, she told Mama something I'll never forget; *"Lela, someday you're gonna have a whole bunch of paychecks."* At the time, I didn't know what she was referring to, but in later years, it all became very clear. She was referring to all of Mama's children, and how someday we'd all go to work and bring our checks home to her. Because traditionally, in the old country, young Mexican boys were taught to bring their earnings home to their mother—a custom to teach responsibility. Mama always allowed me to go with these ladies when they asked for me. She'd visit with them for a little while, sometimes serve them coffee, then, off we'd go. Each time we went, they paid me one dollar.

These were very important days in my life as a young interpreter when I began experiencing such gratification in helping others who needed me. It didn't seem like a 'big deal' at the time, because for me, it was fun and I enjoyed the fact that I was important to them. But from their standpoint, it really could have been a 'big deal' just to have me as an interpreter and guide, allowing them the opportunity to take care of important matters, or maybe just a chance to get away from the boredom of staying home.

At the same time, Papa and Mama were the biggest beneficiaries of my interpreting skills. Since Mama seldom left the house, and with Papa working seven days a week, they greatly depended on me as an intermediary to fill in for them. Having learned to read and write, and speak English, it became very convenient for them to depend on me in lots of ways. And the more they used me, the more experienced I became in navigating a world outside the "Y", in their place.

Those early pre-teen years of growing up in the "Y" were very special to me, and I would like to think that I fully capitalized on each situation at hand, whether it be going to school, doing my homework, attending Mass, performing my chores, running errands, interpreting, my music, or even playing with my little white and colored friends, which was all a part of the natural blending into a white society. Already, I had prematurely developed working ambitions in a variety of jobs, such as; a 'young salesman' selling flower seeds door to door, a newspaper route in West Tulsa, selling newspapers at night on the corner of 10th & Boston at an all-night drive-in restaurant, distributing telephone books in the Utica Square area for Southwestern Bell Telephone Co., and a bicycle delivery boy for Crawford Drug Store in the Brookside area. During the summer, I worked the produce farms at harvest time, twelve hours a day for $1.00 per day. And with each endeavor, I always gave my earnings to Mama

CHAPTER 17

▼

THE GREAT DEPRESSION

When the stock market crashed in 1929, almost overnight, nearly everyone's livelihood in America changed for the worse, including the crumpling of America's economy into near ruin and bringing with it, some of the darkest days in the nation's history. For millions of people who had held investments in stocks, bonds, and securities, the 'crash' literally brought them down in financial chaos. Of course, Papa never had any such investments to lose, but nevertheless, he too, was hit hard in other ways. Fortunately he managed to hold on to his job with the Frisco. He was never totally uninformed as to the grim outlook that the country was in, but he did have fears that nationwide unemployment could eventually reach the Frisco, and with a fast growing family, he and Mama definitely worried that things would worsen.

They had every right to worry, as did millions of other people, because the 'crash' initiated one of the severest depressions of all time, and marked the beginning of a long period of widespread unemployment. Soon after the 'crash', millions of people were out of work, as its devastating affect spread without mercy throughout the lives of the rich, the poor, the bankers and laborers, whether white, black and brown. Millions of businesses came to a dead halt. **Mexicans and colored folks were hit especially hard** and were usually the first to get laid off. Before long, hunger and suffering became widespread, as soup lines began to form throughout America to feed the fallen victims of the depression. But by the

Grace of God, however, hunger never got quite that bad for us in the "Y". Even though fellow employees at the Frisco were being laid off right and left, Papa's number had not yet come up.

By the following year, grinding hunger throughout the country was at its worse. And the "Y" being in dead center of freight train traffic, saw many transient hobos filter through the neighborhood begging for food. Mama, who had already known all too well the pitfalls of adversity, greatly sympathized with the hobos and never turned away a single one. She always listened to their sad stories about how long it'd been since their last meal, and by their appearances, there didn't seem to be any reason to doubt their truth and sincerity. Most of their clothes were dirty, tattered and torn, but each one was willing to work for something to eat. Mama sometimes asked them to chop some firewood, which they always did gladly. She never allowed them to come in the house, but when finished with their chore, she'd fix them a plate of hot beans and rice, and a couple of hot tortillas. Immediately, they'd find a shady spot to enjoy a long over-due hot meal. When finished eating, expressions of thanks were written all over their bearded faces as they tipped their hats and departed. Scenes of poverty and hunger were commonplace everywhere, and West Tulsa was no exception. Many fathers and mothers went through months and months of desperation when they had no money to buy food for their families. For a lot of families who were once well to do would now be experiencing humiliation when standing in a soup line at the north end of Quanah street. Each morning by seven O'clock, people would be standing in line with empty one-gallon syrup buckets or other small containers, waiting for the doors to open. The soup lines that formed outside the Cosden two-story building on Quanah could sometimes be at least a block long. Many times, nearby farmers from Midco road, 21st Street to Berryhill, could be seen on the streets walking alongside their mule-drawn wagons loaded with fresh watermelons yelling repeatedly; "Watermelons!" "Watermelons!" "10 cents!" "Watermelons!"

The colored communities on the north side of Tulsa seemed to be hit even harder than the west side. Ruby Rodrigues, a close friend of the family who lived among the coloreds on East Independence Street, suffered a great deal. But the fact that her husband worked three days a week on the Frisco railroad, didn't qualify her for free soup like many others in her neighborhood. Those who did qualify, were given numbered labels to post in a conspicuous location near their front door to signify how many dippers of soup they were entitled to, because soup was being dished out according to the number of members in the household. Others stood in long commodity lines to receive free handouts of rice, flour, cabbage, and canned beef.

As the depression lingered into the thirties, chronic poverty forced many Westsiders to resort to extreme measures not previously necessary. Gardens sprang up in many backyards for growing vegetables to deal with hunger and the loss of jobs. Housewives everywhere resorted to canning vegetables and fruit. Raising chickens in back yards also became essential for many to provide meals and eggs. Burning firewood also became necessary for a lot of folks. And in extreme hardship cases, families moved in with each other. Once in a while, grown men could be seen rummaging around in trash bins for food.

I'll never forget one terribly unfortunate victim of the depression, a young friend of mine by the name of Bob Glance. We, at our house, knew we were poor, but his parents were even poorer. The incident I'm speaking of happened during the lunch hours at Celia Clinton School, when my friend Bob had nothing to eat, nor could afford lunch at the cafeteria. Every day, he came to school with no more than a pocket full of pecans, and for lunch, he just walked aimlessly around the school yard cracking and eating pecans. He didn't seem to mind it, but what he didn't like, was the obvious sympathy brought on by other kids taking notice of a poor little country boy with no lunch to eat.

Depressive times were not new for Papa and Mama who had already experienced practically every facet of hard times. Papa was only earning 36 cents per hour, and when his hours were cut back, it immediately called for tightening the belt just a little tighter. It was then that Mama decided to take up sewing. After much skimping, Papa was able to buy her a sewing machine, and before long, she would be making dresses for the girls and shirts for the boys—all from feed sacks and flour sacks. When purchasing chicken feed, or a 50-pound sack of Red Star flour, she would be very selective in the prints and colors of the cloth sacks. Of course, anyone could tell that the clothes she made for us weren't exactly 'store bought', but they served our needs very well.

Besides making a lot of our clothes, and on top of the heavy load Mama was already committed to, she took in washings and ironings to supplement Papa's income. I remember watching her do her ironings, how she'd get the fire going in the stove in our front room to heat up the hand irons. She had three of these one-pounders, each with a detachable wooden handle. While she pressed a garment with one iron, the others would be getting hot, then, she'd switch irons again and again, until she finished. As for her washings, she charged 50 cents to wash one load of clothes, which she washed outdoors in boiling water, and five cents for each shirt that she starched and pressed. Sometimes, she could make as much as $2.50 per week.

Beyond Mama's washings and ironings, Papa did his share too, by mending our shoes. Shoes were a big problem because we wore them out so fast, and besides, they were so expensive—much more expensive than dresses or shirts. But Papa handled that problem quite well. From Burgess Hardware, on credit, he purchased a cast-iron shoe stand and four different sizes of shoe molds adaptable to the stand. Plain and simple, it was a complete shoe-mending device that came in real handy when mending our shoes. Additionally, Papa went to **Brock's Shoe Shop** to buy rubber half-soles and heels. After a while, Papa got pretty good at this 'cobbler business', but once in a while, the soles would come loose, and when this happened, we had to be very careful how we walked, because every time we took a step, the shoes would make a 'slap', 'slap', 'slap' sound which made us walk with a funny little kick and with a little more precision to keep the sole from folding up under the shoe. At times, it could be very embarrassing, particularly at school, when walking in the classroom or down the hall.

During those desperate days, when the country was 'down and out' so to speak, people everywhere came together in a common effort to help one another in any way they could—even when it meant self-sacrificing. The "Y" folks too, were always there for each other, never hesitating to extend a helping hand. They faithfully turned to each other when a neighbor lost his job or when food was in short supply. It was not out of the ordinary for Mama to prepare a meal for a neighbor or arrange for them to dine with us in times of hunger

The depression years of 1929 thru' 1934 were absolutely the hardest, and it would be years before the economy turned itself around.

CHAPTER 18

▼

EDELIA FINDS HER MOTHER

Two years after the 'crash', 1931, **marked the 15th year that Edelia last saw her mother, Domitila.** She was just ten years old when she left Waco to go with Angela, the boarding house lady. On that tearful day of separation when Domitila gave Angela permission to take little Edelia with her—destination unknown at the time—it was mutually understood that the parting would only be temporary. But that arrangement was doomed from the beginning because as it turned out, mother and daughter were separated, seemingly forever. Mama never expected to see her mother again..

Since their separation, much had transpired in Mama's life. She was now completely settled down and happily married with a fast growing family. But as the fleeting years came and went, not one single day went by, that she didn't miss her mother, worrying and wondering where she could be, praying constantly that they would someday be reunited.

After all these years, Mama hadn't given up hope. Wanting to make one more attempt to find her mother, she begged Papa to start a new search. Knowing how desperately she missed her mother, he didn't hesitate at all. He, himself, had already been down that same path in missing his own mother.

Papa began with a correspondence approach like he'd done before....inquiring about Domitila's whereabouts by writing letters to the friends and acquaintances whom they'd known in Waco. But as before, this turned out to be a dead end. It was obvious that the people whom they'd known had apparently moved on or returned to Mexico. So Papa decided to try something different.

In those days, there was a newspaper in San Antonio that circulated throughout the State of Texas called "La Prensa". This periodical was completely in Spanish and therefore, would be widely subscribed to by a great number of Mexican families. Papa was already a subscriber, so he decided to place an ad for the 'lost and found'.

Ad in La Prensa

Familia Perdida:

> *Buscamos a la Señora Domitila Almeida Flores, una soltera approxima edad 40 años, nacida en Colotlan, Jalisco, Mexico. El ultimo domicilio conocido fue Waco, Texas, en el año de 1914.*
> *La busca su hija Edelia Almeida Flores de Gomez.*

Juan Gomez
P. O. Box 562
W. Tulsa, Oklahoma

[Lost Family:

> I am searching for Mrs. Domitila Almeida Flores, a single person, approximate age 40, born in Colotlan, Zacatecas, Mexico. The last known residence was Waco, Texas, the year 1914. Her daughter, Edelia Almeida Flores de Gomez is the searching party]

Having submitted his ad with the missing persons department of La Prensa, they waited for a response. At first, nothing. Once again, gloom was turning into despair, until six months later, when Papa finally received a positive response. It was a letter from Domitila written by a friend. The letter came from a little town not far from Waco, called, Marlin, Texas. It read:

Sr. Juan Gomez:

> I am Domitila Flores. In 1914, I left my daughter Edelia in the guard-
> ianship of one Angelita Castro in Waco, Texas. Is she that person?
> Please reply as soon as possible.

Domitila Flores de Salazar
(By: Anita Avila)

No sooner did Papa finish reading the last word of the letter, when Mama leaped from her chair and gave out a loud yell, "Ay, Juan!" "You did it!" "You did it!" *"Ay Diosito." "La hallaste."* "You found her!"

She grabbed Papa hysterically and began kissing all over him, jumping for joy. He, too, got caught up in all the rejoicing as they embraced each other in celebration. In an instant, his loving wife was bubbling over with happiness...and yes, even tears. Amid all the joyous shouting, even the children contracted the infectious emotion and joined the excitement. With tears still trickling down her cheeks and a choking in her voice, Mama clutched her hands prayerfully, then made the Sign of the Cross. Looking toward the heavens, she gasped, *Ay Santo Niño, Gracias a Dios."*

That very evening, Papa was on his way to the Post Office. In his hand, was a letter addressed to:

> Domitila Flores de Salazar
> c/o Anita Avila
> 910 Oak Street
> Marlin, Texas

Before depositing the letter, he made absolutely sure he had correctly printed his return address on the envelope and affixed a three-cent stamp. The letter was too important to risk getting lost. It was the reply to Domitila's letter, which read:

> Yes. I'm your daughter. I want to see you.
> I'm coming to see you. I'll be there in two weeks..

Edelia Almeida Flores de Gomez
September 1931

The next day, Papa applied for a travel pass.

On the train bound for Marlin, Texas, Mama was on pins and needles. Outwardly, there were expressions of laughter and overwhelming joy, but inwardly, she was filled with anxiety and suspense. Her heart was glad, and yet sad. Sad, because in her solitude as the train sped onward, she couldn't help recalling some of the hurtful experiences of the past when she and her mother still lived together. Like the times when there was very little food on the table, seldom new clothes to wear, and how her mother had to slave every day to make ends meet. And also, when her mother gave birth to her two little brothers—Faustín and José—and how that 'good for nothing' Tacho didn't even bother to be at her side. But the most painful memory of all—the hurting that wouldn't go away—was when she and her mother said good-bye in Waco, Texas. Because when the tragic realization of her mother's disappearance had grossly anchored itself in her mind, she could have died out of sheer desperation by the very thought of never seeing her again. But now, en route to Marlin, Texas, those days would soon be gone forever, and thanks to The Almighty, the past was just that—the past. Today, everything was beautiful in her world.

As the taxicab pulled up in front of a humble weather-beaten shack at 910 Oak Street, amid a cluster of run-down shacks, the entire family in the cab was nervous from anticipation. But in a split second, two little dark-skinned boys, shabbily dressed in blue faded overalls, homemade shirts, and wearing scuffed, high-top shoes, came racing toward the cab. Right behind the boys, was their pretty sister, wearing a cotton print dress that hung loosely well below her knees. She too was excited and curious, but walked hesitantly toward the taxi.

And then.........**Domitila! Yes—it was her.** She scrambled hurriedly off the porch, still wearing her apron and her faded high-top tennis shoes. With outstretched arms and tears streaming down her face, she cried out,

"Edelia!" "Edelia!" *"Ay, hija mia,"*

Crying, laughing, and screaming, she rushed to Mama. Sobbing bitterly and practically unable to speak, she threw her arms around her little girl, almost in a daze for the miracle that just happened. Trembling, she kept muttering, "Edelia." *"Ay, hija."*

Mama, too, was crying tears of joy, tears of sorrow, and yes, tears for the mere touch of her precious mother's waiting arms.

"Mama!" she shouted, embracing her mother with all her might. *"Ay, Mama. Ay Diosito del Cielo."* Thank God I found you. Oh, Mama, I've missed you so much." Trembling with excitement and disbelief, she kept repeating, "Oh, Mama. Oh, Mama."

For a few moments, tightly embraced in each other's arms, only the sounds of love and yearning could describe the fabulous end to the years of sorrow and emptiness. At last, no more suspense or fears of the unknown. They were reunited.

All the children bashfully began stepping out of the taxicab. First one, then two, three and four—**Cecilio, Cenobio, Manuela, and Juanito**—while **Virginia,** Mama's latest arrival—remained in the front seat of the cab. For Domitila, it was the shock of her life. She was totally overwhelmed and almost unbelieving that the little girl she lost 15 years ago, was now the mother of five beautiful kids…five little grandchildren she never knew she had. Immediately, she began showering them with hugs and kisses.

Also, for Mama—it was beyond her wildest dreams to meet two more little brothers, a little sister, and Domitila's new husband, **Bentura Salazar.**

Once inside Domitila's little house, reminiscence, joyful tears, and outbursts of laughter continued, as Domitila's eyes remained fixed on her precious daughter. In awe, she remembered her little girl as only a mere child. Still overwhelmed with emotion from the great surprise, she kept repeating *"Ay, hija mia. Bendito sea Dios."* Continuing in disbelief and tears still in her eyes, she said, *"Es increible el milagro que estoy viendo."* "The miracle I'm seeing is incredible."

Clutching her hands and wiping her eyes, she motioned for Mama

"Ven hija. Sientate aqui con migo."

"Come Edelia, sit here by me. I want a good look at you."

On introducing Papa to her mother, Domitila was most respectful, as she politely shook his hand

"Este es mi querido esposo." This is my loving husband," Mama said. "He's the one who found you."

"Mucho gusto de conocerte, Juan. No sabes la felicidad que me trajiste este dia. Que Dios te lo pague." "I'm so pleased to meet you, Juan," Domitila said, "You've no idea the happiness you brought me today. God bless you."

Papa, also, very humbly acknowledged her warm hand shake, and with a slight embrace and friendly smile, said, *"De nada, Domitila."* "Ever since the day we got married, you're all she ever talks about. She loves you very much." Kiddingly, he added, "almost as much as I love my mother who is still in Mexico. Her name is Felipa."

"Sientate Juan. Mi casa es tu casa." "Sit down Juan. My house is your house."

Domitila, now 40, short and pudgy, had remained sweet and jolly all through the years and still possessed that affectionate tenderness that immediately sparked love from all her grandchildren. Bentura—significantly older—was a tall lanky man whose mustache was almost totally gray. He couldn't speak one word of English, nor could he read or write, but he was the friendliest gentleman in the world with a very pleasing personality.

Mexico was all he could talk about.

Mama was most anxious to get acquainted with her new brothers and sister...**Benito**—the youngest at age five, **Bernardo** age nine, and especially **Carmen** age eleven. Embracing each one separately, humorously she kidded with them, asking, *"¿Deveras son mis hermanos? No lo creo."*

Top: Carmen & Edelia. Lower: Benito, Domitila, Bernardo

"Are you really my brothers and sister? I don't believe it. Come over here, Carmen," she said, "let's see if you're as tall as I am." Instantly, the two sisters became pals.

Benito and Bernardo were more reserved and bashful, not leaving Domitila's side all during the acquainting. But when Mama winked at them, it forced a smile, and soon, they loosened their shyness and gave in to her affectionate persuasion and came and sat next to her.

As she squeezed the boys tenderly, she couldn't help remembering her two previous brothers—Faustín and José—who were left with their father Tacho many years ago in San Antonio. The fond memory of her two little brothers just never went away, and now all of a sudden, as she warmly embraced Benito and Bernardo, it was as though Faustín and José had finally been found.

"Mama," asked Edelia, *"¿En todos estos años pasados, porque sería que Tacho nunca te buscó?"* "Mama, after all these years, I wonder why Tacho never looked for you?"

Pausing for a second, she continued, "Mama, I've sure missed my little brothers."

"*Hija, solo Dios sabe,*" said Domitila. "*Pero cuando perdí mis hijos a ese demonio de Tacho, ya mero me volvía loca. Tú te acuerdas que tanto sufrí por ellos. Y hasta el dia que me muera, me golpeo por que los abandone. Le pido a mi Dios que donde quera que esten, que me los guarde y que no esten sufriendo.*"

When the subject of Tacho came up, the hurt and bitterness in Domitila's voice was unmistakable, when she responded, "Only God knows, Edelia, but when I lost my boys to that devil Tacho, I almost went crazy. And until I die, I'll torture myself for having abandoned them."

Pausing for a second with a sigh of regret, she continued, "I pray to God that wherever they are, He'll watch over them, and that they're not suffering."

On seeing renewed hurting in her mother's eyes, Mama replied mournfully, "Yes, I remember. And I've prayed too. I'll always wonder where they are. Do you think they're still somewhere in San Antonio?" she asked.

"*Hija, yo no se. Ese diantre de mal-tratador no estaba contento en ningun lugar. Menos, San Antonio. Yo creo que se devolvio para Mexico con mis hijos.*"

"I don't know, *hija,*" replied Domitila. "That abusive louse wasn't happy anywhere, especially San Antonio. He probably went back to Mexico and took my boys with him."

Lingering pain was still visible on her face, as she continued. "*Ojala que tú no haigas sufrido como yo. Desde que tú nacites, la vida para mi fue muy pesada y los sufrimientos y sacrificios de la pobreza no dejaban felizidad. ¿Te acuerdas de los tiempos cuando andabamos pidiendo limosma solamente para existir? Pero esos sufrimientos no comparan al dolor en mi pecho cuando yo y tú nos perdimos en Waco, Texas. Ya las lagrimas me inchaban los ojos por tanto llorar, y hasta mis rodillas me dolian, dia y noche, por tanto rezar.*"

"Lelita, I hope you haven't suffered the way I have. Ever since you were born, life for me has been hard and heavy. And because of all the poverty and suffering, I never knew happiness. You remember the times when you and I went begging for food just to survive? But even those days of hardships won't compare to the pain in my heart when you and I lost track of each other. I cried so many tears that my eyes stayed swollen and my knees were callused from praying that we'd find each other again.

"It wasn't your fault, *hijita.*" Domitila continued, "God only knows why it happened. After you left with Angela to go North, I got very sick with an acute case of appendicitis and wasn't able to work, and when I could no longer pay the rent, I was forced to leave. When I didn't hear from you after two months, I almost went crazy. I didn't know what to do. But God was there for me when Bentura took me in. Soon after that, he moved here to Marlin, and brought me with him. This is where we were married."

"I've hurt too," Mama said, "and just like you, I've cried a river of tears. Never a day went by, that I didn't pray for the day when we'd find each other again. Praise God, I found you now, and I'll never lose you again." "I promise."

For the next two days, Mama and Domitila spent hours on end, getting reacquainted.

Though neither had many pleasant memories to talk about, their reunion absolutely put an end to fifteen years of worrisome suspense over each other's whereabouts.

It didn't take very long for Papa and Bentura to hit it off. Both being railroad workers, found they had much in common even though at the present time Bentura was out of work. The more they talked, however, the more Papa was getting ideas about *why couldn't Bentura and his whole family move to West Tulsa?* What with the Frisco constantly expanding, surely Bentura could find work with them. It didn't take long for Papa's idea to take hold, because the following month, with a little financial help, they made the move, but not to West Tulsa. Instead, they moved to Sapulpa, Oklahoma, where he actually found work on the railroad. For the next several years, it was pure bliss for Mama and Domitila. Living only six miles apart, Mama was able to make frequent trips to see her mother, and with each visit, they tried to make up for all the lost years.

But as luck would have it, when Bentura's health broke down and no longer able to work, their livelihood declined drastically, forcing Domitila and Bentura to move to Oklahoma City to live with Bentura's brother, a younger man named **Chicho Salazar**. Although it became more difficult for Mama and Domitila to see each other, thanks to Papa's eligibility for free travel passes, she continued making occasional trips. Most trips had never been a problem, except for one unfortunate trip

It began one day when Mama had not seen her mother, Domitila, for quite some time and was beginning to worry. So Papa ordered a travel pass and soon, we'd all be going to Oklahoma City. On the day of our trip—without Papa—it was up to me to get us a taxicab. Now that I was older and speaking English a lot more, Mama looked to me to be the spokesman and interpreter. So to call a cab, I had to go to Mr. Matthew's Cafe to use his phone, since no one in the "Y" had a phone. Quite simply, I gave directions to the "Y" and promised to meet the driver at the railroad crossing for further directions to our house. On his arrival, the cab driver got very tickled when we all piled in his cab. He hadn't counted on so many of us. But he was a nice man and helpful with Mama's suitcase, tossing it on the luggage rack on top of the cab. Right away, I instructed him to take us to the train station on Cincinnati Street in Tulsa.

The train depot that day was as busy as a beehive. I didn't realize that so many people traveled. Inside the train station were ticket offices, concession stands, shoe shine stands, bell-hops, a coffee shop, magazine stands, and even public rest rooms. Train conductors and bell boys in their shiny blue serge uniforms, wearing little black and red caps, could be seen scurrying all over the station's main floor.

Before departure time, which was 10:15 AM, all of us were already on board waiting for movement of the train. We found a seat and got comfortable, then waited for that clickety-clack train ride to Grandma's. We had taken this trip before, and as a matter of fact, the same 10:15 departure schedule. But this trip turned out to be different. No one told us that this particular train—the Silver Bullet—had been reserved for local dignitaries going to Oklahoma City for a political rally, and that employee travel passes were not valid on this special train. To our great shock, we had boarded the wrong train. By the time the conductor finally entered our coach to validate everyone's tickets, 45 minutes had elapsed since leaving the station. When he finally reached our seat, Mama politely handed him our pass, quite relaxed and unaware of our mistake. And just as he was about to punch our pass for validation, he noticed it was a Frisco employee pass. Peering over the rim of his bifocals at Mama, and taking one more look at the pass in his hand, he said, "Ma'am, I'm sorry, but this pass is not good on this train. I hate to tell you this, but you'll have to get off at the next stop." Even though Mama didn't understand every word the conductor said, she knew something was wrong. After I explained it to her, not wanting to contest his order, she said, "*Dile que esta bien. Ahi nos bajamos.*" "Tell him it's alright. We'll get off."

Bristow, Oklahoma was the next stop, and that's where he dumped us off. Humiliated and disoriented, we began walking aimlessly toward Main Street. For us, it was the sheer pits, walking down a strange street like a bunch of lost sheep not knowing where to go or what to do next. Luckily, Mama had a few extra dollars, so she decided that the only choice we had, was to rent a room at one of the hotels on Main Street. At a nearby hotel, we rented a small upstairs room with only one bed, which would have to suffice until we figured out the seriousness of our problem.

After getting settled in our hotel room, I went back to the depot to inquire about the validity of our pass. Lucky for us, our pass would be valid the very next morning. Now we could all rest easy. The snacks that Mama had packed for the trip, we enjoyed thoroughly, while sitting all over the floor and on the bed. The next morning, with a sigh of relief, we were on board the train again. This time, it was the right train.

Looking back on some of those trips we made to Oklahoma City as a youngster, I saw first hand, the reality of Grandma's meager living conditions. One day in particular, when Bentura invited me to go with him on his early morning rounds to the Farmers produce market, a mile away. By 6:00 A.M., we were on our way, on Walker Street, pushing a two-wheel wooden cart in the direction of town. I thought it was fun, getting to push that wagon along the edge of some partially abandoned streets. Bentura enjoyed having me along. With me along, it would make his day less dreadful, because we weren't going to buy produce or fruit, we were going to salvage discarded stuff—that's right—throw-aways! Each morning, the market vendors culled their produce and fruit, separating the fresh from the 'not-so-fresh' and the ripe from the over-ripe, tossing the non-fresh and the over-ripe into large open-top bins, which would later be hauled away to 'who knows where'. Not surprisingly, there were other people pushing carts same as us, scrounging around, hoping to strike a generous haul.

By mid-afternoon, we'd be on our way home with some bananas, perhaps with some apples and oranges, some tomatoes, and maybe some lettuce. After arriving home, Bentura took his load of salvaged produce and fruit to the back porch where the clean-up process would start all over again. Carefully, he cut away the spoilage, keeping the edible remains for Domitila to cull even more.

The days of the great depression were disappearing for a lot of people, and from all indications, things were beginning to improve nationwide. But for Grandma and her family, it may have worsened. I often wondered if things were really that destitute at her house, or was it Bentura who just had to have something to do. It might have been a little of both.

▼

CHAPTER 19

WEST TULSA TOWN—1934

Of all the cities in the United States, Papa and Mama could not have chosen a more pleasant city to settle down in, as this quaint little Oklahoma town on Highway 66. Any other town would, no doubt, have been too big with too many people, too much traffic, and too much commotion. But the people of West Tulsa were never too busy to be friendly and neighborly, or to take the time to stop and get acquainted. And they could very well do without the hustle and bustle of uptown city slickers scurrying in all directions. It wasn't unusual for Westside families to go next door to borrow a cup of sugar or some salt, or maybe a cup of flour. Neighbors here, did this all the time, and gladly, while people in the big city didn't always trust each other.

One might wonder; was *West Tulsa merely an extension of the City of Tulsa?* Well...yes...but not exactly. Of course, it wasn't a municipality all its own, but this little town was more than just another town. It was a perfect little business district on a two-lane street with no stoplights, and also, comprised of an urban community autonomously separated from the 'mother city' by the Arkansas River, which created a certain independence from town central. And besides, it had everything the big city had, except, on a smaller scale, which was just the way the Westsiders wanted it. Nothing fancy, nothing outlandish, no need for high-pressure sales people or tall buildings boasting national prominence—just a plain and simple community of ordinary down-to-earth people away from the streams of busybodies in a hurry to prove something. So, since our little town already offered just about everything the big city did, why cross the river to shop or do business over there, when West Tulsa already had it all.

Early on, Papa and me gradually became quite familiar with many of the streets of West Tulsa, and patronized a variety of the stores, particularly, the grocery stores and the clothing stores. To help out with the language, Papa always took me along. He knew the merchants who found his broken English comical and amusing, and knowing this, he took advantage of it by inviting a friendly and comical response when shopping in their store. They, in turn, enjoyed teasing him when he mixed Spanish words with English. Sometimes, jokingly, they'd say, "speak English, Juan, you know I don't understand Greek."

The busiest grocery store in West Tulsa, without a doubt, was **Fred Walker Grocery.** They did a fantastic business year round, and for good reason. Fred was a great grocery man with a terrific, appealing personality—loud and comical when he talked, and always with a joke and a hearty laugh. He was a heavy-set man with lots of black hair, and probably weighed 200 pounds. I never saw him without a cigar in his mouth. He was very good to our family, and every payday when Papa paid off his bill, Fred always threw in a free sack of candy, cookies or some kind of treat for the kids. Fred's brother, Scotty, usually made all the deliveries and he knew which house in the "Y" was ours. Papa's grocery bill was always pretty high, requiring most of his paycheck, but Fred never worried about it. He knew how conscientious Papa was about settling his account. He once referred to Papa as 'honest as the day is long'.

Some of the items Fred stocked can't be found in today's grocery stores, such as; peanut butter in the bulk at the butcher counter, pure lard in a three pound pail, Calumet Baking Powder in the little red can with an Indian Head profile, Blue Ribbon Bread for seven cents a loaf, Red Star Flour and Mother's Oats—the cereal with a prize inside the box, like; cups, saucers, cereal bowls, all made from pink depression glass. Fred also carried Hale's Leader Ground Coffee, Prince Albert Smoking Tobacco in the little red flip-top can, Golden Grain and Bull Durham Smoking Tobacco in cute little cloth sacks with draw-strings, Nehi Soda Pop in the water coolers, Licorice Sticks, Babe Ruth and O'Henry candy bars, Holloway Suckers, Kracker Jacks, and many other favorite items.

I never understood why West Tulsa—as small as it was—had so many grocery stores. Of course, for us, Fred Walker was the only one, but there were others, like; **George Bunch Grocery, Frank Baker Grocery, Elmer Cline Grocery, Banther Grocery, Crow's Grocery, Seaton's Grocery**, and even a **Safeway.** We never traded very much at any of these stores, they were either too far away, didn't extend credit, or perhaps, Fred Walker was Papa's favorite.

One of the merchants in town that Papa really liked was Whitey Cox, owner of **Cox's Dry Goods Store**, a super friendly blonde-haired man in his mid forties. From the minute Papa and I walked in his store, he and Whitey would start in on each other, kidding, teasing, and joking, especially about Papa's badly broken English—which was not always intelligible when he mixed his limited English vocabulary with Spanish, using a 'rolling R' accent characteristic to his native tongue.

"Ha lo, Parna" Papa would say (Hello Partner)

"Hi, Ju'ann. (Juan) Where've you been hidin'?"

"Me weh'keh. Tu macheh weh'keh. No time to chop."

"Are you kidding me? C'mon now, you don't work all the time."

"Ges ah doo. Me weh'keh siete diaz."

"Seven days? Ju-ann you cain't fool me. If you worked seven days a week all the time, then how come you have so many kids. Answer me that," Whitey would say with a foxy laugh.

"Me no weh'keh de noche," nights. Papa came back, with a silly chuckle, nudging Whitey's arm with his elbow.

"Ha macheh ju choose hoy. Ma boy needeh som choose."

"Ju'ann, I don' t sell choose, I sell shoes. How many pairs do you need today?"

"Jus wan par, but me no gotta no maney. Poot on ma beel, Okay?"

"You mean your account, don't you Ju'ann?"

"Ges. Ha macheh ju choose for heem?"

"How much? Today, they're a dollar ninety five."

"Oh, das tu macheh."

"Too Much? Aw c'mon, Ju'ann. Tell you what, for you, only one dollar and fifty cents. Okay?"

"Okay, I buy."

"By the way, Ju'ann, where's your other boys. They need some choose too. Good God, Ju'ann, now you've got me talking like you." he joked.

"Parna, nex jeer they get som choose."

"Okay, Ju'ann. But I cain't make any money unless you bring in all your kids. How's the wife?"

"Mama Okay. Che in la casa mekeh frijoles and tortillas and anudder bebe."

"Another Kid? Ye Gads, Ju'ann! You better give her a break. How many does that make now?"

"Tu many/"

"No Ju'ann. Never too many. You've got a great family. Come over here. I want to show you some new overalls that just came in."

This is just a typical conversation between Whitey Cox and Papa each time we came to his store. He always got a kick out of the way Papa grossly mispronounced every word, jabbering and gesturing, trying to make conversation. Papa always knew what he wanted to say, but didn't exactly know the words, and even if he did, he still couldn't have pronounced them right. And that's what tickled Whitey so much. He never embarrassed Papa with his teasing, and both had lots of fun taking jabs at each other. Each time we came in to his store, I always knew I was going to be outfitted with some new clothes, perhaps, a pair of hi-top shoes, a shirt, or maybe a pair of long-handle underwear—the kind with the rear flap. The exciting part was when Papa bought me some blue overalls just like he and the Frisco employees wore.

Another clothing store that Papa liked real well was **Julius Jacobson's** on 17th Street. Here, too, Papa felt totally relaxed when shopping for clothes, because Julius also happened to be an immigrant from another country...somewhere in the Middle East. The commonality they shared was the language. Neither could speak it properly, and they often teased each other for their stuttering dialect. Although Julius could speak English much more intelligibly than Papa, he still had a terrible accent. Julius was a large, heavy set man, with long, course eye brows and a broad plump nose. On the times when we came into his store, he and Papa spent a lot of time just talking about the old days back home, and each time, they re-hashed the past as though they'd just met for the first time.

The other clothing store in West Tulsa—**Shepherds Dry Goods**—wasn't as popular as the other two. Papa didn't care for 'old man' Shepherd. Mister Shepherd didn't like shoppers who came in his store just to browse. And when they did, he followed them close behind, as suspicious of pilfering. But Mama liked Shepherds. She thought Shepherds was the best place in town to buy sewing material, because they stocked such a wide variety of fabrics that would serve almost any purpose. This would include an assortment of plain white material, prints, seer-sucker, striped linen or cotton, buttons, bows, ribbons, lace and thread. Shepherds had it all. What Mama especially liked, was the patterns for making shirts and dresses which not only came in the exact sizes she needed, but also, came pre-cut.

For the people of West Tulsa, drug stores were as important and necessary as doctors.

In particular, I'm speaking of **Ozark Pharmacy,** owned and operated by Doc Reynolds on Quanah Boulevard, just off 19th Street. He was not a large person, balding slightly and wore glasses. He was a graduate pharmacist, and drugs were his primary sales product—prescribed or otherwise. But you wouldn't believe this was necessarily so, because the minute you walked in and looked around, you'd see all kinds of neat household items, trinkets and novelties. In the center of the floor, were two sets of quaint black wrought-iron tables and chairs for his soda fountain customers. Malts and shakes were just ten cents and plum delicious. Papa had a charge account with Ozark Pharmacy and used it quite often, but only for medicine. Many times, when someone in our family got sick, Mama would send me to *la botica.* I would describe the symptoms to Doc Reynolds, such as fever, nausea, diarrhea, etc., then he would go to the back room and mix up a bottle of 'get well' medicine, type up a label with instructions, prepare a charge ticket for me to sign, then I'd be on my way home. Doc Reynolds was truly an asset to West Tulsa, a real friendly man who was always there for us in times of illness.

We had another drug store in West Tulsa. It was the **Dooley Drug Store** also located on Quanah on 22nd Street. For some reason, we didn't patronize them very much. Maybe it was because of the automobile traffic on Quanah that Mama was afraid of.

When it came to serious illness in our family, for us, it was none other than **Doctor J. H. Taylor**—a practitioner of General Medicine, about 55 years old, and already balding on top. His office, along with other business offices, was located upstairs on West 17th Street above the Cameo Theater. He probably wasn't the only doctor in West Tulsa, but he was our doctor—and because of the size of our family and the many illnesses that came along, we would eventually get to know him quite well. Doctor Taylor made house calls and wherever he went, he always carried his little black medicine bag at his side, which by all means, contained a stethoscope. My...how well I remember those squeaky wooden stairs and the narrow hallway leading to his two-room office. He knew me by my first name, and more than once, I rode in his long black Studebaker when I went to fetch him.

Across from Ozark Pharmacy—also on Quanah Boulevard—was the most unique hardware store in the country—Yes...it was **Burgess Hardware.** Mr. Burgess, a fairly large man, six feet or more, operated one of the most vastly stocked hardware stores to be found anywhere. From the minute you walked in the front door, you would stand in awe—amazed at the enormous mixture of inventory that covered almost every inch of floor space. He carried every size of nuts, bolts, screws, and nails imaginable. Tools, wrenches and outdoor equipment could be seen everywhere. Guns, rifles, shotguns, you name it, he had it. He also carried a variety of wood stoves and outdoor water pumps, which were always in big demand for people living in the bottom lands of West Tulsa, including us. When things needed fixin' around our house, Burgess' is the first place Papa would go, and me right alongside. Mr. Burgess shared the same building with **Bumgarner Furniture**

West Tulsa also had its own lumberyard. It was the **Long Bell Lumber Company**, located on 19th Street, just around the corner from Quanah. They stocked just about everything in the way of building materials; lumber, roofing, fencing, chicken pens, cattle pens, and offered free delivery. Leon—the manager—was a great man to do business with, and very obliging when we needed credit for taking care of small projects around the house. They knew Papa by his first name, and eventually, they would know mine too. From our house, their lumberyard was just a hop, skip, and a jump across the tracks.

And, how about a movie theater? Well…West Tulsa had one of those too. It was the **Cameo Theater** located on 17th Street just around the corner from Quanah Boulevard. Gosh, this movie house was one of the hottest spots in town. Admission was only five cents. Can you imagine that? Just a nickel. And while you're at it, imagine this…most of the time, I didn't have a nickel. However, empty milk bottles could be redeemed by any grocer in town for a nickel, so, I'd start looking for empty milk bottles to sell so I could go to the Saturday afternoon matinee. It was imperative not to miss any of those serials and westerns, because how else would I know if the good guys with the white hats and white horses rounded up all the outlaws. My favorite good guys were; Gene Autry, Buck Jones, Randolph Scott, Tom Mix, Ken Maynard, Hop-along Cassidy, Richard Talmage, and others by Zane Grey. Also, every Friday night was family night, when during intermission, they turned on the house lights and from the stage, they raffled off a $50. basket of groceries. It was important not to lose our ticket stub, because it just might have the winning number. Of course, we never did win, but we had a lot of fun trying.

Another important business establishment in West Tulsa for those having financial difficulties, which was a lot of people a lot of the time, was the **West Tulsa Loan Company** located on 17th Street, upstairs, next door to Dr. Taylor's office. When Papa needed some quick cash, he could always go here and borrow small amounts—say 5,10,20 dollars, usually with terms of a 30-day payback. Papa was a good customer of theirs, because quite frequently, he needed a few extra dollars to tide him over 'til the next payday, as was probably the case with many other Westside customers. Many times, instead of appearing in-person to request a loan, Papa would send me. All that was necessary was a hand-written request with his signature on it. One thing about Papa, he was a man of his word and had established a very good credit reputation.

Even though our little town didn't compare in size to the central district across the river, we still qualified for our own post office. Absolutely! Our **West Tulsa Post Office**, located on Quanah Boulevard, next door to the nickel and dime store, had everything the main downtown post office had: a General Delivery window for those who didn't have a private mail box, a stamp window, and hundreds of little glass-front mail boxes with combination locks and box numbers. Since we didn't have an official mailing address in the "Y", Papa rented one of their boxes for receiving our mail. Our box number was #562. I remember going there many times with Papa when he mailed money to my grandmother, Felipa. I can still see me and Papa standing at the center island-counter, as Papa very meticulously addressed the envelope after inserting a money order, licking it closed, and affixing a 3-cent stamp on it.

Also in our little town, we had a bakery. Yes…it was **Cox's Bakery and Cafe.** It was owned and operated by Mr. R. L. Cox, a tall slender man with blonde wavy hair, and very pleasant when waiting on customers. His biggest volume of customers was young school children who attended Celia Clinton School across the street, including me. His bakery-cafe was long and narrow, serving donuts, sweet rolls, and other pastries on one side, and a long counter with bar stools on the other. Imagine this, his hamburgers were two for a nickel, his donuts were two for a nickel, and a pint of milk was only 3 cents. This was his 13 cents lunch special.

At the end of Quanah Boulevard on 17th, just behind our **Fire Station,** was a five-acre field where our **Medicine Show** held its fantastic parade of stage shows. They didn't come to town every year, but when they did, wow! Everyone in West Tulsa, and probably for miles around, came to enjoy a night of spectacular events, watching it come alive with exciting vaudeville routines, minstrel acts, girlee dancers, Suwanee river skits, and those flashy stage shows pushing the sales of snake-bite oil and cure-all liniment. Papa took me there once, and I'll never forget it.

I remember **Sunset Park,** an exciting amusement park located at the south end of West Tulsa on Quanah Street near the streetcar crossing. Saturday nights were special. That's when many local people from West Tulsa, Red Fork, and Carbondale came to have a good time. Even if they didn't have much money to spend, they could still come and join a lively Saturday of fun and excitement, strolling over the grounds eating roasted peanuts and cotton candy. If nothing else, it gave them someplace to go, or something to do for entertainment. Sometimes, on pretty Sunday afternoons, families would gather for a picnic. It was a dandy little park, complete with a variety of rides, a Ferris wheel, a Roller Coaster, a swimming pool, and even a playground area for small children equipped with sliding boards, teeter-totters, and swings. Of course, we never went swimming, we just watched the others from a distance. But the big attraction was the Jack Rabbit Roller Coaster—a very exciting ride. Its elevation was not dangerously high, but the fast sharp curves and dazzling steep drops were absolutely breath taking. Papa took me to Sunset Park only once and let me ride the roller coaster—and boy, oh boy—what a ride.

Not too far from Sunset Park, along the railroad tracks south of 25th Street, was another place where Papa and I went a few times. It was the **Frisco's cattle feeding pens.** Papa liked this place because on seeing cattle herds, it always reminded him of the days when he rounded up strays on Panfilo's ranch back home in Mexico. At varying times, this is where the Frisco Railway Company unloaded cows and steers from cattle cars for feeding and watering—then loaded them up again, bound for other destinations. Sometimes, this process continued round the clock and for days. Frisco employees, who herded the cattle through the cattle chutes, hollering and yelling as they cracked their leather whips, weren't real cowboys, but they sure knew how to handle the herds. Papa enjoyed being around cattle. They seemed to bring back nostalgic memories of the simple country life back home in Villa de Reyes. Sometimes, in his own way of talking, he'd strike up a conversation with some of the colored workers who operated the feeding pens.

Once in a great while, Papa and I went to **Ermawitz BBQ** on 25th Street, right off of Quanah Boulevard to buy a small order of barbecue ribs for supper. But this only happened when Mama was sick or unable to cook. The Ermawitzes were fine Catholic people who always spoke to us in church on Sundays. Albert, their oldest son, was a good friend of mine, as were his sisters; Veronica, Virginia and Mary.

I'll never forget **West Tulsa Park**, located on 22nd Street and Olympia—for reasons both good and bad. I liked the fact that the **West Tulsa Library,** just north of **Eugene Field Public School,** was located near the sprawling grounds of the recreation park that covered one entire city block. I remember how on certain weeknights during the summer, they offered outdoor movies. Lots of people gathered around a giant movie screen to watch free picture shows. Many brought their own hand-made fans for fanning themselves during the hot evening breezes as they sat on the grass, and others brought their own chairs. In the park, there was a tennis court and a nice swimming pool, including a bathhouse and rest rooms. Even though I liked this park, I seldom went there for recreation because of the bullies and little white boys who didn't want Mexican kids in their park—and liked us even less because we were Catholic. Many afternoons on our way home from St. Catherine School—they'd be waiting for us. They'd call us 'catlickers' and chase us out of the park. Occasionally, we had to fight our way out of the park. As for the West Tulsa Library, it really was a neat place. I remember Mrs. Ungerman—the librarian—who always sat at the front desk wearing those heavy rimmed eyeglasses, and how no one ever spoke above a whisper while in the library. Those were the rules back then, and Mrs. Ungerman saw to it that silence was observed, especially, if other people were in the library reading. If anyone talked out loud, she'd take off her glasses and get your attention by pointing her pencil at you, or tapping it on the edge of her desk.

Another unforgettable event in West Tulsa was **Halloween.** Quanah Boulevard was the great attraction on Halloween night. There were no house-to-house or trick or treat invasions by little goblins, but playful tricksters were plenty. Quanah came alive at dark, as most Westsiders converged on our two-lane street to participate in the Halloween parade of clowning show-offs. After roping off Quanah Boulevard from 17th to 21st Street, it would be completely packed with paraders and spooks. Halloween costumes were not necessarily the style…people just painted up their faces, wore scary masks, and dressed shabby and silly as they paraded up and down the street in droves. Not too many people could afford store-bought costumes, so they made their own out of old raggedy worn-out britches, old shirts, old hats, checkered hankies, or anything else resembling craziness or just plain wacky. Halloween was a great fun-making night for all the local folks, and even for the tricksters. Those guys carried wooden paddles, and if you dropped your guard just for a second, you might get whopped on the 'rump'. As always, however, there was some mischief and pranksters to beware of, but most of it was playful tricks without any serious destructive intentions—*except for the tricksters who pushed over outdoor toilets.* The climax of this great evening of spooks and ghosts would be music and a street dance in the middle of the intersection of 17th and Quanah Boulevard.

Away from Quanah Boulevard on West 21st street, was the **Annual Soap Box Derby.** This was still another exciting sports event that brought Westsiders together on certain warm Sunday afternoons in the community of Berryhill—just two miles west of town. This event was simply racing little home-made race cars, made out of lumber and empty wooden soap boxes, brightly painted in a wide variety of colors and fancy designs. Since all these motorless race cars were gravity weight-driven, it required a steep hill for coasting. And the perfect hill for this grand racing event for young boys, would be none other than the highest hilltop around...in the community of Berryhill, on 65th West Avenue, near the High School. Just a pre-teen myself, I recall how the boys would line up at the starting line and wait their turn. As their numbers were called, two at a time, and at the toot of the whistle, the coaches would quickly release the blocks from under the front wheels...and away they went—downhill—as fast as their little cars could coast. Practically half of the population of West Tulsa waved and cheered their favorite little competitor from both sides of the grassy embankments of the quarter-mile raceway. The winners were picked for their racing speed, distance, and the uniqueness of construction. Yes—the days of West Tulsa's Soap Box Derby racing days were absolutely exciting and memorable for the people of our little town.

Besides the establishments mentioned above, there were numerous others absolutely worthy of mention. They were: **Community State** Bank between 16th & 17th Street, **Hardesty Jewelers** next door to the post office, the **Rita Theater** across the street from the bank, the **Bailey Ambulance Service** which was noted for its prompt response to westside emergencies in their long, bright purple vehicle stationed at 18th and Phoenix, and there was **Cantrell's Feed Store** where Mama sent me to buy chicken feed, and sometimes, baby chicks for 8 cents apiece. Next door to Cantrells was the **Ice House** that supplied ice in small size blocks for the community. And how about **People's 5 & 10 Cent Store** next to the Post Office where people could buy practically anything imaginable in the way of household and kitchen supplies, sewing material, cosmetics, toiletries, school supplies, novelties, trinkets, knickknacks, arts, crafts and thousands more items—including a soda fountain. By way of restaurants, there was the **Silver Castle** on 23rd & Quanah Boulevard, the **D &D Barbecue** at 24th Street, operated by Dick & Dale Glove, the **Deluxe Cafe, Bar T's Grill, Paul Barr's Restaurant** located in the Mid-Continent Refinery complex, and a **Greek Restaurant** behind **Oklahoma Tire & Supply.** Bars and Parlors also were plenty: **Dick Perry's Billiards** on 17th, **Rex's Beer Parlor** also on 17th, **Rex's Pool Hall** east of the Cameo Theater, and **Nancy's Bar** nicknamed "The Bloody Bucket" where the rough and tough guys of West Tulsa hung out. Then there was the **Potato Chip Factory** which later became **Cotton's Club,** and just another beer joint near 23rd Street which had a policy of hiring only bar maids who weighed at least 250 pounds. On Saturday nights, Cotton usually had five bar maids; two behind the bar, and three serving customers, while other fun-loving customers danced in the middle of the floor to the music of a fiddle and guitar. And how about **Tony Rego's Bar?** Tony had previously played baseball for the Tulsa Oilers as catcher. Inside his bar, he had private booths with draw curtains for his best customers. Other stores were: **Glencliff Dairy, Webbers Root Beer, Port Annex Ice Cream Parlor** across the street from Fred Walker's, **Fields Candy Store** on Olympia Street, the two-story **Baker Hotel** across the street from the Cameo Theater that also served as the boarding station and turn-around point for the electric trolley cars, **Mrs. Ada Sales** who ran an apartment house directly behind **Charlie's Hamburgers,** the **Excel Cleaners, Linde Air Products** along the Frisco railroad tracks on 17th Street, **Fox's Cement Block Foundry** on Olympia street, and **Gay Welding** at 16th and Quanah. Lastly, was the **Glenn Sand Company** located at the northern tip of Quanah Boulevard at the **Arkansas River Bridge.**

Nostalgically speaking, West Tulsa was more than just a typical little town—it was a town of pride and dignity—the perfect model of a small-town transformed into a close community of Westsiders, instead of a city. Despite the energetic ambitions of our town's entrepreneurs, it never lost its quaintness of hometown America…all of which, evolved around the magic of our stately **Quanah Boulevard.** From the beginning, West Tulsa was destined to become famous world-wide with two of the world's biggest oil giants; the **Texaco Oil & Refining Company** on 25th Street, and the **Mid-Continent Petroleum & Refining Company** on 17th Street, both of which became major oil suppliers around the world. Lastly, I must also include **The St. Louis-San Francisco Railway Co.,** for its enormous contribution to West Tulsa for having established one of the largest Railway Freight and Transportation Hubs in the Southwest—right here in our own little town.

From top to bottom, from A to Z, and without exception, **all of the above,** in my opinion, created their own healthy economy by employing literally hundreds, and perhaps thousands of Westsiders during the tough post-depression years.

In the shadows of West Tulsa, was **The Colored Community** on 21st Street, across the tracks from the "Y". They were still not completely accepted by the white community, but ever since the race riot of 1921, peace seems to have settled over the two peoples. There was no more animosity from the colored people, but if there was, at least, it wasn't apparent. They moved about West Tulsa freely and without fear, some holding low level jobs with some of the merchants in town, such as dishwashers, janitors, shoe-shine boys, and bicycle delivery boys.

But the majority of the working adults—those working in the Greenwood Colored District in north Tulsa—still had to sit in the rear of the bus when commuting. The West Tulsa colored community, much like the "Y", and also being bounded on all sides by Frisco's busy rail yards, consisted of about 20 families, and extended southward to the foot of Red Fork Mountain. These families were a lot like us, large in numbers, but poorer. Many of them were unemployed, while some worked for the Frisco alongside Papa. As a young boy, I sometimes wandered to their side of the tracks to play with young colored kids. Playing with them is where I learned my first English words. We didn't pay any attention to the different color of our skin, and therefore, never gave it a second thought about racism. In their community was a small four-stool Cafe housed in a rickety old shack less than one block from our house. It was owned and operated by Mr. Mathew, an elderly gentleman, and his waitress, Roberta. Every night, a loud jukebox could be heard blaring away continuously with Jazz and Soul music. Mr. Mathew didn't exactly have a thriving business, but I'll always remember two of his specialties—they were his 5-cents fried pies and his delicious 5-cents hamburgers. And as often as I could scrape up a nickel, I'd run to Mathew's Cafe with it. Next door to his Cafe, was a boxing arena where every Friday night, young aspiring boxers—myself included—and half of the colored community would gather for the evening boxing matches. It seemed that every boxer who entered the ring, had aspirations of becoming another 'Joe Louis'.

Having settled in West Tulsa, thus far, was only the beginning of a new dawn for us, as our family slowly began making headway toward easing the language barrier. Little by little, Papa was becoming braver and braver, as he attempted to become better acquainted with the local store owners. And in doing so, he gradually picked up a few English words that allowed him to venture into town more frequently. For the most part, the merchants always treated Papa very friendly, and seldom, a sign of discrimination.

CHART OF ESTABLISHMENTS ON SOUTH QUANAH BOULEVARD—1939

Address

1428 Glenn Sand Company	1505 West Tulsa Pipe
1512 Smith Filling Station & Used Cars	1601 Gay Welding
1602 Faaut Restaurant	
1604 West Tulsa News	
1604 l/2 Rooms for rent	
1608 Baptist Tabernacle	1609 Henry Auto Salvage
	1615 Kettle Oil Co
	1617 McDowell Restaurant
1638 Voss Truck Lines	
1648 Reed Filling Station	
1704 Westside Cleaners	1705 Beauty Studio
1706 Radkey Barber Shop	1707 Dr. R. C. Farris
1708 Westside Restaurant	1709 Westside Beer Tavern
1712 West Tulsa Bank	
	1713 l/2 West Tulsa Lodge #64
1716 Rexall Drug Store	1719 Westside Cafe
1722 Martin Grocery	
1724 Davidson Barber Shop	
1726-A West Tulsa Post Office	
1726-B Hardesty Jewelry	
1728 Shepherds Dry Goods	
1730 Fine Grocery	

1730 l/2 Grand Apartments

1732 Peoples 5 & 10 Cent Store

1734 L. R. Billiards

1736 Baltimore Hotel

1738 Cox & Sons Dry Goods Store   1801-07 Okla Tire & Supply

1802 Safeway Grocery Store

1806 Bailey Shoe Repair

1810 B & B Grocery   1817 Used Car Lot

1820 McLuckie Restaurant

1824 McCulloch Used Cars   1825 Southland Filling Sta

                                         1901 Wilkerson Used Cars

1904 Davis Yank Ser Sta

                                         1905 l/2 Kaufman Hotel

                                         1909 Quanah Grocery

                                         1909 l/2 West Tulsa Beauty Shop

                                         1911 Bumgarner Furniture

1920 Ozark Pharmacy

                                         1926 Brock Shoe Repair

1928 Banther Grocery

2004 Carpenter Blacksmith

2012 Fred Walker Grocery Store

2014 Bob Lyles Barber Shop

2014 l/2 Tulsa Tribune Sub Station

2016 Frank Baker Grocery

2018 Tony Rego Beer Tavern

2020 Cox's Bakery & Hamburgers

2100 Celia Clinton Elementary School

2027 Glen Seaton Grocery

2101 Frazier Restaurant

2105 N & B Foods

2107 Harvard Cleaners

2109 Auto Repair Shop

2111 Fruehauf Trailers

2127 Tire Shop

2131 Aldridge Linen & Towel

2139 Boyd Blacksmith

2144 Johnson's Beauty Shop

2150 Church of the Nazerine

2211 Upchurch Restaurant

2218 Cantrell Feed Store

2219 Bunch Grocery

2232 Filling Station & Welding Shop

2234-A Anthamatten Barber Shop

2234-B Dooley Drug Store

2234-C Till Grocery

2239 Brownie Potato Chip

2250 Magness Barber Shop

2252 Stegall Grocery

2301 Ingram Fillng Station

2305 Pop-In Restaurant

2317-A Russell Auto Repair

2317-B Risner Used Cars

2323 H & S Tires

2327 Silver Castle Cafe

2331 Baker Tourist Court

2402 Clinton Service Station

2409 Covert Used Cars

2413 Halstead Electric

2500 Howard Park

CHAPTER 20

▼

PAPA'S MUSIC AND OUR OLE' CHEVY

It was during the early years of the depression, when I first learned about music. Since Papa was a musician, quite naturally, I discovered a musical talent of my own. My very first instrument was an eight string mandolin, the one Papa always kept hung on a nail in the front room. It must have been awfully expensive, because he always handled it with extreme care and cautioned me to do the same. Every time I practiced, he watched me very closely and was really pleased when he realized I had a natural ear for music. He encouraged me to practice regularly and promised me a nickel when I learned to play my first song. The first song I learned was 'Rancho Grande'. In the years that followed, Papa taught me many beautiful Spanish songs, *corridas y valses*. Somehow, the songs he liked most, were love ballads, and songs that told sentimental stories about family life and hardships in Mexico.

Mama was very proud when I began learning to play music, but also apprehensive. She, too, loved music a lot and often reminisced on their early days of their marriage when Papa used to play and sing for her. But now, she recalled that everywhere she'd ever been, where there was music, there was also drinking. And that's what she didn't like. In her mind she envisioned that if I became a musician, I, too, would someday pickup a drinking habit, particularly since Papa had already started drinking. And of course, this troubled her. She used to say that only 'no good' ever came from drinking, and later, I would come to believe that she was right.

I remember when I first became old enough to listen to Papa play the mandolin, and how I wanted to learn to play like him. I remember the great musical jam sessions we used to have, before he started drinking. He dearly loved music, and loved having a good time. And when Papa felt good, we could all have a good time, even if he did get a little tipsy.

Most of Papa and Mama's friends with whom they visited regularly, were **Moses Casas** who played the guitar and also a beer drinker, and his wife **Maria.** And there was **Refugio and Catarina Hernandez**, a very friendly couple who also enjoyed having company, and often invited my parents for a visit.

One evening, Papa and Mama were invited to Moses and Maria's house near 24th Street & Rosedale for an evening of music. Mama agreed to go along, since it would give her an opportunity to visit with Maria and get away from the house for little while. Moses had also invited his brother **Ignacio**. When the music started, I, too, was having a good time, because Papa liked for me to set in with them when they played.

The evening started out great, and for the first couple of hours, it couldn't have been any better. Maria had plenty of snacks and pastries on hand for her guests but of course, the men preferred their beer. As the evening approached midnight, I was stuck with the guitar, accompanying their singing. By this time, Papa and Moses were beyond making any sense of their singing, but still wouldn't call it a night. In the end, I'm the only one playing, except now, I'm totally disgusted and wanting to quit, but Papa keeps saying, *no mas otra*, just one more. The singing lasted way past midnight, and even though I was dead tired and sleepy, he still wouldn't let me put down the guitar. Barely able to stand on their feet, they continued their singing which by now sounded more like 'three caballeros' lost in a brewery.

Mama had been begging Papa to stop drinking and to settle down. She had been ready to go home hours ago. When he finally sat down on the sofa—that was it—he had passed out. Mama was so embarrassed at his humiliating binge and ever so apologetic to Maria. The problem now, was, how were we going to get home? Ignacio had already gone home, and Moses was too drunk to drive. Mama suddenly realized that I would have to drive us home

After much tugging, wrestling and balancing Papa, we finally managed to get him in the back seat of the car. Although I was too young to have a driver's license, I felt confident that I could get us home. So, in the wee hours of the morning, I cranked up our old '29 Chevy and headed for the "Y" via Rosedale Avenue, just barely able to see over the steering wheel. Mama was absolutely scared to death, afraid that if I wrecked the car we would all wind up in the hospital, or if I got caught driving without a license, Papa and I would both go to jail. And she prayed and she prayed—all the way home, *"Ay Dios, Ay Diosito, Diosito mio, Jesus, Maria y Jose, Ay Santo Nino de Atocha.* Arriving home, she was so elated and thankful to all the saints in heaven for seeing us home safely, that I think she could have kissed the ground—and me too.

Our Old Chevrolet

Concerning **Our Ole' '29 Chevy,** perhaps I should explain. When Papa purchased our black, 2-door Chevy. I could never understand why he bought it, because everything we ever needed was within walking distance. His job wasn't that far away either, and besides, we certainly needed other things worse than a car...at least that's what Mama thought. Even though he only paid $65 dollars for it—on credit—she considered it a fortune. At any rate, we were now the proud owners of a family automobile.

Papa had a hard time learning to drive—the clutch was the big problem. It took him forever to get the hang of it. At first, when taking the car into town, he'd take the side streets of Quanah to avoid the main street traffic, but later, as he became more familiar with the car, he drove it to work everyday. The best use we ever got out of owning that car was the frequent trips to Sapulpa to see grandma Domitila. It was just a six-mile trip, but driving on that narrow two-lane road on highway 66, for him, it wasn't easy. There were times when we had some narrow escapes and hair-raising experiences, particularly, on the curves and downward slopes. When Papa would catch up to a slow-poke and felt courageous enough to pass......then, Lord have mercy. Not again.

Papa would push the pedal to the floor and make his move around the car up ahead. The down slopes on highway 66 didn't exactly allow enough time for passing, much less, offer enough time to adjust for on-coming traffic. And this is where it paid to pray. At the top of her lungs, Mama would be yelling at Papa, and again, calling out to her *Virgen Purisima* and all the other saints. When Papa would finally make the pass, here's where we had to hold on to our hat, because that old '29 Chevy would start zigzagging and weaving from side to side, and all the time, Papa fightin' the steering wheel trying to get this thing under control.

Sweaty hands? You bet! Tears? Yes! Laughter? Plenty!

This same experience occurred more than once and only the good Lord knows why we're all still here to talk about it

The day that **Mama wanted to learn to drive** was another hair-raising experience. It all started one Sunday afternoon, when Albert Perez jokingly suggested taking her out for a driving lesson. Since she'd never tried it before, forgetting her fears for a moment, laughingly, she agreed, thinking there was nothing to it. So, off we went. Instead of heading west on Midco road where there was virtually no traffic, she opted to go straight into the business district of West Tulsa, which was a serious mistake for anyone's first driving lesson, because as soon as we got to town, she became scared to death and regretted consenting to the crazy idea. How we ever got to Quanah Boulevard in one piece, I'll never know. Because from the minute she got in the car, she screamed. Every time she released the clutch and the car lunged forward, she screamed. And when she turned a corner and over-corrected, she screamed. When she finally got our old Chevy turned around, we were on 21st street heading toward the "Y". Now it just so happened that Mr. Banther, owner of Banther's Grocery, lived in a pretty white house on 21st Street. And just as we approached his house, zigzagging all over the road, Mama became petrified and refused to go any farther. In sheer panic, she let go the steering wheel and forgot where the break pedal was. Head on, she smacked a telephone pole right in front of Mr. Banther's house. Fortunately, she had just been driving at a snail's pace and no one was injured. However, the crash was so loud that it awakened Mr. Banther from his afternoon nap and he immediately dashed outside thinking someone had crashed into his white picket fence. But seeing that no damage was done to his property, he simply asked, "Is anybody hurt?" Of course, Mama was crying and terribly shaken, so Albert had to drive the rest of the way home. Papa was not too happy when he saw the broken headlight and bashed-in fender. Mama never again attempted driving. Thank goodness.

Still another time, we would all have another unforgettable scare. That was **when Papa was underneath our old Chevy changing the oil, and how it rolled backwards pinning his head against the framework.** He had changed the oil several times before, and always made sure to place the gears in park position and to put blocks behind the tires. But this time he forgot. While under the car laying flat on his back, he rested his head on a railroad tie he'd placed beneath the car, and this was a mistake. Because as soon as he yanked on the oil drain-plug with his wrench, the car rolled forward wedging his head between the railroad tie and the framework. Instantly, all pandemonium broke loose, because on hearing Papa's desperate screams for help, Mama and I, and all the children immediately ran outside screaming. For the next several minutes, it was sheer panic and hysteria, because all the while, Papa was trapped underneath, kicking and screaming for help. Frantically, I tried lifting the car by its front bumper, but it wouldn't budge. Yelling and panic stricken, I jumped in the front seat thinking that if I could start the car and back it up, I could free Papa. But as fate would have it, being in a hysterical state of mind, when I inserted the key in the ignition, I broke off the key inside the switch. Not knowing what else to do, I quickly jumped back out of the car and was going for help, when out of thin air, I spotted Don Arcadio and Buck Hilton coming up our dirt road with their lunch pails in their hands. When they heard my hysterical yell for help, they came running, and we three lifted the front end just enough to release the steel from Papa's head. In a flicker of a second, Papa felt his head release and came crawling out from beneath the car. Bleeding badly, he made an attempt to stand, but immediately collapsed to the ground. As soon as an ambulance arrived, he was rushed to Morning Side Hospital

To this day, I have never forgotten that horrible accident. Not the helplessness, not the screams of desperation, or the violent scene that almost brought death to Papa. God was there all the time, as he watched me try to start the car but wouldn't allow it, for if I had done so, I probably would have killed Papa.

A year or so later, Papa wrecked our old Chevy. It was totaled. He never again owned a car.

CHAPTER 21

▼

ANGELA REUNITES WITH MAMA—1935

This was the year that Mama would have another great surprise: Angela. **Since 1921** when Mama defied Angela with a runaway marriage, not one word had been heard from her. Now she's back in Mama's life once again. Through former acquaintances in Oklahoma City and former tenants at her boarding house, Angela searched for, and successfully found, Mama.

From time to time, Mama talked about Angela; telling me stories about the days when Angela first hired her mother, Domitila to work in her boarding house in San Antonio; including the ups and downs of her teen-age years. She remembered quite cheerfully, the more pleasant things about her, like; how she always saw to it that she had nice clothes to wear; the times they went shopping; and the Saturday night dances at Casa de Baile. But the one thing hard to forget was the scornful circumstances under which they parted—the fight over falling in love with Papa and her elopement. Mama always started out by telling me what a rigid woman Angela was, but in the end, the uncertainty of her whereabouts always hinted of a lonesomeness for her, and a need to make amends. No doubt she loved Angela, and in her heart, she longed to see her again. Finally, after all these years, they would be re-united. Of all places, Angela was now living in Kansas City, Missouri and still married to that nice man, Manuel.

When Angela arrived at our house, she came alone in a taxicab. The first thing I noticed about her was that her skin was pale white, with scattered liver spots on her arms, and little pitted scars on her face—the result of small pox. The silk blouse she was wearing was the color of grasshopper green and could barely contain her large, well-rounded *Chiches*. Her veiled hat was covered with tiny, black rhinestones, and her patent leather shoes had stylish, cris-cross ankle straps. *At first glance, I thought to myself, this lady is in the wrong neighborhood.*

We all knew the day she'd be coming and anxiously awaited her arrival. Of course, none of us knew what kind of person we expected to see for the first time, but she certainly surprised us all. On seeing her, my first impression was that she was not a pretty lady. She was approximately 55 years old, stone faced, short and heavy-set, and spoke with a loud and forceful voice, totally in Spanish. I soon observed that her English wasn't much better than Papa's. When she laughed, the gold in her front teeth came shining through as if to indicate a woman of means. No one ever questioned or contradicted her, instead, they stood clear of her 'take charge' personality. However, of all the strong and rigid traits she possessed, they were by no means detrimental to her personality. True, she didn't exactly impress people at first glance, but in days to come, we would all find out how truly generous she could be.

From the minute she stepped out of the taxicab and walked through our front gate, passed the wood shed, Angela was overwhelmed by our drabby little shack and its unsightly surroundings. But on seeing Mama standing on the front porch, she couldn't hold back tearful emotions. Rushing to greet Mama with out-stretched arms, she gave out a loud yell. *"Hija! Ay Lelita! Hija de mi vida!"*

She was utterly beside herself with emotion, as she literally clung to Mama.

"Ay Lelita. Mi hijita preciosa." "My precious little girl!"

Mama, too, was overjoyed and filled with excitement on seeing Angela again. As they embraced each other tightly, both were crying joyful tears and laughing excitedly over their happy reunion. The atmosphere at our little house quickly became ecstatic for a few moments with only echoing sounds of sorrow and gladness.

Still clinging to each other, Mama cried out, "Oh Angelita! It's so great to see you again. How did you ever find out where I live?"

Finally separating from their long tearful embrace and brushing aside the tears that trickled down both their faces, Angela and Mama could hardly wait to get re-acquainted.

"Oh, Lela, how I found you is a long story. Here…let me look at you. My. My. I can't believe my little girl is now a full grown woman and still pretty as ever."

"*Pase Angelita. Pase para dentro, pero dispense mi pobre casita,*" "Come in," Mama said, "but don't look too close at my poor little shack."

As Angela entered our front room, it was obvious that she was stunned at the sight of our meager home, but refrained at first from saying anything.

"Where's Manuel?" Mama asked. "Why didn't he come?"

"Oh, he's not able to travel anymore, honey. His arthritis is really bad."

"Gosh. I'm sorry to hear that."

"He asks about you every once in a while; he thought a lot about you, and really missed you after you left us."

"Same with me, Angela. I couldn't have asked for a better Papa than he. Is he still the same jolly person he used to be?"

"I guess. He's a lot heavier now. He hardly every goes anywhere anymore."

"Angela, it's so good to see you again. Are you still operating a boarding house?"

"No, Lelita. Not anymore. We gave that up a long time ago. We're selling cigarettes now, but not the kind you buy at the store."

"Cigarettes? Don't tell me you're selling.….."

"Yes, *Chiquita,*" she interrupted, "*Marijuana. Pero no vayas ha decir nada.*"

"Marijuana? Oh, my! No! I won't say anything. But, isn't that against the law?"

"Yes, but I'm not worried about the law. It sure is a good business; the people in Kansas City really go for it."

"Oh, yes. I remember your letter saying you lived in Kansas City."

"Yes, we're living in Kansas City now. We bought us a little place up there; been there over ten years, now. Sure are a lot of Mexicans in our neighborhood; a lot of Italians too."

"*¿Donde esta Juan?*" "Where's Juan?" she asked, curiously.

Still filled with excitement and curiosity, Angela couldn't wait to acquaint herself with our little house; glancing around at our overcrowded conditions.

"Oh, he won't be home 'til around five O'clock." Mama answered, as they both glanced at the *Big Ben* alarm clock at the head of the bed.

"*Sientese, Angelita.*" "Sit down, Angelita, I'll bet you're tired, aren't you?"

"Yes. I'm really tired," she said, reaching for the chair next to the bed. "Eight hours on the Katy Passenger train just wore me out."

As she sat down, she began loosening the straps on her shoes, then began to take the hatpins out of her hat.

"Lela, don't tell me all these kids are yours! Are they?"

"Absolutely." she replied. "Everyone of them." *"Cuentelos."* "Count 'em—five boys and two girls; and that's not counting my first born who passed away about eight years ago."

"Lela, honey, you're amazing. I can hardly believe it."

Still looking around in astonishment, she paused for a moment, then, added, "I'm sorry to hear your first child died. Boy or girl?"

"It was a little boy, and only seven years old. His name was Juanito."

"Gosh Lela, I'm so happy to see you. I've missed you so much. *Dulce corazon,* are you happy?" Dying to know, she asked, "I mean, really? Has Juan been a good husband?"

"Angelita" she replied, "Juan—the man whom you didn't want me to marry—has been a wonderful husband. He loves me even more now than he did when we got married. And that's the truth. He's a good, hard working, decent man. Yes, I'm happy…and I have no regrets."

On hearing Mama's convincing remarks of happiness with Papa, Angela sighed softly, as though much relieved, saying,

"Honey, it's obvious you're still in love with Juan. I see it all over your face. I'm so happy for you; in fact, I envy you. Even when you were my little girl at the boarding house, I knew that someday you'd make somebody a fantastic wife."

Wiping her cheeks once again, composure was returning to Angela's face as she tucked the little silk handkerchief in the cuff of her sleeve; still moist from wiping away the tears.

But as she continued to look around the room, she couldn't grasp the reality of such cramped quarters. Quite freely, she walked from corner to corner inspecting every square inch of our little *jacal*, amazed, and yet so unbelieving. Unable to resist expressing her opinion, she quipped in dismay, *"Hijita,* how can you live like this? Is this all there is?"

Seeing Angela's disappointment at the meekness of our little house, Mama recalled how Angela had always been a woman of means and could afford almost anything she wanted. So, in defense of her hasty conclusion, she respectfully replied, *"Angelita. No se apure."* "Angelita, please don't worry. We're fine. Yes we're poor, but so are a lot of other people. But tell me," she mused in rebuttal with a happy grin on her face, "how many rich people do you know who have raised seven kids? And don't forget, we've just come through an awful depression. Of course, it hasn't been easy, but we've managed."

Changing the subject, Mama said, "*Hijos, vengan aqui. Saludenle a Angelita.*"
"Come here children, say hello to Angela."

Mama was beaming with pride when she introduced us to Angela. As we bashfully gathered around Mama in our shabby clothes, she said, "This one is **Cecilio**—he's the oldest, this one is **Cenobio**, this is **Manuela**, over there is **Juanito**, and that one is **Virginia**. This little one is **Alberto**, he's two years old. The baby in the cradle is **Miguel**. He's just two months old."

"My goodness" Angela responded with a puzzled smile. "Seven beautiful children. Honey if you have any more, I don't know where you're gonna put'em."

Laughingly, Mama replied, "We've got a full house, alright, but I don't care. Anyway, Miguel, the baby, may be the last one."

One by one, Angela kissed us all, hugging and squeezing my little sisters, and affectionately hugging the boys with a gentle pat on the butt.

After all joyous emotions had quietly settled down, Angela could no longer hold back her feelings of guilt from the past.

"Lelita—*mi corazon.*" she said, "I was wrong. When I refused to let you marry Juan. I was wrong. I was selfish—very selfish. I thought I could keep you as my little girl forever, but I should've known better. But in spite of what you might think of me, I loved you. And I still love you." Pausing with a choking in her voice, she continued, "Only God knows how I've paid for my mistake Can you ever forgive me?"

"Angelita" Mama replied, on sensing her lingering remorse, "Please don't punish yourself. You were only doing what you thought was right, and in a way, I didn't really blame you. I know I was just a crazy, love-sick kid back then, but Juan and I really did love each other. I never have blamed you Angela, and believe me, there's nothing to forgive."

In an effort to lay Angela's troubled mind to rest, Mama continued.

"Angelita, not too long after Juan and I got married, both of us went back to the boarding house looking for you, but you were gone. We found Rebecca and she told us that you'd sold the boarding house and had moved away, but she didn't know where. We wanted your blessing, but I guess we were too late. But Angela," she went on, "all the years I lived with you, you always treated me great. In fact, you treated me as if I were your own daughter. I haven't forgotten how you gave me just about everything I ever needed…and I should have been more grateful. But let's not worry about it anymore, we're together now, and that's all that matters. And remember…I still love you."

With tears in both their eyes, once again they reached out to each other for one more embrace of repentance and reassurance. At that moment, both felt reconciled over an unfortunate event long past.

Looking at the clock again, Mama said, "*Ay Dios. Ya son las cinco. Ya mero llega Juan.*" "Oh my, it's almost 5 O'clock. Juan will be home soon. I'd better hurry and start supper. Will you help me?"

"*Si, como no. Enséñame la cocina.*" "Absolutely! Where's the kitchen?"

As Angela stepped down into our small kitchen, she couldn't help but notice our cheaply constructed kitchen; with its flapping shutters, rusty screens, our wood-burning cook stove, and the long wooden dinner table and benches.

"Lela, Honey," she said, politely complaining, "You amaze me. How you can live like this and still be a contented woman is beyond me. It has to be true love."

"Oh, Angela it's not bad. We're really happy here."

"Where do I wash my hands, honey?"

"Over there in the corner is the *lavamanos*, but wait just a minute. I think we're out of water." Looking at me, pretending not to be embarrassed, she said, "*Chilo, hijo. anda trae agua. Pronto!*" "Go get some fresh water son, Hurry!"

"*Tampoco no tienes agua? Ay Diosito mio!*" "You don't have water in the house either?" declared Angela with a chuckle. "Oh, my God!"

When Papa came home from work, he didn't come inside right away. Instead; he wandered around outside pretending to be inspecting his vegetable garden. He knew Angela had arrived, but was certainly in no hurry to see her. As I stepped outside through the back door with my two empty water pails, I yelled at Papa.

"Hey Papa! *Aqui esta la señora, Angelita.*" "Mrs. Angela is here"

"*¿Que dices, hijo?*" "What did you say son?" he asked, pretending not to have heard me.

"Angelita is here!"

"Angela, did you say? Oh, yeah! Alright son, I'm coming."

When he finally decided to go inside, he felt very uncomfortable, unsure of what to expect. He was no longer bitter over the way Angela had treated him at the boarding house, in fact, he had forgiven her a long time ago. But still, he was in no hurry to get re-acquainted. *There was no love lost as far as he was concerned.*

Stepping in to the kitchen through the back door, simultaneously, they caught each other's eye, forcing a smile as though glad to see each other.

"Angelita!" Papa shouted in a happy pretense. "*Que tal sorpreso!*" "What a surprise!" he said, extending out his hand for a welcoming handshake

"*Juan!*" she shouted back. "*Ay Juan. ¿Te acuerdas de me?*"

"Oh Juan! Do you remember me?" she asked.

"Como no." he replied, as he returned her smile. *"Como me puedo olvidar."* "Of course I remember you. How could I ever forget?"

"Juan, you're sure looking good. Fourteen years hasn't changed you a bit. In fact," she said jokingly, "you're still that handsome guy that gave me so much trouble at the boarding house."

"Aw, c'mon, Angela. You're making me blush."

"Gave you trouble?" he shot back, with a chuckle. "I thought it was the other way around. By the way, where's Manuel?"

"Oh, he didn't come. He's getting pretty old, you know."

"Aren't we all? Just think; I'll soon be forty-six. You're looking good too, Angela. Do you ever hear from my old friends in Oklahoma City? Antonio? How about Rebecca?"

"Not any more. I did for a while, but it's been a long time now."

"I sure would like to hear from Tony." Papa remarked. "But he's probably gone back to Mexico by now. Sometimes I wish I were back there myself."

"Really, Juan?"

"Someday, maybe. But not yet."

After a few casual reflections on the day of the big fight at the boarding house, they moved on to a lighter conversation, but with very little genuine enthusiasm.

Trying to ease any remaining chill between them, Papa asked, *"¿Como le paresen mis hijos, Angela?"* "What do you think of all our kids?"

"Oh, Juan," she answered, "they're all sweet little darlings." Jokingly with a chuckle, she asked, "Can I have one?"

After supper, the entire family proceeded outdoors to cool off in the shade, as they continued reminiscing on some of the better times at the boarding house, including Linda and Rebecca and some of Papa's old railroad working friends. Papa could tell from the beginning that Angela wasn't too happy about our little shack in the "Y", and he certainly didn't like it when she rattled off her opinions so freely; which was one of the reasons why he couldn't accept Angela as whole-heartedly as Mama. He resented the way she threw her voice around, and he certainly didn't need her pity about our standard of living. But he was the perfect gentleman and welcomed her into our home. Even though he didn't always like or agree with everything she said, he wouldn't stand in the way of Mama's happy reunion. Still however, he remembered the 'old' Angela and the awesome confrontation they had when she ordered him to leave the boarding house, and it was with this in mind, that Papa braced himself for the 'new' Angela.

Despite her crude bluntness, we all soon discovered another side of Angela, and even though she immediately took control over our household routine, we all loved it. On this, her first visit, she bought us all a whole new wardrobe. She made it look so easy. Just call a cab, hop in, direct the driver to 5th and Main street in downtown Tulsa, hop out, and there you were…standing in front of some of the fanciest clothing stores in Tulsa. What made it so exciting was that we seldom went to the big City. That day, all of us would be completely outfitted in dress clothes of our own choosing. And before returning to Kansas City, Angela bought Miguel a new baby bed, and for Mama, a brand new 'chambers' four-burner cook stove, then, stocked our kitchen full of groceries.

Angela was like a different Santa Claus in July. Looking back at that generous shopping spree—one of several others—it occurred to me that perhaps she felt like she was our grandmother and just couldn't wait to spoil us. Or maybe, it was all those years of absence from Mama that made love that much stronger; making her more determined than ever to make up for it. But whatever the reason, she took great pleasure in showering us with quite an extravaganza. After a week, or so, Angela returned to Kansas City. But before leaving, she handed Mama one hundred dollars. She said it was for a rainy day.

All the time Angela was at our house, Papa respectfully stepped aside from the center of attraction and let her take over. In doing so, however, he continued to indulge himself in a beer or two in her presence and sometimes deliberately, three or four, knowing that she disliked his drinking. All this splurging on the family while Angela was at our house was all well and good, as Papa saw it, but inside, his feelings were hurt because seemingly, he had been decimated to a lowly provider. He never let his resentment show around Angela, however, nor did he ever stand between her and Mama. But, it was obvious that he harbored feelings of jealousy and perhaps a touch of resentment.

In subsequent years, Mama stayed in touch with Angela through me. I wrote the letters.

CHAPTER 22

▼

MID-CONTINENT OIL
COMPANY STRIKE—1936

The following year after Angela reunited with Mama, a very unnerving event took place within rock-throwing distance of our house in the "Y". And that was the unfortunate labor dispute between Mid-Continent Oil Company and some 2000 employees, causing a strike that lasted from **1936**, until **1939**. From the beginning, it was a bitter fight between management and labor that immediately made headlines, putting Tulsa in the national spotlight. The conflict was so widely reported that the site of the strike, at one point, became a curiosity attraction for gawking motorists. Shortly after the strikers walked out, things around our house were becoming very uneasy. Papa worried for our safety and cautioned me explicitly to be on the alert for any hostile activity nearby.

As it was reported in the beginning, many Mid Continent employees were very dissatisfied, not only about working conditions, but especially their wages. The popular consensus was that the Company was generating huge oil profits, while suppressing wages, and still enjoying one of the highest levels of oil refining in the country. When the negotiating demands of approximately one-third of the company's employees were stymied, the walkout began; thus, setting off one of the most alarming and dangerous strikes in the country.

These were indeed very troubling times for the employees of Mid-Continent, many of whom lived on the company-owned residential grounds **directly across the tracks from our house.** Because as soon as the strike began, it created mass confusion and division among friends—some in favor of the strike and others against it. The strikers numbering into the hundreds, after losing their bid to form an Oil Workers Union, became violent, causing critical tensions and chaos. Soon after the shutdown, replacement employees called 'scabs' were recruited by the Company, and that's when the strike became even more hostile. The strikers refused to let any of the scabs past the front gates without a physical confrontation, but once past the gates, those inside were blocked off and refused exiting; thereby causing an entrapment for all those inside the refinery compound. Oil transportation rigs, suppliers, workers, and many others were denied entrance by the strikers. This in turn, created an immense problem for the Company after strategic points of egress and regress were blocked and jammed by the striking forces. Out of necessity, Mid-Continent prepared a makeshift airplane landing strip using small planes to bring in urgently needed supplies and provisions. Another counter move by the Company was to use the Frisco with its locomotives and boxcars to bring in supplies and equipment by way of a rail spur leading into the gated grounds of the refinery. **Using the tracks directly behind our house—no more than 60 feet away—**I could view the attempts made by the Frisco's locomotive engineers to penetrate the striker's roadblock. Sometimes the locomotives would sit idle for hours, apparently waiting for instructions or permission to crash the picket line or to back off.

Now, for the locomotives to crash the lines that picketed the Company's southeast gate with engineers on board could be very risky and confrontational. But when orders came down for the locomotive to go forward…here's how they did it. The engineer backed off some 100 yards; disconnected the couplers of the gondolas loaded with supplies, then at full speed, all throttles open, wheels spinning, and whistles blowing—they charged the striker's blockade with the disconnected cars. At the precise point of impact, the engineer slammed on the brakes, allowing the disconnected, unmanned cars to crash the blockade and coast free and unstoppable passed the gate into the refinery grounds. Once inside, the non-strikers intercepted the welcomed cars, guiding them into safe and appropriate locations using their own motorized rigs. This trick by the Frisco definitely prevented a physical confrontation with the strikers.

For months, a tense atmosphere of violence hovered over the "Y", West Tulsa, and the Mid-Continent Refinery, never knowing when or where the next point of disturbance would take place. And when all peaceful negotiations failed, Governor Marland had no choice but to intervene by calling out the Oklahoma National Guard comprising of approximately 100 guardsmen. Armed with bayonets, guns and barbed wire barriers, they took their positions at all the entrances and hot spots leading into the refinery.

I remember how sometimes in the dead of winter, I'd cross the tracks from the "Y" into the Mid-Continent compound carrying my water pails for fetching fresh water, and how I'd spot some of the guardsmen on duty on the embankment of the railroad tracks. They were always in small groups, dressed in combat uniforms with leggings on, and rifles on their backs. On real wintry days, the soldiers gathered firewood and pitched a fire on the park grounds to keep warm, while they stood guard around-the-clock. Sometimes when I approached them with my pails of water, I'd stop to chat with them. They were always friendly and anxious for someone to talk to.

This terrible labor strike, which ended approximately in March of 1939, turned many friends into enemies, as former striking employees gave up the fight and disbanded. Striking employees who had once lived in one of the fine homes of the Company's housing addition, no longer had a home to go to. Immediately, the tired and beaten strikers faced another dilemma—unemployment. And with no jobs to go to, many who had previously been well-to-do, now found themselves among the ranks of the poor. I know how humiliating it must have been, because I could see it in the faces of several of my friends whose 'striking parents' lost the good fight. For them to step down to an unaccustomed lower standard of living, was truly a heart breaker; as was the case of the parents of my friend Murray Chapman and another friend—Jack Glance—who was employed by Mid-Continent at the time.

CHAPTER 23

▼

STAND-IN FOR PAPA

I was only 14 years old when the Mid-Continent Strike ended, and the stature of my life was changing quite rapidly—as was maturity. Unknowingly, I was beginning to develop certain qualities of leadership and good judgment, of which both my parents were well aware of. It was during these early teen years that things around our house, regarding obligation and responsibility, were becoming confused and in disarray. Mama had far too much to deal with, and Papa, seemingly, was becoming insensitive to this fact. That's when I was drawn in to a subordinate role of authority. Papa was already convinced that I could handle responsibility and was expecting it more and more. Gradually, as he was releasing his hold on me, it forced me to start using my own judgment on certain family matters when they came up, and in doing so, on my own initiative, I strived to earn my own place at the top, *next to Papa.*

Mama taught me responsibility intentionally. She saw from the beginning that I had matured far ahead of my time, and cultivated my instincts for making grown-up decisions. Since her task and responsibility over such a large family was so enormous, and considering the fact that Papa wasn't very helpful in the personal, intimate needs of the kids, she badly needed someone to share her burden. Papa was 50 years old now, and definitely slowing down. That in itself was understandable, what with a family our size and Papa working seven days a week. Moreover, he was gradually loosening his strictness toward the children, including relinquishing control over household matters. He had become perfectly satisfied with all things in general around the house, which for sure, indicated a lessening of ambition or a lack of motivation. It was circumstances such as these that gave Mama no choice but to give me an alternate degree of 'big brother' authority over my little brothers and sisters. When she turned to me, that's when I began answering the call of growing up. Having unofficially granted me a certain charge over my siblings, now it was becoming understood that they should come to me for help and answers when they needed it. So, alternately, they were becoming my responsibility too, and for some reason, I didn't mind it at all; as a matter of fact, they didn't either. Being their older brother, they began looking up to me and willingly accepted me as a 'father figure', so to speak, and began coming to me when they needed help with their little problems. And so it was, that an unspoken degree of secondary authority had been established. I loved my siblings, and with a built-in protective nature about me, I willingly accepted this degree of responsibility, *next to Mama.* So…as Papa was quietly stepping aside, and Mama needing help badly, I gladly welcomed the opportunity to assume this new role.

For years, having worked along side Papa, watching and studying every thing he did, like; working on the house, the fences, the car, the yard, the garden, etc., I must say, I learned quite a lot. It definitely prepared me for handyman projects around the house. Always before, the things that he did as a provider and father were driven by his natural sense of tireless responsibility. Now, those same ambitions were tugging at me, and I needed to find some way to prove myself.

It was during those days of growing pains that I was becoming more and more dissatisfied with our meager existence in the "Y" and began building dreams of my own. Every time I went to a friend's house, immediately I could see a world of difference between their neatly structured house and our little shack. On seeing their nice modern homes, their pretty decorated rooms with polished floors, matching furniture, their pretty lamps and ceiling lights all operated by switches on the wall, I couldn't help being envious and wished for the same things. Of course there wasn't anything I could do about our cramped quarters or the condition of our house, but that didn't keep me from wanting to reach out. Before long, however, my teenage ideas **did** bring a small degree of satisfaction to my persisting desire for improvements, when I began to demonstrate my ability to initiate certain projects of my own—projects that Papa never took care of.

One of the first projects that I tackled was a **walk-in closet**. We needed a clothes closet in the worst way because after all these years, we didn't have a single closet in the house. Always before, we hung our clothes on a piece of 1/2" pipe diagonally stretched in the corner of the front room that Papa had positioned for this purpose. I'll have to admit, however, that for the time being, as unsightly as it looked, these crude hanging rods worked. But even so, by now, our family had grown so rapidly that we drastically needed more closet space.

As a very young kid, I loved working with wood. I remember how I liked tinkering with a saw and hammer and driving nails; how I used to make my own wooden toy hand-guns and rifles, and like the time I made a wooden scooter. So, with a natural inclination to work with wood, I felt confident that I could build a closet for our family and I was anxious to try it. When I explained it to Mama, because of our dire need for more closet space, she encouraged me to go for it.

To construct a clothes closet, would require some carpenter skills for which I had none. Papa was definitely not a carpenter either, but he had saws and hammers and plenty of other tools, so that wouldn't be a problem. Also, he had stacks of random used lumber varying in sizes and lengths, so it appeared that all the materials I would need were already on hand.

For our new closet, there was no space inside the house, so I would do the next best thing; attach it to an outside wall of the house. My plan called for the elimination of one of our exterior windows and converting it to a door-opening by way of a step-down. First, I brought in several flat rocks to be used for the foundation, leveled them as closely as I could, then I built the wooden floor. Next came the walls, the framing, and lastly, the roof. Finally, I cut out the window and converted the opening to a doorway. When all the rough-in was complete, I proceeded to install hanging rods, shelves, and remounted the window on an exterior window for light.

After five days of sawing, hammering and fitting, I could finally stand back and take a good long look at what I had built; my first wood-working project. Mama was very pleased. She too, had watched this piece-by-piece construction turn in to a beautiful walk-in clothes closet. The truth is, however, it wasn't beautiful at all. But to her, it was, and she wasted no time in utilizing it by rearranging all our clothes. She bragged about my work to all who came to the house.

I don't remember asking Papa's permission to tackle the closet project, because at this particular stage in his life, he just wasn't too keen on changing the size or conditions of our little house. Apparently, to him, the house was just fine the way it was. Maybe it was the lack of money, or it could have been other things, but Papa just never saw the need for such things as a closet; his attitude toward growth and improvement was becoming dormant. It might have been different a few years back, when his domestic awareness was keener and when he was more energetic. Even though I didn't get Papa's permission to build the closet, he never objected to it. In fact, as construction got underway, he kept a watchful eye on my progress. He never offered to help or give me any suggestions, but for the five days it took to complete it, he stayed pretty much out of the way.

I might never have fixed **our leaky roof** either, had it not been for one evening of humiliation. For weeks, Mama had been after Papa to fix it, but he kept putting it off. But on this particular evening when we had company at our house—Doroteo and Jesus Perez—we were all sitting outside in the shade when storm clouds began rumbling around overhead. All of a sudden, the rains came pouring down so fast and furious that the Perezes never had time to make it to their house. In a frenzy, everyone scampered inside. After everyone had swished away the raindrops from their wet clothing and seated in our front room, the same usual leaks began to hit the floor. Immediately, Mama rushed to the kitchen for her pots to catch the leaks. Soon, all we could hear were musical pans, 'ping' 'ping' 'ping' 'splat'. Each drop that fell, chimed in harmony with the others as they splatted in their waiting targets—*how embarrassing*.

While everyone was sitting around, commenting on the loud thunder and the heavy rain pounding our roof, Don Doroteo, laughing and still swishing at his wet shirt, happened to look up to the ceiling watching the rain drops collect into tiny water pools, when…splat….right in the eye. A new leak had just been born. He yiped and jumped backward, saying, *"Ay Caramba!"* Looking at Papa, jokingly, he remarked, *"haste para alla Juan, deja me sentar ahi junto de ti."* "Move over Juan, I'm coming over to your side." By this time, everyone was laughing hilariously, making light of this humiliating situation. Mama looked at Papa, pretending not to be embarrassed, saying, *"Juan, no tienes verguensa."* "Juan, you ought to be ashamed" But Papa just chuckled. He wasn't ashamed. If he was, it sure didn't show because laughing and jokingly, he just brushed it aside and promised to fix it right away. He meant well, but other things continued to take priority over fixing our leaky roof.

Mama continued to plead with Papa to repair our roof, but he paid her no mind. One day, after her patience was growing thin, she asked me if I thought I could do it, and, of course, I told her I could. Because after having built our walk-in closet, her confidence in me and my ability for this kind of work had now gotten stronger. But…there was one little problem; Papa, and the lack of roofing materials. All this came up at a time when we were over budget, and certainly, this was no time for piling on more bills. Mama knew the seriousness of our financial problems, and realized that if we bought the materials on credit, Papa would have a fit. But shutting her eyes to the additional expense and risking a fight with him, she gave the 'go-ahead'...*and off I went.* .

Since Papa had done business with Long Bell Lumber Company, Leon, the manager, didn't question my order, thinking that Papa had sent me. On arriving back home with a single roll of roofing, galvanized nails, and roofing tacks, immediately, I climbed up on the roof and began making the repairs.

When Papa came home from work and saw what I had done, he was furious. He ranted and raved, first with Mama, and then with me, as if the project had cost a fortune. I don't know if it was the amount of money we spent that angered him so, or if it was the fact that I hadn't asked his permission. Either way, he was very upset over it. Later, he inspected my work rather hurriedly, then went into the house and never said another word.

All during the roofing project, I had been up tight, wondering if Papa would be reprehensive toward me for charging the materials to his bill, because at times, he had a tendency to be intolerant with me. Sometimes he went overboard, I thought, and could be unreasonable, not only with me, but also with Mama. Of course, there were times when she and I did conspire against him in order to get things done; things that he should have taken care of and didn't, but it was always for good reasons. Nevertheless, when his drinking was becoming a top priority, just about everything came to a standstill. So, when Mama wanted certain repairs done around the house, instead of asking Papa to do it, she'd ask me.

Other times, when Mama needed immediate cash for some special reason, or an important project around the house, she'd ask Papa to borrow the money from the West Tulsa Loan Company, but he could never get in a hurry to do so. After waiting as long as she could, she'd ask me to prepare a note and sign it, as though prepared by Papa, and take it to the Loan Company for a small advance on his paycheck. I never had any problem getting the money, since I'd been there with Papa many times before. The real problem was explaining to Papa later why we did this without his knowledge. And that would be another time when he'd be furious and all hell would break loose. So then, I wondered, who was right— Mama or Papa. *Either way, I can still feel his belt across my you-know-what.*

When we over-rode his authority to fix the roof and created more debt without his permission, understandably, I would be nervous. But from my point of view, I was only growing older, more eager and ambitious, and just exercising some responsibility of my own. As for the job I had done on the roof, I was hoping Papa would be proud of me, like; a pat on the back, or even one word of praise or encouragement, but no, it never came.

During those years of bursting energy, I was determined to tackle one more challenging project—**a new front porch.** When my friend Nick's house burned down, of course, they all moved away, leaving the ruined remains behind. Soon after the fire, I went to see if anything could be salvaged; perhaps some firewood. What I found, was that an entire floor section of a bedroom had escaped the fire and still in reusable condition. I really wanted this 12'x12' wooden floor section badly. I wanted it to replace the floor on our old porch, which had deteriorated beyond repair. I watched the ruins for a few days, and when I was convinced that no one was coming back, I was ready to bring the floor slab to our house. When I told Mama what I wanted it for, at first, she hesitated. She was afraid that people might think we were stealing. This time, we talked it over with Papa, and for some strange reason, he didn't offer any resistance. He just said if I thought I could do it, to go ahead and try it. This was his permission.

Immediately, I encountered a problem. The wooden floor slab seemed to weigh a ton. *How would I ever get it to the house?* After much studying and sizing up the situation, it finally came to me; I'd tumble it all the way, a distance of about 60 feet. And it worked. With the help of my little brothers Noble, Johnny, and our little neighbor friends Raymond and Edward, together we tumbled it over and over and over, until we got it to our house.

The next couple of days, I spent preparing for my new project. Little by little, I carefully dismantled our old dilapidated porch, saving every piece of reusable wood and pitching all the bent nails into an old empty pure lard can, like I'd seen Papa do. No telling how old our porch was, but it had seen its better days. Finally, it was time for it to go. The first thing I did, was to straighten out all the used nails. Next. I built a small sawhorse I'd need for the job, and finally, I was ready to start.

I don't think I slept a wink all night, the night before, just thinking and studying on how and where to start. I kept telling myself over and over how important it was for me to do a good job, because I knew that eventually, my friends would see my work.

By the time I started the framing, Joe Perez came over to visit. He must have heard all the loud hammering and decided to check it out. Joe was a good friend of mine—several years older—and for a long time, we had enjoyed a swell boyhood relationship. I often looked up to Joe as an older brother, and likewise, I think he had a tendency to treat me like a little brother. He was a handsome guy and stood about 5' 9" tall, had a great muscular build, black wavy hair, and a pink birthmark on his right cheek. I think Joe wanted to try his hand at carpenter work also, but from what I had seen of some of his previous projects, I wasn't sure if he would ever make the grade. Some little something always seemed to be lacking in his projects; like the time he built a front door for Mrs. Chewy's house. He wanted me to come over and see it, so I did. I sensed that he was very proud of it, so I was careful not to make any negative comments. After seeing it, I didn't have the heart to tell him, that even though the door was practical and sturdy, it was not the way I would have built it.

Practically all day long, Joe watched my every measurement and saw-cut and watched me fit every piece of wood in place. He didn't try to supervise the job, nor did he try to help. We just made casual conversation, but all along, I felt self-conscious. When he finally went home, before leaving, he complimented me on my work and my meticulous precision. Of course, his compliments did wonders for my ego, and yes, even inspired me to continue as though I had known what I was doing all along.

The porch when completed, turned out great, and once again, I was very proud of my accomplishment. To most people, it was probably just another porch, but to Mama and me, it was something very special. Every time she bragged on my developing skills as a carpenter, it was like beautiful words from my biggest fan, and music to my ears. As always, a few words of encouragement from her, could immediately dispel any shadow of doubt that might have entered my mind. Sure, it was just another porch…constructed entirely of used scrap lumber, *but it was my porch,* and besides, no one else in the "Y" had one like it. Now our new porch, complete with overhead shelter, would be safe and dry, and we wouldn't have to worry about cracked flooring giving way under foot.

After this, I enjoyed many evenings sitting on our new front porch after supper, playing my mandolin and guitar, watching that old silvery moon and the stars dance around in the night. Somehow, the serenity of a quiet evening with no other night-sounds in the air besides the chitter-chatter of locusts and crickets, just naturally seemed to pacify my mind, allowing me to scheme away to bigger and better things.

City Water Comes to the "Y"
1939

This was the year that the "Y" families would experience a world of relief and a most welcomed commodity—**fresh drinking water.** After all these years since moving from Sapulpa in 1927, everyone had to 'carry in' fresh drinking water almost daily. Finally, this was about to change. It all started when our neighbor Arcadio Gonzales—a kind of resourceful man who had learned to speak English, or at least good enough to make himself understood—decided to look into the possibility of bringing city water to the "Y". Now you would think that someone would have looked into this matter long before now. And quite possibly someone did, but ran into a stone wall at city hall. A better probability, however, could be the fact that most of the "Y" families being of Mexican decent and unable to speak English, might have been either too timid or just plain incapable of initiating an inquiry.

Immediately, on Don Arcadio's first attempt with the Water Deprtment in downtown Tulsa, he was denied. Reason given was that only the Frisco could make the request, since they owned the land. Pursuing their requirements, after several visits and much wrangling with both parties, the Frisco and the City Fathers finally approved his application. Stipulations were, that only one meter would be authorized to serve all the families, providing that Don Arcadio would accept full responsibility for all water consumption, to which he gladly agreed..

Only one water tap meant that only one continuous water line would be installed. Like a chain reaction, each family would install their own section of line, one at a time, until all families were connected, with the family closest to the meter going first. That would be Don Doroteo.

So far, all was going well and on schedule, as all the families anxiously awaited the arrival of fresh water to become a reality, *all except Papa*. It seemed that he wasn't concerned, one way or the other. Mama, however, had been hinting indirectly that it would soon be our turn to tie on and we should be taking steps to be ready. But Papa, in another one of his apathetic moods, remained unmoved.

"Juan," she said finally, hinting again, "it looks like Don Doroteo has completed his portion of their water line, because I see that the Edisons are starting to dig their trench line. It'll be our turn next. I can hardly wait for us to have our own water. I'm so tired of having to carry water from so far away, day after day. I've prayed for this day so many times, and now, it's almost here. By the way, Juan, where are we going to get the money for the material? Have you thought about it?"

Papa just shrugged his shoulders a bit, indicating an unimportance of the matter, but after a brief pause, he responded saying, "Yes, I've thought about it, but there's still plenty of time. Maybe next payday we'll have a little extra money for the pipe."

"Juan," Mama snapped back, "next payday is still two weeks away, and besides, I don't think there'll be any extra money. Fred Walker's grocery bill is already over one hundred and fifteen dollars."

"Don't worry Lela," he replied. "Everything'll be alright. If not this payday, maybe the next."

Obviously, Papa was not easily motivated. His cool and calm attitude toward this urgent matter was a clear example of what Mama thought was pure procrastination. But she, on the other hand, was most anxious about taking advantage of this long over-due opportunity.

All day long, she watched the two Edison boys dig away at their trench line from Don Doroteo's house and knew that very soon, it would be our turn. So right after supper, she mentioned it again.

"Juan, the Edisons are almost finished. What are we going to do? Can't we borrow the money somewhere?"

But Papa still didn't show much reaction to her concern. It was as if over the years he'd become quite satisfied with the way we'd managed our water needs and was not yet ready to commit to change.

Finally, Mama couldn't wait any longer for him to take action.

"Juan" she said, quite angrily, "You may not give a darn if we get drinking water or not, but I do. If you won't borrow the money somewhere, I will," then turned and walked hastily out of the kitchen.

The following day, being Sunday, she knew that **Francisco (Frank) Moreno,** her *Compadre,* a bachelor, would be coming over to pick up his clean laundry and pressed shirts, so she had decided she would ask him for a small loan. Not having anyone to support but himself, she felt quite sure that he'd have the money. So, after Sunday Mass, she waited anxiously for him to arrive, and for a while, she thought he wasn't going to show up. But he did. She had prepared a fried chicken dinner, complete with *mole* and all the trimmings, then, waited for the perfect opportunity to approach him for the loan. Very slyly at the dinner table, she opened the conversation about our water project.

"Compadre, it won't be long before we'll be getting city water here in the "Y". Isn't that great? Just think, after all these years, we'll have fresh water any time we want it, right here at the house."

"I'm glad for you, *Comadre,*" he replied. "I really am. I wish I was that lucky," referring to his little shack north of town near Archer and Greenwood Avenue.

"But there's just one little problem," Mama continued, with a slight hesitation "We're gonna have to borrow some money somewhere." Looking over at Papa with a sly grin on her face, nervously,she added, "But we'll manage, won't we Juan?"

Frank immediately picked up on the hint of a loan that Mama was alluding to, because he sensed her nervousness and could see the trouble she was having getting the words out about the shortage of money. Being such a close friend of the family and eager to help, without hesitation, he said, *"No se apure, Comadre. ¿Que tanto necessita?"* "Don't worry Comadre, how much do you need?"

Relieved and smiling from ear to ear, Mama thanked him excitedly saying, *"Ay Compadre, que tanto se lo agradesco, muchisimas gracias."* "Oh, compadre. I sure do apprecite it. Thank you so much."

The next day after work, Frank was at our house with twenty-five dollars and handed it to Mama. A tremendous relief had just been lifted off her shoulders.

That same evening, Mr. Edison came to our house and knocked on our screen door. Still in his dirty blue overalls and wiping away the perspiration from his balding head, the first thing he said when Mama answered the door, was, "OK Mrs. Gomez, we're through digging our trench for the water line. Anytime ya'll are ready to connect to our line, have at it. My ain't it hot today?"

Mama graciously smiled at Mr. Edison saying, *(as best she could)* "Yes, it's very hot. Thanks for coming by. We'll get started as soon as we can."

Early the following morning, Mama handed me the twenty-five dollars, saying, *"Bueno hijo, parece que este proyecto de la linea de agua es tuya. Anda a comprar la pipa que necessitamos, y ten much quidado que no vayas a perder el dinero."* "Well son, it looks like this water line project is all yours. Go and buy the pipe we need and please be careful not to lose the money".

Now, Mama was depending on me to install our water line. But she was really peeved with Papa for ignoring the importance of bringing drinking water at our house. With my material list in my hand, I walked all the way to East Tulsa to a pipe supplier, then, located at 1st and Elwood. The man behind the all-metal counter was very nice.

"Can I help you son?" he asked, as I politely handed him my scribbled order for pipe and fittings. Looking at my list, he asked, "What are ya'll doing out there, laying a water line?"

"Yes Sir" I replied.

"Is all this pipe for you, or for some one else?" he asked.

"It's for me." I answered. "I'm laying a brand new line at our house. We've never had water at our house before."

"Do you know how you're gonna do it, son?" he quizzed, sensing that I was too young to tackle the job.

"I think so," I replied.

As he was calculating my order, we continued to carry on a casual conversation about plumbing, but all along, I felt he was unsure of my ability to install our water line. And, he might have been right.

Having tallied up my order, he said, "That'll be nineteen dollars and fifty cents, please."

Just for a moment, as I handed him the money, I felt rich. After all, it was very seldom that a young boy my age ever came in contact with that much money.

"Lookie here son," the clerk said, reaching for a blank piece of paper. "Here's what you do." Then he proceeded to sketch a rough diagram of an eighty-foot water line complete with all connections; collars, freeze drain, shutoff valve, riser, and faucet. *And boy, was I glad!*

"Thank you very much, Sir," I said, putting the sketch in my pocket. "I think I know what to do now."

At that, I began giving him detailed directions to our house in the "Y". The clerk was very helpful and promised same day delivery. Sure enough, by mid afternoon my order had arrived. Now all I needed were shovels and about four men with plenty of muscle.

Immediately, I started staking out the path of our trench line. By 6:00 O'clock, lo' and behold, Frank pulled up to our house in his 1937 two-tone green, Dodge sedan. Still in his dirty overalls, he stepped into the front yard and saw the galvanized pipe laying on the ground. Cheerfully, the first thing he said was, *"Bueno Chilo, ¿donde commensamos?"* "Ok Cecil, where do we start?"

Was I ever surprised. I hadn't expected him to come over to help. I soon learned that he didn't know anything about plumbing either and was leaving it all up to me to engineer the job. But that was alright by me, because the more I studied the project, the more convinced I was that connecting all the pipe and fittings couldn't possibly be that complicated.

"Did you really come to help?" I asked, glad but curious to know if he'd been kidding.

"Of course I came to help." he replied. "That's why I brought my own shovel."

That was all I needed to hear to get the job underway. Papa owned two shovels. I took one and gave the other to Cenobio. Immediately, we three commenced digging. After about thirty minutes, Papa decided he wanted to help too. He went to Doroteo's house to borrow a shovel, then jumped right in, saying teasingly, *"Haganse un lado, porque aquí viene el mero trinchero."* "You all move over, because here comes a real ditch digger."

It made my day to see him working right along side the rest of us. Somehow, it had never dawned on me before, just how much he had needed me in the past, and now, how much I needed him. For the rest of the evening, his jovial humor completely distracted from our minds, the hard work ahead. *By ten o'clock, the digging was complete.*

By the time Papa got home from work the next day, I had already finished connecting our entire water line. Immediately, I informed Mrs. Strickland, *the next family in line,* that we were finished with our line. Now, the remaining families could continue with their portion of line extension. When the entire project had been completed, we all waited for the city inspection.

When that day came, it was a banner day for the "Y". It was something just short of a miracle that after so many years of carrying water through blistering summer heatwaves and freezing winter temperatures, we could now enjoy the same luxury as everyone else in West Tulsa. **Never in a hundred years, could anyone ever imagine the fabulous feeling this was for us and all the families in the "Y". At last, our own fresh, clean, cool, water.**

Needless to say, everyone was deeply indebted to Don Arcadio for his vigorous efforts to obtain water for us all. I, too, thought he had done a great service to our little community. But despite his applaudable efforts, that didn't change my opinion of him. Ever since I was a little boy, I always felt uncomfortable around him. He possessed not a single spark of humor, and when he spoke, it was always with a firm, authoritative tone with very little allowance for disagreement. If ever I knew an arrogant person, it was he. Don Arcadio never did anything to me personally, and from that standpoint, I had no reason to dislike him. But I couldn't forget two good reasons why my esteem for him was low. One, was because of the humiliating way he physically battered his wife, Viola; sometimes in the presence of other people. And the other was when he physically beat up his brother. It so happened that his brother **Hipolito**, an amputee who wore an above-knee prosthesis, was my godfather. Even today, I can still see my *Padrino* lying on the floor, helpless. So maybe my feelings were justified, and maybe not, but one thing for sure, Don Arcadio certainly came through for us on this one.

The water line project had been a tremendous experience for me and I was very satisfied with the results of our work. I was particularly happy for the opportunity to play a leading role in this crucial undertaking and was beginning to enjoy this youthful authority and position of leadership. And Mama...well, she felt so sorry for me all the while, treating me so special and so sympathetically, thinking that I would die from heat exhaustion.

Shortly after completion of our water line, I began entertaining another idea, which was to **install a water line to Mama's kitchen.** This little project too, I completed quite successfully with the balance of the twenty-five dollar loan from

Frank. Hereafter, the wondrous convenience of water inside the house at Mama's fingertips, though unprofessionally installed, was absolutely beyond words to describe. *And she truly deserved it.*

Now that we finally had water at our house, I began entertaining one more great idea. With summer nearing its peak, I began thinking how super nice it would be to have a place to take showers. Taking baths at our house was absolutely hectic. In the first place, we were now all getting older, more modest, and required much more privacy. But the real hassle was carrying in the bath water, the rinse water, heating it, dumping the water after bathing, putting away the tubs and cleaning up the mess. *Like I said. For a family our size, it was a real hassle.*

As before, there was no room inside the house for a shower stall, so again, that was out of the question. Instead, I would do the next best thing; **build an outdoor shower stall.** And that's exactly what I did. About fifteen feet away from the house, under our cottonwood tree, just in front of the chicken pen, and near the outdoor toilet, I built a completely private 4'x 6' open-sky enclosure, complete with a wooden platform. Afterwards, I used a garden hose for the water supply, hanging it overhead and attaching a water sprinkler to the end of it for showering. Another first for me and for the whole family.

After this, there would be no more bathing indoors in a #2 washtub, at least, not in the summer time. Of course it was just a crudely built bathhouse. I was too young to have done a professional job on it, and besides, using scrap lumber with no special tools or training, in my opinion, it was perfect. If not in appearance, then in the essence and practicality of what I thought was a small wonder and just one more simple convenience for our family.

Getting water in the "Y" was like a giant step forward, but only in a manner of speaking, because in reality, we were still worlds away from being modern. I never knew how other families in the "Y" utilized their newly acquired water supply, same as us, I guess. But one thing for sure, *for Mama and me, it was a blessing. Our water-carrying days were over.*

One more stroke of good fortune followed this same year, when **electricity also came to the "Y"** and we were finally able to put away our coal oil lamps. Also, at last, we could have a small radio like everyone else in West Tulsa.

CHAPTER 24

▼

DOMESTIC PROBLEMS
TAKING A TOLL—1940

In the most recent years, Papa seemed to have entered a mid-life crisis regarding his position as head of the house and his responsibility toward the family. His once admirable dedication as a husband and father was changing, and at times, he appeared disconnected from the happy family atmosphere that once was so warm and prevalent in our house. His once youthful vigor was losing steam. There was never any doubt that Papa loved us all very much, but his love was becoming a silent love, difficult to discern. It troubled me to see him so withdrawn from the family. *Had the dream of success in America for Papa reached a dead end? And was poverty in the "Y" the problem?*

I wondered about these things a lot, because it appeared that somewhere along the way, something good may have gotten lost between my parents. They didn't pull together as a team anymore like they once did. I knew that the love between them was still there, but Papa's willingness to hold up his end of marital obligations and responsibilities had all but disappeared. Granted, I could see how endless problems and struggles could easily stymie Papa's ambition and motivation. And when coupled with the demands of raising such a large family during suppressive times, especially in a place like the "Y", yes, it's conceivable that he is becoming disillusioned and losing sight of the dream he once pursued so vigorously.

In the beginning when Papa left Mexico—still a very ambitious and energetic young man—he'd always been mindful to forge ahead, despite the many obstacles that kept interfering, but now, the dream goal doesn't seem to surface like it used to. Gradually, he's stepping aside, letting his world around him take care of itself. It all began dissipating when Papa's drinking was becoming a compulsive habit–the reasons for which were hard to understand. But as the drinking began, that's when problems for Mama began to escalate, marking the beginning of my involvement in their lives, and eventually, a greater role to play on behalf of Mama and the family.

I probably was too young to remember when Papa began to like beer. Maybe he'd always liked it and I just didn't notice. But gradually, he wanted it more often. Sometimes, when we'd go into town for supplies, he'd duck into a tavern for a 'quickie' and make me wait outside. At first, I never saw anything wrong with Papa indulging himself in a beer or two, because to me, he simply enjoyed it.

But Mama saw it differently. Especially when she learned about his dodging into a tavern and leaving me outside. She scolded him good, accusing him of setting a bad example. And at this very opportune time, she'd remind him that already we couldn't afford adequate food and clothing, much less, an expensive beer drinking habit. In that particular instance, I believe Mama was probably right. Still Papa didn't see anything wrong in a few beers every night and just fluffed off her objections. Obvious changes, however, were taking place in Papa: his attitude, his behavior, and his need for solitude.

All this drinking business translated into an unusual change in Papa—a change that even he was unaware of. He had moods in which he could be happy and jovial, and other times, he'd be on the warpath when things went wrong. His temper flared, and if he'd been drinking heavily, he would use foul language, much of the time directed at Mama. The foul language itself was bad enough, but back talk and heated arguments only fanned his temper all the more. And the louder the arguing, the more I'd yell at Papa to leave Mama alone. On these occasions is when I'd step in and get involved, especially when he made Mama cry. He resented my taking sides, and at times, appeared to take his anger out on me, because that's when he'd take off his belt and whip me for interfering..

Every time these fights occurred, there never seemed to be a justifiable reason. Something was troubling Papa. Always before, it had been obvious that he and Mama were happy, but now, disharmony was growing between them and somehow, things were now taking on a different perspective. As for Mama, she'd always had a heart of gold, but in recent years, her very existence had found its way into the confines of a marriage seemingly going nowhere. Because; hard times, hard work, no money, a house full of children to raise with less and less help from Papa, and with very dim expectations of better days, it certainly didn't paint a very pretty picture for the future. So now...her heart of gold and all the love in it was mostly being devoted to the children, *not Papa.*

When I try to speculate why Papa's drinking habit was becoming compulsive and why my parent's marriage was in trouble, there were several probable reasons that come to mind. First, it could have been money problems. Jealousy could be another reason, or it could have been the death of my older brother Juanito. Lastly, and the most probable, could have been the death of Felipa, his mother.

Money Problems. Realistically speaking, money—or the lack of it—had undoubtedly put a serious financial strain on their marriage. One reason was that every payday, just like clockwork, Papa sent money to his mother in Mexico, and also his sister and brother. Not much, of course, but still enough to cause a shortage at home. Each payday, he cashed his check, paid off his grocery bill, then went straight to the Post Office to mail support money to his folks. After which, he pocketed enough to see him through 'til next payday, including beer money. The remaining balance, he gave to Mama, which was never enough to see *her* through to the next payday, much less, enough money to buy little extras for the house, the kids, or herself for that matter. The bare-bones conditions arising out of the shortage of money from payday to payday, just never seemed to go away. *Who's fault was it?* It was no one's fault, of course. These were just the results of trying times. Mama always tried to be fair, realistic and practical, not making any unreasonable demands on Papa, but seemingly, her concerns fell on deaf ears,

Papa too, with a heart of gold was constantly worrying about his folks back home in Mexico; wondering if they were going hungry. The letters he received from them always sounded so pitiful, but Mama didn't always believe their hardship stories. Nevertheless, Papa lived with their plight daily and with such compassion that he couldn't turn a deaf ear to their pleading. So, it could have been a never-ending argument without solution or compromise. If money was their problem—a problem of insufficiency—then perhaps one could understand it as being a probable cause of a growing frustration between them.

Still yet, I could never condone his ill behavior when he drank. Thank goodness, most of the time those tension-filled arguments and displays of ill temper were short lived. Invariably, however, shortly after each argument or after the sobering process kicked in, Papa would be ever so apologetic and conciliatory. He always tried to explain his way out of it by saying such things as, *Perdoname Edelia. No se que me pasó anoche. Te lo juro que ya nunca voy a tomar ese mugrera. Ya no voy a tentar la botella.* "Forgive me, Lela. I don't know what got into me last night," and, "I swear I'll never touch the bottle again," etc. He meant well, but it was yet to happen.

Jealousy could, in fact, have been a psychological factor in trying to explain Papa's quarrelsome behavior, because for him, it wasn't easy sharing Mama with just anyone. He often resented her being the focus of attention when friends came over to visit, particularly if any of the men paid more attention to her than him. And understandably so, because after all, Mama was quite an attractive lady and such a delight to be around. Her enthusiasm and charismatic personality quite naturally made her the center of attraction wherever she went. In the evenings when we had company, everyone just automatically displayed a respectful admiration for her candidness, her humor and incredible frankness.

Papa's jealousy could also have stemmed from feelings of instability due to the decline in that all-important #1 status as the man of the house, *and no longer 'first' in Mama's life.* It's true that Mama had gradually been taking over the helm. When any of the kids needed something, they'd come straight to her or me, not him. This trend didn't just happen over night; it had long been in the making and perhaps Papa could have prevented it, at least in part, had he been there for the children. But be that as it may, Mama's attention had gradually shifted from Papa toward the children, and this is where he could have begun to feel rejection and demoralized—and perhaps just another reason to hit the bottle that much more.

Juanito's Death. When Juanito, Jr.—Papa and Mama's first-born son—became deathly sick with an acute case of typhoid fever, they were terribly worried. After having tried several household remedies earlier, without relief, they decided to summon Doctor Taylor. But apparently, after his examination and diagnosis, no decision was made for hospitalization. Instead, medicine was prescribed and no cause for alarm was indicated.

I'll never forget that cold wintry evening, only two days after Doctor Taylor's visit, when Mama was holding Juanito in her arms, burning with fever, sitting next to the pot-belly stove trying to keep him warm. All of a sudden, Juanito stopped breathing. Hysterically, Mama and Papa started screaming, beseeching all the saints in heaven to save their little boy. At the time, I couldn't comprehend what all the crying was about, but it frightened me, and I, too, began crying. Papa quickly snatched Juanito from Mama's arms and started shouting his name and shaking him violently attempting to restart the breathing, utterly refusing to give up his son. Mama then took Juanito and sat down in front of the stove holding him tightly to her breasts, *trembling and screaming, and calling for Jesus.* **Papa started pounding the walls with his fists,** insanely yelling and cursing his wretched fate and the whole world that came crushing down on him. He blamed himself, because earlier that day, he had brought home some ice cream for Juanito, and now, he was sure that this was what worsened his condition. Also, just minutes before this dramatic display of piercing agony, Papa had tried to give Juanito medicine with a spoon, causing tendencies to choke and gag, and Papa blamed himself for that too. There's no way to describe the agony in Papa and Mama's hearts, as they wailed over Juanito's lifeless body. **Juanito died on November 7, 1928.**

For the next two days at our house, numerous friends from the "Y" attended all-night vigils for Juanito's wake. I remember peering into his casket as though he merely lay sleeping, but more so, I remember my parent's excruciating pain through the day of his internment. For the longest time after Juanito's death, Papa suffered immensely, seeking solace and refusing to let go of the precious memory of his young vibrant son. I was just five years old when Juanito died, and just like Papa, I'll never forget it either.

Death of Felipa—his mother. There were probably many reasons floating around in Papa's mind that caused him to become so disillusioned. One in particular could have easily been the one that killed the will to pursue his dream in America. It was a letter that Papa received from Hilario, his brother, **only three years after the death of Juanito. The letter might as well have been edged in black,** because the bad news it contained was that of his mother. **She had passed away.** Liken to a little boy with a broken heart, he sobbed bitterly. Once again, he was devastated beyond words. And to make matters worse, he found himself a thousand miles away from Villa de Reyes, and flat broke. He adored his mother, and her memory was never more than a split-second away. Now with her passing, it was as though his whole world had come tumbling down—again.

Trying to ascertain why Papa's drinking had become so compulsive and sometimes unruly, I may never know the true reasons. But some of the things he did in the course of satisfying the habit, and all the needless worry he brought on Mama and me, and later to some of my younger brothers, in my opinion, was inexcusable. Because many times when he got off work, instead of coming straight home, he went to local bars. There, he found friends much like himself; steady customers who could also drink away the evening hours without a moment's worry about the needs at home. Papa was never a trouble-maker at the bars, he just wanted to drink and drown away his ever-present sorrows and listen to sad country music. On the evenings when he failed to come home for supper, Mama worried about him because she knew he was out drinking again. And each time, about nine or ten O'clock, if he still hadn't come home, she would tell me, *"Hijo, anda busca a tu Papa"* "Son, you better go look for your Papa."

So here I'd go, first to one bar then another, until I found him. Most of the time, he'd be in a friendly mood, a little tipsy, but outside of that, no problem. On finding him, I'd sit down beside him and immediately, all smiles, he'd introduce me to his drinking friends and proudly start bragging about me, telling them what a good boy I was, and so on. But right away, I'd start coaxing, *"Ya vamonos, Papa. Mama quere que te vengas para la casa."* "Let's go home, Papa. Mama wants you to come home."

At first, he'd refuse, but after a few minutes of pleading, he'd give in and we'd start for the house. The next day, it would be as though nothing ever happened, and off to work he'd go

It was routine, at times, for me to go and fetch Papa from the bars, usually on paydays. Later on, as my younger brothers were growing older, they too, were called on to do the same. Unfortunately, on one occasion when Papa didn't come straight home, he gave all of us the fright of our lives. It was on a night when he had been beaten and robbed of his entire paycheck. When little brother Johnny went looking for him, he found him in the alley at the rear entrance of Tony Rego's bar with severe head lacerations, bleeding and unconscious. He was hospitalized for seven days.

Papa's Home Brew In those days of prohibition, it was illegal to buy or sell alcohol and also illegal to make home brew. Papa knew this and chose to ignore it. He couldn't see any harm in making homebrew just for personal enjoyment. He probably figured that if he made beer at home, he wouldn't have to patronize the taverns as frequently and would spend more time at home. It would have been a noble thought, but it didn't exactly turn out that way. Because making his own homebrew, only deepened the wounds of an already shaky situation at home. *Why? Because of me!* I would be the focus of new grounds for more family strife.

After having successfully brewed a few crocks of beer, Papa insisted that I learn how to skim the fermentation from the crock, fill the bottles, and apply the bottle caps. I had no choice in the matter and neither did Mama. But did she ever protest! Yes Siree! Loud and clear. She accused Papa of teaching me how to make beer and later becoming an alcoholic like him. She absolutely couldn't stand it when he involved me in his beer production. I don't know how many times they fought over me, and the new role Papa made me play in making beer. But each time, he rejected her demands and refused to listen, saying there was nothing wrong in what he was doing. If ever there was a time when Mama hated Papa for his stubbornness, it would be a time like this, when he forced me to be a part of his repulsive beer habit.

Eventually, however, Mama would all but surrender to Papa's insistence on making home brew. If for no other reason, her concession would be only to prevent this explosive issue from resurfacing and to avoid further outrageous arguments over a 'no win' situation. After that, it became routine for me, and each time, I did as I was told.

Each time when he was ready for another crock, Papa would send me to town for supplies. First, Burgess Hardware for bottle caps and then to Fred Walker Grocery for the malt, sugar and yeast. I always felt so stupid and embarrassed when I asked for these items, because Fred liked to quiz me about it. He'd say, "What's your daddy gonna do with the malt and yeast, son?" I hated it when he'd ask me that. He knew very well what Papa was going to do with it. But I'd just say, "I don't know."

Police Raid. Apparently, during those days of prohibition, there were other people making home brew because Pabst Blue Ribbon Malt was a hot item at Fred Walker's grocery store and beer-bottles and bottle caps could readily be purchased at Burgess's Hardware. It was during Papa's home-brewing days that we found out Lawrence Strickland, directly across the road from our house, was also a home brew maker. One day when police were raiding his house, nearing suppertime, we heard weird noises coming from his house. When we all went to look, we saw that the noise we were hearing was the explosions from beer-filled bottles that the police were crashing against some rocks in Lawrence's back yard. As we watched this frightening raid, of course, Papa's first thought was that we would be next.

Perhaps Papa had anticipated something like this because some time previously, he had cut out a trap door in our floor directly under the bed that led under the house. It was barely big enough for one person to get through. *That person was me.* All of us were scurring around inside the house like frightened rabbits, wondering what to do. We certainly didn't want Papa going to jail. So, frantically, he ordered me to get under the house through the trap door on the double, which I did, lickety split. No sooner had I'd gotten under the house, when here comes Papa's entire stock of beer-filled bottles of home brew. Mama and Papa were tossing them to me in such a frenzy that I could hardly keep from bursting them. When the last bottle came down, I came topside and we all waited to see if we would be next. Naturally, we all pretended to be calm and peaceful, like any other ordinary law-abiding unsuspecting family. But no! The police never came. This was a lucky day for us, but not for Lawrence. They took him to jail. We never found out how the police were tipped off, but afterwards, we laughed and laughed many times over this hair-raising close call.

Papa never learned a lesson from the night he was beaten and robbed, nor the police raid on our neighbor, Lawrence, because he continued making home brew for quite some time. And all it did was reduce the number of visits to the bars, not the beer intake. Somehow, he still never saw anything wrong with making home brew at home, and of course, Mama never agreed and continued to wage war against it.

The younger kids never really worried much about Papa's drinking and our disturbing situation at home like I did, but I learned to despise it, same as Mama. I was partial to her beliefs and convictions, mostly because I had personally witnessed some of his harsh treatments of her—*some of which turned physical.*

All this conjecture about possible reasons for Papa's drinking and being out of touch with the family, was difficult to understand. Thank goodness those moments of anger and fighting moods were infrequent. We all loved Papa, despite his beer obsession. When he came home from the bars, often times, he'd be in a playful mood and felt like singing. When he came home in a good mood, we would ask for our payday which was usually a nickel, and sometimes he'd oblige by pulling out his little snap-top coin purse and dig around until he came up with some nickels. Other times, however, when sorrows weighed heavy on his mind, he'd easily become tearful and mutter things that didn't make a lot of sense. And being such a sentimentalist, the slightest thought of any misfortune in the lives of his family in Villa de Reyes, would easily trigger an emotional sob story. It was times like these when he obviously needed someone's love and attention, because, he sure wasn't getting Mama's…at least not one hundred percent.

One day during those trying days with Papa, after a bitter quarrel, I happened to see Mama standing in front of the screen door of the kitchen just looking out into blank space, softly crying. I put my arm around her waist and asked, "*¿Que tienes Mama?¿Porque lloras?*" "What's wrong, Mama? Why are you crying?" At first she hesitated; then, with a cracking in her voice, she answered, "Son, I wish you'd never have to grow up." "*La Vida es muy dura*" "Life is so hard…." She never told me why she was crying, but at that moment, I didn't need an explanation.

Divulging other sides of Papa perhaps never should have been brought to light, because just like Mama, he was a fantastic person with an endless pride for his family.

"*Soy rico,*" he would say. "*Soy rico con mis hijos*" "I'm a rich man. Rich in all my children." Absolutely true. Though dirt poor in material wealth, truly, he was a rich man surrounded by a loving family.

From the beginning, Papa pushed the hardest for the American dream of success and prosperity. But now that his dream no longer seems important, it raises the question, "What's next? End of story?"

Absolutely not! As it will be seen, he merely passes the dream torch to Mama, *and the pursuit continues......*

When Papa and Mama moved into the "Y" in 1927, they never dreamed that thirteen years later, they'd still be living in the same little old shack unable to afford anything better. But unfortunately, their fate thus far had not allowed otherwise, and their beautiful dream of someday owning a small cottage all their very own, seemed to be fading. And now that the dreadful Japanese war has started, the whole country's future is in a state of uncertainty.

Me.....well, I'm still trying to grow up and trying to help out as much as I can.

Let's continue.....

PART IV

▼

SUCCESS IS FINALLY IN THE OFFING FOR JUAN AND EDELIA

CHAPTER 25

▼

PRE-WORLD WAR II
ACTIVITY IN THE "Y"—
1940

All the years in the "Y" when Papa was working my butt off, were finally beginning to pay off. **Now 16 years old**—like him—I loved to work and it seemed that the harder the work, the bigger the challenge for my young ambitious body. A trait of responsibility for my family, out of necessity, had been instilled in me, which made it even more challenging to become a wage earner like Papa. The depression was not yet a thing of the past, but jobs were slowly beginning to open up. Particularly after President Roosevelt's Federal Relief Agency had been set in motion, which included the formation of the Civil Conservation Corps—CCC camps—an agency designed to take young unmarried men from relief rolls and put them to work in Federal projects, such as; restoration of forests, parks, beaches, flood control and other relief projects. Men of all ages who had previously been out of work, quickly applied for jobs in the CCC camps. Obviously, the CCC camps were out of the question for me, because we weren't on any relief rolls, but I still wanted to find work for the summer.

Many unemployed men, at the time, were going to the downtown unemployment office at 2nd Street and Elwood, and of course, I thought I'd give it a try also. Each day, Mama fixed me a small lunch and off I'd go, to the unemployment office. As usual, there was always quite a gathering of other men standing around waiting to be dispatched to a job somewhere, perhaps for one or two days work, or maybe just a few hours. On arriving, I'd sign in, giving my full name, then I'd join the other fellows—most of whom were old enough to be my father—and wait for a call. For a solid week, I waited and waited, eating my lunch on the premises so as not to miss my name, should it be called. But this endeavor was to no avail. I was never called. Soon after that, however, my luck changed.

As I walked toward our house a few days later, I noticed a ditch digging crew of approximately eight men, working near the Frisco Hotel on 21st Street, parallel to the Street Car line. On second glance, I saw that my friend Joe Perez—one of Doña Salome's older sons—was one of the ditch diggers. Needing to work and eager to take on anything, I ran up to Joe and started inquiring about the possibility of hiring in also. Laughingly, he tried to discourage me, saying that ditch digging was extremely hard and back-breaking and that I should forget it. But yielding to my persistence, he finally pointed to a fellow at the far end of the trench, saying, "Go talk to that man over there. He's the foreman."

Immediately, I did as he said. With a lively step, I walked up to the foreman and said, "Sir, my name is Cecil Gomez. I live right over there," pointing to our house across the railroad tracks. "I was wondering if you're hiring any extra help today?"

Now the foreman saw me coming and probably knew that I was looking for work and had already decided that I was too young, because his first words were, "Son, I don't need any more help today." Grinning, he continued. "Besides, this is man's work. This kind of work is too hard for you."

From the answer he gave, I was almost sure he might be persuaded to reconsider, so I pleaded, "Sir, the work isn't too hard. I can do it. I can handle a shovel and a pick pretty good."

"Have you ever done any manual labor like this before?" he asked.

"Yes Sir, I have. I dug a water line to our house," again pointing to our house.

Scratching his head, wondering what to do, he finally said, "OK young man. I'll try you for a few days." Pointing to his Company truck parked alongside the streetcar tracks, he said, "Go over there and get a shovel and start digging."

Was I ever surprised. My persistence had paid off. Immediately, I took my position next to Joe and started digging.

Now the work was hard. A lot harder than I'd expected. Trying to prove my strength and stamina, I fought at the ground fiercely, and soon, I was feeling signs of heat exhaustion. Joe noticed my face was red as a beet and in a fatherly tone of voice, which I took as a slight scolding, he said, "Cecil, I told you to take your time. Don't work so fast in this hot sun, it'll kill you. When you get tired and out of breath, stop and rest for a minute." Pointing to a 5-gallon container of cold water, he said, "Go over there and get a drink and rest for a minute. You'll be alright."

He was absolutely right. I definitely was trying too hard. After that, I began top pace myself as Joe had advised.

The job lasted for two weeks and finally, I had gotten a taste of some extremely hard manual labor. Now I knew just how hard people like Papa who worked on the railroad, had to work day in and day out in the hot sun, just to make us a living. This experience taught me that digging a gas line five feet wide and five feet deep, a quarter of mile long, was not the kind of work I would want on a permanent basis. But the best part was my paycheck—my first real paycheck with my name on it. Right away, I cashed it, then gave it to Mama

Looking back at all the work I'd done, it was beginning to look like manual labor was the only kind of work out there for me. Because my very next job this summer would again consist of hard manual labor.

It happened one sunny afternoon, when in the "Y", several of us boys were playing softball in front of Don Arcadio's house. It was my turn at bat, and just as I stepped up to the plate, I noticed a long black car drive up alongside and toot the horn. I'd never seen this car in the "Y" before, and I thought surely the driver must be lost. Just then, the man in the car motioned for me to come closer, so I did. As I stepped up and braced my hand on top of his car, I asked, "Yes sir. Can I help you?"

Giving me the once over, he replied, "I'm looking for someone who might be looking for work. Would you know of anyone?"

Instantly, all kinds of thoughts were going through my mind, because the only person I knew looking for work, was me. So I answered, "No Sir, I don't know of anyone around here looking for work, but I could sure use a job."

He grinned amusingly, took a couple of puffs on his pipe then responded. "I'm afraid not, son. The kind of job I have is hard work and it calls for a much older person."

I could see immediately that this man was quite friendly by the way he chuckled. So jokingly, I made a pitch for the job again, saying, "Aw c'mon mister, give me a chance. I've done hard work before."

Of course I knew that, but he didn't. I could tell that he thought I was big enough, but just not old enough, when he said, "I'd get in trouble with your mother if I put you to work.

Immediately, I suggested. "Let's go ask her."

"Alright," he said, still smiling. "Where do you live?"

"Right here," I said, pointing to our house.

Mr. Fox was a nice chubby man. When he laughed, one couldn't help but notice the narrow spaces between his little white teeth. My guess is, he weighed about 200 pounds, stood right at 5' 8" tall, and was wearing overalls. He stepped out of his shiny Buick Sedan leaving his wife waiting, while we walked to our front door. When Mama came to the door, he introduced himself very politely, tipping his old work hat, saying, "Good afternoon Ma'am, my name is Fox. I'm in your neighborhood looking for a man to hire for the summer. Your boy here says he's looking for a job and wants to go to work for me. He looks a bit young for the kind of work I have, so I thought I'd better ask you to see what you think."

Mama was certainly surprised. She wasn't prepared for a knock on our door from a total stranger, much less, an employer looking for men to hire. When she asked for more details, Mr. Fox began explaining that he was in the concrete block business and was looking for an older person to hire—until I applied for the job. He continued to express concerns about my age and the possibility that the work he had in mind might be too hard. Mama already knew that I was a young workhorse, and also, how badly I wanted a job.

Apparently, a job was on her mind too because without thinking twice, she said, "Yes. He can work for you. My boy is a good worker."

And with that, I got the job. Mr. Fox turned to me and said, "Young man, I'll pick you up at 8"00 O'clock tomorrow morning right here at your house." Grinning from ear to ear, I thanked him. "Thank you sir. I'll be ready."

Sure enough, the next morning Mr. Fox was right on time, and I was waiting. His residence, located on the corner of 19th and Olympia Street was a super nice bungalow. In the rear of the house, next to the alley, was his concrete block assembly shop, which housed five flat rail cars. Each car was miniature in size, open top, only 4' wide x 8' long, and no more than 30 inches high. The kind of concrete blocks that Mr. Fox fabricated were the kind used in foundations for houses and commercial buildings, each weighing about 40 pounds. I could tell he had a fair size business in West Tulsa and surrounding communities because his phone rang quite often as customers called to place orders.

Getting started that first day was not bad. The first thing we did was to push the five little rail cars outside to their proper position for receiving ready-mixed concrete. Then, we placed pre-oiled dividers and panels inside each rail car that would ultimately form a concrete block with a wavy design on the front side. Each little rail car produced 36 concrete blocks. When everything was ready to go, we'd start up the one-cubic yard cement mixer and start mixing concrete and filling the 36 empty slots. Once commencing, there was no stopping until all five rail cars were filled and dressed out—four hours later.

The third day consisted of removing all the panels and dividers from each car and prepare for unloading. And here's where the real work began. One by one, I had to remove each block from its casting mold, carry it 50 feet out to the yard, and start stacking. Sometimes the stacks could easily exceed six feet high. Hard work? Absolutely! By the end of the day, every muscle in my body had been severely strained beyond aching—they hurt.

My pay was good, I thought—45 cents per hour. Mr. Fox and I got along great and I could tell that he was pleased with my work. Now, I really did have a steady job. Mama was very happy too, because now, we could afford some little extras for the house.

After having been employed at Mr. Fox's for over a year, one Saturday morning, we had a terrifying accident at the shop. While pouring concrete, me on the far side of the huge cement mixer and he on the opposite side, the 12" conveyor belt began squeaking noisily and needed lubricating. So Mr. Fox casually picked up a tube of belt dressing, stepped over to the speeding belt on the drive shaft and began applying the waxy lubricant as it revolved—round and round. All of a sudden, his hand slipped and the fast revolving conveyor belt sucked his entire left arm under the belt and wedged it over the steel drive shaft, crushing his arm. Immediately, he started yelling for me and I knew something terrible had happened. I flung my shovel to the ground, came around the cement mixer and leaped over the rail cars to the other side. Mr. Fox had been thrown to the ground with his arm still caught between the belt and the shaft all the way up to his shoulder, and bleeding badly. The motor was still grinding away, and on hearing the hum of the stifled motor, as fast as I could, I ran to the electric breaker box and flipped off the switch, then ran back to Mr. Fox. I knew that I'd have to find a way to free his arm, so in sheer panic, I immediately took hold of the thick 12" belt and with both feet propped against the frame, I pulled the belt in reverse direction with every ounce of strength in my body. Fortunately, inch by inch, I was able to reverse the belt just enough to free his arm, and with each yank, he screamed in sheer agony. As his upper body had been partly suspended off the ground by the driving force of the belt, as soon as I freed his arm, he fell to the ground, bleeding and in enormous pain. His shirtsleeve had been completely shredded. Excitedly, I ordered Mr. Fox not to move, while I called for an ambulance. Leaving him sprawled on the ground, I ran to the house frantically, and started banging on the back door as hard as I could until Mrs. Fox finally answered. Instantly, I yelled, "Quick! Call an ambulance! Mr. Fox has been hurt." Screaming and in shock, she did exactly as I ordered, then I ran back to Mr. Fox and held his head in my lap until the ambulance arrived. After the ambulance drove away with Mr. and Mrs. Fox, I felt like it was my turn to collapse. Even though I had remained cool headed throughout this horrendous ordeal, my whole body felt jittery and limp as if I was about to go to pieces.

The next day, I visited Mr. Fox at the hospital and learned that he would be alright. His arm was broken in several places and severely fractured, but otherwise, he would recover in good time. Needless to say, he expressed his gratitude time and time again, and each time, he declared that I literally saved his life. In the days and weeks that followed—with a nice increase in pay—I was given complete authority to continue operating the shop as I deemed necessary, including hiring whomever I chose, which I did.

Working for Mr. Fox as a teenager, while still in school and receiving a nice paycheck every week, boosted my confidence enormously. I was gradually learning the value of the almighty dollar and what it could do, and I really liked it. Taking my place among the adult work force was giving me proud strains of a budding manhood that naturally wanted more. So much so, that I didn't want it to stop. I even considered dropping out of school and start searching for full-time employment. I didn't like high my school anyway.

Attending Holy Family Catholic High School, now in my sophomore year, was anything but enjoyable. I felt out of place. No, it wasn't the school, nor the sisters, and certainly not the wonderful priests. I really liked serving mass at the beautiful Cathedral. At least, when serving mass, there was no distinction between the rich and the poor. It was the school's snobbish classmates that I didn't like, nor the way those spoiled catholic brats flaunted their wealthy attitudes and their fine clothes. The shabby clothes that I wore was a dead giveaway as to our humble circumstances at home, and many times, I felt shunned. Also, not being able to afford noon lunches at the cafeteria, made me feel all the more inferior. There was no denying that my inferiority complex constantly reminded me that I wasn't one of them. At any rate, it was resentment hard for me to deal with.

Wrestling with the idea of dropping out of school at the start of my junior year, was really tearing me up. I knew how Mama felt about the importance of my education, and I hadn't forgotten how tough and trying all her sacrifices had been in getting me this far. We had discussed this subject several times before, but she never yielded. Her wisdom was always far greater than mine when she explained the implications and the pitfalls of the lack of a good education. She could have consented to my dropping out of school, considering our need for supplemental income, but for her, the importance of an education far out-weighed all other considerations. I had tried thinking positive and making allowances for feelings of inferiority among my classmates, but all I could think of, was, 'who needs it'.

Finally, after much mind wrenching, I got the courage to tell Mama about my decision to quit school. Of course, she was very disappointed and tried to make me reconsider, but she knew my mind was made up. Knowing how much my education meant to her, I promised that someday, I'd go back to school for my high school diploma (Which I did) *At the time, however, I had every intention of finding a good-paying job, but had no idea that we would soon be at war with Japan.*

Just before Japan attacked Pearl Harbor, I had celebrated my 18th birthday. The war in Europe had already been going on, but as far as I was concerned, there was not yet cause for me to be alarmed. After all, the "Y" was worlds away from Pearl Harbor and Germany. Until now, I had not yet taken the war news very seriously and was still pretty naïve as to the war problems of the world. Even after the attack on Pearl Harbor, I still wasn't convinced that young boys my age would ever be called off to war. Things around our house remained peaceful and quiet, and though the continuing news of war found its way into the "Y", we tried to keep it pushed aside and go on with our daily routines. On occasion, however, Mama would bring up the subject of war, worrying of course, unable to hold back signs of fear. And when she prayed, she prayed for the war to end soon, because in her heart, it was me that she worried about. The possibility of me going off to war, was constantly on her mind. Within a year, however, that possibility was becoming more and more a reality.

That stark reality came in January 1942 by way of a notice from the Tulsa Draft Board for me to register within 60 days. When I received the notice, it was the 'wake-up' call I wasn't prepared for. My friends Joe Perez and Jerry Edison had already enlisted in the Navy, and now, finally, it dawned on me that, I too, would soon be added to the induction list for active military service. All this draft business started when President Roosevelt—foreseeing the impending possibilities of our entering the war in Europe—signed into law the Selective Service Act in which every male between the ages of 18 and 65 had to register. Accordingly, two months after turning 19 in mid-January, 1942, I registered for the draft, and within a week, I received my draft card. My classification was 4-A. What else!

Shortly after having registered for the draft, I finally found the job I had been looking for. It was with Maloney Tank and Manufacturing Company, located at 38 N. Peoria in Tulsa. Prior to Japan's attack on Pearl Harbor, the Company manufactured oilfield storage tanks, but when the war came along, they too united with the rest of the country in the mass production of war equipment. Their war product consisted of fabricated steel airplane landing mats to be installed and used by the military in building emergency airfield landing strips in war-torn areas abroad. So urgent was the production assembly line, that the company worked around the clock—three full shifts—employing over 100 factory men and women.

As soon as my application was accepted, I was called in for preliminary instructions and orientation. After having passed a rigid physical exam. I was photographed for identification, given an employee number, a war badge, and a gate pass. My starting pay was 59-1/2 cents per hour.

My foreman, Chester Moore—a peach of a fellow—was greatly impressed with my output on the job. Every once in a while, he'd come over to where I was working and whisper in my ear, "I got you a three cent raise." Sometimes, it was 4-1/2 cents, and other times, it would be 5 cents.—and my hourly rate just kept climbing and climbing, and certainly, a great alleviation to our financial struggles at home.

I continued working at Maloney all through the winter months knowing all along that the day was fast approaching that I would be drafted into the Army. Never a day went by, that the thought of going off to war didn't prey on my mind. Filled with apprehension, I couldn't understand why it was, that—when I finally landed a good job and able to assist in providing for our family—almost as much as Papa—I'd have to chuck it all in. I didn't want to go off to war and leave Papa and Mama in the "Y", groping daily under serious unstable conditions.

Continuing to worry about the fate of our family, should I be drafted, I thought surely there had to be an exemption from service for me if I'm bound by obligation to provide support for our family. No one knew better than Mama and me, the seriousness of our financial woes. Papa's income at the Frisco fell far short of what the family needed to get by, and it was with this deep concern that prompted me to seek deferment from military service. But when I visited my

Draft Board requesting deferment on grounds of my duty-bound responsibility, my request was denied. After that, all I could do was wait.

Waiting was extremely worrisome because I didn't want to go into the Army. The Army, to me, meant being a soldier. And in wartime, being a soldier meant killing. I never did like guns, and the very thought of arming myself with weapons that could kill another person, nearly turned my stomach. So....what was I to do? Gradually, in the far reaches of my mind, I resigned myself to the fact that sooner or later, I would be compelled to join some other branch of service. And since the Army was not for me, I attempted to enlist in the U.S. Coast Guard, only to find that current quotas had already been filled, and the same, when I tried to enlist in the Merchant Marine. In this light, I had no choice but to volunteer for enlistment with the U.S. Navy.

To my great surprise, one week later, I received my induction papers from the local Navy department ordering me to report for enlistment on January 26th. On receipt of my induction papers, I immediately notified my employer, Maloney Tank Company, for which they were very understanding and promised me that after the war, my job would be waiting for me.

The next ten days would be filled with much sadness, a lot of emotion and soul searching. **Josephine Garcia**, my childhood sweetheart and I, had become very close and the thought of leaving her behind was extremely hard. Mama tried her best to remain calm and unemotional, but at times, the pain in her heart gave way, making it impossible to hold back the tears any longer. All she could think of was the uncertainty of the war and the ever-present possibility of me becoming a war casualty.

CHAPTER 26

▼

WORLD WAR II—1943

The beginning of this year, after having received my 'greetings' induction from the United States Navy, it has caused me to seriously reflect one last time on the "Y", including Mama and Papa and all my little brothers and sisters. Little did I realize that this would be my last year at home as a member of the household. Soon, I would be leaving, and in doing so, I would leave behind the most wonderful family in the world. Even though leaving would be heartbreaking, it wouldn't be near as painful as the overwhelming concern that I was bound to take with me when I left, worrying that my family's inability to maintain a decent livelihood would worsen.

In my absence, Mama would, of course, continue to slave away every day with no end in sight to the demands of raising our large family. She would continue to make many personal sacrifices for the betterment of the children, and of course, Papa would continue working seven days a week and being himself, tinkering around the house and yard, sporadically attending to the needs of the family, and with an occasional self-indulgence at the bars or his homebrew at home.

My brother Cenobio (Noble) is now age 17 and deeply committed to his friends and good times. But still very stubborn and filled with animosity toward our living conditions in the "Y" and the inescapable fact that he happens to be a member of such a large Mexican family. But despite his blunt rejection of our lifestyle, he still has a tremendous love for Mama, Papa, and the whole family, as well as love and respect for me.

Manuela (Nellie) is now age 15 and starting to be a big help to Mama. But like most young teenagers, she too, is feeling the strains of the humdrum boredom of the household and starting to look for exciting pastime pleasures and social life outside the "Y", as I had done.

Juanito (Johnny) now 13, is a carefree young boy with an easy-going personality and with a warm and tender heart, also, with a very entertaining sense of humor.

Virginia, now at age 11, is developing a most pleasing and compassionate personality. Her resemblance to Mama is very striking and she readily accepts our adverse living conditions.

All the rest of the children are still in tender growing stages and still a bit too young to characterize, but no doubt, each one will develop his or her own unique personalities. I'm absolutely sure that their waiting future will be much like my past—romping all over the "Y" and exploring West Tulsa. Alberto is 9 years old, Miguel (Michael) is 7, Guadalupe (Lupe) is 5, and Felipa (Phyllis) is 2.

On the morning of January 26, 1943, a cool brisk day—typical of Oklahoma winters—I was ready for my departure to the U.S. Navy and had already said a heartbreaking farewell to Josephine the night before. Mama had been up early this morning and had already lit a candle at our little prayer alter and prayed the rosary. As she stirred around in the kitchen scrambling me some eggs, she was crying softly and almost speechless from anguish and worry. I knew her heart was breaking in two, when she called out to me, *"Bueno, hijo. Ya esta tú almuerzo."* "Your breakfast is ready son."

"OK, Mama. I'm coming."

As I stepped down into the kitchen, she broke down in tears, clutching her apron to her face. And as she leaned against the wall, trembling and unable to contain the hurt of saying good-bye, she cried out pitifully, *"Ay corazon ya te vas! Ay Papasito, que dolor tan pesado tengo en el pecho! No se que voy hacer sin ti."* "Oh, son, you're leaving. I can't stand this pain in my chest." Continuing with a cracking in her voice, she said, "Son, I wish you didn't have to go. I don't know what I'm going to do without you."

"Mama! Mama!" I said, rushing to her side. Turning her around, I embraced her gently once more and tried to console her.

"Mama, please don't cry. I'll be alright. You'll see. I'll write you as soon as I get to California." By this time, Papa had joined our embrace, adding his misty tears of farewell.

On finishing my breakfast, still sobbing softly, Mama motioned for me to come to our little prayer alter, saying, *"Hincate hijo."* "Kneel down, son." And so I did. Looking at Papa, she said to him, *"Dale la bendicion a tú hijo."* She was asking him to give me his blessing. As I knelt before my parents, Papa made a bold sign of the cross over me and gave me his blessing. "In the name of the Father, and of the Son, and of the Holy Spirit

After embracing each of my siblings, I said good-bye, as Papa walked me to the front gate for a final embrace.

As I walked away from the house to catch the bus at 21st and Quanah Boulevard, I was overcome with all sorts of crazy feelings and thoughts going through my mind. In a way, I felt big and important because I would soon be in uniform serving my country. But also, I felt small and too young to leave home, certainly unprepared for what lay ahead. Moreover, it was the sadness I felt in seeing the hurt in my parent's eyes. Personally, I wasn't afraid of going off to war. By now, I had been keeping abreast of the daily war news and knew of the war's ongoing devastation, as well as the lives being lost in the Pacific and on the European front. But at the moment, I was having trouble with true patriotism. Of course, I loved my country and had great pride in being an American. But going off to war and leaving Papa and Mama in a state of destitution, was my deep concern. My feeling of obligation and responsibility for them sliced through me from all sides. I was certainly not ready to be whisked away from the dire needs of my family.

On the train bound for San Diego, I found myself in the company of dozens of other young recruits just like myself. Some appeared to be excited, some quiet, and others like me, sad and lonesome. I wanted to be alone to unscramble my clouded mind and the confusion of this sudden change of direction in my life. After all, California was still three days away. As I sat there in the farthest corner seat of the passenger coach staring aimlessly out of the window, watching the turned-brown countryside swish by, I knew I'd have plenty of time to clear my troubling thoughts. The lonesome clickety-clack rhythm of the train was already beginning to soothe my mind, shutting out the exuberant, noisy laughter of some of the other recruits in the jam-packed coach. Soon, the somber reality of who I was, where I was going, and why, began to self-explain. Why....of course! This is America, and I'm an American. And the reason I'm here is clear as a bell. I'm just like all these other Okies sitting around me. We're all going to fight to protect our great country. Funny I'd never looked at it like that before. At this conclusion, I began to feel better about myself.

Sitting there quietly in a cloud of cigarette smoke, staring out of the coach window, it was as though the fast moving countryside was responding to my thoughts, which were holding fast to the lonesomeness I was feeling. At that particular moment, it dawned on me that the Christmas just passed would be my last for quite some time. All of a sudden, sweet and sad recollections began to appear, particularly this last Christmas in the "Y". Even as poor as we were, we couldn't help but feel the joyous season approaching and cheerfully welcomed the spirit of Christmas. I guess for people all over the world, Christmas is a most special time of the year, and at our house, it was no different. I've heard it said, that 'for everything there is a season' and certainly if this reference applies to the season of love and family togetherness, then the Gomezes would rank among the top. The spirit of Christmas never failed to find its way into our little house and family, and even though down through the years there had been many bumps along the way, at Christmas time, no matter how lean or simple, all the hardships of the past were forgotten and forgiven.

Christmas Eve always found Mama extremely busy in the kitchen, and just like all Christmases past, this was the season when she made a huge batch of the tastiest hot tamales in town. True to the Mexican custom and tradition, hot tamales were in the making throughout the "Y". By mid-afternoon, the aroma of slow cooked, steaming hot tamales filled the whole house and neighborhood. By suppertime, Mama would have prepared stacks of *tortillas de maiz, tortillas de arina, bacon flavored pinto beans, steaming brown rice sprinkled with green peas, mole, salsa,* and for desert—*juicy buñuelos* sweetened with *canela,* cinnamonin sticks. Finally at the supper table, when the whole family sat side-by-side enjoying a meal fit for a king, our Christmas feast began. At that very moment, when the entire family was together and the joyous sounds of chatter and laughter noisily vibrated our little house, it became the festivity everyone had been waiting for. Truly, the spirit of Christmas had completely embraced our bulging little house, allowing us to forget the hovering cares of the day, and join the whole world as we celebrated our own little family Christmas.

From the first day I was old enough to talk, Mama taught us to always give thanks after each meal. Not a blessing of the Lord's bounty, nor a beseeching for the nourishment of our bodies, etc. Very simply, it was '*Gracias a Dios*'. Each of us, as we finished eating our humble Christmas meal, gave thanks to God in the way we were taught—*Gracias a Dios.* After our Christmas feast, the whole family celebrated the birth of Jesus Christ at St. Catherine midnight Mass.

As I sat there on the train—my eyes glued to the fleeting countryside—I couldn't help reflecting on many wonderful memories of the past. Funny how the memories we treasure the most, we don't really treasure until we suddenly come face to face with their disappearing, as though they were being dejected from our minds. That's exactly how I felt on the train when the full realization of leaving home finally hit me. Fond family memories began to collect in my growing lonesomeness.

Memories like…..

The time when our little house was about to be blown away by a tornadic windstorm, and strewn debris was flying wildly through the air, and how at the same time, when we were being pounded by hail and a deluge of rain and lightening, Papa grabbed a large butcher knife from the kitchen and rushed outside under extreme turbulent conditions. And with the knife in his hand, looking skyward at the monstrous storm, he made a huge Sign of the Cross, defying the devil, shouting, "*Vete de aquí, Demonio.*" "Be gone, you devil"…..

And how about the chickens we raised; the Rhode Island Reds, the White Leghorns, and the Dommineckers, and how Mama always kept their wings clipped to keep them from flying over our chicken wire fence; and how she'd ask me to wring a chicken's neck on Sundays so we could have chicken for dinner…..

Serving Mass as an altar boy, too, was very special. How could I forget serving Mass at Our Lady of Guadalupe—the all-Mexican church where I made my First Holy Communion…..

Nor will I ever forget my first guitar—the one Angela bought me at Sears Roebuck in Kansas City, and the many times I played country music with my jamming buddies Bob Glance and Luther Todd, and how music became such a big part of my life when I became an avid fan of Bob Wills and his Texas Playboys, frequently attending their 12 O'clock live noon broadcasts, and later, going to the Saturday night dances at Cains Academy…..

How good I felt, too, when I made it possible for our neighbor Antonio Chaves to return home from a trip to Mexico after he was robbed of all his money and passport. Stranded in Mexico, he wrote me, desperately pleading for my help, asking me to re-establish proof of his legitimate residency in West Tulsa. Even though I was only fourteen years old, he had great confidence in me when he asked me to procure official notarized documents from his employer—the Frisco—and various West Tulsa creditors who could attest to the validity of his residence in Oklahoma—a and how appreciative he was for all my efforts on his return…..

And how could I ever forget **the day a total stranger came to our house** looking for Papa—a handsome well-built Mexican, also in his early 50's, and who obviously couldn't speak much English. It was the way the electrified reception took place, that no one could ever forget—especially me at age nine. When Papa opened the door, instantly, he recognized the man. And from the way Papa yelled out at the top of his lungs, as if suddenly seeing a long lost relative from Villa de Reyes, **Pedro! Pedro!** immediately I knew who the man was. It could be none other than 'Pedro', his hobo friend—that train-hopping guy—the one whom he'd often talked about when recalling his initial journey to America. In sheer delight, they embraced each other extremely excitedly, shouting crazy, affectionate greetings of surprise, then grabbed each other and began scuffling and tumbling all over the floor, laughing uncontrollably. At first, their initial contact appeared as though they were fighting mad, but no—they were just overjoyed in having found each other again. Afterwards, for hours on end, they reminisced on the past, sometimes sentimentally, and other times hilariously, about their incredible adventure to America. For two whole days, they feasted happily over food and beer. I later learned that Pedro had found Papa through Rafael Peña in Seguin, Texas.

These memories and many more, no doubt, I'll carry with me no matter where this war takes me, particularly the one about Mama, how at suppertime when she always made her daily 8" stack of delicious hot tortillas and how that mouth-watering aroma of tortillas hovered all around the house. And how **she always called me to supper** by stepping outside, wiping away the perspiration from her face with her apron, and how at the top of her voice, so I could hear her wherever I might be playing, she'd yell, **"C e c I i o"...."C e c I i o."** What a beautiful sound and such a precious memory. One that I will forever keep engraved in my mind and soul.

It was getting dark outside and our slow moving train was still in Oklahoma. So far, it had made four stops: Stroud, Oklahoma City, El Reno, and Elk City. And each time we stopped, we picked up more recruits. I thought at this slow pace, we'd be forever getting to San Diego. The tone of the enthusiasm in the coach was already beginning to sound like a victory celebration. At that moment, as I found myself heading West as a Navy recruit, it just naturally forced a reality check in my life; like the war in the Pacific—a subject that I had previously ignored, thinking that war was for someone else—not me.

Now that I was wide awake to the reality of a war that included me, looking back to the days just before the attack on Pearl Harbor, I distinctly recalled the national news broadcast; how they'd not been good, and how the on-going fighting in Europe had begun to worry a lot of folks in Washington, and how their worries over the winds of war were beginning to spill over, dissipating the tranquility on the home front. Back then, however, I was too busy growing up to let it affect me. Still, it was hard to push it out of my mind altogether because the news media continued to expound on the fighting abroad. Even at the movies, one couldn't escape the newsreel accounts of the horrors of the European war and the German atrocities. They constantly hammered away on the aggression of Hitler and Mussolini.

I recalled how the words "Hitler" and "Germany" were just about on every tongue. And I thought, *Adolph Hitler? Who is this guy? How can one man on the other side of the world cause so much fear and unrest here in America?* Being so naïve at the time, I didn't worry about it that much, nor seriously concern myself with the news abroad. But I should have known that I couldn't look away from the truth indefinitely and pretend there was no possibility of war. To be convinced of war's inevitability, all one had to do was read the news accounts about the power-hungry motivations and ambitions of this madman in Germany who thinks he can conquer the whole world. Reportedly, his conquest had already seen the occupation of Netherlands, Czechoslovakia, Belgium, Norway and Poland, including France. By now, millions of courageous men had been trampled to their death by Hitler's war machine and his rage for world power,. So, with hundreds and perhaps thousands of men dying daily on the battlefield from Germany's conquest and the war news dominating the airwaves, it was becoming almost impossible to think that America could continue to remain neutral much longer.

Finally it happened. For whatever reason Americans might have been trying to stay cool to the drumbeat of war, they would no longer be kept in suspense. The grim news was out. America was finally drawn into war, **except—not with Germany or Italy—but with Japan.**

I'll never forget that Sunday morning of December 7, 1941, when all America was awakened to the full realization that war was not only imminent, but already knocking at our back door. It was a most tense and frightening feeling when the news of Japan's invasion of Pearl Harbor came over our radio. All the radios and loud speakers in the United States, and probably throughout the world, broadcast the astounding announcement by President Franklin Roosevelt; *"We interrupt this broadcast to bring you this special news bulletin—Pearl Harbor has been attacked by the Japanese."* As we listened intently to our radio, the news continued with broader details of the hideous events, and for hours, it seemed the news of the attack were being repeated over and over. At last, the shocking reality of America going to war had finally arrived. Papa immediately became worried because he still had vivid recollections of frightening troop movements and military activities that he'd witnessed during the days of World War l, just before settling in Oklahoma City.

It was reported that the Japanese attack had destroyed or damaged over 200 fighter planes and bombers. The battleships Utah, the Arizona, and the California, had been sunk, the Tennessee, the West Virginia, and the Pennsylvania were badly damaged, the Nevada had been beached, and the Oklahoma was capsized. Many other ships anchored in the bay were also damaged. Over two thousand men had been reported killed and many were missing.

The following day, a Monday, December 8, at 12:30 P.M., President Roosevelt gave one of the most courageous and inspiring speeches of his presidency when he *declared war against the Japanese Empire.* The next day, December 9, newspapers carried this headline: *Pacific battle widens—Manila area bombed.* Again, the following day, December 10, the headlines read: *Japanese invade the island of Luzon—Fight in Manila. Two British warships sunk.*

On December 11,1941, the United States declared war against Germany and Italy.

Shortly after Japan struck the first blow against the United States, Japanese Nationals living in America began paying a heavy price for their country's aggression. Even though most of them were innocent, President Roosevelt signed an executive order creating 'relocation camps' for all Japanese living in the United States. Later, it was reported that 120,000 Japanese-Americans had been rounded up and placed behind guarded camps to be detained for the duration of the war to guard against possible Japanese espionage.

Despite the horrid traumatizing war news, somehow I always felt confident that America would respond overwhelmingly, and my belief that America was still the greatest country in the world, never wavered. And, I was right, because immediately after the bombing of Pearl Harbor, all America began mobilizing for war. Almost overnight, from East to West, every sign of internal conflict within the government or division among citizens had vanished. War plants and ship building yards became one hundred percent operative from coast to coast, building guns, planes, tanks, ammunition and everything else that would support our military forces. Within the first year after Pearl Harbor, practically every freight train in the country was steaming back and forth from East to West—including

West Tulsa's congested Frisco train yards—with military shipments loaded to capacity with troops, armored tanks, field artillery, jeeps, trucks, and every other type of front line fighting equipment and supplies. Millions of Americans freely converted their life's savings into war bonds to build a war chest of billions of dollars to finance the war. Besides the thousands upon thousands of men enlisting in the armed forces, young women too, were joining the Army as WACS, and others in the Navy as WAVES. So urgent was the need to provide for our fighting men and women, that by late 1942 and early 1943, America was experiencing critical shortages of many basic commodities essential to the war effort and was forced to create a War Rationing Department nationwide. In Tulsa, our Rationing Board was set up at 616 S. Main for issuing ration books to families according to their size and need for purchasing precious items such as: gasoline, soap, sugar, rubber products, and even shoes.

As our troop train continued westward, huffing and puffing over the mountainous ranges of New Mexico, the black smoke of the engine and the constant sounds of clickety rails continued their musical rhythm, reminding me that our destination was still far away. This was our second day on the train, and I was already beginning to get homesick. Luckily, sitting next to me, was another recruit from around Oklahoma City way, who was a full blood Apache Indian. His name was Maynotonah. It was easy striking up a conversation with this young boy, because we quickly identified with each other. I believe it was the same color of our skin that sparked a brotherly friendship that would last for quite some time.

Also aboard the train, were dozens of colored recruits who sat apart from everyone else. But for them, there was not much hospitality. Quite to the contrary. Not only were they shunned, but occasionally snickered at by arrogant, prejudiced white boys. Every time I saw this, I couldn't help feeling sorry for them, especially when our troop train stopped en route for dinner at the Harvey houses and the Howard Johnson restaurants located inside the train stations. Like the time we stopped for dinner in Albuquerque. Hundreds of us were marched inside in an orderly manner where fine tables and chairs, eloquent silverware and place settings awaited us. But not the colored boys—they were segregated from everyone else and led into the kitchen or to the rear of the building for their dinner away from the main dining hall. Every time I saw this, I could feel their humiliation

After three days and nights, we finally arrived at the San Diego Naval Training Base where I would receive ten weeks of boot camp training. California was the farthest I'd ever been from home, and it seemed like an entirely new world. Within the hour after arrival, I learned first-hand the rigid regimentation of the military—and I didn't like it. First order of business was to be completely outfitted with a new wardrobe of Navy Uniform, including hat, underwear, shoes, leggings, pea coat, linens, blankets, and a sea bag. They offered us boxes for shipping our street clothes and personal belongings back home, but I had no valuables, and besides, the clothes I'd been wearing were ragged, so I trashed them all. The rest of the week, we stood in endless lines for inoculations of every kind imaginable.

Mr. Inglekey, our Company Commander, was a short medium build, hateful little man, barely taller than five feet, in his early 40's, and as humorless as a chicken. I don't know what his game plan was, but he had no intentions of making friends with anyone—to the contrary—I believe his primary purpose was to make our lives a living hell, in which he fully succeeded. From the very first time I laid eyes on him, I suspected there would be rough days ahead. From his podium, as he began introducing himself, he wound up yelling and shaking his arms wildly, trying to put the fear of God in our every thought. His last remarks from the podium that first day were "give your soul to God, because your ass belongs to me." Somehow, I knew what he meant. Many were the times when I saw him chew on a fellow recruit for a simple smirk or chuckle in ranks by getting right in his face and spewing saliva as he yelled, as though the unforgivable sin had been committed. And believe me, this characterization of Mr. Inglekey's tough disciplinary enforcement, is putting it mildly. For ten straight weeks, that little man literally gave us holy hell each and every day to the point that we were almost afraid of our own shadow.

When boot camp was finally over, Mr. Inglekey's mission had been accomplished, which was to remove any remaining signs of adolescence in his young recruits and to transform us into tough mature young men. Although I hated his guts, I respected him for his tough, unrelenting drilling tactics in order that I might grow up quickly and enter the real world of a country at war.

On completion of my boot camp training, all of us were given an aptitude test in order to determine our next immediate assignment. Lucky for me, I qualified for a supervisory position over four complete mess halls and kitchens. Some fellows from my camp were sent to gunnery schools, some to administrative posts, while others who weren't so lucky, were assigned to waiting ships for overseas duty. As their assignments were carried out, I never saw so many disappointed faces in my life, as those shipping out—and for good reason—they all knew that within 30 days they'd be in dangerous enemy waters. One young boy from New York cried like a baby and wanted to go home. But for me, it just wasn't my time yet, I guess, because for six weeks I had plush duty on the base. I was given complete authority over dozens of new incoming recruits and continued to enjoy stateside duty.

Not long after completing my boot camp training, I received a letter from home that completely devastated me. It was a letter about Papa. He had been fired from the Frisco, and of all things, the letter said that he was fired for stealing a pair of gloves. *Fired? For stealing?* No way! Papa would never steal. But being fifteen hundred miles away, I felt totally helpless. The only thing I could think of was, *what will happen to Papa and Mama and my siblings now?* The next day, I went to the Administration Office on the base and applied for leave, but of course, it was denied. However, when they heard my persisting story of urgent concern and verified the bad news contained in my letter, they—the Navy—came to our rescue authorizing a monthly allotment of $68.00 dollars for my family. Shortly afterwards, I went shopping in downtown San Diego and purchased a variety of clothes for my young siblings and shipped them home. Fortunately, two months later, I received word that Papa had been reinstated to his old job, and that the firing was all a mistake—Papa had been wrongfully accused by his prejudiced white foreman. The real thief had been found and fired.

All during the war, young girls and young mothers, all over the country were hopping trains, planes, and buses to be with their loved ones, even if just for a few days. Train stations, airports, and bus terminals were constantly overflowing day and night with travelers heading in all directions, and often, were stranded for lack of available lodging. The war had definitely awakened every loving heart in America and created a blanket of desperation among young lovers everywhere. Somehow, their love and feelings for each other were further intensified because of long periods of separation

Josephine and Cecil

and the uncertainty of their future. When listening to all those beautiful love ballads on the radio by Vaughn Monroe, Tommy Dorsey, Harry James, and Glenn Miller, it either excited the heart or made it more lonesome, depending on where your sweetheart was. And of course, Josephine and I were no different. She had come to be near me at Treasure Island Naval Base in San Francisco. After several weeks of living in constant suspense, waiting for our orders to ship out, we decided to get married. Hurriedly, we procured our marriage license and were married on the base by a Catholic Navy Chaplain only two days before shipping out to overseas.

My ship—the P.C. 782, a Patrol Craft—was a 185 feet long submarine chaser, so named because of its speed and maneuverability. The ship had just been recently built and launched for sea duty, but had never been thoroughly tested in ocean waters. However, after eight weeks of intensive sea and gunnery drills and exercises, we finally departed from San Francisco, which marked the beginning of a long stretch of overseas duty.

Most of that first day at sea went great. We had been sailing at a pretty good clip, perhaps 18 knots per hour, and at last, we had reached a distance far, far, from land. As far as the eye could see in any direction, only a blanket of green ocean swells could be seen swaying eternally against each other. For a young Okie like me, it was a beautiful experience to watch the ship cut its way through the white foamy waves and to feel the cool, brisk wind sharply brushing against my face, and all the while, listening to the constant mist of salt water spraying the bow, the port and starboard walkways, as the ship endlessly pushed onward.

The second day was much like the first, except that by nightfall, things began to change very drastically. A storm had been brewing at sea and heading toward the mainland. What started out as a pleasant voyage, turned out to be a nightmare. The storm became furious and deadly with dangerous crosswinds that kept trying to alter our course. The bow of the ship constantly kept nose-diving into 50 and 60 foot, fierce waves, as the torrential rains and 80 mile per hour winds tossed our ship around as though it was a matchbox. I never dreamed the Pacific Ocean could become so violent. Was I scared? Absolutely! Not just me, but most everyone else also, because none of us had ever seen or experienced anything so deadly. The oblivious storm was so intense that the possibility of capsizing was on everyone's mind. The only person aboard ship with enough experience to pull us through this tempest was our skipper—Mr. Thomas, a 25-year Navy veteran. He knew instinctively that we couldn't survive the storm without capsizing unless we altered our course. And so he did. He deliberately turned the ship squarely into the face of the deadly storm and prepared to meet its fury head on. But this didn't alleviate the ship's bucking and tossing, nor did it reduce the tremendous charge of the storm—to the contrary—it increased the impact of the giant crashing waves.

Late into the night, the violent storm continued to batter our ship, pounding at it from all sides. Life jackets had already been ordered on. Hardly anyone had eaten a thing since late afternoon due to the constant bucking, nor did they want to, since everyone's unsettled nerves had already been strained to the limit. So eating was the last thing on anyone's mind.

Now at this late night hour, not a single man would be safe on topside. Most of the crew, except for those on watch at the quartermaster deck and the fantail, were below deck. Unfortunately for me, however, I was stuck with the 12 O'clock midnight fantail watch. And I soon became the first casualty of the storm.

From my quarters near mid-ship, there was no way to get to the fantail without going topside, and for me to get back there, 90' away, would require split-second timing due to the dangerous bucking and listing of the ship. First, I had to unlatch the hatch door, jump to the outside, relatch the hatch door, all in split-second timing when the ship tilted to the opposite direction. All this, was so I wouldn't get inundated by the giant waves once outside. I knew this would be a dangerous sprint, particularly since all other personnel had already been ordered to stay off topside. But as my watch came up, those orders didn't apply to me.

For a few seconds, as the adrenaline surged through my body in fear of what I knew was waiting for me outside, I studied the listing of the ship. First starboard, then port, and again starboard, then port. Now—on my mark! Get set! Ready! Go! In a flash, I unlatched the door, jumped outside into a wall of water, flung the hatch door shut, relatched it, and as fast as humanly possible, I began making my way aft, gripping the life line cables with all my might to keep from being pitched overboard. At that frightening moment, I knew I was face to face with an angry wrathful sea, producing huge gigantic waves that nearly dwarfed our 185' vessel. I was praying the 'Our Father', soaked and wet, gripping the life line hand over hand, when all of sudden, a monstrous wave hit me broadside. It was so powerful that I lost hold of the lifeline and it flung me through the air inwardly, dropping me against an ammunition box and striking my face on its metal frame. Still conscious, laying flat on the deck, I grabbed hold of the ammunition box and hung on for dear life. I knew my face was cut badly, but I was not yet ready to panic. Of course, I was badly shaken, but I realized I still had a long way to go to the rear of the ship. Timing my advances for the remaining distance between thrusts of killer waves, I finally made my way back to the galley in the midst of one hellacious storm. Hours later, as I lay stretched out on one of the mess hall tables, the ship's doctor was finally able to tend to my facial wounds. But because of the storm's brutal rage and the ship's continuous lunging and tossing, it would not permit suturing, particularly above my right eye where most of the lacerations had occurred. The vicious storm and all its madness continued all through the night, and after the fourth day at sea, we finally pulled into Puget Sound Naval Yards in Seattle, Washington.

The next day, I was transported to the Naval Hospital in Bremerton, Washington. Our ship checked in to the Naval dry dock for minor repairs and leaks caused by the storm. After five days, the ship continued its course to the Aleutian Islands, while I remained behind. Our shipper assured me that on complete recovery, I would rejoin my ship. And sure enough, six weeks later, I too, was on my way to the Aleutian Islands.

The island of Attu was the farthest of all the Aleutian Islands in the far northwest stretches of the Bering Sea. Prior to the attack on Pearl Harbor, the island had been safeguarded by the presence of the Navy, but when Japan began its daring sweep through many of the South Pacific islands, they also hit Attu. Several ships in the bay, that day, were sunk. By the time our ship arrived, most of the war damage inflicted by Japan had already been repaired and the damaged ships restored. After Japan's initial attack on Attu, the strategy by the War Department was to place a string of warships from Attu to Dutch Harbor, then to the entire western coast of the U.S. mainland, and continuing southwest to Pearl Harbor. The plan, as we learned later, obviously, was to keep Japan away from striking distance of the western shores of Washington, Oregon, and California.

Our orders in the war, along with our sister ships, was to maintain vigilance around the entire island for enemy submarines, especially to the west in the direction of Japan, should they attempt another strike. Days on end, night after night, out of sight of land, through frigid temperatures and icy waters, our patrolling and maneuvering at sea remained on continuous alert for Japanese submarines.

In the early months that followed our arrival, we actually did make contact with Jap submarines on two different occasions. Each time, one was just as frightening as the other. The instant our radar detected a foreign sub, the sonar system went crazy with its continuous sounds of alarm, "ping," "ping," "ping." Immediately, the Radarman contacted the officer on deck, and instantly, 'general quarters' were barked out over the P.A. system, over and over, "Man your battle stations!" "Man your battle stations!" When the shrieking siren sounds of general quarters came blaring through every loud speaker throughout the ship, whether asleep, at mealtime, on duty, or wherever one might be, every man jumped feverishly into action. In most cases, there wasn't time to strap on a life jacket, because within 45 seconds, all battle stations had to be manned and awaiting further orders. There's something very sobering about the sounds of general quarters. The very bone-chilling sound sends out a shockwave of immediate dangers, and instantly, the body is heaped with fear and reacts accordingly. The entire ship's crew becomes like a panic-stricken ant pile with everyone running frantically at top speed in every direction.

Our captain and our ship also jumped into action. On determining the distance and the exact location of the enemy sub, immediately, instructions were relayed by earphones to the Boatswain stationed at the fantail to start pre-setting the timers on the depth charges, some to explode at 50', some at 75', and others at 100'. Then at full speed ahead, we charged the target's position. As the ship approached its underwater target, the captain poured on the coals and commenced dropping the bombs off the fantail from both port and starboard chutes. As we repeatedly released the depth charges—one every fifty feet or so—we could literally see and feel the underwater explosions aimed at the enemy below. Turning sharply and returning to the same target area a second time, we continued dropping the depth charges. Each nerve-wracking minute was tense and feverish, to say the least, and remained so, until the 'all-clear' sounded.

We never learned if we sank an enemy sub, probably not, since we never saw any physical evidence of debris after our night engagements. Nevertheless, after each hair-raising encounter, each man reacted differently, some, noticeably scared, and others excited and laughing, pretending not to be scared. But even so, each man, no matter how brave or courageous, surely must have felt at least a twinge of fear. I did.

Although America was also at war in Europe and in the Atlantic, my main concert was always Japan and the sea battles being fought in the Pacific. Sometimes at night, I'd lay awake trying to piece together this whole mess about the war and wonder about the awesome dangers facing all of us—not just us on my ship, but also my brother Noble and all my boyhood friends from back home. It seemed unreal that we'd all become grown men overnight and each of us were now on distant shores, thousands of miles from home.

I eventually received word that brother Noble had also enlisted in the Navy. By the time I learned of this, he had already completed his boot training and had been assigned duty aboard an LST amphibious ship—the kind used for beach invasions. I also learned later that he was pulling duty somewhere in the South Pacific. Knowing this, I couldn't help but wonder about Mama, and how agonizing it must have been for her to give up her two oldest sons to the terrible Japanese war. Getting letters from back home was always the highlight of my days, particularly since we were lucky if our mail reached us sooner than six weeks. Nothing could bring more excitement, than to hear from Mama with news of the whole family. It didn't matter that she couldn't write her own letters, or that Manuela, Virginia, or Juanito had to write the letters for her, it was still an incredible uplifting. Invariably, when receiving letters from Mama, it was always at a time when I needed it most. I never told her about my injuries at sea. I knew that she already worried constantly, and to tell her now from this far away, would only add more cause to worry.

By the spring of 1945, rumors aboard ship had begun to circulate that we'd soon be going back to the States. Those kinds of rumors, however, were usually too good to be true. The war was certainly not over yet, even though we had received some positive news about General Douglas MacArthur re-taking some of Philippine Islands from the Japanese. Nevertheless, hopes and expectations were clearly vivid on everyone's face. Sure enough, by the first week of March, after thirteen months in Attu, we were relieved of duty in the Aleutians. Finally, we were headed back—back to the States

After two whole weeks homeward bound on what seemed to be a slow boat to China, we finally eased into the port where it all started—Treasure Island in San Francisco. I don't remember any welcoming committees, bands playing, or crowds cheering us home, but it didn't matter. All that mattered was that we were back home on American soil. Immediately, everyone aboard ship was granted a 30-day leave.

There were no words to describe that wonderful, nostalgic feeling of being back home again. The feeling of seeing that familiar high-rise Philtower building and the beautiful triple towers of Holy Family Cathedral, were absolutely indescribable, as the train slowly eased into the Tulsa train depot blowing its whistle announcing our arrival. At that wonderful moment, all I could think of was seeing Josephine and Papa and Mama again.

As soon as possible after spending some time with Josephine, she and I caught a taxicab to the old home place in the "Y". I could hardly wait to see my family again. As I approached the door, I saw that Mama had proudly displayed the 'gold star' emblem on our screen door to signify that she had sons serving in the war. Immediately, I got goose bumps all over. The minute I saw that beautiful mother of mine, with tears in my eyes and outstretched arms, I ran to her. The minute she laid eyes on me, she praised God and fainted—literally. Luckily, Manuela was standing behind her to break her fall. To her, all her prayers had just been answered. God had granted my safe return home, if only for a few days. Even Papa had tears in his eyes as he approached me for a father and son hug.

CHAPTER 27

▼

VICTORIOUS END OF
WORLD WAR II—1945

Shortly after returning to my ship in San Francisco from my 30-day leave, I was admitted to the Oak Knoll Naval Hospital in Oakland, California for further treatment to my facial wounds. It was here—now in mid-March of 1945—that I said farewell to my fantastic family of shipmates, as they continued their voyage to the East Coast for their next assignment. I'll never forget my great shipmates, like: Felix Irving, Allen, Tolbert, Picentini, and Steven.

While at the Naval hospital undergoing radiation treatments, I came face to face with the shock of my life. It was the war casualties. Of course, I knew there were many, but to witness them before my very eyes was absolutely unbelievable. Because what I saw, was ward after ward bursting at the seams with hundreds and hundreds of broken bodies of sailors and marines, some with a missing hand, an arm, a leg, some with severe burns, while others were blind. Each ward was overflowing with the likes of casualties in wheel chairs and on crutches. The fortunate ones who were spared severe injuries, were writing letters home, some playing cards or dominoes, and still others were listening to music on the radio. As I myself was admitted to the hospital, time after time, I realized how fortunate I had been, because my facial lacerations—though they were deep and had disfigured my face—wouldn't compare to the injuries I was seeing. For a long time afterwards, I kept seeing the faces of these countless war casualties and couldn't help wondering if I would make it through the war, *particularly, after I had just been reassigned to an Aircraft Carrier headed for Japan.*

Shortly thereafter, however, **on May 7, 1945,** it was announced on the radio, and no doubt all over the world, that **Germany had surrendered** and that the war in Europe was ended—a momentous day, long to be remembered as V-E day, "Victory over Europe."

At last, the death and devastation which the Nazis had inflicted upon other nations had come full circle, as the United States, Great Britain, and Russian troops avenged Germany's onslaught, bringing them down in total defeat without mercy. Berlin—the German Capital—lay in complete shambles. The news media also reported that the allies were liberating prisoners by the thousands that had been held in notorious prison camps, many having the appearance of walking skeletons from starvation. Concentration camps that were overrun by the allies, exposed the mercenary brutality inflicted on prisoners and innocent people, including the torture chambers in which millions of Jews had been put to death.

At last, the war in Europe was over. Millions celebrated this great victory by going to church to thank God for restoring peace and the return of long over-due freedom. Soon, hundreds of thousands of American soldiers would be coming home, including General Dwight D. Eisenhower—the Allied Supreme Commander of the Allied Forces in Europe. Even in our barracks, jubilation spread with great enthusiasm, because the surrender of Germany, most definitely, signaled a positive sign that the end of world conflict was in sight.

All during the time I was waiting to board my new ship for departure from stateside, I felt sure the surrender of Germany would bring about a major turning point in the war with Japan. The newspapers were full of optimistic reports of the war's progress, and according to one article, the fighting in the South Pacific had intensified in recent months, and that Japan was now feeling the full might of America, as General Douglas MacArthur and the U.S. Navy were retaking the Philippine Islands. As I followed the news events of the war more closely since returning from the Aleutian Islands, I learned of the many sea battles that had been fought in the South Pacific. Like: the battle of Leyte, Manila, New Guinea, Soloman, Guadalcanal, Saipan, Guam, and Luzon. Most recently, the U.S. Marines had landed on the tiny island of Iwo Jima, triggering one of the fiercest land battles of the Japanese war thus far. The marines suffered extremely heavy losses, but were victorious nonetheless. Also, as recently as April, the Marines landed on Okinawa—another heavily fortified Japanese island, and secured it by late June, again, a horrendous number of casualties. Tokyo also, by this time, had been hit by our Air Force. As heavy air attacks were being brought to the outer gates of Japan, from all indications, a strategic noose was being stretched around Tokyo, and the final blow was about to be struck.

Lo' and behold, on August 6, the invincible might of America unleashed the 'mightiest of all bombs' on the Japanese City of Hiroshima, which undoubtedly marked the beginning of Japan's defeat. It was reported that in 60 seconds, 60% of the City had been obliterated by a single most powerful weapon—the atomic bomb.

Even more convincing of America's resolve to bring the dreadful war to a quick ending, occurred only three days later, when the second atomic bomb was dropped on the City of Nagasaki—again, creating an incredible incineration of the city. It was reported that out of 50,000 buildings, 18,000 were destroyed and very few others escaped damage. Nearly 30,000 people were killed. Now, in no uncertain terms, the unleashing of America's new weapon was driving Japan to its knees.

A few days after dropping the Atomic Bombs on Japan's cities of Hiroshima and Nagasaki, I was standing in the breakfast chow line reading the newspaper about the two deadly blows inflicted on Japan. From the ecstatic enthusiasm in the chow line, apparently, many others had also read the news of our new weapon, and how we were closing in on Japan. *The smell of victory was everywhere.* No doubt, every soldier, sailor and marine was beginning to envision the days when they'd be going home—I among them. I couldn't help being extremely proud of our country, and like the others, I was very much relieved. But on a personal level, I felt somewhat remorseful at the thought of the tremendous price Japan paid, in terms of human lives, for the restoration of peace and freedom. No question about it, though, Japan asked for it—and they got it. From this day forward, throughout the entire Treasure Island Naval Base, everyone remained abuzz with excitement. All were optimistic that the war couldn't possible last much longer. For certain, this had been a long and hard fought war. Now, with a bright glimmer of victory in the air, from here on, it would be just a matter of time.

Sure enough! Just as had been expected, only eight days after dropping the Atomic bombs, on **Tuesday, August 14, 1945, at 4:00 P.M.,** President Truman gave the formal announcement to all Americans and to the whole world that Japan had unconditionally surrendered. At that exact moment, celebrations of triumph began. **The war in the Pacific was over.**

I had just eaten lunch on this historic day, seated at my bunk listening to the news of victory, when I received an urgent tap on the shoulder from the Officer of the day. Frantically, he explained that in downtown San Francisco, all hell had broken loose on Market Street, and that overflowing jubilation had gotten completely out of hand. Hastily, he sought as many Shore Patrol (S.P.'s) police as possible to be mustered downtown on the double. Before I could turn around, he had slapped an armband around my right arm, gave me a billy club, a pair of handcuffs, and a 45-automatic handgun. And as soon as I could lace up my leggings, I, along with two-dozen other sailors were swiftly driven downtown and dumped out on Market Street near Fisherman's Wharf with orders to keep the peace.

How ridiculous, I thought, that anyone in their right mind would even want to silence thousands and thousands of people on such an historical day. The minute I stepped off the Navy Patrol van, I knew that keeping the peace was virtually impossible, since every inch of Market Street, from one end to the other, as far as the eye could see, was literally alive, elbow to elbow, with swarms of electrified men, women, and children. The atmosphere of triumph and jubilation was like a joyous haze over the City of San Francisco. Trolley cars were being blocked unable to move, as were taxicabs and busses. Movie theaters were being disrupted as people danced and celebrated on the theater stages. Many jewelry stores, clothing stores, and the like, ceased doing business as they locked their doors for fear of being swarmed by happy mobs. The overwhelming outburst of enthusiasm and excitement was absolutely uncontrollable. If I'd caught anyone disturbing the peace, or better yet, in the act of expressing sheer joy over our victorious defeat of Japan, could I have arrested them? And even if I did, could I have taken them to jail or the brig? Absolutely not! So—what did I do? Well....I did the same thing the other S.P.'s did. I took off my armband, concealed my handcuffs and 45-automatic under my blouse, threw away my peace-keeping club, stripped off my leggings...and joined the thunderous celebration. After all, the war was over and we won, and I had just as much right to celebrate as anyone else.

From San Francisco to New York, and probably every city and town in between, including rural neighborhoods, people rushed into the streets to celebrate and to hail a glorious American victory. People everywhere embraced. Even strangers became instant friends. Triumph reigned among men in every branch of service, as they celebrated throughout Navy camps, Army camps, Marine camps, and airfields. Even barriers between high-ranking officers and enlisted men dissolved instantly, realizing they'd all soon be civilians again. Every G.I. on Market Street cheered ecstatically as they set out to kiss and be kissed by every girl in sight. Unfortunately, however, a few over-enthusiastic citizens did get out of hand, and isolated instances of personal injury or property damage was reported, but mostly, it was caused by the overflow of jubilation over a grand and glorious fete. What mattered most, for the moment, was that peace had finally come. The killing was over.

The takeover of Japan was history in the making and would undoubtedly rewrite the book of American History, because on the morning of September 2nd, General Douglas MacArthur accepted the unconditional surrender of Japan. The official signing took place aboard Admiral Halsey's flagship, the mighty Battle-ship, USS Missouri, as it was anchored in Tokyo bay. Simultaneously, as the signing was taking place, over 200 American planes led by B-29's, roared over the ship in a mighty display of invincibility.

One week later, General MacArthur, Supreme Commander of the Pacific forces set foot on Tokyo soil and began establishing control over the Japanese Empire. First, he ordered the dissolution of the enemy's high command, then he ordered the arrest of the entire cabinet members in office on the day of the attack on Pearl Harbor, considering them responsible for the infamous 'death march' in the Philippines after the fall of Bataan and Corrigidor. Finally, he liberated all the Japanese prison camps. MacArthur's mission was to completely destroy Japan's power and capability to ever make war again.

The weeks that followed the end of the war with Japan, absolutely brought relief and peace of mind to every man and woman in the military, especially me. Particularly, after my orders to report for duty on board an Aircraft Carrier were cancelled—as was my deep concern of going back overseas. Filled with anxiety and much anticipation, each day thereafter, I waited for the day of my official dis-charge. After nearly three years in the Navy—mostly at sea—I was ready to go home.

At last, on November 4, 1945, I was discharged from the United States Navy at the Algiers, Louisiana Naval Base with an honorable discharge—a docu-ment I'll cherish for the rest of my life. Also, I was given $100 dollars and a bus ticket to Tulsa, Oklahoma. On board the ferry boat that was taking me across the bay from Algiers to New Orleans where I was to catch my bus bound for Tulsa, I couldn't believe I was actually on my way home—this time—home to stay.

No doubt, the Navy had made a man out of me and now, after 33 months, I was definitely much more mature and wiser. When I first left home, I was just a young boy without any legal obligations or responsibility. But that had all changed, because now, I found myself a married man, and besides, the day had finally come for me to cut the ties that had bound me to my loving family in the "Y" for 22 years.

As for brother Noble, I didn't know when he would be coming home. The last I heard, he was still in the South Pacific. But no matter where he's at, I know he's safe, and now that the war is over, he'll surely be coming home in a few months. However, just before the war ended, I had reason to worry for both of us. Because if Japan had not surrendered when they did, both of us might very well have taken part in a last thrust against Japan. Because we learned later that the United States had been preparing to launch an all-out invasion, and that several million Marines, Soldiers, Sailors and Airmen had been slated to participate in that last fearsome battle. Anyway, thanks be to God, the war was over and all America could now start a new beginning.

On arriving at the greyhound bus terminal at 4th & Detroit Avenue in Tulsa, I immediately hailed a Yellow Cab that would take me to mine and Josephine's new apartment at 12th & Zunis. Needless to say, the great surprise as I entered the door, was fabulous. For my new wife and I, the war was over and we could start anew—beginning with the honeymoon we never had. Even more excitement awaited me at the old home place.

As Josephine and I stepped out of the taxi cab in the "Y", Mama and Papa spotted me right away, and together came running toward the cab. From a distance, I could hear Mama shouting and screaming. As they swung open the old dilapidated gate and approached me, all I could feel was my heart throbbing with excitement, as my face gleamed from ear to ear. This was truly the fabulous moment that had alluded us all for the past three years. As that beautiful mother of mine leaped in my arms, crying and laughing at the same time, she couldn't stop shouting for joy.

"*Mi hijo,*" "Oh son!" she yelled. "You're home! Thank God. Oh, thank you Jesus." "*Ay hijo*" she continued, "*"Ya se acabo la Guerra. Ay Padre Nuestro del Cielo, Gracias."* "The war is over, thank goodness. Thank you Father in heaven."

Mama could not find enough words to express her joy over my return home. She held on to me until Papa came and pulled her away. It was obvious he was holding back tears, but misty-eyed, he said, "*Ay hijo. Dejame verte. Ay hijo querido, como te hizimos menos. Por fin, se acabo la Guerra."* "Oh, son, let me look at you. Oh son, we've missed you so much. Thank God the war is finally over."

As I continued to embrace my loving parents, I too, was at a loss for words. The wondrous feeling of their mere presence and familiar surroundings of the old home place was absolutely incredible, as was the happiness and relief I felt over the end of a long warring ordeal. All I could say was, "Mama. Oh, Mama, I'm home."

As the three of us walked arm in arm into the house, including my younger brothers and sisters, who were walking ahead of us, Mama was still repeating, *"Ay hijo,* this crazy war is finally over and you're home at last—safe and sound. *"Bendito sea Dios."* "Blessed be God."

Once inside, the exuberance over my return from the war, followed by continuous questions and chatter, was coming at me from all directions. As we all gathered around our pot-belly stove, everyone around me, some sitting on the bed, and others sitting on the floor, wanted to know down to the last detail, all about the war and my experiences in the Navy. The rejoicing seemed to go on for hours as we talked about everything that had happened during the last three years. The fabulous feeling of 'home again' was almost unbelievable, and how about this—at age 40, Mama was pregnant again expecting her twelfth child. She continued to bring me up to date on the unchanged routine around the house and the few visits to see grandma Domitila in Oklahoma City, and Angela in Kansas City. As for the old home place and general living conditions at home, there wasn't a dime's worth of difference since I left home. Struggling to make ends meet was still the norm. But despite the long ordeal brought on by the war and the untold hours of worrying and praying, Mama still looked great. She had not lost one ounce of charm or sense of humor. Papa was still Papa, and doing fine. He was now making $1.75 per hour at the Frisco. Mama says his drinking is subsiding, but once in a while, he still likes to check out some of the local taverns.

Could there have been something special about the "Y"? Maybe God just thought we were special. On the other hand, it could have been Mama's endless prayers on bended knee that brought protection to Noble and I, and all my friends in and around the "Y". The reason I wonder about this, is because every single one of us returned home safely from the war. I'm referring to Joe and Raymond Perez, Nick Fernandez, Bud and Bob Glance, Burtis and Wayne Carpenter, Jerry Edison, Benny Neely, Virgil Harris, and of course me—and soon, Noble. What a wonderful feeling to know that God was with us all along as we cris-crossed the wide Pacific from corner to corner during dangerous war times.

My Terrible Accident

After spending a few days of leisure at home with Josephine, I returned to my former employer, Maloney Tank & Mfg. Company, where I would start all over as a welder's helper in the shop. Already, I had high hopes of amounting to something someday. For the first couple of weeks, things couldn't have worked out any better. I felt so fortunate to have come home and automatically have a job waiting for me. But very soon, things changed dramatically. My life would be abruptly jolted with a devastating crisis, all because of a serious industrial accident in the shop that would leave me physically handicapped for the rest of my life.

The date was **November 20th, just 16 days after being discharged from the Navy**, that an overhead crane carrying a huge plate of 1/2" steel, dropped it to the ground where I was standing below. Without warning, that enormous 20' long sheet of steel came crashing to the ground severing my right leg in a split second. Shop whistles and sirens from every corner of the shop immediately began sounding the emergency alarm. As I lay on the ground in a blur of pain, still conscious and aware of what had just happened, I was surrounded by dozens of shop employees. Then I remember being loaded onto a stretcher and into a waiting ambulance. I was having great difficulty coming to grips with my horrible accident, thinking such things as, *dying, call Josephine, call Mama, call Papa, someone call a priest*. Bewildered and in shock, I took my rosary from my pocket and began praying. In my mind, it felt like my life had just ended.

Josephine came immediately, after she was summoned to Mercy Hospital. Several hours later after recovery from surgery, together we cried, and tried to reassure one another that we would overcome this terrible accident. Mama, who was seven months pregnant, was absolutely devastated and in tears, as was Papa. Even Mr. Fox, my former employer from the concrete plant, was at my bedside. He too, cried in everyone's presence as though I was his son.

After spending 30 days in the hospital, I was released to complete my recovery at home. By this time, Noble had been notified of my accident. Later, when he tried to get emergency leave from San Francisco, it was denied. Determined to come home to see me, he jumped ship—AWOL—then purchased a train ticket and rushed home. I'll never forget that Sunday afternoon, as Mama, Papa, Josephine and I, and some of the kids were seated outside in the back yard near the outdoor shower that I had built. With my crutches at my side, chatting with my family, I saw Noble get out of a taxicab and walk straight toward me. He looked so tall and handsome in his tailor-made bell-bottom blues.

"Noble!" I shouted, reaching out to him.

"Bud! Oh, Bud," he shouted back, looking at my missing limb.

Instantly, we embraced each other, each with misty eyes.

"Here, Noble, Let me look at you. My goodness! How long has it been? Two years?"

"Yes. At least two years, but it seems more like five."

"Bud, are you okay? I came as quick as I could."

"Noble, I'm fine." I replied, noticing signs of worry on his face. "As soon as my stump heals, the Company is buying me a new prosthesis, and before you know it, I'll be as good as new."

"Oh Bud. I'm so sorry. You made it all through the war, safe and sound, and now this. My God."

Slowly he put his handkerchief back in his hip pocket.

Looking at Mama, he said, "Come here, Mama," squeezing her tightly and kissing her repeatedly. "The war's over," he said. "Ain't that great? You don't need to worry anymore. Cecil's home now, and before long, I'll be coming home too. Love you, Mama."

"Yes, *mi hijo,* the war's over now, and all my prayers have been answered. Both my boys are home once again. *Gracias a Dios.* "

"Papa, you doin' alright?" Noble asked. Giving him a warm embrace.

"*Sí hijo. Estoy bien. Pero que mala suerte le toco a tú hermano, verdad?*" "Yes Son. I'm doing alright, but your brother sure had some bad luck, didn't he?"

"Yes, Papa, he did. But knowing Cecil, he'll be alright."

"Sure is good to be home. Wish I didn't have to go back, though."

For the rest of the afternoon, we continued chatting in the back yard, catching up on all the local news, but mostly about the war being over. At last, Mama seemed to be happy and worry free—including Papa. Later, Mama prepared a delicious dinner and we all went inside for a small feast.

Noble remained at home for only a couple of days then hurried back to his ship. He had been missed, of course, and immediately placed under ship's arrest. Later, he was court-martialed for having gone AWOL, and spent five days in the brig, besides having had all his hair cut off. The love for his brother was pure evidence of our roots and the kind of love and affection instilled in all of us by Papa and Mama. True, Noble could rant and complain about our lowly standard of living conditions and the unsightly condition of our little shack, but no one could deny the outpouring of love in his heart for his brother.

The day I was fitted with an above-knee prosthesis, was another worse day in my life. I had tried preparing myself psychologically for this day, but my mind was closed and filled with self-pity, embarrassment, humiliation, and even anger over my ill-fated condition that seemingly had turned me into half a man. From the outset, I couldn't help but form a mental rejection of my new artificial limb, blaming anything and everything for its strangeness and awkwardness. But thanks to our Lord, Jesus Christ, time has a way of healing the human spirit, and yes, even the worst of handicaps. With constant encouragement from Mama, Papa, Josephine and all my friends, my attitude quickly changed from that of negative to positive. Soon, I was bound and determined to defeat my misfortune, and to that end, implement my God-given talents toward building a future for me and my family.

CHAPTER 28

▼

EASTER SUNDAY—1948

During the three years following my terrible accident, I had plenty of time to fully recover and accept my misfortune. Josephine and I soon saved up a small down payment for our first home located on the Sand springs Trolley Line. It was a nice 2-bedroom house with a large 12' x 18', one-room basement, costing only $8,000—and our monthly payments were only $54.

One big problem remained, however, and that was getting accustomed to the idea that I was no longer a member of Papa and Mama's household. My roots in the "Y" constantly beckoned me back home. Out of concern for the family, I still felt obligated to remain close at hand and assist in their daily lives as often as possible. Mama still relied on me, as before, and still hinged all her important household decisions around my judgment. Even my siblings looked forward to my visits. One in particular—an Easter Sunday picnic.

It was a beautiful April afternoon, when in my recently purchased 1941 Chevy Impala, Josephine and I drove up to our house in the "Y" and parked along side our old fence. Papa was at the woodpile and had been chopping some kindling, still wearing that old sweat-stained work-hat that had just about out-lived its usefulness. His face, bright as copper, was beaded with perspiration from working in the warm Sunday afternoon. We'd just been to the 10:00 O'clock Mass at Holy Family Cathedral.

¿"Que esta haciendo, Papa?" "What are you doing, Papa?" I asked.

"Aquí no mas, hijo, cortando poquita leña." "Not much, son" he answered, "just chopping a little wood."

¿"Como esta mi hijo?" "How's my son today?"

"Muy bien, Papa."

Looking at Josephine as she was entering the gate, he asked, quite affectionately,

¿"Como te va, Josefina?" "How are you today, Josephine?"

"Pasen para dentro. Ay esta Mama en la cocina. Ella los esta esperando." "Go on in. Mama's in the kitchen, and she's waiting for you."

As I stepped up onto the front porch, that familiar aroma of fried chicken saturated the outdoor breeze. It really was a beautiful Easter Sunday, and we'd made plans earlier to have a picnic at Mohawk Park. Like we'd done before, we'd all pile in, in two cars and drive 'til we found a secluded spot for the younger kids to hide Easter eggs. The younger ones were: Linda, my sister Nellie's one-year old daughter, brothers; Alex 2 and Tommy 5, and sisters; Phyllis 8 and Lupe 10.

Josephine stepped up onto the porch and entered the house carrying on a chummy conversation with Phyllis and Lupe, admiring their cute, pink Easter outfits that Mama made, and complimenting the pretty pink lace beautifully stitched around the collar and sleeves. She gave each one a snugly hug, patting them on the back as she opened the warped screen door. Mama was in the kitchen, as usual, with her apron on, wiping away the perspiration from her forehead. She had fried two chickens for our picnic.

"Ay Josefina, no te vide. Pasa!" "Oh, Josephine, I didn't see you. Come in."

"Buenos dias." "Can I help you do something?" replied Josephine, as she stepped down onto the kitchen floor.

"Sí Josie, you're just in time." *"Ayuda me espantar estas moscas fregadas para afuera, que me dan tanto asco."* "Help me shoo these darn flies out of here. They're making me sick of my stomach."

Picking up two dish towels, Mama started at the far end of the kitchen and began swishing the towels wildly, shooing the flies toward the front door while Josephine held the screen door wide open. And all the while, as Josephine laughed out loud, Mama was saying, *"Vayanse para afuera moscas cochinas."* "Beat it outside, you nasty flies." Again and again, she shoo'ed flies until most had been unwillingly evicted to the outdoors.

"Gracias, Josefina." "Honey, bring that fruit basket over here please, and we'll use it to carry the food."

The basket happened to be the one Mama used for dampening her clothes when she ironed. She was still taking in ironings and washings from railroad workers.

Obediently, Josephine picked up the laundry basket off the floor and set it on the wooden bench, and carefully began to fill the basket with Mama's fried chicken, including some sweet potatoes left over from the day before, then she proceeded to place the colored Easter eggs in the basket, and finally, the red checkered tablecloth.

"Here, *Josie,*" Mama said, handing her a thermos bottle. "We sure don't want to forget Juan's coffee."

About that time, Tommy came in. "Mama, I'm hungry," he said. He'd been out on the front porch peeling the cork from pop-bottle caps hoping to win a 'free' soda.

"That's too bad, son." *"Anda vete afuera a comer hongos."* "You'll just have to wait, son." Jokingly she added, "Go outside in the yard and see if you can find some mushrooms."

"Where's Alex? I thought I told you not to let him go outside. He'll just get dirty!"

"He's in the other room, Mama. He's jumping on the bed."

"Dile que venga para aqua." "Tell him to come here."

Pretty soon, noisy laughter by Alex, Phyllis and Lupe was coming from the bedroom. Alex had just farted. The girls thought it was nasty, but hilarious as well.

Phyllis, the little tattle-tale, yelled, "I'm gonna tell Mama on you."

Running into the kitchen, she said, "Mama, tell Alex to stop farting."

"Alejandro, chacho feo! Ven aqui!" "Alex, you naughty child, come here!" she yelled.

"Ay Dios mio!" Mama exclaimed. *"Como le hacen fiesta al pedo."* "My goodness, all that hullabaloo over one little old fart."

Turning to Josephine, she said, "Now you see what it'll be like when you and Cecil have children of your own."

"We're not gonna have any kids," she replied, with a silly grin on her face.

"Si, apoco no." "Oh yeah," replied Mama. "That's what I thought too when Juan and I got married, but you see what happened?" Continuing her amusing humor, she said, *"Dicen que las mujeres son locas por el amor, Josie. ¿Sera cierto?"* "Josie, they say that women are crazy for love. Do you think it's true?"

"Don't ask me," she replied, with a surprised chuckle. "I never heard that one before. Why do you ask?"

"Well....I don't know how true it is, but that gal, Maria—the one who comes over to see Mercedes—she always has a man hanging on her arm. And it's not always the same beau. She openly admits, *"me gustan los hombres."* "I like men."

"You might be right, Lela, but it sounds like Maria has more of an appetite for men, than she has for love."

"Beats me, Josie, but more than one man is too many."

Looking at Tommy, Mama said, *"Dile a tu Papa que se venga a cambiar."* "Go tell Papa to come in and change his clothes because we're almost ready to go."

Holding the screen door wide open and letting more flies come in, Tommy yelled out, "Papa!" "Hey Papa! Mama said for you to come in and get ready."

"Guat?" "What?" Papa replied, unsure of what Tommy just said.

Again he yelled at Papa, "Mama said to come in and get ready!" then slammed the screen door shut.

On hearing the screeching screen door slam shut with a loud bang, Mama cringed, shaking her head, saying, *"Ay Diosito."* "Oh my God!"

After a few minutes, Papa came in like he was told and stepped down into our walk-in closet to change out of his dirty work clothes.

"Hi, Mama," I said, as I finally made my way into the kitchen to give her my usual bear hug. "Is Noble going with us today?"

Responding affectionately with a kiss on my cheek, she said, ¿*"Como esta mi hijo?"*

"How's my son today." "I don't know if your brother is going with us or not."

Just then, I heard a horn honking. It was brother Noble and his pretty wife, LaJuana, who had just driven up in their '39 Ford. As usual, he was neatly dressed and well coordinated in a sporty lookin' shirt and slacks, and he was wearing his brown leather loafers with a lucky penny tucked in the top seams. Since his return from the Navy, and now a married man, never again, would he be seen in shabby dress wear. Also, he had completely divorced the "Y", and only the unpleasant memories remained as evidence of being the son of a poor railroad worker who had way too many kids. I already knew, even before asking, that he wouldn't be going with us today—too many kids.

"Hi Mama," he said, also reaching to collect his hug. Looking over at me, he said, "Hi Bud. You doin' okay?"

"Hi Noble. Yeah, I'm doin' okay. We're all going to Mohawk for an Easter picnic so the kids can hide Easter eggs. You coming with us?"

"Can't go today, Bud. We're leaving for Stamps, Arkansas pretty soon. I just landed a construction job over there and I have to be there by tomorrow morning. We just came to say bye to Mama and Papa. And besides, LaJuana hasn't been feeling too good."

I could see that she was about seven months pregnant.

"Hi, Mama. Gee, something sure smells good in here." LaJuana said, with her usual cheerful smile, as she joined the others in the crowded kitchen, also reaching to embrace Mama.

"Hi, Juana." Mama replied. "It's the fried chicken you smell. It's for our picnic. Sure wish you were going with us. How've you been feeling, honey?"

"Oh Mama, I feel just fine. Fat as a cow, but otherwise, okay."

"What's it going to be, a boy or girl?"

"I don't really care," she answered, "but Noble wants a boy."

Just then, Mama looked over at Josephine and said in Spanish, grinning and knowing LaJuana wouldn't understand an off-the-cuff remark in Spanish, *"Cada vez que veo una muchacha con panza soplada, se me frunse la cola."* Jokingly, but dead serious, she said, "Every time I see a girl with a blown-up belly, my crotch just naturally contracts."

"I'm not surprised," Josephine said, unable to keep from laughing.

Nellie and Virginia decided to join everyone else in the kitchen. They'd been back in the elongated bedroom dressing Nellie's little girl, Linda, in her satin and lacey Easter dress. Everyone was in such a vibrant mood today, and why not, this was a beautiful Easter Holy day, and just one more gathering at Mama and Papa's, where our little old shack could barely keep from bustin' at the seams. Nellie's marriage to that Yeager fellow had not worked out very well, so she had moved back in with Mama and Papa. She was olive complexioned like me and Papa and Noble, and her skin soft and smooth, and the color of *Caramelo*. Now at age 20, she was so very pretty, always friendly and definite in her goals and objectives, and possessing definite ambitious qualities.

Unlike Nellie, though, Virginia, now 17, was more extroverted, very friendly and charming. Always courteous and could put a bright face on any dim circumstances. Her complexion was just like Mama's—rosy white, and both with natural wavy hair. Even her personality was the splitting image of Mama, always bubbly, filled with excitement and enthusiasm, unselfish, and never finding fault in anyone. Also, she'd become a true work-a-holic—just like Mama, which had proven to be a tremendous help with the younger ones.

Albert, 15, the light complexioned one, and Michael, 13, the darker one, were outside near the coal shed playing catch ball. Both were neatly dressed in their Sunday best and anxious for the picnic. They had just returned from gathering

Quelites y Verdolagas along the banks of the railroad tracks where 'edible greens' grew wild and abundantly. These were pure delicacies for Papa and Mama, and they'd probably have them for supper.

"Lupe," Mama ordered, *"Anda ver si tu hermano Juanito ya viene."* "Lupe, go and see if Johnny has arrived yet."

Johnny, now nearing 19, had served Mass at St. Catherine today and was running late in getting home. He was a good-looking kid with a full head of cold, black, wavy hair, a great personality, a comical sense of humor, and an artist to boot.

After a little while, Noble said, "Gotta go, Mama," giving her another peck on the cheek and a gentle hug.

"Bueno hijo, ten much cuidado. Que les vaya bien." "Okay, son. Be careful and have a good trip."

¿"Que le pasaría a mi compadre?" "Where's my compadre?" she wondered out loud. Francisco (Frank) Moreno was running a little late. He would be going with us on our picnic and providing the additional transportation that we needed. After a few minutes of waiting, he drove up. He was still driving that two-tone green Dodge, the same one he had when he gave me my first driving lesson. Frank was also godfather to two of the children. Every few weeks or so, he came to visit Mama and Papa, usually on a Sunday afternoon, and if I was around, we'd play music.

"Mama, Mama," yelled Tommy. "Frank's here!"

"Bueno. Dile que se pase." "Alright, tell him to come on in."

"Andale Juan, date aprisa!" Mama yelled. *"No seas tan despacio. Yo no se porque te corre la sangre tan despacio."* "Hurry, Juan! Don't be such a slow poke. I don't know why the blood in your veins runs so slow."

She no sooner got the words out, when Papa stepped out of the closet looking rather spiffy, considering the age of his black gabardine trousers, his white shirt, and his old black hat. This was a special day for him. Seldom did he ever have a good reason to dress up in his finest clothes.

¿ "Te lavates las manos, Juan?" "Did you wash your hands, Juan?"

"Sí. Como no." "Yes I did. I sure am hungry," he said, as he began rummaging around in the picnic basket. Right away, he noticed the sweet potatoes.

¿"Camotes?" he asked. *¿"Vieja, para quien son los camotes?"* "Who are the sweet potatoes for," he asked.

"Son para tí, para que te peas bonito." She replied, with a foxy grin on her face, and winking at Josie. "They're yours, Juan….so you can let some sweet smelling farts."

"Mira, mira, Edelia," he snapped back, sort of blushing and grinning, while holding his hand over his mouth so as not to expose a missing front tooth.

"Mira quen habla. Apoco los tuyos huelen a perfume!" "Oh, look whose talking. I'll bet you think your smell like Perfume."

Still chuckling over Mama's witty humor, he bent over to take a couple of swipes at his black dress shoes to brush off the dust, then, after tightening up on his belt one more notch, he said, *"Ahora si, vieja Ya estoyo listo. ¿Vamos en el carro de Ceeso?"* "Now I'm ready," Papa said. "Are we going in Cecil's car?"

"I wanna go with Cecil!" Albert hollered." Me too!" yelled Michael, and then Tommy chimed in, "I wanna ride up front!"

At last, Mama was ready. She untied the straps from her apron and gently wiped away the perspiration from her face one more time. Reaching for her bonnet and her white linen hanky, the one with the knot in it where she kept her money, she said, *"Ahora sí. Haver si ayamos la coneja de la pascua."* "Okay, I'm ready. Let's go see if we can find the Easter bunny.

This of course, was just one more typical day in the daily lives of Juan and Edelia. Purely, a simple unglamorous lifestyle whose high-point on any given day, could be just another unpretentious family gathering. A gathering with all the usual everyday sounds and activity that one might expect in their little over-crowded shack Such as: the noisy slamming of doors, the wrangling with tattle-tale kids everywhere and underfoot, sometimes laughing crazily or hysterically, some crying because they want something someone else has, girls playing jacks on the floor, while the boys might be bouncing a rubber ball off the wall or climbing our mulberry tree that stands next to the coal shed.

As usual, Mama has mousetraps in most corners of the house and under the bed, set to go off. Or she might be curling up her apron, filling it with chicken feed so she can go out to feed the chickens, always checking her shoes for fear of stepping on some chicken *caca* and tracking it inside.

Sometimes, Mama likes to pretend to keep a tight rein on Papa, and at times, he obeys like one of the kids but only when he wants her to feel like she's the boss. Most of the time, he can be found outside tinkering or pulling weeds in the garden, but never loafing. Usually, there's a lighted candle burning in Mama's prayer altar.

Without a doubt, for a family as big as ours, living in a small shack amid non-stop conversations, both in English and in Spanish, pure simplicity blesses Papa and Mama's humble home. Within it, lies a blissful atmosphere that many other families might never know.

This final chapter reaches the highest point of culmination in the lives of Juan and Edelia Gomez, when at long last, after having navigated an ever-challenging road of poverty, were nearing their ultimate reward. A reward bought and paid for many times over, via years of living in the valley of the poor. Finally, lush green pastures of peace and happiness are in sight.

But not before one more steep mountain to climb.

CHAPTER 29

▼

EVICTED FROM THE "Y"—
1948

I don't know who coined the phrase, "When it rains, it pours," but it could have easily been someone from the "Y". Because as long as I can remember, our lives in the "Y" had always been filled with too many problems. No sooner did one problem get resolved, than another problem would crop up. Maybe that's the way life is with poor people who remain suppressed by the lack of means or the ability to better themselves. I'm speaking now of one more bombshell to hit Papa and Mama and the "Y". It was the same year of our Easter picnic.

The bombshell I'm speaking of was the condemnation of all the houses in the "Y". It came in the way of an eviction notice from the Frisco Railway. After all these years, since I was a child, the Frisco suddenly decided to expand its operations at the expense of forsaking every family in the "Y". The eviction notice clearly specified a six-month deadline of October 31. **Immediately, a calamitous shockwave of worry and confusion spread among all the families,** plummeting any remaining hopes and dreams of the future to their lowest level. That very evening, all the "Y" families gathered together in Papa's back yard to discuss the heart-wrenching impact of the eviction notice, hoping that somehow, there was some mistake, or perhaps, something else could be worked out allowing them to stay. But no, there were no alternatives. And to top it all off, not a single family was financially prepared for what lay ahead.

In the months that followed, one by one, the "Y" families began relocating. Don Doroteo and wife Jesus, began looking for a place to rent north of town near **Doña Aurela Nieto,** Jesus's sister. Antonio Chaves didn't know what to do, at first, but later decided to go back to Mexico where he still had a wife and family. The Edisons found a place to rent in West Tulsa, as did Don Arcadio Gonzales. The Stricklands moved in with relatives out of state.

From the beginning, Papa had never taken the eviction notice very seriously and had declared that he would never move out of the "Y". But Mama worried tremendously. She new very well the serious implications they were faced with, particularly since they had no money or no place else to go. She prayed and prayed, wishing this traumatic nightmare would go away. But not a chance. The cold hard facts remained unchanged. Finally with deep concern, she turned to me.

By the time I learned of the eviction notice, nearly all of the shacks in the "Y" had been vacated. Realistically, we should have known all along that the Frisco wouldn't have let us live there rent-free forever. I tried to ease Mama's worried mind, trying to assure her that we'd get through this troubling ordeal somehow. I knew she was struggling with the enormity of the problem, but after a while, she settled down, and once again, left the problem in my hands.

First off, we had to find some other place to live.

A few days later, Mama and I set out to look for a place to rent in the residential area. For most of the day, we walked over practically every street n West Tulsa without any luck. To our surprise, there weren't many houses for rent. To purchase a home was not even thinkable, and to rent a place large enough for our whole family, if we found one, was just not affordable. The situation was beginning to look very bleak.

Trying to stay calm over this compelling problem of 'what to do', I began to entertain a crazy idea that just might work. **I thought to myself, why couldn't I build a house for Papa and Mama?** The idea, admittedly a bit far fetched, was incessantly consuming all my thoughts and energy. True...I was no carpenter, but I had always loved working with wood; like the front porch that I built, the walk-in closet, and that ingenious idea that worked so beautifully when I built the family an outdoor shower. So, with all that experience, I thought rather naively, *what could possibly be holding me back now?* Confident and psychologically fortified for this new challenge, I continued to delve deeper into my crazy idea to see if there was even a ghost of a chance.

When I first approached Mama with my wild idea, she was flabbergasted, a little apprehensive, but still very receptive. She could hardly believe that just perhaps she and Papa actually could own a new home—all their very own. Even I was excited. Mama's big worry, of course, *was where would we get the money?* Expanding on my idea, I told her that if we all pitched in, we just might make it. I knew that she had saved $400 dollars, and knowing that all the working members of the family always gave a portion of their paycheck to Mama, it was definitely worth considering further. Noble couldn't help. He was already trying to make his own living in Arkansas. But Nellie was working at Barnes Manley Laundry, so she could help; Virginia was also working at Barnes Manley part-time, so she could help; Johnny had just gotten a job at Ernest Wieman Wrought Iron Company, Albert was still in school but worked part-time as a sack boy at the Warehouse Market, and Mike had an after-school job at Naifeh's Grocery. Considering the small earnings of my siblings collectively, it definitely appeared at though we had a workable solution. Particularly, since I promised Mama that I would also pitch. So…with everyone in agreement, we decided to go for it.

Again, Mama and I went combing the streets of West Tulsa, but this time, we were looking for a vacant lot. After hours of walking the streets, **we finally found 2 adjoining vacant lots for sale** in the 2400 block of South Olympia Street, an excellent location just two blocks from St. Catherine Church and School, and two blocks from Quanah Boulevard. Immediately, I contacted the owner, Mr. J. T. Chamblee, and in a couple of days, we had a deal. The purchase price was $650 dollars. We used Mama's $400 dollars savings for the down payment, and the balance, would be paid off at $25 per month.

I don't know where I ever got the idea that I could build a house, a complete house from top to bottom, that is. It must have been a bottled-up ambition that stemmed from wanting to shake the "Y"'s dust from our shoes once and for all. I'd always possessed a positive attitude that constantly prodded me onward, so obviously, I wanted more out of life—not only for me, but also for my family. Especially after comparing our lowly living conditions with alluring lifestyles of people outside the "Y". There were times when I appeased my concerns, and in weak moments, drew the conclusion that this kind of sub-standard living really was meant to be our cup of tea. *But who was I fooling?* All I had to do, was look around me to see that there had to be better possibilities out there. Noble had always seen these differences and never hesitated one second in expressing his displeasure and resentment. Unlike Noble, though, I wasn't that vocal in expressing my frustrations. I knew how he felt and why, but I tried to be more understanding, knowing that Papa and Mama had always done they best they could. Also, I knew that our way of life was not that of our own choosing, nor that of our making, but largely due to lack of money. Having understood these facts, I accepted our way of life more patiently than Noble, but it didn't suggest for a moment that I would accept this lowly standard forever. And to that end, and in silent determination, I vowed to someday rescue our family from the 'clutches' of an unjust way of life—namely; the "Y".

That someday was finally here. Now came the real moment of truth. *Could I really do it?* Yes, I kept telling myself. In my mind, it was all settled. I just knew I could do it and could hardly wait to prove it. I was being driven by that opportune moment to sever the tenacity of the "Y". But even more than the "Y" itself, it was like a golden opportunity to put a new face on the Gomezes and shed the cloak of a haunting past. The time had come to take that giant prevailing step forward, and take hold of the promise of a better life. I owed it to Mama and Papa, and all my siblings. But my 'all fired up' motivation was really being fueled by the dream they once had. When I was just a youngster, they both dwelled a lot on their dream of owning their own home someday, and becoming a part of the great American society, but as the years came and went, their dream remained in limbo—hard times wouldn't go away, and times became even harder when the depression hit, and if that weren't enough, the number of their children grew almost beyond affordability. Then the dreadful World War II came along to further drive their dreams deeper into despair.. As I look back and weigh in on their forlorn past, and how their dreams had been all but shattered, I said to myself, **Cecil, it's now or never. This is your last chance to make their dream come true.**

Making the decision to build Papa and Mama a new house was easier said than done. I soon learned that without the skills of a journeyman carpenter, it would be next to impossible to get financing. For the next three weeks, everyday on my lunch hour, including Saturdays, I contacted a dozen or more banks and lumberyards, submitting credit applications right and left. Each time, my application was rejected for lack of skills and no collateral. I was beginning to worry that my great idea was about to turn sour. But still, I had to persist.

Finally, in the latter part of May, I knocked on the magic door—the first door to give me hope. It was Square Deal Lumber Company at 4th and Kenosha. The yard proprietor's name was John Burris, a friendly, straight forward kind of man, short and heavy-set, and in his s50's, I'd guess.

"Sir," I asked, as I stepped into the front office. "Could I submit a credit application for some building materials?"

"Building materials, you say?"

"Yes Sir."

"What are you building?" he asked.

"I'm going to build a house for my folks."

"A whole house?" he asked. "That's going to take an awful lot of lumber. What Company are you with?"

"I'm not with any company, Sir."

"We don't usually extend one hundred percent credit commitments to individuals," he said, "just builders and developers. Where are you building?"

"In West Tulsa," I replied, "near the Texaco Refinery."

"How old are you, son," he asked, looking me up and down.

"Twenty-four," I said.

"Where do you work at?"

"I work at Maloney Tank & Manufacturing Company, just up the street from here."

"Do you have any collateral?"

"No sir."

"No collateral?"

"No Sir."

"Well, now," he said, with a funny look on his face "you want a loan, but you don't have any collateral. Now that's a new one."

For a moment, by the way he chuckled, I gathered he was making light of my all-important request and thought there was no way he would ever consider my application.

Quite amused, he scratched his head slightly, then turned from side to side in his swivel office-chair mulling over my unusual request.

"Do you have a vacant lot on which to build a house?" he asked.

"Yes Sir. We just bought two lots on Olympia Street in West Tulsa."

"Are they free and clear?" he asked.

"No Sir. We still owe $225 dollars on them."

"Who holds the mortgage?"

"Mr. Chamblee. He's the man we bought them from. He lives on East 3rd Street.

"J. T?" "J. T. Chamblee?"

"Yes Sir. That's him. Do you know him?"

"Yes! I know him. He's a good friend of mine. Let me get him on the phone."

Easing up out of his chair, he walked into his private office and closed the door behind him. I wasn't too hopeful, judging by the way Mr. Burris kept looking at me. Somehow, he knew I wasn't a carpenter, but I kept my fingers crossed and said a little prayer. Pretty soon, I could hear an excitely one-way conversation.

"J. T," he roared on the phone, "this is me. Hey, when we goin' fishing again? Yeah, this is John."

Right away, he was laughing into the phone with loud enthusiasm. Jokingly, with occasional spurts of laughter, they bragged about their last fishing trip and the amount of beer they consumed.

"Aw, c'mon now, it wasn't that big. The bass that I caught was bigger'n yours. By the way, did you notice how clear Grand River Lake was this time?"

For what seemed five long minutes, they talked and talked. I was beginning to think he'd forgotten all about me. Then the conversation changed.

"Say, J. T. I have a young man in my office who wants to build a house for his folks. His name is Cecil Gomez....says you sold him some vacant lots over there in West Tulsa."

Pretty soon, the conversation became almost inaudible. As I strained to hear what they were saying, the conversation turned from casual chatter to serious business talk. Obviously, the two men were not only good friends, but also business partners. Pretty soon, Mr. Burris hung up the phone and walked back into the front office.

"Cecil," he said. "I might be able to help you. Fill out this application for me and get back with me in a few days. Oh, and by the way," he continued, 'bring me a set of your house plans. I want to see the size house you have in mind."

"I sure will, Mr. Burris. You'll like my plans. I drew them up myself."

With a smile from ear to ear, I reached out to shake his hand.

"Thank you, Mr. Burris. I appreciate whatever you can do for me."

As I walked away from Square Deal Lumber company, I was extremely relieved. Somehow, I just knew my credit application would be approved and felt lucky that Mr. Burris and Mr. Chamblee happened to be good friends.

Five days later, I went back to see Mr. Burris to check on the status of my credit application. Of course, I was nervous, but as soon as I walked in his office, while mumbling a little prayer, I could tell from the positive smile on his face that my application had been approved.

Within a week, after signing some mortgage papers and other legal documents, everything was settled. I was ready to start.

Timing was of the essence. The eviction notice from the Frisco had given us 'til the end of October to evacuate. I knew it was impossible to complete the house in that short length of time, so here was my plan. We would start construction right away, and the family would stay put in the "Y" until sometime in October before the arrival of cold weather. At that time, we would vacate the house **and the whole family would move in with me for the duration of construction.**

No one said it would be easy, building a house. I knew all along that it would require many long hours of hard work, and working late into the night. And I also knew that, basically, most of the time it would be just me and only the help of my little brothers Johnny, Albert, and Mike who were only 19, 15, and 13. I couldn't depend too heavily on Papa, because of his 7-day work-week at the Frisco. And besides, carpentry had never been his calling.

The simple floor plan which I had drawn, called for a small 7-room house; a living room, dining room, kitchen, hallway, 3 bedrooms, one bath, and a large front porch. Right off the reel, I encountered some problems. No electricity. That meant that without electricity, after the sun went down, I'd have to lay the concrete block foundation using the headlights from my car. Every evening, while working on the foundation, I felt so conspicuous knowing that all the neighbors were watching every move we made—including a certified carpenter who lived across the street.

From the very first day after having purchased our two small lots, I started preparing myself for the day of show and tell. Not only had I never built a house, I didn't know how. Knowing this, I set out to learn.

In those days, right after the war, many housing projects were underway all over Tulsa, and G.I. homes were springing up everywhere. So again, everyday on my lunch hour, I visited various construction sites. On scratch pads, I drew sketches, layouts, and rough drafts of specific phases of construction in progress; floor joists, sub floors, wall studs, ceiling joists, rafters, and the whole bit. All along, I was taking down notes to myself on specific skills and techniques used by the professional carpenters. Occasionally, I'd talk to some of them and pick their brain for pointers, which they were always happy to oblige.

From the day my first order of lumber arrived in mid-June, all of us worked super hard and very long hours. Every evening after work, I'd rush home, grab a fast bite for supper, then rush to the "Y" to pick up the boys. On occasion, Victor

Leos, my brother-in-law, came over to help, as did Frank and Papa, but mostly, it was just the boys and I. On weekends we literally took advantage of every minute. From early morning 'til late at night, we never let up. By the time construction had reached 25 percent completion, the boys had become quite familiar with the working end of a hammer. Since we had no electric tools whatsoever, I personally handsawed every piece of lumber going into the house. Together, we made a great working team, but with very little time off for recreation. As we got deeper and deeper into construction, my relentless push to meet our deadline had become urgent. And because I had promised Mr. Burris a completion date of six months, I became very strict with the boys and any notion of time off for recreation was quickly quashed. But in the end, they were always obedient and understanding, and at the same time, proving their ability to work under pressure.

Toward the latter part of October, with the weather beginning to cool down and the deadline for completion nearing, it was time to relinquish the family's house in the "Y". By this time, the new house had been completely framed, roofed, and shingled, and I felt satisfied that we were right on schedule.

Moving the entire family to my house was filled with much sentiment, as well as a sundry of emotions. What was once our ugly little broken down shanty, now seemed beautiful with many precious memories locked up inside. As Mama walked through our lonely, empty house for the last time, the hollow echoing sounds of her voice revealed a deep sadness from the fond attachment to her little shack. On her way out, she paused for a minute to take one last look, as if to capture one more special memory. Other families had already moved away, and only the empty shacks stood still and worthless. As she looked around the yard at her dried up flowerbed and Papa's deserted garden spot, I could feel that she was about to cry. When I escorted her to the car, holding my hand, she whispered softly, *"Adios, mi jacalito."* "Good-bye, my little shack."

On the way to my house, Mama was very quiet. She seemed motionless and almost despondent. The very thought of leaving her little old house was like saying good-bye to a dear deceased friend. As I looked at her sitting next to me, I could see tears trickling down her cheek. At this very moment, I knew she felt as though her life, again, was at another heart-breaking crossroad. *What she was leaving behind was certainly no paradise, but it was her home sweet home. Now, after21 years, we were all saying good-bye to the "Y".*

On the day we vacated the old house, everyone had been transported to my house—all except Papa. I had already made several unsuccessful trips to the old house and West Tulsa looking for him, and it wasn't until late that night when I decided to make one more trip to the empty house, that I finally found him sitting on the front porch, all alone.....he had been drinking.....such a sorrowful sight. Not his appearance, nor the fact that he'd been drinking, but instead, it was the scene of the heart breaking ties that bind. Because even if he had freely consented to moving away, it would've been extremely painful for him to just walk away from 21 years of toil, sweat, and contentment, and yes.... even the place where he had enjoyed a million times, the fun and laughter of his children, watching them grow up. Now, the house stood deathly quiet and empty—childless, with not even an echo or a faint sound of their playful voice. Moreover, his estate in the "Y", though worthless, had become a haven from an outside world that he never became a part of. Now the Frisco had taken it all away.

As I saw him sitting there on the porch in front of our dark empty house still wearing his dirty work overalls, he was muttering things to himself and softly crying. I walked up to him and asked in an admonishing tone of voice, ¿"Papa, donde estabas? Esta es la tercera vez que te vengo a buscar, y no te hallaba. ¿Porque estas llorando, Papa?" "Where've you been, Papa? This is the third time I came looking for you and couldn't find you. Why are you crying?"

As I approached him closer, immediately, I knew he was in mental distress, a dejected man with a broken spirit.

"Why are you crying, Papa?" I asked again.

At first, he ignored me and turned away. I knew all along that it wouldn't be easy for him to leave the "Y", and somehow, knew why he was grieving. As I sat down beside him and gently put my arms around him, trying to relate to his sorrow, I asked again, this time softly and with a more compassionate voice, ¿"Que tienes, Papa?" "What's wrong, Papa?"

On looking at me with painful mixed emotions, and yes, with feelings of having been forsakened, his sobbing increased so pitifully, asking,

¿"Donde esta Mama?" "Where's Mama?"

Papa already knew that the day was nearing when they'd have to move out of the "Y", but kept it pushed out of his mind, thinking it would never happen. As he continued to stare blankly at the ground, brushing away the tears with his handkerchief, I could feel his grief when he asked in a trembling voice, ¿"Donde estan mis hijos?" "Where are my kids?" ¿"Porque me abandonaron todos? Ay hijo de mi alma, ya se acabo todo." "Why has every one abandoned me? Oh son of my soul, it's all over."

"Vete hijo. Dejame aquí." "Go home, son. Leave me here."

"No, Papa! I'm not leaving you. C'mon, we have to go now."

At first, he resisted and pulled away, insisting that this was his home and he would never leave it.

"Papa, Please?" I pleaded. "C'mon. Let's go. You'll see Papa. In just a few more weeks you and Mama will have a brand new home—the one you've always wanted.

"Go home," he insisted. "Leave me alone. I'll be alright."

After a few more minutes of tugging and pleading, he finally gave in.

As he got in the car, totally disheartened, he turned around to take one last look. And even though memories are invisible, I could almost see the binding strands of love, happiness, sorrow, and despair, all wrapped up in one, that was tearing him apart. For him, only precious memories were left, as well as fading reasons to continue the good fight. No doubt this very evening, in a web of confusion, he was thinking of his far away home in Villa de Reyes, wondering where he had failed, and burdening himself with his seemingly ill-fated destiny.

It didn't take very long to move the family's meager belongings to my house. One whole day is all we needed. Mama insisted on living in my over-sized basement, and yes, it would be crowded—very crowded, but she would see to it that everyone was comfortable. She was already used to living in cramped quarters, with children underfoot anyway, so these arrangements would be nothing new. Still holding on to her 3-burner kerosene cook stove, we also moved in two full-size beds, tables and chairs and all personal items. The entire family, with the exception of Noble, had now moved in with Josephine and me. Altogether, there was: Papa and Mama, and the small children, Alex, Tommy, Phyllis, Lupe, Virginia, Nellie and Linda, occupying the basement. In my outdoor detached garage with a dirt floor, we set up another full-size bed for Johnny, Albert and Mike. For the next six weeks, these overcrowded conditions would be their home. Mama had no trouble adapting to the close confinement of my basement and graciously accepted her new temporary home. Her patience was absolutely virtuous, as she continued to pray and give thanks for what she considered a blessing, instead of an ordeal. Knowing the terrible inconvenience for everyone, was all the more reason to push more vigorously for an early completion of the house.

The daily routine at my house with my newly enlarged family was very strenuous, to say the least. Each morning was a mad house of confusion, as everyone scurried to get to work or to school. Papa was always the first to leave, walking to the streetcar line one block away that took him all the way to West Tulsa and to his job at the Frisco. On occasion, some of the kids also boarded the trolley for transportation to their schools. Nellie and Johnny each had jobs to go to, while Virginia, Albert and Mike were all in school at Holy Family and Lupe and Phyllis were at St. Catherine. With only one car—mine—it wasn't easy making the rounds each morning. The sole consolation was that this strenuous schedule was only temporary.

Finally, an Uncloudy Day

By the early part of November, the boys and I had made a vast difference in the structure of the new house. Already, it was taking on the appearance of a neatly constructed bungalow fit for a king and queen. The siding was installed, as were the windows and doors, the electricians had completed the wiring and we now had ceiling lights and light switches on the walls in every room, as well as receptacles throughout the house. The plumbers had also completed their work and at long last, the floor furnace was set. The bathroom was finished, complete with flush toilet and with hot and cold running water. At last, the floor plan was coming alive with individual room divisions.

Even though we still had a ways to go, the excitement was beginning to beam on the faces of all the kids who were anxiously waiting for their new home. Especially Mama. When I brought her to the building site to show off our carpenter skills, she was thrilled to death and floating on cloud nine. She was completely overwhelmed at the job her boys had done and unbelieving that this new house was actually going to be her very own.

At this stage of completion, however, I decided that it would be best for the family to go ahead and move into their new house, even though it was not quite finished. I hadn't wanted them to move in prematurely, but the cold weather was creating a serious problem, particularly for the boys who were sleeping outside in my unheated garage. All things considered, however, we made the move. *The whole family could now take up permanent residency at 2427 South Olympia, in West Tulsa, Oklahoma. Now at last, the family had an official street address.*

We continued working nights and weekends, finishing the trim work and painting. When this was finished, I immediately began building Mama's kitchen cabinets, complete with kitchen sink—something she never had before. Next, came her new gas cook stove with a large oven. No more, would she have to burn wood or coal when fixing dinner. Last, but not least, was her brand new washing machine. Never again, would she have to build a fire under black washtubs in the back yard, or wash and scrub clothes on a scrub board outdoors on washday.

By the time the house was completely finished and the last piece of trim fitted into place, it was mid-December. From the time we started construction until now, it had taken almost eight months to build the house. Considering all the problems we faced, like; the children's commuting morning and night, limited working hours comprised of evenings and weekends only, and certainly our unskilled labor using minors for helpers, I'd have to conclude that we did a fantastic job in record time.

When the final tally was in, our total turnkey construction costs amounted to $5,093. On April 30, Josephine and I deeded the house to Mama and Papa, thus, climaxing the most memorable fete and accomplishment of my life.

As wonderful as it was, when my family moved into their new home, it was also an incredible milestone when they moved out of the "Y". But for all the years we lived there, I must admit it was a peaceful haven for all its inhabitants. Especially for those who were content to live out their lives from day to day, never wanting or demanding more than what just came naturally. But not for me. I would never have settled for a permanent residence as that offered by the "Y". My aspirations and ambitions would never have allowed any resemblance of stagnation. That cruel day, when Papa and Mama received the eviction notice from the Frisco, could now be viewed as a blessing and a signal to go forward. Looking back, however, it's so sweet to wallow in those wonderful moments of triumph and success of building a new house for Mama and Papa and all my siblings. Certainly, it was not a fete that I accomplished single handedly. The boys were superb, as was the patient endurance and sacrifices by Mama and Papa. And it didn't end there. From that day forward, every single working member of the family contributed to the early payoff of the mortgage.

Was it easy? Absolutely not! Times were still tough, But by the grace of God, we all had taken a giant step forward.

Conclusion

When Papa and Mama moved into their new house, it brought the entire family one of the sweetest and most pleasurable periods of adjustment known to man. Including Papa, who usually kept any thoughts of praise to himself. We all knew that for him, it would take some time to adjust. At first, he was like a fish out of water. He had become a creature of habit and still longed for the solitude and seclusion of the "Y" and to be away from any resemblance of city life. He had been happy in the "Y", living the 'down to earth' life of a poor man, which was the only kind of life he'd ever known. But in due time, however, he began showing great pleasure and enthusiasm over his new home, and at times, was very complimentary over our achievement. In his excitement, he was already laying out plans for his new garden spot in the back yard.

As for the entire family—far from the screeching sounds of freight trains—there would be no more dangerous railroad crossings like *el cruzero del Diablo,* there would be no more walking long distances to school, or to the bus stop. No more outdoor showers in cold water or snuggling up to a coal-burning potbelly stove on those cold winter days and nights. Also, there would be no more hauling and chopping railroad ties for firewood, and no more trips to the outdoor toilet, especially on dark spooky nights. Almost every disadvantage born out of life in the "Y" had all but dissipated into thin air. Including the constant hazards of allergies, colds, and the flu'—all caused by our drafty little trackside home.

Moreover, the move from the landscape of the "Y", not only brushed away many dreadful discomforts, but now, the family could begin a new life of pride and dignity. No longer would they be ashamed to bring home a friend. The feeling of inferiority, too, had been swept away, as the move to their new home breathed new life into them all. **At last, Juan and Edelia's dream of owning their own little home was no longer a phenomenon.**

As for Mama—the queen of my heart—she would benefit the most. For her, the facilitation of indoor plumbing and electricity drastically reduced her burden. Everything was now at her fingertips and a long over-due, well-deserved 'rest' was in order. But being a creature of habit, like Papa, she insisted on drying her clothes outside on a clothesline, even though she had a new dryer. But to her, one of the highest benefits of her new home, was St. Catherine Church, which was just two blocks away. Now, she could attend Mass more often to give God thanks and praise for the gift of a lifetime—truly, a blissful sea of peace and contentment.

From the very first day that my mind conceived the idea of building my family's new home, and all during its construction, until the day she passed away. Mama never stopped boasting of my accomplishment and leadership. And how despite great odds at a time of desperation, I seized the opportunity to reverse their plight into what she referred to, as another miracle. Of course, it wasn't any such thing, but in her mind and in her eyes, her new home was living proof of the triumph over passed decades of economic suppression—a status in her life that, heretofore, showed no signs of improving. And she gives me all the credit.

But I, in turn, give her and Papa all the credit. Because from the very beginning, as each of their children were born, their dream was that each of us would have a better life with more opportunity than was allotted to them. And to that end, they persisted and nurtured each of our lives by way of religion, education, and an upbringing of genuine morality and honor. It was by their love, their beautiful human spirit and endless encouragement that furnished me the deep well of courage and ambition to draw from. *With Papa and Mama leading the way, how could I have missed.*

Soon after moving into their new home and getting settled in a new modern environment, the entire family began establishing new and exciting routines. Each of the children began pursuing different endeavors in school and their jobs, always adhering to their responsibility of supporting the household. Within a few years, as they all became of age, they gradually began dating and eventually, one by one, would marry and leave the nest. Not only did hard times practically disappear for Papa and Mama, but varying forms of success began encircling their wonderful lives. **At last, Juan and Edelia's nearly mission impossible, had become mission completed.**

All eleven children, without exception, received their basic elementary education through the 8th grade at St. Catherine, followed by high-school diplomas from Holy Family and various Public schools. Each in their own way, began cultivating their own remarkable future and destiny. For Juan and Edelia—after all is said and done—there were two more outstanding moments of enormous pride absolutely worthy of mention. First, after all the years of inhibition and voluntary seclusion in the "Y", our whole family had now been warmly welcomed into an all-white society in the fabulous neighborhood of West Tulsa. Secondly, all seven of their sons served in the United States military during World War II, the Vietnam War, and the Korean War. Furthermore, after 30 years of service with the Frisco Railway, Papa retired with a nice pension.

I, Cecil, returned to high school to earn my high school diploma, then went on to graduate from Oklahoma School of Accountancy with a Bachelor of Commercial Science degree (BCS) and pursued a highly successful Public Accounting practice.

Noble attended two years of college at Oklahoma State University (OSU) pursuing a college major in Engineering, and later became International Representative for the Boilermaker's Union, representing Puerto Rico and the Southeast region of the United States.

Nellie became a successful owner and operator of a large local Day Care Center.

Johnny became a supervisor in the department of printing and advertising for a large statewide wholesale grocer.

Virginia married a graduate engineer from Missouri who enjoyed a prosperous position with a local TV station.

Albert pursued the medical profession in Guadalajara, Mexico, and established a private practice as Doctor of Medicine in Nashville, Tennessee.

Michael joined the U.S. Postal Service and became a Postal Supervisor.

Lupe married a career U.S. Marine Master Sergeant and both enjoy a wonderful life.

Phyllis married a career employee of Sun Oil Company.

Tommy pursued the computer industry and became a computer analyst and consultant.

Alex became a building engineer.

Furthermore, besides their 12 children, Juan and Edelia were blessed with 38 grandchildren, 50 great grandchildren, and 14 great, great, grandchildren.

In closing the chapter of the "Y" and all it had to offer, as well as what it failed to offer, there remains a beautiful air of nostalgia, because, as vividly as though it were yesterday, I can still see me playing and running throughout the "Y". I remember the junkin' days, the ice truck, the ice dock, and how I used to kick a tin can all the way home from school. I remember walking the train rails with great ease and balance as though they were a mid-air tight rope, the constant humping of switch engines and the sound of those lonesome freight train whistles. I remember hunting and shooting lizards up and down the Frisco railroad tracks with my 'beenie flip' on blistering hot gravel and sand, barefooted, looking for shade in the shadow of a skinny telephone pole. I remember our old Chevy, Papa's garden, and our cruddy old fence that resembled a stockade, and how I pole-vaulted it many times. I remember, too, that nasty beer that Papa used to make, and all the fun times, as well as the 'not-so-fun' times I had, playing music with Papa, and with Frank, and with Bob, and with Luther. And how could I ever forget the trolley cars and how they swayed from side to side cutting their way through the open countryside. I remember the fun of learning to dance, and watching Papa eat his lunch in the engineer's cab of a locomotive while I pretended to be an engineer, and how about all those wonderful neighbors who put up with me and all my solicitations. And if I close my eyes and listen carefully, I can still hear Papa's voice, and Noble's voice, and too, I can hear Mama's voice calling me to supper.

But looking on the downside of the "Y" for a minute, it also has to be remembered as a holding block for the poor, the suppressed, and the forsaken, many without opportunity, and how it inhabited the helpless, as probably the hopeless who surely aspired for even a taste of prosperity.

But regardless of what the "Y" was, or what it wasn't, what it gave or didn't give, the very fabric of its existence still remains beautiful and unforgettable in my long list of childhood memories. Unlike Noble, who viewed the "Y" as despicable, I prefer to hold its memory dear to my heart, and remember it as a wonderful learning experience and springboard to an exciting future.

I sometimes believe that my life in the "Y", in many ways, was just another repeat performance of the lives of Juan and Edelia, as well as the lives of Cenobio, Felipa, and Domitila, and that only the names and faces of the players were changed. The scenes too, were different, and yet, in many ways were the same when comparing the lifestyles of the "Y" in West Tulsa to Villa de Reyes in Old Mexico—both of which tend to mirror identical forlorn realities of another time and place.

Today, as I try to re-invent the life-long image of Mama, I see a beautiful portrait of the most wonderful person in the world. And even though her face was aged and wrinkled and her hair silvery white, I'll always see that warm beckoning smile that will never go away. From the very beginning, she was that all-inspirational force that constantly sustained us all. She fully accepted her role in life as a total wife and mother, and by her pure sweet bondage of love, she gave a true meaning to our lives. As long as I live, I'll always feel her presence hovering over me as though she were my guardian angel.

Likewise for Papa, sweet and sad memories still come to the forefront quite often. Because how could I ever forget the tenderness of his soul and those melancholy moods of his when he reminisced about his childhood days in Mexico, recalling his mother's love, her sweet smile, and how he loved being at his father's side. And in this regard, I'll always remember Papa's sorrow in having left Mexico and his parents, never to return as he'd hoped. When I speak of Papa's sorrow and his unfortunate past, I can better describe his feelings and memories in one of his favorite songs entitled, '**Cuatro Milpas**', 'the four cornfields'. He sang this song often, and when working outside or in the garden, I could hear him humming it softly. The song itself was a sentimental song whose lyrics spoke of a poor, young farm boy who had left his *'rancho'* to roam in search of life's dreams and fortune. All through the song, it touches on this young man's visions of the past and the beautiful memories of a yesteryear, such as the early morning chirping of the birds, the lovely fragrances of the flowers in the patio, and the enchantment of soft Mexican music being heard from a distance at evening time. As the song's chorus continues to repeat itself, *its last words painfully describe how this young man one day returns home, only to find that all is gone, including his parents.* This is the sentimental picture in which I remember Papa, and how true to the words of the song his life played out. That was exactly the case when I took Papa back to Villa de Reyes in 1952 for a final visit. Only Hilario remained.

When Papa died in 1974, I was absolutely devastated. I became numb and shocked beyond words. Disbelieving the reality of his death, I had extreme difficulty accepting it and couldn't help torturing myself with the thought of his passing. On the day of his funeral and his last rite's Mass at St. Catherine my pain had reached its peak, as I nearly became violently emotional in church. It was as though I wanted to die with him. And even today, 30 years later, I still get a lump in my throat and get misty eyed at the very thought of the sound of his voice. Papa died a natural death, and I suppose at age 84, it was finally his time to go, but the love I had for him will never die, until I do.

Today, as I face the sad reality that my parents are gone, I must also concede that life goes on, and that even though their pictures hang on the walls and their physical memories still hang in the closet, the end is also the beginning. We've no choice but to carry on in hope and in prayer, in love and laughter, and in the songs we sing…and yes, even in tears when there's pain in our hearts. **No question, this is the reality of our lives…..and it all has to happen.**

From the rutted paths of Villa de Reyes, Mexico and the life-giving cornfields where Juan worked cheerfully beside his father….from the dark streets of sleepy Colotlan, Mexico, where on the night Domitila wandered aimlessly waiting to give birth to Edelia….to the memorable little town of West Tulsa, Oklahoma—together, **Juan and Edelia** obediently followed the call of their waiting destiny—a destiny of hardships and sorrow, but sprinkled with happiness, love and laughter—a destiny of hurt and grievance, but always trumped with a promise of a new day. But most importantly, the test of time ultimately rendered its highest reward—an uncloudy day—including a fresh breath of spring that began dissipating the dark clouds of indigence when they abandoned the "Y" and walked victoriously into a new dawn.

Although Juan and Edelia have both passed on to their reward in heaven, there's no denying them their accomplished victory over life's bitter battles, because in the end, they achieved their goals. The twilight that had constantly only flickered in the distance, finally came into full view. And their greatest accomplishment was the passing of the symbolic torch to all their children. That torch was a **Mexican Twilight of hope and opportunity in the Great Land of America.**

Gracias a Dios.

The End

Author Biography

The author, a retired accountant and second born of two Mexican immigrants in the early 1900's, proudly re-tells the true story of how, why, and when his parents came to America. He is also a World War II U.S. Navy veteran and the author of the non-fiction book *Mama & Papa's Twelve Children* and the *Y*.

978-0-595-38017-6
0-595-38017-4

Printed in the United States
64710LVS00004B/1-78

9 780595 380176